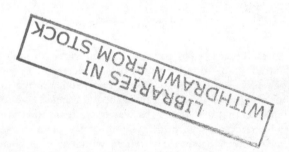

On
SACKVILLE
STREET

A. O'CONNOR

POOLBEG

Published 2016
by Poolbeg Press Ltd
123 Grange Hill, Baldoyle
Dublin 13, Ireland
E-mail: poolbeg@poolbeg.com
www.poolbeg.com

1

A catalogue record for this book is available from the British Library.

ISBN 978-1-78199-893-9

Typeset in Sabont 11pt on 15pt by Poolbeg Press Ltd
Printed and bound by CPI Group UK Ltd, Croydon, CR0 4YY

www.poolbeg.com

About the author

A graduate of the National University of Ireland Maynooth and Trinity College Dublin, A. O'Connor is the bestselling author of ten previous novels. Four of these are historical fiction, including 'The Armstrong House' series which has been translated into German and Russian.

Also by A. O'Connor

Acknowledgements

As always thank you to Paula, Kieran, David, Caroline and all at Poolbeg Publishing. Thanks to Gaye Shortland, whose guidance is always much appreciated. Many thanks also to those who provided me with the historical details, anecdotes and stories of Dublin's O'Connell Street, or as it used to be called – Sackville Street.

For Laura

PROLOGUE

Summer 1916

The traffic was light as the taxi-cab motored down Dublin's main thoroughfare, Sackville Street, on Easter Monday. The street was absent of its usual bustle as most of the stores were still closed for the holiday. As Amelia Robinson chatted away to her grandmother Milandra in the back of the cab, it struck her that it was hard to believe Milandra was now in her seventies. She still had the vigour, poise and alertness of a woman much younger. They were returning to Milandra's home on Sackville Street, having spent the Easter break at Amelia's parents' home in the south of the city in Dalkey. Her parents had tried to persuade Milandra to stay for a further night. In her typical fashion she had insisted she wanted to go home. Amelia realised it had been a triumph even to get her grandmother to leave her beloved home to stay with them for the Easter weekend, as she rarely left her house these days.

"Next house on the right, young man," Milandra ordered the taxi driver and he dutifully pulled over in front of the mansion townhouse at the upper end of Sackville Street.

The taxi driver jumped out and opened the door for his passengers. Amelia got out first and then went to assist her grandmother out of the vehicle.

"I'm quite all right, Amelia," said Milandra, waving her away as she stepped out onto the street.

"Of course," conceded Amelia, moving back.

"There you go, young man," said Milandra as she opened her purse and paid the driver, tipping him generously.

"Thank you, ma'am," he said with a smile.

"Ah!" she declared as she crossed the pavement and walked up the steps to her front door. "I look forward to spending tonight in my own bed! Your parents' house may have a lovely sea view, but I wouldn't give tuppence for the mattress I had to endure!"

"Yes, Grandmama," said Amelia, smiling to herself as Milandra let them in through the front door.

"I always think you can judge a person by their mattresses, and your mother's are hard and cold!" said Milandra.

"Mama always speaks very highly of you too!" teased Amelia, fully aware that her mother Petronella and Milandra rarely saw eye to eye on anything.

Amelia took off her hat and coat and placed them on a chair. She followed her grandmother down the huge hall of the house, past the dining room and parlour, to the central staircase that swept upstairs.

Amelia knew better than to offer assistance to Milandra as they walked up the staircase.

"Where is everyone?" Amelia asked as they reached the top of the staircase and headed down the landing to the drawing room that occupied most of the first floor.

"The servants aren't due back until tonight. I gave them the full holiday off," Milandra informed her.

"Oh, Grandmama! I wish you had said that before we left Dalkey! I thought I explained I'm meeting Rupert from the boat in Kingstown in two hours. I can't stay that long with you!" Amelia felt quite cross. She would never have allowed Milandra to leave Dalkey with her if she had known she would be alone in her house for so many hours.

"My dear Amelia, I could not bear spending another minute under your mother's roof! If I had told you the servants were gone, I'd still be marooned there! I shall be quite all right for a while on my own, I assure you. You go and meet your young man as planned and there is no need to worry about me." With that she sat down on one of the luxurious velvet couches.

Amelia sat opposite her in an ornate armchair. "I really do wish you would reconsider Mama's suggestion that you move into our home in Dalkey, Grandmama. It would be much safer for you and we wouldn't worry about you so much."

"My dear girl, I will never leave this house. I have lived here for over fifty years, and I will only be leaving it one way now!"

"Grandmama! Don't speak like that!" Amelia chastised her.

"Well, it's the truth. This is my home. I came to live here as a young woman. I hardly ever knew any other life."

Amelia looked up at the gigantic portrait of Milandra painted as a young woman which was hanging over the fireplace. She thought her grandmother still bore the signs of the raving beauty she had been in her youth.

"I remember the first day I came to live here as if it were yesterday," Milandra said, a distant look coming to her eyes. "I was Milandra Carter then, a recently widowed young woman. I knew nobody and I built my life from there. Everything you see in this house I chose. I spent months deciding on the curtains, the carpets, the furniture. Nothing has changed since then. How could I leave it, when everything here is part of me?"

"I know all that but, as Mama says, we need to be practical."

"Practical!" scoffed Milandra. "When was Petronella ever practical? Not one day of her life, I can tell you. No, she is just worried about her inheritance! But she may rest assured – as I have only one child and one grandchild her inheritance is quite safe. I think she worries I will leave everything to the Cat and Dog Home in my dotage – that's the only thing I can think of."

Amelia stifled a giggle. "Oh, you are bold. Mama does care about you very much, despite everything."

"Well, she can care from a distance – that will suit both of us just fine," said Milandra. "I sometimes wish I had more grandchildren. But Petronella was like me – once was enough!"

"Perhaps," said Amelia and her face became sad. "Although maybe it was a blessing you don't have grandsons . . . they would be fighting the war in France now, at risk of being killed every day."

Milandra saw the frightened look on her granddaughter's face. "You're worried about your young man."

"Of course! Rupert writes that the war is so much worse than what we are hearing and reading."

"Well, I don't know what has got into everybody! Why are we all fighting this war? What's it even about? I've never heard of so much death in the world, not since the Famine!"

"I just wish it would end and Rupert would be home for good. We've been engaged for two years. We should be married by now, and would be if it weren't for this wretched war. There was no reason for Rupert to volunteer to fight!"

"How do you mean?"

"I mean, of course, that there is no conscription in Ireland though there is in the rest of the United Kingdom!"

"True – but he has gone to war because of a sense of duty, I daresay."

"A sense of duty to whom?" Amelia became agitated and angry. "Ireland should be independent by now, and it would be if it wasn't for this war delaying Home Rule."

Milandra smiled to herself. Never one who was too interested in politics herself, her granddaughter's fervent Irish Nationalism was a cause of bewilderment to her. But she was not surprised, as many of Amelia's friends in Dublin's writer and artist circle were Irish nationalists.

"Well, look, Rupert is arriving home today and you will have two weeks together. Forget about everything and just enjoy your time together."

"And then when he goes back? This might be the last time I ever see him. As a captain in the army, he's in the front lines all the time."

"Rupert strikes me as a very capable young man. I'm sure he knows what he is doing."

"He might, but do the men in charge? Doesn't seem like it. I would have married him last time he was home on leave, but he refused. He said if anything happened to him, he wouldn't want to leave me a young widow."

"Very wise of Rupert! I know what life is like as a young widow, and would urge you to avoid the same fate!"

"At least I would be his wife, and that's all I want," Amelia whispered.

Milandra reached forward and patted her granddaughter's knee. "It will be all right, just wait and see."

Amelia quickly wiped away the tears that were threatening and smiled brightly. "Of course it will be, I'm just being silly . . . Grandmama, I'm writing an article for the newspaper that I was hoping you could help me with."

"Oh?" Milandra was interested. She took pride in her granddaughter's burgeoning career as a journalist.

"Yes, I'm investigating some old unsolved mysteries."

"I would have thought there are too many new mysteries to bother with old ones," said Milandra, sitting back into the couch.

"Well, my editor said anything that helps take people's minds off the war . . ."

"And how could I help you with anything?"

"I'm investigating the disappearance of Lucas Hempton," said Amelia.

Milandra's face tightened as her eyes opened wide. "Lucas Hempton . . . now that's a name I've haven't heard for quite a while."

"From my research I discovered he was some kind of business partner of your first husband's?"

"Yes, he was – and a good friend of his also. When Ambrose died and I moved to Dublin, Lucas was a good friend to me too. He helped me as much as he could."

"Excellent! Then you *can* help me?"

"Well, not really. I can't tell you any more than I just said," said Milandra.

"But it's the most curious situation. He was a well-respected, wealthy businessman and he just disappeared one Christmas. Vanished into thin air. I've been looking through all the old newspaper articles about it."

"Well, then you have discovered as much as anybody ever knew – as I remember, the newspapers covered it widely at the time."

"He left his house one Christmas and was never seen again. It was against his very nature, as he was meticulous, dedicated to his work and commitments, and reliable."

"Oh, Lucas was all those things, yes . . . but I always imagined he had one drink too many that Christmas and fell into the river and was washed out to sea."

"But he was a teetotaller and never drank – that's what the newspaper articles said!"

"Well, the front people present to the world may be very different to what they actually are. He may have been a raving alcoholic behind closed doors."

Amelia shook her head. "Doubtful. I've seen statements from his servants, all of whom said he didn't even keep alcohol in his house on Leeson Street."

Milandra's eyes widened again. "My! You have been looking into this quite carefully, haven't you?"

"I think it's an intriguing story."

"Well, I don't know why people would be interested in one disappearance fifty years ago when there is so much death every day in the war."

"As I said, it's to take people's minds off what is happening," said Amelia. "Everyone likes a mystery."

"I suppose. But, as I said, how could I possibly help you with it?"

"I was hoping you could tell me more about him? What was he like, who were his friends, where did he like to go?"

"He was Ambrose's friend, not mine. I really didn't know him that well, nor was I that interested in him, to be honest. He had a habit of poking his nose into everything, that's all I remember."

"The police suspected foul play. Murder."

"But who would want to murder Lucas Hempton?"

"Well, that's what I'm trying to discover," said Amelia, sitting forward. Then she caught sight of the clock on the wall and quickly stood up. "Oh, gosh, Grandmama, I'd better run! Rupert is docking in Kingstown soon and I can't miss him arriving."

"Yes, dear, run along to your fiancé," said Milandra.

Amelia looked worried. "Are you *sure* you'll be all right until the servants arrive?"

Milandra waved her away. "Of course I will. Now don't delay or you will miss Rupert."

Amelia bent down and kissed her cheek. "Rupert and I will visit you tomorrow."

"I shall look forward to that." Milandra smiled up at her.

"I'll lock the front door behind me with my key. Goodbye, Grandmama!"

"Take care! Give my love to Rupert!"

Milandra sat back and listened as she heard Amelia's heels rattle down the staircase and across the hallway. She heard the front door open and slam.

"Lucas Hempton!" Milandra whispered to herself, sitting back into the couch. She shook her head. The very mention of his name brought the memories flooding back – memories of when she arrived to live on Sackville Street as Ambrose Carter's widow. For a while Lucas had been important to her as he had helped her establish herself.

She looked up at her portrait hanging over the fireplace. She might look different from the beautiful young woman she had been, but she still felt the same on the inside.

She hadn't changed that much – had she?

Time seemed to last an eternity as she thought of those early weeks when she came to live in Dublin back in the 1860s. It was a different world then, a different Sackville Street.

Suddenly a loud crash downstairs snapped her back out of her memories.

She sat up quickly and called, "Amelia?"

There was no answer, but she could hear somebody downstairs. Concerned, she stood up. It might be one of the servants back early. They had a new scullery maid who was forever breaking everything. If she had broken one of her exquisite vases, she would dismiss her on the spot.

Milandra walked out of the drawing room and across the landing to the banisters. She looked down on the hallway.

"*Who is down there?*" she called, but there was no answer.

She walked to the top of the stairs and called again. "*Hello?*"

Suddenly she saw a figure race across the hallway and up the stairs towards her. She stepped back in fright, leaning against the wall behind her.

The man reached the top of the stairs and stopped.

"What do you want?" she demanded.

But the man said nothing as he raised a revolver and pointed it at her.

PART 1

1869

CHAPTER 1

On the day of Ambrose Carter's funeral everyone said it was a tragedy that his wife Milandra had been left a widow at the early age of only thirty. However, most people privately thought that, if she had wanted to avoid such a tragedy, Milandra had been somewhat careless in marrying a man some three decades her senior.

The church on Henry Street was within walking distance of Dublin's main boulevard Sackville Street. Perhaps because of that, the great, the good and the not so good had all turned out to pay their respects to Ambrose Carter, widely recognised as one of the country's premier wine merchants. But the attention of the congregation packed into the church was not trained on the solemn service being conducted on the altar, but on Ambrose's young widow.

As chief mourner, Milandra was seated in the front pew, her expressionless blue eyes focused straight ahead of her. The front pew looked a lonely affair, with just Milandra and Lucas Hempton occupying it.

Lucas was sixty-two years old, a tall thin man, with silver hair combed back. He had inquisitive but honest blue eyes, and round spectacles permanently perched on the end of his nose. He had been Ambrose's best friend and business advisor through the decades and, as Lucas had supported Ambrose through life, he now supported his young widow on the day of his funeral. As Ambrose had no other relatives still living, and his marriage to Milandra was childless, the congregation silently acknowledged how grateful

11

Milandra must be for Lucas's support on the day – and, in the months to come, how she would rely on his support and advice during the process of winding down Ambrose's business affairs.

As the Reverend said the final prayer, the pallbearers stepped forth and, raising Ambrose's coffin aloft, ceremoniously began to carry it down the church aisle. They paused after they passed the first pew to wait for Milandra to follow them. Lucas stood first and, stepping out of the pew, indicated to Milandra to walk in front of him directly behind the coffin.

"I'm just behind you," he whispered reassuringly into her ear as she began to follow the pallbearers down the aisle.

Agatha Fontenoy strained to get a good look at Milandra. She and her husband Daniel were seated halfway down the church, their son Nicholas beside them. As Milandra walked serenely past them, Agatha was hoping to catch her gaze and offer a sympathetic and supportive smile. But Milandra was not looking left or right. Her eyes continued to focus ahead, as if the rest of the congregation wasn't there.

"Well, she's not what I expected – not what I expected at all!" Agatha whispered into her husband's ear after Milandra had safely passed by. "She's young enough to be Ambrose's daughter – and then some!"

"Agatha!" chastised Daniel. "Remember where you are!"

"I am remembering! And I am remembering the cross old cantankerous miser Ambrose Carter was, and wondering how on earth he ever managed to marry such an elegant beautiful young woman!"

"Agatha! You really must not speak ill of the dead, particularly on the day of his funeral!"

Agatha shrugged unapologetically, confident she was only voicing what everyone else was thinking.

The truth was, it had come as a surprise to Dublin society when Ambrose Carter had married some eight years previously. But what was more surprising in Dublin's close-knit social world was that nobody in Dublin had ever heard of his wife or knew anything about her. The marriage ceremony had been in France and nobody, not even Lucas Hempton, had been invited. Afterwards the couple had gone straight to live on Ambrose's estate in the country. Apart from his frequent business trips to the capital, never accompanied by his wife, he and Milandra never left his country estate where they lived, in what everyone assumed was a state of marital bliss. And so, since the marriage, his funeral was the first time anyone had laid eyes on his wife in Dublin.

The congregation filed out of the church and followed the young widow and the pallbearers into the adjacent graveyard where Ambrose's eternal resting place was waiting for him.

As the coffin was lowered, Milandra stood between Lucas and the Reverend who said the prayers loudly in order that the large crowd should hear.

"Ashes to ashes and dust to dust, may the soul of Ambrose Carter be granted eternal rest," the Reverend concluded and then, turning to Milandra, he whispered words of solace to her.

Agatha Fontenoy observed Milandra whisper something to the Reverend who then cleared his throat and said loudly, "Ladies and gentlemen, after you have expressed your condolences, Mrs. Carter would like to invite you all back to a reception at the Gresham Hotel on Sackville Street to honour her late husband's memory."

"Well!" whispered Agatha to her husband. "That's the first time Ambrose Carter ever offered hospitality to anybody! He didn't do it in life – how surprising he's doing it in death!"

"Agatha!" admonished Daniel. "A little respect, please!"

As the crowd filed past Milandra and Lucas, offering their condolences, the Fontenoys took their place amongst them.

"Shall we go back to the Gresham, Daniel?" asked Agatha.

"I can see no reason why we can't go for a short while. Though I suspect your reason for going is not to honour the memory of poor old Ambrose, but to be nosy about his widow."

"I admit I would like to see more of Milandra Carter, and I suspect this will be the last opportunity we'll ever get to meet her."

"What about you, Nicholas? Will you come as well?"

"I don't think I can, Papa. I need to get back to the college this afternoon," said Nicholas.

Daniel nodded approvingly. "Duty first."

"Will you be seeing Constance this evening?" asked his mother.

"Yes, I told her I would be having dinner with her family."

It was Agatha's turn to nod approvingly.

The Fontenoys fell silent as they reached Lucas and Milandra.

"Lucas, I was so surprised to hear of Ambrose's demise. I thought he would outlive us all," said Daniel, shaking his hand.

"A shock to us all, Daniel," nodded Lucas sadly.

Daniel stepped in front of Milandra and shook her hand. "My sincere condolences, Mrs. Carter. My name is Daniel Fontenoy. I knew Ambrose all my life. He grew up in the house down from ours on Sackville Street. Although I hadn't seen him for a long time, I have fond memories of him."

Milandra nodded, but her face remained expressionless. "Most kind, thank you."

"And I'm Mrs. Fontenoy, Daniel's wife," said Agatha, stepping forward. "I knew Ambrose too. He was quite a character!"

"Most kind, thank you," Milandra repeated.

Seeing that Agatha looked as if she was about to try and engage Milandra in conversation, Daniel grabbed her arm and moved her on.

She looked back at Milandra. "We'll see you at the Gresham! We can have a proper chat there!"

Nicholas then stepped forward and shook Lucas's hand.

"Nicholas, good of you come," said Lucas.

Nicholas nodded and then stepped in front of Milandra.

"Sincere condolences on your loss," he said as he shook her hand.

Milandra took his hand and held it for a few moments as she stared into the tall young man's face – a distinctive face set off with a square chin. He had fair hair and light-blue eyes.

"That is most kind of you," she said and smiled at him.

Nicholas nodded and followed his parents.

When the last of the sympathisers had shaken her hand, Lucas turned to Milandra and said, "You did very well, my dear. Ambrose would be proud of you."

"Thank you, Lucas." She then stepped forward and looked down at Ambrose's coffin for a moment before turning to the gravediggers and ordering, "Carry on."

Lucas escorted Milandra out of the graveyard. Her eyes were trained on Nicholas Fontenoy as he climbed into a carriage with his parents in the street outside.

"Who is that man?" she asked, nodding over at the Fontenoys.

"I thought he introduced himself to you? That's Daniel Fontenoy. He's a barrister and judge and a neighbour of Ambrose's when he lived in Dublin."

"No, not him – the young man with them?"

"Ah, that's their son, Nicholas. A very bright young chap, from everything I've heard. A law student at Trinity."

"I see. He has a kind face."

"Well, one would expect he would have – at a funeral," said Lucas as they reached their carriage and the driver held open the door for them.

CHAPTER 2

As the carriage travelled down Henry Street, Milandra sat in silence, looking out the window.

"It's such a tragic time for you, my dear, losing Ambrose so suddenly – I can only imagine how lost you must be feeling." Lucas reached out and took her hand. "I want you to know you can rely on me completely. I know all of Ambrose's business affairs, all his interests and investments, and I don't want you to worry about any of that. I will look after everything for you."

"Thank you, Lucas."

Lucas sighed loudly. "It will be a monumental task dismantling his empire. But rest assured, I will not allow anybody to take advantage of you and will protect your interests to the very best of my ability."

"I know I can rely on you, Lucas."

The carriage got to the end of Henry Street and turned onto Sackville Street which was, as ever, a hive of activity. Dublin's main boulevard stretched wide and far, from the thriving commercial end of the street full of stores and shopping arcades at the south end near the Liffey, to the elegant townhouses that ran along the north end of the street. The carriage joined the busy procession of carriages and headed northwards towards the Gresham Hotel, Dublin's finest hotel, situated in the residential section of the street.

"Where is Ambrose's house?" Milandra asked.

Lucas looked surprised at her question but pointed to a grand four-storey townhouse the carriage was passing.

16

Milandra stared up at the imposing building where all the windows had their shutters closed.

"It's big," she commented.

"Yes. He never brought you to see it?"

"He never cared for the house. I think he had an unhappy childhood there and was always happiest at his estate in the country."

"True, especially after he married you, my dear. Even when he came to Dublin on business, he either stayed at my home or at the Gresham."

"What condition is the inside of the building in now?" she enquired.

"I don't know, Milandra. I haven't been inside since Ambrose's parents died. I believe Ambrose just used it as a warehouse to stock wines for the business. But that shouldn't stop you from achieving a good price for it when you put it on the market. It's a very fashionable part of town."

Milandra nodded as the carriage pulled up outside the Gresham Hotel.

Agatha and Daniel Fontenoy had arrived at the Gresham just before Milandra and Lucas and, as they made their way through the expansive and ornate foyer, Daniel paused at the reception.

"Where is the Carter funeral party, if you please?" he enquired.

"On the first floor, in the Drogheda Suite."

"Thank you," said Daniel.

He and Agatha made their way towards the marble staircase and set off up the stairs.

"I was thinking we should have Constance over for dinner at the weekend?" suggested Agatha.

"Splendid idea," answered Daniel.

They were directed to the Drogheda Suite by a member of the hotel staff when they reached the landing upstairs. As they entered the suite they saw it was already filled with guests seated at the tables, waiting to be served.

Agatha's lively blue eyes danced around the room, searching for what might interest her the most. She noticed that Milandra and Lucas hadn't arrived yet. Then, to her delight, a waiter showed them to two of the only four seats left available – at the top table. The remaining two empty seats were obviously for the chief mourner and her companion.

"I wonder how much all this will cost?" Agatha whispered to Daniel as they sat down.

"I doubt it will be of any concern to Ambrose wherever he is now," he said.

"No. But it will be of concern to his widow!"

"Are you sure we're all right sitting here?" asked Daniel of the waiter. "Is the head table not reserved for the family?"

"It's perfectly fine, sir. Mrs. Carter did not express any instructions for reserving the head table – apart from herself and Mr. Hempton."

"How sad!" whispered Agatha to Daniel. "For the man to have so few family and close friends to mourn him."

"You get what you put into this life, Agatha," he said. "And Ambrose has got what he put into his life. He put the pursuit of fortune before all else. And that can be a lonely place."

"At least we'll get a chance to speak to Milandra before she disappears back to the country," said Agatha.

The function room fell silent as Milandra entered, followed by Lucas. All eyes looked on as a waiter escorted them to the top table where he pulled out a chair for Milandra. Lucas sat down beside her.

Agatha smiled sympathetically at her. "At least you have the worst of it over now – the service and the burial. Although I'm sure the time ahead will be very lonely and heart-breaking for you."

Milandra nodded and surveyed her guests who were being served a sumptuous feast of lamb. "I'm sure Ambrose would have been delighted that there was such a turn-out for him."

"Well – everybody knew him over the years," smiled Agatha. "He was a well-known man."

"Indeed – he was many things," said Milandra.

"Had Ambrose been ill?" said Daniel. Nobody seemed to know the circumstances of the death, as he had gathered from the other mourners at the funeral.

"He hadn't been ill. But his heart gave out – it was quick, which

18

was a blessing," said Milandra as she looked sadly down at the tablecloth in front of her.

"How tragic!" Agatha shook her head in dismay.

"There was nothing that could be done for him," Milandra assured her as the waiters began to serve the top table.

By the time the dessert plates had begun to be cleared, Agatha had decided Milandra was quite a mystery. She kept her cards close to her chest and, though her conversation was polite, Agatha couldn't get any information from her however much she probed. Milandra was very vague in her answers and Agatha realised she must be still be in shock from Ambrose's death.

As Lucas and Daniel left the table to step out on the balcony to have a cigar, the two women were left alone.

"What are your plans now for the future, dear?" queried Agatha.

"I haven't given them much thought," said Milandra. "I relied on Ambrose for everything."

"Indeed. He was such a capable man. It's such a pity you didn't have children. They would have been such a comfort to you at this time."

"It obviously wasn't meant to be," said Milandra.

"Yes, it's best to be philosophical about these things. But you're still young – I daresay you can have them yet. You will be able to marry again . . . in time."

"That is the last thing on my mind right now, Mrs. Fontenoy."

"Of course. I apologise if I'm being insensitive," said Agatha.

"What of your own children? That was your son accompanying you at the funeral earlier?" queried Milandra.

Agatha's face lit up in pride. "Yes, that was Nicholas."

"He was unable to attend this afternoon?"

"I'm afraid he has exams coming up and had to attend lectures."

"He is at university?"

"Yes, he's in his final year of law at Trinity."

"A very busy year for him."

"Yes, and next year will be even busier."

"How so?"

"Nicholas is engaged to be married to Constance Staffordshire, Bishop Staffordshire's daughter. They will be married as soon as he qualifies as a lawyer and settles into his career. A busy time ahead for all of us! Do you know, we were trying to decide on a wedding venue – and, having seen the excellent service here today, I think I'm going to suggest the Gresham." Agatha smiled as she looked up at the elaborate ceiling.

Milandra nodded and managed to keep smiling distantly as Agatha rattled on about the relative advantages of numerous potential wedding venues.

On the balcony, Lucas and Daniel stood smoking their cigars as the evening began to draw in. Beneath them Sackville Street was still buzzing with activity as the day's business was drawing to a close.

"Milandra seems like a very pleasant lady. She conducted herself very serenely today," commented Daniel.

"I've always found her so when I visited them at their estate," agreed Lucas.

"She's not what I would have expected at all," said Daniel.

"I'm sure she isn't. I have become accustomed to seeing Ambrose and Milandra together, so I'm used to them as a couple."

"It was a happy marriage?"

"I never heard Ambrose complain."

Daniel smiled. "Well, then it must have been a happy marriage, as it was seldom that I ever heard Ambrose *not* complain!"

Lucas chuckled at the memory of his friend. "True! Well, he's gone now and I'm going to be very busy winding up all of his affairs."

"I imagine Milandra has been left in a very wealthy position?"

"Yes, but she is young and naive and knows nothing of the world or of business affairs. Ambrose kept her very protected on their estate. I have to protect her and make sure she is not compromised by unscrupulous vultures." Lucas's face was set in determination.

"She could not have a better ally than you."

Daniel looked across Sackville Street to the row of fine townhouses leading up to Rutland Square. All the lights were coming on in the windows, apart from one. Ambrose's house sat amongst its neighbours in darkness, the shutters firmly closed.

"And what of their house here?" enquired Daniel, nodding over to the building down the street.

"Oh, that will be put up for sale without delay. I was always urging Ambrose to sell it as he never used it, but he was reluctant to let it go. It will just be a further worry for Milandra, and she needs to get rid of it before the house falls into further disrepair and loses value."

"You will get an excellent price for it, positioned as it is on the main street of the city."

"Yes, I've already had numerous enquiries," said Lucas.

Daniel's face suddenly creased with worry. "Not from any commercial enterprise, I hope? We really would hate to see the commercialisation of this end of Sackville Street."

"Well, there have been a number of interested parties," said Lucas, indicating that the building's continuance as a residential building was not assured.

"Oh, I really hope you exercise caution in the sale, Lucas," urged Daniel, now very anxious. "It is bad enough that the southern end of Sackville Street has become full of stores, shops and arcades. We really don't want this end of the street to become commercial also. I remember when I was a boy growing up, the whole street was residential, apart from a small arcade in the middle. I'll be honest with you, I was furious when even this hotel opened here on the residential side."

"You can't stop progress, Daniel," said Lucas. "And, as I said, I have to look after Milandra's interests first. So whoever offers the best price will be the purchaser."

"Well, that does disappoint me." Daniel's face looked more angry than disappointed as he put out his cigar. "Shall we return to the ladies?"

The Drogheda Suite was emptying out of guests and Milandra stood at the door beside Lucas as she accepted the guests' gratitude for her hospitality and further condolences on her loss.

The Fontenoys brought up the rear.

"It was a real pleasure to meet you, despite the circumstances," said Daniel, shaking Milandra's hand.

"Thank you," she said.

"Lucas informs us you'll be returning to your estate tomorrow," said Agatha.

Milandra nodded.

"We wish you every happiness for your future," said Agatha. "Time is a great healer, and you have the rest of your life in front of you."

"It's so hard to think of the future right now," said Milandra.

"I only regret we have had so little opportunity to get to know you," said Daniel. "If you are in Dublin again, please do call on us. We live just at the top of Sackville Street on Rutland Square."

"I'll bear that in mind," said Milandra.

"Please do call – any time," said Agatha as she and her husband left.

Milandra sighed as she turned to Lucas.

"Well, you certainly gave Ambrose a fine send-off," he said. "One he would be proud of."

"I hope so," said Milandra.

He offered her his arm. She took it and they walked out of the room and down the corridor towards the staircase.

"I really must meet you tomorrow before you return to the estate, Milandra. I want to go through some immediate affairs with you."

"Of course. I'll meet you in the hotel foyer at eleven if that is convenient," she said.

"Perfect. And I can give you a lift to the train station afterwards."

"One thing, Lucas . . . do you have a set of keys for the house on Sackville Street?"

"Yes, I do. Ambrose left me a set in case of an emergency."

"Good. Could you bring them with you in the morning? I should like to take a look at the house before you employ an auctioneer. I would have brought Ambrose's keys with me from the estate, but he had so many I didn't know which was which!"

Lucas nodded, realising his new charge really was clueless as to all her late husband's affairs, right down to his keys.

"Well, I could, Milandra," he said. "But I don't see the point? As I told you the house is full of dust and in a very dilapidated state."

"Even so, I would like to see where Ambrose was brought up and spent part of his life," she said as they reached the foyer.

"Of course. I wonder did he ever know how much you cared for him?"

"I hope he did." She looked down at the expansive cream marble floor.

"Anyway, I shall bid you farewell. You must be exhausted. I'll let you rest and shall see you in the morning."

"Thank you, Lucas – for everything."

He smiled then turned and left.

Milandra's suite was on the top floor and was one of the best in the hotel, large and luxuriantly furnished, with several tall graceful windows.

Milandra unfastened the top button on her black crinoline mourning gown and walked across to one of the windows and opened it. She breathed the air in deeply as she looked across Sackville Street to the city beyond. She then turned and crossed over to the bed. She flung herself on it, staring up at the ceiling.

She smiled. And then began to giggle with relief. It wasn't long before her giggles turned to laughter.

CHAPTER 3

Nicholas Fontenoy hurried across the main square of Trinity College under the darkening sky, realising he was running very late. He had been tempted into going to the college bar with fellow students after his afternoon classes and was now an hour late for dinner with his fiancée's family, the Staffordshires. He raced through the main arch of Trinity and out onto College Green where he quickly flagged down a hansom cab.

"No 31, Mountjoy Square, quick as you can!" he instructed the driver and the carriage took off and joined the rest of the traffic.

As the carriage crossed over Carlisle Bridge and into Sackville Street, Nicholas racked his brains to try and think of an excuse as to why he was late. He could always say his classes had delayed him. But the smell of alcohol on his breath would give him away. And Constance's father, Bishop John Staffordshire, was known for his disapproval of needless alcoholic consumption. It would be much better to say that one of his lecturers had insisted he come to his office to discuss a dissertation, and the dastardly man had insisted Nicholas join him in a glass or two of sherry – no, brandy would be better. Out of sheer politeness and fear of offending his lecturer, Nicholas had obliged. What else was a chap to do? Even Bishop Staffordshire would have to see the pickle he had been put in. Yes, it was all Dean Gratton's fault.

Content with his excuse, Nicholas relaxed back into his seat and looked out at the luxuriant stores on southern Sackville Street. As he passed Carter Wines he wondered if the store had closed for the day out of respect for its dead proprietor. Nicholas imagined old Ambrose Carter probably had left instructions for the store not to close. The carriage continued into northern Sackville Street, past the fine townhouses there and on to Rutland Square. Sackville Street and the Georgian squares beyond were where the merchants, bankers and clergy who ran the city had their homes. In comparison, the Georgian squares to the south of the river, like Merrion Square and Stephen's Green, were the city homes of the country's aristocracy. Nicholas's father always maintained this division made Sackville Street and its environs the most important part of the city, as this was where business was done.

They passed Nicholas's family house which was situated on the eastern side of Rutland Square. At the top of the square the carriage turned a corner and headed towards Mountjoy Square.

In the Staffordshire's dining room at 31 Mountjoy Square the clock chimed, indicating it was half past eight. Bishop Staffordshire sat at the top of the table, a mixture of worry and irritation written on his face. He had a large frame and exuded a strong physical presence which was at variance with his neat brown hair, and immaculately tidy dress. But his most striking feature was his grey unforgiving eyes.

Opposite him at the bottom of the table sat his wife Henrietta. Thin and pale, her hair greying, she always seemed to fade into the background, even at her own dinner table. She glanced nervously at her husband, then lowered her eyes.

The Bishop's eldest daughter Constance sat to his right, and his other daughter Emma to his left.

The seat beside Constance was empty.

"Will I begin to serve dinner, Your Grace?" asked the butler, Reeves, as he stepped forward. It was the third time he had asked in the past hour.

"No, not yet," the Bishop snapped. "And please don't ask again. I have told you already that we are waiting for Mr. Fontenoy."

"Very good, Your Grace," said the butler, stepping back.

"Are you sure you have not got your arrangements mixed up, Constance?" asked Henrietta.

"Mama, it was you who invited Nicholas to dinner yourself last Sunday," said an exasperated Constance.

"But perhaps he told you he couldn't come in the meantime, and you've forgotten?" queried Henrietta.

Constance raised her eyes to heaven. "I'm not stupid, Mama! If he told me he wasn't coming, then I think I should remember!"

Henrietta sat back and sighed. "Well, I don't know what we shall do in that case. Sit here until midnight waiting for him?"

"Papa, the servants will be starving, waiting for their own dinner after we have ours," said Emma. "Is it not best we allow them to serve dinner and Nicholas can join us whenever he does?"

"Of course we can't do that!" snapped the Bishop. "It would be unforgivably rude to start without our guest."

"And what of Nicholas's rudeness arriving so late?" asked Emma.

"Emma, please don't further irritate your father with mindless questions," ordered Henrietta.

"Yes, Emma, stop bothering Papa." Constance shot her sister a warning look across the table.

Suddenly the sound of the front-door knocker echoed loudly through the four-storey townhouse.

"At last!" sighed Emma.

"If you will excuse me, I shall let young Mr. Fontenoy in," said the butler as he turned to leave.

"No, it's quite all right – I will answer the door," said Constance as she stood quickly and left the room.

She closed the dining-room door behind her and hastily walked down the hall to the front door.

Unlatching it, she found Nicholas standing there.

"Thank goodness! I thought you'd had an accident!" she said as he stepped inside.

Closing the front door behind him, she enveloped him in an embrace.

Nicholas held his fiancée away from him and admired her, thinking how lucky he was.

Constance was of medium height, with an attractive figure. She had intelligent brown eyes set in a heart-shaped face, with a pale complexion and glossy brown hair pulled back in a bun. Although often her expression was demure, it was when smiling that her natural loveliness shone through.

She wasn't smiling now.

"Why are you so late?" she demanded.

"I got delayed by a lecturer – there was nothing I could do!"

"Papa is not pleased, I warn you."

"You should have just continued without me," said Nicholas.

"Oh, Nicholas, as if we would! You know what a stickler for etiquette Papa is!"

The irritation on her face faded as she looked into Nicholas's handsome face. She leaned forward and kissed his mouth.

"You've been drinking!" she accused him then, drawing back in horror.

"Yes, I had to!"

"Nicholas, is that you?" asked the Bishop as he came out of the dining room and peered down the hall.

"Yes, Father, it's Nicholas," Constance answered as she gently pushed Nicholas down the hallway to the dining room.

"Bishop Staffordshire, I can only apologise for my late arrival," said Nicholas, smiling broadly as he shook the Bishop's hand.

"We were becoming quite worried about you, my boy," said the Bishop as he smiled back and led Nicholas into the dining room.

"Good evening, Mrs. Staffordshire, Emma," Nicholas greeted the others as the butler pulled out his chair and he sat down at the table. "I must apologise for my lateness but I'm afraid it was due to circumstances quite beyond my control. My lecturer, Gratton, insisted I come to his study to discuss a dissertation and proceeded to insist I join him in a brandy."

"Brandy!" exclaimed Bishop Staffordshire, horrified.

"Yes, brandy, sir!" nodded Nicholas, looking equally outraged.

"Could you not have said no?" asked Emma from across the table.

"Hardly, Emma! And risk insulting his tutor!" snapped the Bishop.

"And risked not getting as good a grade in his dissertation?" added Henrietta.

"That's exactly what I thought!" said Nicholas. "I couldn't risk offending!"

"So you chose to offend us instead by being so late," Emma whispered under her breath.

"Pardon, Emma?" Nicholas smiled over at her.

"Ignore her, Nicholas," encouraged Constance, giving Emma another warning look.

"I don't know what the country is coming to," the Bishop shook his head disapprovingly, "when the teachers of our finest young minds are foisting alcoholic beverages on their charges!"

"I feel a little sorry for old Gratton," said Nicholas. "I think he might have a drink problem."

"Obviously!" said Henrietta.

Reeves stepped forward. "May I now serve dinner?" he said loudly.

"Yes, and as quick as you can – Master Nicholas must be hungry," said the Bishop.

With an audible sigh of relief, Reeves withdrew to fetch the food from the kitchen where the cook was struggling to keep it warm.

"Yes, I am hungry," said Nicholas. "I missed lunch as I had to attend that funeral today."

"You poor thing!" said Constance and she reached for his hand in concern. "I'm surprised you didn't faint in the lecture theatre."

Nicholas chuckled as he squeezed her hand. "I'm made of hardier stuff than that, Constance."

"Was that Ambrose Carter's funeral you attended?" asked the Bishop.

"Yes, I attended with my parents. I didn't see you in the congregation, Your Grace?"

"No. I had to attend a charity meeting. Were there many there?"

"Yes, it was crowded," nodded Nicholas.

"I suppose we should have gone?" fretted Henrietta.

"I told you I was otherwise engaged," said the Bishop harshly.

"But perhaps the girls and I should have attended?" Henrietta said.

"We, unlike Nicholas's father and many more, didn't know the man, Henrietta. We didn't grow up here and know him through the years . . . though I had occasion to meet him on a few occasions to ask for charitable donations for the city's disadvantaged. Needless to say he lived up to his reputation and gave me and my requests short shrift."

"He didn't give you a penny?" asked Nicholas.

"Not a penny," confirmed the Bishop. "Which was his prerogative, of course. But I wondered how a man who had so much could give so little."

"My father said he was a complex character," said Nicholas.

"I just found him plain rude when I met him," said the Bishop.

Reeves entered with a large tureen and quickly began to serve the soup as the diners helped themselves to dinner rolls.

As they began to eat, Constance said excitedly, "Never mind poor old Ambrose! What of his widow? I've heard rumours all day that when she turned up there were near gasps from the congregation as she is an exceptionally beautiful young woman, with all the grace of a royal princess. Is it true, Nicholas?"

"A royal princess?" repeated Emma in a rare show of excitement.

"Eh, yes, I guess it is," said Nicholas. "His wife is much younger and prettier than what you would have expected of Ambrose Carter, the little I knew and saw of him."

"How intriguing!" said Constance. "I think we should have gone to the funeral just to take a peek at her, Mama!"

"Funerals are not a vehicle of entertainment for your pleasure, Constance, and should not be treated so," the Bishop chastised her.

"Well, I know that, Father – but I still would have liked to take a peek at her. And it is probably the last time we'll see her. I've heard from friends that she's returning to her country estate without delay to continue her life as a recluse!"

"What a sad future for her," sighed Henrietta. "Without chick or child, husband or family."

"At least she'll have plenty of money," commented Nicholas with a smile at his fiancée.

CHAPTER 4

The next morning Lucas Hempton stepped from a hansom cab outside the Gresham Hotel and paid the driver. He checked his pocket watch and, seeing it was exactly eleven o'clock, climbed the steps briskly. The hotel doorman opened the glass door, letting him into the foyer. He glanced around, looking for Milandra, and spotted her sitting on her own in a Queen Ann chair at a low table in a corner. Smiling, he approached her. But, as he neared her, his smile dropped as he saw she was dressed in a green satin flounced dress with a resplendent, elaborate green hat.

"Ah, good morning, Lucas!"

Slowly he sat down in the armchair opposite her.

"Would you like some tea?" she asked as she reached forward and lifted the silver teapot on the table.

"No, thank you. I had tea just before I left my house."

"Very good," she said and replaced the teapot.

Lucas was studying her hat and gown in dismay.

"Is everything all right, Lucas?" she asked, seeing his concerned expression.

"I'm just – it's just – I'm slightly –" He couldn't seem to get the words out.

"Yes, Lucas?"

"You're not wearing black!"

"No," she agreed, looking down at her gown, unconcerned. "I'm wearing green."

"Yes, but – do you think that is appropriate?"

"I've always thought green rather suited my complexion. Do you not?"

"Well, I'm sure it does. But – my dear – you have just buried your husband! Black is the appropriate colour to wear – for some considerable time!"

"Ah, yes, black. I've never cared for black. It always seems to make me look washed out."

"Washed out or washed in, Milandra, black is what you should be wearing and I suggest you return to your room with haste to change your garments!" Lucas's words sounded more like an order than a suggestion.

"Lucas, I only brought one black outfit with me and, after the dreadful day yesterday wearing it, I've no wish to ever wear it again. As for Ambrose, he hated the colour black on a woman as well. And he insisted that if he should go before me, always the likelihood given our ages, I was to wear black for one day and no more."

"But –"

"One day and no more. And I have fulfilled his wishes – I could not go against what he requested me to do," she said with downcast eyes.

"But what will people think? What will they say? A widow dressed as if she is about to be presented at court the day after her husband's funeral!"

She reached forward and took his hand. "Dear Lucas, I know how much you mean to protect me, but I can't really see what difference the colour of a gown will make."

"Well . . . I suppose it won't matter for long, as you're returning to the country today. I doubt you will have many visitors at your estate to see what colour you're wearing."

She smiled broadly and stood up, picking up her pink silk shawl and arranging it around her shoulders. "In that case, shall we go and take a look at the house? You brought the keys?"

"Eh, yes," said Lucas, looking even more shocked at the sight of the shawl. "I did want to go through that paperwork first, though."

"Oh, we can go through all that after. I really want to have a look at the house." Milandra picked up her embroidered purse and began walking towards the hotel entrance.

"Well, in that case . . ." said Lucas as he stood up and quickly began to follow her.

They walked out of the hotel and down the steps onto the street. The pavement was busy with people coming and going and the street was filled with carriages making their way along the thoroughfare.

"One of the most important papers we need to deal with, before you get your train, is the signing of the proxy of the wine merchants over to me," said Lucas., "so that I can enable the smooth running of the business before it is wound down."

"Are you sure you can manage all that, Lucas? I mean, you have your own business to see to."

"It will be my pleasure to assist you, Milandra. I will find the time, no need to worry on that score."

As they arrived opposite Ambrose's townhouse they began to make their way across the street, careful to avoid the carriages.

"A proxy? Is that similar to a power of attorney?" asked Milandra as they waited to cross from the middle to the far side of the street.

"Yes, my dear. I will make all the decisions for you. You don't have to worry about a thing."

"I don't know what I'd do without you," smiled Milandra as they crossed to the far side of the street.

They stopped in front of the house. Milandra looked up, studying the monumental four-storey, double-fronted, terraced townhouse, standing proudly amongst its neighbours.

Lucas climbed the three steps that led to the double teak door and fumbled in his pocket. He took out a key and unlocked the door.

"It's quite stiff," he complained as he pushed it open.

Milandra followed him in and looked around. They were in a huge hallway. There was a staircase at the back which led up to a landing with a large arched window that let the light flood in. The hallway was filled with wooden boxes marked 'Carter Wines'.

"As I said, he stored stock for the wine business in here," said Lucas, inspecting one of the boxes.

Milandra crossed over to the double doorway to the right of the hallway and entered a shuttered room, which she could just make out was a dining room in the semi-darkness.

She came back out and crossed over to the other side of the hallway and through another double door that led into a parlour. Lucas followed her.

"It's many years since I've been in here, but I think the main drawing room is on the first floor," said Lucas.

Milandra silently came out of the room and headed towards the staircase.

"At the back of the stairs is a stairway that leads down to the basement – which is where the kitchens are and what used to be the servant's quarters," said Lucas.

Milandra nodded and began to walk up the stairs.

"It was a fine house in its day," said Lucas as he followed her. "I remember coming here as a child visiting Ambrose growing up. It was never a happy house though. His parents' marriage was strained and he was an only child – but you know that."

Milandra didn't answer. As she reached the first landing she paused and looked out the arched window down at the long garden which was overgrown and looked as if it had not been tended to in decades.

"He should have sold it years ago," sighed Lucas, looking down at the garden.

Milandra walked around the banisters of the staircase and through a double door that led into the drawing room.

"Be careful!" warned Lucas as she made her way through the disarrayed furniture and boxes there.

She walked towards the front of the house and began to open the shutters of the six tall windows there, flooding the room with light.

Lucas blinked a few times as his eyes became accustomed to the sunlight.

"What a mess!" he declared, looking around the giant room which was completely topsy-turvy.

Milandra walked around, studying the fine ornate ceilings and the chandeliers which hung from them. She examined the large fireplace. And then she looked through a window at busy Sackville Street below.

"At least I've got my bearings of the house now before I show the auctioneer around," said Lucas.

Milandra stood in thought, staring out at the street below.

"My dear, I really hate to hurry you," said Lucas, "but we need to return to the hotel and sign the papers before I get you to the train station. You don't want to be arriving back home in the dark."

Milandra made no response.

Lucas waited, puzzled by her silence.

Then she said: "Lucas, I'd like you to contact the auctioneer and arrange a viewing without further delay."

"Of course," nodded Lucas.

"For the sale of the estate in the country," she said.

"*What?*"

"Put the estate in the country on the market at once. I no longer wish to live there," she said assuredly.

"But this is the first time you have mentioned this! Where will you live?"

"Here! I plan to live here in this house!" she announced.

"On Sackville Street?" Lucas's eyes widened in shock and his mouth dropped open.

"Yes, on Sackville Street."

"Have you taken leave of your senses, Milandra? The estate has been your home for the last eight years. Why would you move to Dublin? You don't know anybody here!"

"I know you – isn't that a start?"

"But, you love the estate."

"I loved the estate when Ambrose was alive, but it would be unbearable to live there now that he's gone," she said, looking sadly down at the floor.

"But –"

"Far too many memories. No, I need a fresh start, and here's as good as anywhere."

"But Ambrose would turn in his grave if he knew you were selling his beloved estate."

"Ambrose is dead, Lucas. He will not be turning left, right or centre any more. I have to make a new future for myself. I can't just stagnate on the estate for ever more, lost in memories of my beloved Ambrose."

"Well, I am quite shocked, I don't mind telling you. I never dreamed you would want to live anywhere else, or want any other life than the one you had there," said Lucas.

"And indeed I wouldn't have, if Ambrose was still alive."

"But the house here is barely habitable – it is a disgrace!" objected Lucas.

"Then I shall employ the best interior designers to renovate it. Money is no object. I will turn this house into the best on Sackville Street – nay, in Dublin," she said confidently.

"I think it's wise you do nothing in haste. Return to the country, think on this matter and decide what you want to do."

"No need, I have already decided. I won't be returning to the country. I will stay at the Gresham Hotel until work here on the house is completed," she said.

"But what of all your things, your belongings in the estate?"

"Flancy shall pack them all and bring them here to me," said Milandra.

"Flancy!"

"Yes, you know, my cook and maid."

"Oh, I know her all right!" Lucas shuddered at the thought of the woman.

"Dear Lucas," she smiled and walked over to him, taking both his hands in hers. "I'm so glad we have come to this decision and that you support me in it. I truly don't know what I would do without you!" She let go of his hands. "Em . . . I should look at the bedrooms . . ."

With that, she walked out onto the landing.

CHAPTER 5

Constance waited patiently at the front gates of Trinity College in the afternoon sunshine. She had spent the day looking through the shops on Grafton Street and now waited for Nicholas as pre-arranged. Her eyes searched among the young men who were teeming in and out of the university. She smiled as she spotted him heading in her direction. As always her heart lightened just at the very sight of him. She knew that was as it should be, as she was deeply in love. But Nicholas seemed to have a similar effect on everybody who met him. He had the ability to lift a person's spirits, lighten their hearts, charm them from bad form into good form. Even her father the Bishop adored him. She knew how lucky she was to have him.

"Sorry, I think I'm late!" apologised Nicholas as he reached her.

"Nothing new there!" she said, smiling at him.

He smiled back and offered her his arm. She took it and the two of them began to stroll in the direction of Sackville Street.

"How were your classes?" she asked.

"It's just all about the exams now." His face creased in concern at the thought of them beginning the following week.

"Don't fret, my love. I know you will come top of your class," she assured him, reaching forward and kissing his cheek.

"I wish I had as much faith in me as you do! If I just pass the bloody things, I'll be happy," he said.

"You will!" she said.

"Just think, in three weeks' time I will be free of all this study. Free from exams and lecturers lecturing me!"

"And you will be a qualified solicitor working in the esteemed practice of Fetherston & Sons." She said it almost dreamily, as she anticipated the glorious future before them.

"All the other chaps are so envious I've got a position at Fetherstons'. Most can't even get a position at a solicitor's practice and are starting their careers as clerks. I guess I owe that to my father's reputation and connections."

"Nonsense! You would have passed the interview regardless of whose son you were. Any solicitor's firm would realise they'd be privileged to have you, as soon as they met you!"

"Perhaps. But Father's connections still were a deciding factor with Fetherstons', I imagine!"

"Anyway – the wedding! Your mother is now insisting the venue is the Gresham after she attended that funeral function there. She's made an appointment for us to meet the management. What do you think?"

"Darling, as long as it is you that I'm getting married to on the day, I don't care about anything else," he said. "We could have the reception in an alleyway for all I care."

She hit his arm playfully. "Oh, be serious, Nicholas! I need your opinion on this!"

"I would be delighted with the Gresham in that case. And anything else you suggest," he added with a smile.

As they strolled across Carlisle Bridge and along Sackville Street, Constance had many further suggestions about the wedding. Nicholas tried to concentrate as Constance went into great detail about flowers and pageboys and church music. He smiled to himself as the thought struck him that Constance was putting more work into their impending nuptials than he was into his law exams.

"Mother says we should book a special carriage to carry us from the church to the –" Constance stopped speaking abruptly and stood still.

"What's the matter?" he asked.

"Look!" she said, pointing across the road to Ambrose Carter's house.

Nicholas peered across the road. Workmen were coming in and

out of the front door. Boxes and furniture were being carried out and brilliant luxurious furniture was being carried in. The shutters were all open and the windows were being cleaned. Inside the windows they could see curtains being put up.

"My gosh," said Constance, "I've never seen a soul going in or out of that shut-up house for years. It's a surprise to see all that going on. It must be the new owners."

"It can't be sold yet," Nicholas said. "The funeral was only last week and Lucas Hempton told my father he hadn't even employed an auctioneer then."

"Well, sold it must be, my darling. I wonder who bought it?"

"Somebody with a lot of money, that's certain," he said.

"Oh Nicholas, imagine if we could afford to live in such a house! Instead of having to live with your parents for the beginning of our marriage."

"One day we might live in just such a house," he assured her. "And living with my parents won't be for that long. Once I start earning we'll be able to afford something of our own."

"Yes, but what?" She sighed. "A shoebox of a house somewhere in one of these new suburbs that are being built."

"It will only be for a while. I promise you we will be back living around here very soon." "I have every faith in you and believe we will. But, do you know, if I had to live in a shoebox for the rest of my life, I'd be happy as long as you were there with me."

They reached the Fontenoy house. Nicholas took out his key and let them in. The house was a very bright house with cream tiled floors that stretched down the hallway to a winding staircase which swept upstairs.

Constance always loved being there as it was a cheerful happy home. It was not a large family: apart from Nicholas there was only one other sibling, Frederick, who at twenty was five years younger than Nicholas. He was also a student at Trinity.

They could hear voices coming from the drawing room and they headed into the room.

Like the hallway, the parlour was large and bright with light flooding in through the bay windows. The room was elegantly furnished, with a dark-timber floor covered by a Persian rug. Over the fireplace, pride of place in the room, was a portrait of Nicholas which Constance always thought showed him at his most handsome best.

"Good afternoon," said Nicholas as they entered.

Agatha and Daniel were seated together on a couch in front of the fire and they were in conversation with a woman, dressed in dark red, who occupied a Queen Ann chair beside the fireplace. Constance felt she knew nearly everybody in Dublin society, and certainly all of the Fontenoys' relatives and friends, but this beautiful woman was a stranger to her.

"Ah, my boy, we have a lovely surprise guest – Mrs. Carter," said Daniel, standing up.

"Please, Mr. Fontenoy, call me Milandra," urged the woman.

"Milandra, you remember my son from the funeral? Nicholas?" asked Daniel.

"Of course I do – lovely to see you again, Nicholas," said Milandra, standing up and crossing over to shake his hand.

"And you too, Mrs. Carter –" Nicholas saw Milandra's disapproving expression and corrected himself: "Milandra."

Milandra then turned and smiled brightly at Constance. "And you must be Constance. I've just been hearing all about you."

"All good, I hope?" asked Constance, who found herself strangely intimidated by this woman.

"Nicholas's parents have been singing your praises – singing both your praises." Milandra flashed another smile at Nicholas.

Constance took Milandra's outstretched hand and shook it gently. "I was so sorry to hear about your husband. I didn't know him, but I can only imagine your loss."

"Thank you, most kind of you." Milandra nodded and returned to her seat.

"Join us for tea, children," urged Agatha, reaching for the teapot in front of her.

Nicholas and Constance sat on armchairs on the opposite side of the fireplace from Milandra.

"We were just talking about you too," said Nicholas as he smiled over at her.

"Oh? How so?"

"Well, we were passing your house and there seems to be a great deal of activity there," explained Constance.

"Is it sold?" asked Nicholas.

"No!" said Agatha as she carried two cups of tea over to Nicholas and Constance and placed them on a small table in front of them. "Milandra is moving into it herself! Imagine!"

"Oh!" said Nicholas. "I thought Lucas had said –"

"Lucas says many things and knows many things, but doesn't know what's in a woman's heart," said Milandra. "And my heart couldn't return to the country after Ambrose died."

"I think it's a very wise decision," said Agatha, retaking her seat. "Milandra was just explaining to us that she has no family where they lived, so why should she stay there? And I'm being completely selfish in my opinion, as it will be wonderful to have a bit of glamour around here."

"Well, I don't know if I can bring any glamour to you, but I can certainly promise to be a very good neighbour," said Milandra with a smile.

"And isn't that all we could wish for?" said Daniel.

"You're very brave," said Constance who was studying Milandra intently. "Moving to a strange city and starting again."

"I don't call it brave, I call it sensible," interjected Agatha. "Milandra is in her prime, and needs to get on with her life."

"Yes, indeed," said Constance as she studied Milandra's deep-red gown and wondered where on earth her widow's weeds were. She was also confused as to why the Fontenoys weren't scandalised by Milandra not wearing mourning dress not even a week since the funeral. She only hoped her own father would not see Milandra on Sackville Street or he would denounce her from the pulpit.

"I hope you don't think me forward, Nicholas," said Milandra, "imposing on your parents' hospitality by just arriving to the door unannounced, but they did ask me to call on them at the funeral . . . and I am in desperate need of good friends in this metropolis at such an awful time for me."

"Not at all!" said Nicholas.

"Not in the least!" said Agatha. "I meant it when I said you were to call on us, and am delighted you did. I just know we're all going to be the very best of friends."

"Thank you," said Milandra. "And, Nicholas, I also came on a purely selfish mission to ask some business advice from your father, he being a judge and so familiar with the legal profession in the city."

"Yes!" said Agatha, clapping her hands together. "Milandra was looking for a recommendation for a law firm to handle Ambrose's affairs now that he is deceased – and your father has recommended Fetherston & Sons!"

"I believe you are due to start work there yourself, Nicholas, so your father tells me, once you qualify next month?"

Nicholas was taken aback. "Yes, but didn't Tattingers' always handle your husband's affairs – correct me if I'm wrong?"

"They did, but old Mr. Tattinger, well, is exactly that now – old! I don't think he's up to the job, and Ambrose did recommend I employ somebody younger, if he should pass away before me. I have so many legal affairs to sort out."

"Oh, I see," said Nicholas, thinking that Lucas Hempton would not be impressed with a change of solicitors from his own friend Douglas Tattinger. "Well – in that case I'm sure Fetherston & Sons would be delighted with your business."

"I'll call into Fetherstons' tomorrow on my way to the courts and set up a meeting for you," offered Daniel.

"Isn't that a wonderful idea?" declared Agatha. "And, Nicholas, she would like you to help take care of her affairs!"

Now it all made sense to Constance. No wonder the Fontenoys were looking so happy. Certainly, whatever colour Milandra Carter was wearing in mourning was insignificant to them! To land a client as big as Carters for Fetherstons' before Nicholas even began to work there would assure his career would be made. Although as thrilled for Nicholas as his parents were, she sometimes wondered if things came too easily for him. A charmed life.

"Thank you – Milandra – we would be delighted to get your business," said Nicholas. "And I will be more than delighted to play my part."

41

"And I will be delighted to have my affairs in safe hands. As Lucas keeps telling me, there are so many vultures out there."

"So many!" agreed Agatha.

Milandra smiled at Daniel. "You must be delighted, Daniel, that your son is following you into law. Does the legal profession run in your family?"

"Yes, my father was a barrister," said Daniel.

"Although, Daniel is also related to aristocracy," said Agatha importantly.

"Really? How so?" Milandra's eyes widened.

"Daniel is the cousin of an earl in England," boasted Agatha unashamedly.

"How exciting!" declared Milandra.

"A distant cousin," said Daniel, looking irritated at his wife's inappropriate boasting. "I hardly know him. I believe he is a decent fellow, but his son is quite wayward, from what I understand."

It was Agatha's turn to give him a disapproving look for being so unnecessarily honest.

"Shame," said Milandra. "Anyway! I must not detain you any longer." She picked up her beaded purse and stood up.

"Oh, will you not stay for dinner?" asked Agatha.

"Most kind, but I have an appointment with a table restorer. I'm afraid I'm running late for him and have already kept him waiting in the Gresham foyer this past half hour. It was so nice to see you again and thank you for all your help."

They all stood and shook hands with her again.

"Thank you for the tea, Agatha," she said. "I will no doubt be seeing you soon, Nicholas, at Fetherstons', and it's been a pleasure meeting you, Constance."

"I'll show you to the door," said Daniel and he escorted her out.

Agatha sat in excited silence, beaming at Nicholas, until Daniel returned to the room.

Then she clasped her hands together. "Oh Nicholas! Isn't that wonderful news? Carters as your new client!"

"As my only client," said Nicholas, his head still spinning from the news.

Daniel returned and took his seat. "Fetherstons' won't believe it when I tell them the news – it will be the making of your career, my dear boy," he said.

"I thought that Carter Wines would be closing down?" asked Constance.

"Well, whatever its future, Milandra will bring a huge amount of work with her," said Daniel. "She's selling the estate in the country for a start. You can handle all that, Nicholas."

"This is all very sudden – Milandra Carter becoming a neighbour, employing your firm, having tea with you," commented Constance.

"Well, she is to be our neighbour, so we may as well be on good terms with her," said Agatha. "And why should Nicholas look a gift horse in the mouth?"

"I'm not saying he should. It's just – it's just –" Constance blurted out what was uppermost in her mind – "where are her widow's weeds?"

There was a pause before Agatha said, "Milandra said Ambrose insisted she didn't wear them."

"But why would he do that?" asked Constance.

"Ambrose Carter was a most peculiar man, liable to say anything that is not of the norm," said Daniel.

"But, even if he didn't want her to wear black, and she is merely doing what he wished, is she not worried about her own reputation? What people will say about her?" said Constance.

"Evidently not!" said Nicholas with a smirk.

"I think it's quite shocking," said Constance.

"Well, I think she's a young woman who should get on with her life without much delay," said Agatha. "She doesn't want to waste her best childbearing years while she's dressed in widow's weeds!"

"Well, I hope the rest of Dublin can be as liberal in their attitudes as you, Mrs. Fontenoy," said Constance. "To me she's coming across as a scarlet woman!"

"I think that's enough of that kind of talk, Constance." Daniel's face was disapproving. "It's up to Milandra – Mrs. Carter – to conduct herself in whatever manner she wants and she certainly has the means to do so. She could be the making of Nicholas's career, and certainly a very big help up the ladder for him. We welcome her with open arms."

Constance knew not to say any more. The Fontenoys had made their minds up to like Milandra Carter, and nothing would dissuade them. Constance reckoned Daniel and Agatha first considered her a creature of curiosity but, on finding out she was liable to be a client of Nicholas's new firm, were quite willing to put the interests of their pride and joy, their son, before anything else. They were also sufficiently confident about their position in society not to worry about what others would think of their having a guest in their house not wearing black, when she should plainly have been.

"Are you staying for dinner, Constance?" asked Agatha pleasantly, changing the subject.

"I'm afraid not – I'm expected at home this evening," said Constance.

CHAPTER 6

Constance was deep in thought as she turned the corner into Mountjoy Square. She was unsettled by meeting Milandra Carter and she really wasn't sure why. The woman had been charming, friendly and was likely to be an amazing support to Nicholas's career. But there was something about her that she mistrusted and she was uneasy that the Fontenoys had struck up an instant friendship with her. She supposed she was just aware that Milandra Carter was set to be a permanent fixture in the Fontenoys' life. And Constance didn't like change. She liked their life just as it was, and was uncomfortable about this mysterious beautiful woman suddenly invading it. As she made her way around the park in the centre of Mountjoy Square to their home, she realised she was being uncharitable. The woman had just lost her husband, was in a strange city where she knew nobody and she, Constance, was just being selfish – and perhaps jealous of this woman's beauty, confidence and, yes, wealth.

She reached the house, climbed the steps to the door and knocked. A few moments later the butler, Reeves, opened it.

"Good evening, Miss Staffordshire," said the butler.

"Hello, Reeves," she said, walking past him then removing her shawl and handing it to him.

Seeing the time on the clock, she hurried down the hallway to the dining room where she found her family just being seated for dinner. Nicholas might get away with being late with her father, but she never would. She quickly took her usual seat.

The Bishop said grace and then Reeves began to serve dinner.

"Did you have a good day, Constance?" asked her mother.

"Yes, I had to check some plans for the wedding and then I met Nicholas and spent some time at the Fontenoys'."

"And how were they?" smiled Henrietta.

"Good, as always . . . they had a guest having tea with them."

"Anyone we know?" asked Henrietta.

"Milandra Carter," answered Constance.

The Bishop's face turned red as he slammed down his fork and knife on the table.

"Ambrose Carter's widow?" he asked.

"The very one," answered Constance.

"What!" he exploded. "Having tea with the Fontenoys! And her husband not cold in his grave! And that's the least of it!"

Constance hurried to explain. "She was there to ask for advice on her business affairs."

"Nonsense! I am truly shocked by the behaviour of this woman!" said the Bishop, his face becoming angrier. "I have heard nothing but talk about her over the past week from various sources. The woman is prancing around the city in a variety of different coloured expensive frocks – shopping!"

"Shopping?" asked Henrietta.

"Yes – shopping!" confirmed the Bishop. "Seemingly she is due to move into that relic of a house Ambrose Carter left her on Sackville Street and is busy renovating it and refurbishing it at great cost, from what I hear."

"Hardly the behaviour of a grieving widow." Henrietta became concerned.

"It certainly is not! And I have heard far worse about her than that!" continued the Bishop.

"Do tell!" pushed Henrietta.

"She dines in the Gresham Hotel in the restaurant on her own most nights – and drinks wine with her supper!"

"No!" Henrietta looked horrified but Constance saw a glimpse of excitement on her mother's face as well.

"She has been seen during the day and night in the foyer and the lounge of the hotel, meeting with a series of different *men*!" The Bishop's voice rose several octaves on the last word.

"I think – I feel – a little dizzy!" said Henrietta, picking up a napkin and fanning herself.

"And where does she go with these men after having met them?" asked Emma excitedly.

"It is not for young ears to hear where a woman dressed like a trollop staying in a suite in a hotel brings her assortment of men," pronounced the Bishop.

"Father!" interrupted Constance. "I believe Mrs. Carter has been very busy meeting a variety of furniture restorers, plasterers, painters, polishers, curtain-makers and gardeners! These, I imagine, are the assortment of men you are referring to, and there is nothing more untoward about the meetings than the price of a yard of fabric!"

"I've never heard anything like it! She should be dressed in black for at least two years after the demise of her husband and should not be even seen out for six months." The Bishop spoke as if he was on the pulpit. "Not meeting furniture polishers, if that is who these men are, but it all sounds very dubious to me! And as for socialising – it is just out of the question! Having tea with the Fontenoys!" ·

"Well, tea was what she was having," said Constance as she cut into the lamb Reeves had just served her.

"I'm shocked that Daniel Fontenoy would even receive her in his house," said the Bishop.

"Well, he could hardly slam the door in her face," said Henrietta, beginning to fret.

"That's exactly what I would have done and told her to behave herself in a proper manner as fitting for a recently bereaved widow, and not go around acting like a common . . ." The Bishop searched for the right word but was unable to find one that was fit to be said in front of his daughters.

"Well, perhaps the Fontenoys are a little more liberal than us," suggested Henrietta.

"Or more charitable!" Constance felt the need to defend her future in-laws. "The woman is alone and without friends in Dublin, and they are merely holding out the hand of friendship to her."

"While she is sitting there dressed like a – a –"

"She looked perfectly respectable, Papa. If she hadn't been recently widowed, we wouldn't even pass comment." Constance found herself getting angry.

"But you are missing the point – she *is* recently widowed!" The Bishop was getting angrier. "I think I will make my sermon this Sunday all about reminding the congregation about the correct manner in which a wife must mourn her husband!"

"You're not going to name her on the pulpit!" Henrietta's fretting turned to panic.

"I nearly think I should!" said the Bishop.

"Papa!" It was Constance's turn to slam her fork and knife down on the table. "Under no circumstances are you to mention Milandra Carter's name on your pulpit!"

"It's not for you to decide what I speak about in my sermons, young lady!"

"Papa! If you mention that woman's name on your pulpit, then you are also casting aspersions on the Fontenoys who have taken her under their wing. Do you really want to do that? To my fiancé's family? You need to hold your tongue!"

"I think you forget yourself, young lady!" snapped the Bishop. "You may be soon to be married but you are still my daughter and still living under my roof!"

Father and daughter glared at each other.

"If you will excuse me," said Constance, abruptly standing up. "I am no longer hungry."

"Constance!" pleaded Henrietta as Constance marched out of the room.

That night Constance was sitting in her room reading a novel beside the lit fire. She hadn't gone back downstairs after her disagreement with her father.

There was a knock on her door.

"Come in!" she called.

The door opened and her father walked in.

She looked at him warily.

"You didn't finish your dinner," he said, standing by the fire.

"I wasn't hungry," she said coolly.

"I'll get Reeves to send you up something from the kitchen," he offered.

"No need," she said and continued reading.

"I don't wish to quarrel with you, Constance. But what's right is right and what's wrong is wrong. We need to uphold values and correct behaviour. And from all accounts I've heard, and there have been many, Milandra Carter is setting the most dreadful example to the young women of this city. One bad apple can turn the barrel rotten."

"I think there are enough bad apples already in this city and I doubt Milandra Carter will be responsible for turning any more apples bad. If you don't wish to quarrel with me, then why bring up the subject again?" she asked, slamming her book shut.

"I – I do admire your loyalty to Nicholas's family – that I commend you for," her father said, his voice becoming gentler.

"I'm sure if Daniel Fontenoy feels there is nothing wrong in receiving Mrs. Carter, then there isn't," she said.

The Bishop looked at his stubborn daughter and then bent down and kissed her head.

"Goodnight. I will see you at breakfast," he said.

"Goodnight," she muttered as he turned and left.

CHAPTER 7

Milandra had spent the day visiting the boutiques, shops and arcades in Lower Sackville Street. As she walked down the street, her reputation had gone before her. She was attracting many glances, stares and disapproving looks. People whispered about her as she walked by, staring at the lush purple gown she was attired in. She was greeted with dismay by the shop owners as she ordered a series of exquisite shoes just delivered from London, and glamorous gowns from Paris, the proprietors' moods only lifting at the realisation she was depositing a small fortune in each of their outlets.

She finished her shopping trip in a chocolatier's. As she walked into the shop a hush descended on the other shoppers and the staff. She walked slowly around, inspecting the array of chocolates, toffees and cream cakes on offer behind glass.

"May I help you?" asked the proprietor through thin lips.

"Yes, thank you," smiled Milandra and she delivered an extensive order of different treats. "And if you could have them delivered to my house. 71 Upper Sackville Street."

"Quite a large order, madam," said the proprietor. "When do you need it delivered?"

"I'm expecting guests," said Milandra as she opened her purse to settle the bill. "So, if you can have them delivered within the hour? Good day to you."

Milandra left the shop and continued walking up the street. As she passed the General Post Office, she recognised a woman coming towards her who had been at Ambrose's funeral. Her name was

Mrs. Vickers, a matronly woman who looked very pious and proud.

"Good day, Mrs. Vickers," smiled Milandra as their paths crossed.

Mrs. Vickers barely nodded at her as she hurried past her with a look of disgust on her face.

Unconcerned, Milandra continued her journey until she reached her house. The door was open and a workman was painting it.

"Afternoon, Mrs. Carter," he said cheerily.

"Afternoon," she said, walking past him indoors.

Inside, the house was a hive of activity with workmen everywhere.

She spent a while inspecting the work. Then there was a knock on the door. The messenger boy from the chocolatier's had arrived with several boxes.

Milandra led him into the dining room. "You can just leave them here on the table," she instructed before going back into the hall and calling loudly, "Gentlemen! Down tools! I have an array of treats here to reward you for your hard work!"

The next day Bishop Staffordshire was seated at his office in an annexe to the church, when his assistant knocked on the door.

"Pardon me, Your Grace, there is somebody here to see you."

"Who is it?" asked the Bishop, looking up from his paperwork.

"Mrs. Milandra Carter," said the assistant.

The Bishop's face turned from surprise to anger. "Tell her I cannot meet her."

"Very good, Your Grace," said the assistant who hastily retreated and closed the door. The Bishop sat thinking for a moment, then shook his head in bewilderment and continued with his paperwork.

A minute later there was another knock on the door and the assistant came in again.

"What is it?" snapped the Bishop.

"It's Mrs. Milandra Carter, Your Grace. She says it's very important and she won't take up much of your time."

The Bishop's face erupted in rage at the audacity of the woman. "Tell her to –"

He was suddenly silenced by the sight of a beautiful woman dressed in a cream gown sweeping past the assistant into his office.

"I am so sorry to barge in on you like this, Your Grace, but I really needed to speak to you." Milandra positioned herself in front of his desk.

The Bishop sat with his mouth open as he looked her up and down.

"I will only take five minutes out of your busy day, I promise you," she said, smiling graciously at him. "Judge Fontenoy suggested I pay you this visit."

The Bishop fought the urge to tell this harlot to leave his premises immediately. But he knew to do such a thing would risk offending Daniel Fontenoy if she was speaking the truth.

He looked at his assistant and said, "You may leave us."

The assistant beat a hasty retreat and closed the door behind him, leaving them alone.

Smiling, Milandra sat down in the chair on the other side of the desk. The Bishop's face became crosser, as he had not asked her to sit.

"Well – what do you need to see me about?" he asked coldly.

"I know how busy you are, Your Grace. So, as I said, I won't take up much of your time." Milandra was smiling sweetly.

He sat in stony silence, waiting for her to continue.

"I know this is a big imposition, but I need your advice," she said.

"In what area could I possibly advise you?" he asked, his eyes trailing up and down her gown, lamenting the waste of money that had gone into its purchase.

"Were you acquainted with my late husband?" she asked.

"Not really. I had met him on occasion, but that was the sum of my relations with him."

"Well, I want to talk to you about Ambrose's good works."

The Bishop squinted in confusion behind his spectacles, wondering if they were talking about the same man.

"What good works? I never knew Ambrose Carter to do any good works."

"Ah, yes, that was Ambrose. Such a modest man." She nodded knowingly.

"The little I knew of your late husband would never inspire me to describe him as modest."

"Oh, but he was, Your Grace. He was always donating to various good causes, but he did it anonymously. He didn't want gratitude or attention."

The Bishop took off his spectacles and sat back in his chair. "I can hardly believe it."

But, as Ambrose Carter had shocked everybody in Dublin by his choice of wife, the Bishop considered the fact that there might have been many different sides to Ambrose Carter that he kept well hidden.

"Well, if Ambrose did give anonymously throughout his life as you suggest, then I am glad for his sake, for the good of his eternal soul," he said.

"Indeed."

"You still haven't said why you're here?" Although his interest had been piqued, he still wanted this vainglorious creature gone from his office as quickly as possible.

Milandra sat forward and spoke earnestly to him. "It is my intention, Your Grace, to continue with Ambrose's good works. I want to donate considerable sums to charity."

"I see!" said the Bishop, shocked but now very interested and sitting forward himself to hear more.

"But I don't know where to begin! What cause is worthier than the other? Which charity is more deserving than the next? That is why Judge Fontenoy suggested I meet you. He said that you may be able to offer some guidance, a helping hand, to make sure that the funds I donate get to the most deserving."

The Bishop's eyes widened in amazement "Well – I – well –"

"But, if you're too busy, or have not got the time needed to help me, then I completely understand and will ask for another's guidance," Milandra said.

"No! Of course I have the time!" he said, and managed a smile for the first time that day.

"You do?" Her eyes widened in surprise.

"My dear Mrs. Carter, this city is crying for wealthy patrons such as yourself to help the disadvantaged. I am the head of several such charities, and the help you could give us would be invaluable. I – I can't tell you how much we would appreciate it."

"Oh, you would be doing me such a favour," she sighed. "I know nothing of such things, and a guiding hand like yours will make the process so much easier. I will be able to rest assured that the money is going to the right causes."

"You can rest assured, Mrs. Carter! Not one penny you donate will go to the undeserving or the ungrateful. I myself will be eternally grateful to you if you support the charities I run."

"Then I won't take up any more of your time, Your Grace," she said, standing.

He stood up quickly. "I sincerely hope you don't feel you must rush off now? If you would like to discuss the matter further, I will make time for you."

"How kind, but I really must be going. I'm meeting an interior designer at my house in Sackville Street at three."

"Yes, I heard you are moving in there?"

"Yes. It should be ready next week and hopefully I will be ensconced by then."

He rounded his desk and escorted her to the door. She waited for him to open it for her. He did so and followed her out to the office where his assistant was sitting at his desk.

"Let us arrange to meet next week to discuss your plans in much greater detail," the Bishop suggested.

"That would be excellent."

"Shall we say next Thursday? At three?" he suggested with a smile.

"Splendid!" she said.

"Write that in my diary," he instructed his assistant. "Mrs. Carter – next Thursday – at three."

"Good day to you, Your Grace."

"Good day, Mrs. Carter!" said the Bishop cheerily and stood there staring after her as she walked out.

"What a remarkable woman!" he said to his assistant who stared at him in confusion and shock.

CHAPTER 8

Nicholas's best friend Tom Fitzgerald lived in rooms at Trinity College. It was late on a Friday afternoon and both of them were due to start their final law exams on the Monday. But instead of being in the library studying, they were in Tom's small drawing room enjoying bottles of beer with Nicholas's younger brother Frederick.

"So –" pressed Tom as he swigged from his beer bottle, "who is it to be?"

"I told you, I haven't decided yet," said Nicholas who was stretched out on a couch.

"But it's not fair leaving us in the dark!" complained Frederick, seated by the window.

"There's plenty of time to decide yet," said Nicholas.

"When are you thinking of letting us know then? The night before your wedding?" asked Tom, half laughing.

"It's not fair putting such pressure on a chap!" laughed Nicholas, sitting up.

"It's a simple question and deserves a simple answer – who is to be your best man – Frederick or me?" pushed Tom. "You won't leave this room until you tell us!"

"You have to pick me – I'm your brother!" said Frederick. "It's what is expected!"

"Nonsense! You have to choose me! Traditionally it should be your best friend!" insisted Tom.

As Nicholas looked at the two of them, he realised that despite the good-humoured banter both very much wanted the role. And rejection could cause offense.

There was a knock on the door. Tom put down his beer bottle and crossed over to the front door which led directly on to the main square in Trinity College.

To his surprise, he saw Constance standing there.

"Constance!" he said.

"Hello, Tom. Is Nicholas here?" she asked.

Hearing the others talking inside, she walked in past Tom.

"I thought I might find you here!" said Constance, looking down at her fiancé. "I tried your home, and the library, and as your classes are now finished this was the next place on my list!"

"Eh, myself and Tom were just doing some last-minute swotting!" explained Nicholas, looking embarrassed and amused all at the same time. "Isn't that right, Tom?"

"Yes, just going through the finer points of – invitation to tort!" said Tom as he sat back down in his chair.

"Invitation to drink, more like!" said Constance, taking the near-empty bottle of beer from Nicholas's hand and examining it.

"Don't be mad, my pet, all work and no play . . ." Nicholas said.

"Hmmm." Constance tried to look disapproving but a smile crossed her face and she started to giggle.

"That's more like it! You see, Nicholas, you couldn't find a more supportive and gracious wife in the whole of Dublin," said Tom, as he uncorked another bottle and handed it to Nicholas.

"That is to be your last one, Nicholas," said Constance, sitting down beside him on the couch. "Your father would be furious if he knew you were wasting precious days before your finals drinking!"

"Oh, Nicholas doesn't need to do any more study, Constance – he's going to come top of the class," Tom assured her. "Unlike me who will be lucky to pass!"

"In that case, Tom, you shouldn't allow Nicholas and Frederick to distract you from your own studies," said Constance.

"I'm a lost cause at this stage! Nothing I can do between now and Monday will save me. So I might as well have another one of these!" Tom uncorked another bottle of beer. "Can I tempt you to a glass yourself, Constance?"

"Certainly not! My father would throw me out of the house if he as much as smelled liquor on me!" said Constance, grimacing at the thought of it.

"Actually, Constance, now that you are here, you can settle an argument for us," said Frederick.

"Oh?"

"Yes, Nicholas hasn't said yet who will be his best man. Both Tom and I have put ourselves forward for the position. But he won't decide. I think the decision should be left to you."

"I have enough problems sorting out my bridesmaids, let alone involving myself in Nicholas's best-man dilemmas!"

"Excellent idea!" agreed Tom. "Constance, you should pick."

Constance turned to Nicholas who looked amused and unworried by the suggestion.

"Well, if the decision is left to me, then I think I will never be able to choose," he said, "so you would be doing me a favour, my darling. And, after all, you are making every other decision about the wedding." He took her hand, smirking at her.

"As it should be!" declared Tom.

Constance's forehead creased as she looked at Tom and Frederick. She knew both of them adored Nicholas, and from their faces both were eager to be by his side on his big day. Frederick, his brother, would be a natural choice. But Tom was such a good friend, and normally a man's best friend should be best man. As she looked at the two, she tried to imagine which of them would look better at the top of the church on the wedding day. Both looked very well, and would not let them down. But as she observed Frederick, he did look very baby-faced and even younger than his years. Whereas Tom looked like an adult and would look very impressive.

"In that case – I choose Tom!" she declared.

"Aha!" shouted Tom in delight, jumping up and shaking Nicholas's hand and then kissing Constance on the cheek.

"I'm sorry, Frederick." Constance looked over sympathetically at a crestfallen Frederick. "But it usually is a best friend rather than a brother, after all. Now, we really must go!" She took the bottle of beer out of Nicholas's hand and placed it on the table. "I want to speak to your mother about the Gresham, which will barely leave me enough time to be back at home for dinner."

"The perils of being engaged to a Bishop's daughter! A curfew of seven thirty every evening to be seated at the dining-room table!" mocked Nicholas.

Tom saw them to the door.

"And I will prepare a list of all your best man duties, Tom!" said Constance as they stepped into the main square.

"I look forward to receiving them!" Tom called after them.

Constance took Nicholas's arm as they walked across the cobbles of the university's front square.

"Thank you for saving me from that unpleasant job of choosing," said Nicholas.

"Well, I knew if it was left to you, you would be so frightened of offending either of them we would end up with no best man!"

"Why did you go for Tom?"

"Well, as I said, a best man is normally one's best friend rather than one's brother. But, also, I think he is older and more mature – he will be able to carry out the duties better."

"Wise thinking!" He bent down and kissed her cheek. Then he smiled down at her and gently led her over to one of the arches that led off the square.

"What are you doing?" she asked as he led her into the darkened empty laneway.

He enveloped her in his arms and began to kiss her. She held him tightly, kissing him back.

"I can't wait for our wedding night," he whispered into her ear.

She thought she could stay with him there forever as she gazed into his blue eyes.

"Well, wait we must!" she said, smiling at him. "I really need to speak to your mother!"

"All right!" he sighed and offered his arm to her again.

She held his arm tightly as they walked back into the square.

CHAPTER 9

Lucas Hempton hastily made his way down Sackville Street towards Ambrose Carter's house. He chastised himself that he must now stop referring to it as that, as it was now Milandra's house. He paused as he reached it, looking up at it. It was barely recognisable, from the cleaned stonework to the sparkling unshuttered windows, to the shiny freshly painted black door and the polished brass knocker.

He climbed the steps and, taking out his key, let himself in.

Inside, the house was transformed. The vast hallway now had new black-and-white Italian tiles throughout. The staircase had its wood polished and a thick luxuriant red carpet swept up the centre of it. To either side of the staircase the French windows at the back of the house were now unshuttered for the first time in years, flooding the foyer with light. Through these open windows Lucas could see gardeners busy at work transforming the garden. He peered into the dining room to the right and saw that had been equally transformed into a lavish room fit to host Queen Victoria. The parlour to the left of the hallway was now a tasteful room with exquisite French Renaissance furniture.

"*Milandra!*" he called at the top of his voice, which seemed to echo through the building.

He stood in the hallway waiting for a response and a few moments later he saw her walk around the banisters upstairs and stand at the top of the stairs, the light flooding in behind her from the arched window there.

"Lucas! I wasn't expecting you!" she said.

"I hadn't heard anything from you all week, and so I thought I'd better call in as I was worried about you," he said, climbing the staircase up to her.

"You are so thoughtful," she said and kissed his cheek when he reached her.

She turned and began walking back to the drawing room she had come from.

"I hardly recognise the place," he said, following her through its double doors.

There was a young girl standing in the middle of the room, unpacking some wooden boxes. She gave a brief curtsy to Lucas.

"Do you like what I've done?" Milandra asked.

"It's certainly impressive," he said, staring around what was now an ornate and elegant room. He marvelled at the luxuriant curtains swishing down from the tall windows at the front of the room and gold-leafed-framed couches and chaises longues perfectly placed around the room in front of the giant marble fireplace that took centre stage.

"Do you think Ambrose would approve?" she asked.

"Well, I don't know if Ambrose ever approved of the spending of money," said Lucas, crossing over to the curtains and examining the thick drapes.

"Kitty, go and fetch us some tea," said Milandra to the girl and she went off to carry out her task.

"You've been hiring staff as well?" he asked.

"Yes, not many, but I thought I'd better make a start," she said, taking out a silver ornament from a box and unwrapping it from its paper.

"Is this all new?" asked Lucas, peering into one of the boxes.

"No, these are items I've had Flancy send up from the estate. Items I want to keep."

She crossed over and placed the ornament on the mantelpiece. She stepped back and admired it, then made a small adjustment to its placing.

"Flancy has been very busy packing everything and having it sent up here," she said.

"I imagine she has!" said Lucas, reaching into a box and taking out another ornament to inspect. "So – when are you moving in?"

"Oh, I've already moved in! Yesterday."

"I see! But have you enough staff?"

"Quite enough to get me by for now. I will interview for more shortly."

"I know a good butler, if you require one," Lucas offered.

"No, I can make my own arrangements, thank you,"

"Very well."

"And Flancy is due to arrive soon. Flancy is so capable, though she has a history of not getting on with butlers!"

"I can well imagine!" H raised his eyes to heaven. "Well, you appear to be settling in very well . . . I feel quite unneeded around here."

Milandra abruptly stopped unpacking and looked at Lucas with concern.

She crossed over the room to him, took his hand and led him over to one of the couches. They sat down.

"But, my dear Lucas, I couldn't have got through this time since Ambrose died without you," she said urgently. "You've been my rock, my anchor, my lighthouse in the dark, my harbour in a stormy sea."

"Well – I tried to do what I could," he said, somewhat embarrassed.

"Lucas, I think if it weren't for you I'd have ended up in the grave beside Ambrose by now."

"Now, now, don't say things like that, my dear," he said, patting her hand.

"But it's true! You have rescued me from despair and made me realise I can go on, albeit without my precious Ambrose."

"Well, I hope I have been of some comfort to you."

"More than you'll ever know! And I will need you even more than ever from now on."

"How so, my dear?"

"I've decided not to sell the wine merchants."

He blinked a few times. "Not sell Carter Wines?"

"Yes – I mean, why sell it? Carter Wines is extremely profitable and one of the most well-known company names in Dublin. Why give all that away?"

"But you don't know the first thing about the wine business!" He was flabbergasted.

"More than you realise, Lucas. Dear Ambrose taught me everything he knew about wine."

"He did?"

"Yes, I used to accompany him on all his trips to the wineries in France when ordering the stock."

"I wasn't aware of that!"

"And when we lived on the estate we spent every evening tasting and sampling the stock, with him training me in the art of fine wine."

"I see!" He was trying to picture the scene and failing.

"So you see, I have a duty to Ambrose after all that training to continue the family business," she said assuredly.

"But it's his family business, not yours," Lucas said.

"Well, it's mine now," she said, smiling sweetly. "And that's where you will be vital to me. For I know that you maintained the bookkeeping, and that's what I need you to continue to do for me."

"But a woman in business, Milandra! It's out of the question!" objected Lucas.

"Why ever so? I met a couple of lovely ladies who run a hat shop here on Sackville Street."

"But this is the liquor business, no place for a woman! And Carter Wines is a far bigger enterprise than a hat shop! You will be eaten up and thrown to the wolves!"

"Not with you by my side, Lucas Hempton!" She almost sang the words. "Did Wellington retreat at Waterloo? Did Victoria shy away from her throne? Did Columbus turn back for home when he first set eyes on the America? Fortune favours the brave!"

"And fools rush in where angels fear to tread!"

As Kitty carried in a tray with tea things and a cake-stand with an assortment of small cakes upon it, Lucas stared up at the chandelier in bewilderment.

Kitty unloaded the tray onto the low table in front of Milandra.

"Shall I be mother?" asked Milandra as she picked up the teapot.

"Indeed – why not?" Lucas sat back and studied Milandra in amazement.

"Oh, Lucas, I wonder would you accompany me to church on Sunday? I was hoping to become a regular at Bishop Staffordshire's service."

"Of course, Milandra . . . although I do suggest, nay insist, that you wear mourning to Bishop Staffordshire's service. Otherwise he's likely to throw you bodily from his church and damn you forever!"

"Goes without saying, Lucas," she said, smiling as she handed him his cup of tea.

CHAPTER 10

Constance had got into the habit of attending her father's Sunday service with the Fontenoys. She would call down to their house and walk the few streets to his church.

That morning she found Nicholas distracted and, on the way to church, he confessed to her that he was very concerned about his exams, due to start the next day.

"I have every faith in you, Nicholas. Everyone knows you will come top of your class," she encouraged him.

"I sometimes wish I had as much faith in myself as everybody else does," he said.

Reaching the church, they followed Daniel and Agatha through the churchyard as they greeted all the people they knew.

Inside, as Constance walked up the aisle with Nicholas to the Fontenoy pew, she yearned for the day when they would be walking down that same aisle as man and wife. She moved into the pew, nodding and smiling to other people she knew in the congregation. She noticed her mother and sister in their usual front pew on the other side of the aisle.

The church was now full and all stood as Bishop Staffordshire came onto the altar with his attendants. On the Bishop's signal everybody sat down and waited for him to begin the service.

At that moment the door opened and loudly closed.

Constance turned around, wondering who had risked her father's wrath by arriving in late. Her mouth dropped open as she saw Milandra Carter beginning to walk up the aisle, dressed in a glamorous red-sequinned gown, followed by a very red-faced and obviously unhappy Lucas Hempton.

"I don't believe it!" whispered Constance to Nicholas as all eyes in the church followed Milandra.

"Good Lord!" said Nicholas, equally shocked.

"What does she think she's doing? In red! And late! Father will denounce her!" Constance had a terrible feeling in her stomach at the thought of what might happen. Was the woman really that stupid? Had she no idea that she was damning her reputation in front of everybody who was anybody in Dublin?

"Oh dear!" whispered Agatha. "Perhaps I should have advised her of the proper etiquette."

"Perhaps you should have!" Constance hissed back.

"I just thought they might do things differently down the country and widow's weeds weren't as important as in Dublin."

"I know that not to be true, as do you!" Constance's voice was harsh.

"But I should have said under no circumstances to come to church dressed like that!" lamented Agatha.

"Yes, you should have!" Constance snapped, causing Agatha to look at her, surprised by her crossness.

There was a chorus of whispers and murmurs through the congregation as Milandra reached the top pew where Henrietta and Emma were sitting in places close to the aisle. Milandra stepped into the pew regardless, forcing the Bishop's wife and daughter to shuffle along the bench to make room for her and Lucas. Head down, face red, Lucas quickly sat down beside her while the congregation looked even more scandalised at Milandra's audacity.

Constance looked up at her father on the pulpit who was staring expressionless at Milandra and she braced herself for what was to come.

The Bishop cleared his throat and then began the service as usual.

At least her father hadn't demanded Milandra to leave straight away, but Constance realised he was waiting for his sermon to make a public spectacle of the woman. Constance desperately hoped her father would glance in her direction so she could plead with him facially to let it go. But the Bishop never looked in the direction of the Fontenoy pew. Instead he seemed to concentrate on the front pew, where Milandra was seated, unconcerned about the stir she had caused.

When it came to the time for the sermon, the Bishop took his position on the pulpit, and Constance's nerves were strained to the limit.

"Dear friends, today I would like to discuss with you – Mrs. Milandra Carter," began Bishop Staffordshire.

Constance gripped her hands together in horror of what was to come. Milandra would get the full force of Bishop Staffordshire's public damnation.

"As we go through life caught up in our own issues, problems and concerns, it is often easy to forget the plight of others. This past week I have had the opportunity to witness the incredible self-sacrifice and example of a young woman putting others before herself. As many of you may know, Mrs. Milandra Carter lost her husband, a native of Sackville Street, very recently in a sudden and tragic way. One might think and be forgiven to think that Mrs. Carter would be immersed in her own private suffering and mourning. Perhaps even unconcerned and uninterested in the plight of others as she wallowed in self-pity and her own tragic circumstances. But no! Not Mrs. Carter! I had the very good fortune to have occasion to meet Mrs. Carter this week and was overwhelmed by the fact that she did not lament her plight once. No! Instead all she expressed was her concern for others in less fortunate situations than herself. As many of you know, I tirelessly raise fund for Dublin's disadvantaged. How many times have I knocked on your doors, pleading for assistance for those in dire circumstances? I am often their only voice, their only hope, in a world that seems not to care about them. And yet, here this week was this bereft young widow knocking on my door, offering her financial and spiritual help to those in desperate need. No need had I to go knocking on Mrs. Carter's door, she came to mine. Refusing to be bowed by the circumstances that are her fate, she is an example to us all. How fortunate we are that she has chosen to come and live in our community! And now to the hymn ..."

As the organ began to play and everyone stood up to sing in chorus, Constance stared at her father in shock. He had made no mention at home that Milandra Carter had visited him or made any offers of assistance with his charities. Her stare turned from her father to Milandra who stood singing in the front pew, looking as cool and calm as ever, as if she hadn't been the subject of the Bishop's sermon. As Constance continued to study her, she guessed that Milandra would look equally cool and unconcerned if the Bishop had in fact denounced her.

The service over, Milandra and Lucas filed down the aisle along with the rest of the congregation.

"Well, I must say, Milandra, that was very unexpected!" said Lucas, whose overriding emotion was relief, as they reached the churchyard.

When he had collected Milandra, he had been horrified to see what she was wearing. He had vocally expressed his outrage to her and warned her of the consequences. She had appeared completely unconcerned and had ignored him as they set off to the church. Outside the church, he had threatened not to go in with her and to leave her to her fate. But, as she continued into the church, he realised he couldn't leave Ambrose's widow to public humiliation on her own, and followed her in.

"I told you there was nothing to worry about," she said.

"Good day, Mrs. Carter," smiled a gentleman as he lifted his hat to her.

"Good morning, Mr. Kelly," she greeted him back.

"Good morning, Mrs. Carter, wasn't it a beautiful service?" said a matronly lady.

It was Mrs. Vickers who had practically ignored her the previous week outside the General Post Office.

"Yes, Mrs. Vickers, very soothing." Milandra smiled back.

"I see you are making plenty of acquaintances," said Lucas.

"Yes, I find people have been most kind since I came to live in Sackville Street. Ah, there's Daniel Fontenoy – we must go over and say hello."

Milandra moved over to Daniel who was with Agatha and the rest of the family.

"Hello, everybody," said Milandra on reaching them, and nodded to Nicholas and Constance.

"Milandra! We weren't expecting you today," said Agatha.

"Oh, yes, this is going to be my regular church."

"Well, you have certainly left an impression on Bishop Staffordshire!" said Daniel with a grin. "I've rarely heard him praise anybody from the pulpit, and certainly not in such glowing terms as he described you!"

"Was His Grace praising me so much? I was so deep in thought and prayer, I must admit my mind wasn't concentrating as much as it should." Milandra smiled at Nicholas broadly.

"Oh, he was praising you all right," said Constance dryly. "You have certainly won him over, a hard feat to achieve, I can assure you."

"You have put the rest of us to shame, Milandra!" said Agatha. "We can never expect to compete with your kind soul, as His Grace said."

"I'm only giving back a fraction of the kindness you have shown me since my arrival," said Milandra.

"What are your plans for the day, Milandra?" asked Daniel.

"Just unpacking the last boxes that have been sent from the country," she said.

"On the day of rest?" asked Constance wryly.

Milandra glanced at her, but didn't respond.

"I insist that you join us for Sunday lunch if you have no plans," said Daniel.

"Oh, yes, do!" Agatha pressed her.

"Oh, well, if I'm not imposing?" said Milandra.

"Of course not – eh, you too, Lucas, are welcome to join us," said Daniel as if he had just spotted Lucas for the first time.

"Most kind, but I think I've had enough excitement for one day. I bid you all good day," said Lucas with a bow.

"Do call in to me tomorrow, Lucas!" Milandra called after him as he walked away.

He didn't respond.

"Well, let us be off then. Lunch awaits!" said Agatha, delighted with herself. "Come along, Milandra!"

"But we shouldn't have Sunday lunch today – Nicholas's exams start tomorrow – he has to study!" Constance blurted out.

As everyone looked at her in surprise, Nicholas gave a little laugh.

"I won't deny the rest of you a good Sunday lunch because *I* have to study, my darling," said Nicholas.

"We are having Sunday lunch as usual, regardless of Nicholas's exams, Constance," said Agatha, wondering what had got into the girl.

Constance knew her comment had been nonsensical and she was sorry she had made it.

"I don't want to impose . . ." said Milandra.

"Of course you're not imposing!" said Daniel. "I sometimes think Constance cares more about Nicholas's exams than he does himself! You come in the carriage with us, Milandra. Nicholas and Constance can walk. I'm sure these two lovebirds will enjoy the time together."

"I'll see you back at the house," smiled Milandra.

She, Daniel, Agatha and Frederick went to the carriage which the driver had parked outside the churchyard.

"That was bit rude!" said Nicholas as he and Constance began to walk back to the Fontenoys' house.

"I just didn't want to lumbered with her for the day."

"So you were being deliberately rude to Milandra! Why? She is a charming, pleasant lady, from what I can see," he said.

"Too charming and too pleasant! Do you know she was visiting your house three times this past week when I called over? Sitting there, chatting away to your parents."

"Well, that's hardly a crime, is it?"

"But who is she? We know nothing of her!"

"Well, your father seems to have given her his seal of approval, in a very public way."

"I know. That's what worries me! If she can twist my father around her little finger, mocking the customs of widowhood in his face and before his congregation, then what else is she capable of? I mean, regardless of her late husband's supposed wishes about widow's weeds, she was really flying in the face of decency showing up dressed like that to church today. And she came out smelling of roses!"

"I really don't know what your problem is!" said Nicholas, exasperated.

"If she wasn't so rich, she wouldn't have everybody running around after her as she does," said Constance.

"Are you suggesting the only reason my parents are friendly with her is because of her money?" Nicholas was annoyed.

"Of course not. It's just . . ."

He put his arm around her. "I think my little lovebird is a teeny bit jealous."

"Of course I'm not!"

"I think she is," Nicholas said teasingly. "And you have nothing to be jealous of from the likes of Milandra Carter. She couldn't hold a candle to my fiancée."

She found his words comforting and smiled at him gratefully.

Milandra seemed to dominate the dining-room table at the Fontenoys'. And, even more annoying for Constance, she seemed to do it without effort. Everyone was fussing and talking to her, and she didn't have to do anything to be the centre of their attention. Perhaps Nicholas was right. It was usually *she* the Fontenoys made a fuss about, but now she seemed to be left sitting quietly in the background. Also Agatha was being quite cold with her and she realised her comments in the church and snapping at Agatha had probably annoyed her.

As soon as lunch was over, Nicholas retired upstairs to his room to study, leaving Constance feeling even more isolated from the conversation. Frederick seemed to be enamoured of Milandra. He hung on her every word, laughed at everything she said, filled her glass frequently and made sure anything she needed be fetched straight away. Constance realised Frederick had a major crush on the woman. It was embarrassing to watch, in her opinion. Also,

Frederick had barely said two words to Constance, and she realised he was annoyed with her for choosing Tom as best man rather than him. Oh, well, she seemed to have done a good job of offending Nicholas's family, the family she was due to live with once they were married.

CHAPTER 11

Milandra was sitting in her drawing room upstairs the following afternoon as she sorted out papers on the table in front of her. Her maid Kitty had just brought some tea when there was a loud knock on the front door downstairs.

"Go see who that is, Kitty. Show them into the parlour downstairs and let me know who it is before I decide if I'm home or not." Milandra continued shifting through her papers.

"Very well, ma'am," said Kitty, then turned and headed off to do her mistress's bidding.

As Milandra tried to concentrate on her papers, she could hear some kind of a commotion downstairs. A minute later she heard somebody walk boldly into the drawing room and looked up to see a slightly overweight woman in her late fifties standing there, with a hat and cloak on, carrying a suitcase which she plonked down on the floor beside her.

A flustered Kitty came rushing in behind her.

"Well, here I am – and who's like me?" said the woman loudly.

Milandra sat expressionless, looking at the woman coldly.

"Sorry, ma'am, but she just pushed past me and barged on up the stairs!" explained Kitty, red-faced. "Will I fetch the police?"

"Police? Where did you find this half-wit?" demanded the woman, jerking her head in Kitty's direction.

"There's no need for the police just yet, Kitty. You may leave us," said Milandra coolly.

"Yes, clear off!" said the woman, pushing Kitty out the door and slamming the door shut behind her.

Milandra looked annoyed at the woman's behaviour and said coldly, "Well, what a day it is – the day that they allowed an old goat like you into Sackville Street!"

"Well, if they allowed you in, then they'd allow anybody in!" the woman shot back at her.

The two women viewed each other suspiciously.

Milandra rose from her seat and walked slowly over to her, stopping in front of her, squaring up to her. The woman glared back.

Then suddenly Milandra's face broke into a huge grin and she held her arms out. "Flancy!"

"Come here to me, my darling!"

They embraced in a huge hug.

"Aren't you as welcome a sight to me as sunshine on a rainy day!" said Flancy.

Milandra pulled back and looked at her. "Oh, I've missed you!"

"'Tis well you missed me, when you swanned off to Dublin and left me to close up that miserable estate you and your late husband called home!"

Milandra led her over to the couch and they sat down.

"I didn't have the time to go back and do anything myself," Milandra said. "I've been far too busy building our new lives here!"

"And very well you've been doing it too!" said Flancy, looking around at the décor and the furniture. "How much did all this cost?"

"We can afford it, and a lot more besides!"

"Well, we had to put up with old Ambrose Carter for years – we deserve a little luxury now."

"Oh, don't mention that man's name!" Milandra grimaced. "All I've heard since I've arrived in Sackville Street is Ambrose this and Ambrose that! If I hear his name once more I shall scream! I thought once he was gone that would be the end of him. But his memory seems to linger around like a ghost, with everybody talking about him. And I don't know why they continue to mention him, because from what I can understand none of them liked him!"

"Well, you can't blame them for that!" said Flancy.

"True."

"So tell me all – what have you been doing while I've been busy slaving away tidying up your affairs back on the estate?"

"Where to start! And what a start I've made! You'll be proud of me." Milandra smiled broadly as she stood up.

She walked to the drinks cabinet, took the decanter of whiskey and filled two crystal tumblers. Walking back to the couch, she handed one to Flancy before sitting down.

"Well?" asked Flancy, taking a swig of her drink.

"I've managed to infiltrate many of Sackville Street's most influential families," Milandra announced.

"Your charm never fails," said Flancy.

"Copious amounts of money played their part too. They were drawn to a rich widow like moths to a flame. Once I got to know a couple of the families, they quickly introduced me to the rest. There's one family, the Fontenoys, who have taken me under their wing." Milandra pulled a sad face. "Poor young widow all alone in the world! They felt it their duty to extend the hand of friendship."

"Who are the Fontenoys?"

"They live on Rutland Square. He's a judge, Daniel Fontenoy, highly respected. And his wife, Agatha, is a socialite – a scatty woman who seems intrigued by me. Daniel knew Ambrose when they were younger which opened the door with them. I sealed my position with them by appointing the law firm their son Nicholas is employed by, as my solicitors."

"What a great tactical move!" Flancy was impressed.

"Once I was in with the Fontenoys, the rest of the families followed suit. Oh, I had some resistance. Most of the good people of Dublin expected me to be dressed in deepest black and not leave the house for the next two years! As if I was going to waste the next two years of my life! I've already wasted the last eight years with Ambrose. From what I understood, there was a certain Bishop Staffordshire who could have made life difficult for me. A pious sanctimonious man who I had heard was furious with my 'carry-on'."

"How did you silence him?"

"I paid him a visit, put on my best bereaved-widow act, and requested he allow me to donate considerable money to his charities. Oh, Flancy, everyone has their price, even Bishop Staffordshire! He even praised me in his sermon last Sunday!"

Flancy burst out laughing. "I'm proud of you! You haven't lost your touch."

"If anything, I think it's become even more finely tuned. I think I could walk down Sackville Street naked now, and nobody would say a word!"

"Cheers!" said Flancy clinking her glass against Milandra's in delight.

"I have them all eating out of my hand, and it's been on my terms."

"You're a smart one, Milandra. By not wearing black and nobody daring to confront you, you've put yourself at the top of the pecking order!"

"That was my plan, Flancy." Milandra sat back in the couch smugly.

"And what of Lucas Hempton?" Flancy frowned.

"Well, he was the only one who did voice opposition to my face. He thought that he was going to take over after Ambrose died. That I wouldn't have a clue about anything and would rely on him for everything. I think he was looking forward to being in charge."

"And how did you handle him?"

"I just ignored everything he said and did what I wanted to do. He has been quite important, showing me around Dublin and introducing me to people. And of course I do need him for the business with the bookkeeping and accounts for now. I'll push him aside when I have a handle on everything myself."

"Best to push that old goat aside as quickly as possible," said Flancy. "I wouldn't be surprised if his plans were to marry you himself as soon as you come out of mourning, just so he can get his hands on Ambrose's money!"

"Please, Flancy, don't! The very thought of it!" Milandra took a gulp of her whiskey.

"Better to be an old man's darling than a young man's fool!" said Flancy.

"I will never be any man's fool, Flancy, young or old."

"So what are our plans now?" asked Flancy, knowing that Milandra would have a plan.

Milandra sat up excitedly. "Oh, Flancy, I've met the most wonderful man!"

"Go on!" said Flancy, smirking knowingly.

"As soon as I saw him, I knew he was the one for me. He's everything I want in a man, and everything Ambrose wasn't."

"What's his name?"

"Nicholas Fontenoy."

"Fontenoy? The judge's family?"

"Yes, he's their eldest son."

"I see!" said Flancy, digesting the information.

"He's handsome, kind, clever. He's doing his law exams. And from one of the best families in Dublin. Everything I want in a husband."

"Sounds divine! Doing his law exams? Is he younger than you?"

Milandra dismissed the question. "Only by a couple of years, but you could never tell when you see us side by side."

Flancy looked at her knowingly. "Well, you certainly didn't waste much time. You will have to wait at least a year before you announce the marriage or else your reputation really will be in tatters."

"Hmmm, yes. There's a few things that have to be sorted first, so I imagine it will take a little time," mused Milandra.

"What kind of things?"

"His fiancée, for starters," said Milandra.

"*What?*" Flancy nearly dropped her glass. "He's got a fiancée!"

"Yes, unfortunately."

"And when is he thinking of telling his fiancée about you?" Flancy demanded.

"Well, as I said, there's a few things to be sorted . . . Nicholas isn't quite aware of my feelings and intentions for him as yet."

Flancy slammed her glass on the low table in front of them. "Are you trying to tell me that this is all in your head? That your love for this man is unrequited, or worse that he is totally ignorant of it?"

76

Milandra stood up quickly and walked over to the end window, taking up a pair of binoculars that lay on a cabinet.

"You can just see the Fontenoy house from this window. I can see Nicholas coming and going through their front door each day on his way to and from his classes."

"Milandra! This sounds all very unhealthy to me! You've just got rid of old Ambrose and you're throwing yourself into another unhealthy situation!"

"I can't deny what my heart feels," said Milandra, peering out the window through the binoculars.

"And who is Nicholas Fontenoy's unfortunate fiancée?"

Milandra put down the binoculars and walked back towards Flancy. "A meek little uninteresting creature called Constance. Quite pretty, I suppose, in an unthreatening way. She's the bishop's daughter – Bishop Staffordshire."

Flancy stood up abruptly. "The Bishop's daughter! Milandra, you haven't thought this through. Have you lost your mind? If you try to do anything with this lad, you'll end up destroying yourself!"

"I don't think so, Flancy. I have the brains, the beauty and now the money to make sure I'm untouchable. And Constance Staffordshire is no competition for me."

"Constance Staffordshire sounds like the kind of girl these Fontenoys want for their son."

"Oh, I'm sure she is. He's their golden-haired boy, they all hang on his every word and he can do no wrong in anybody's eyes."

"Well, would they want their precious son married to you?" asked Flancy.

Milandra's face turned sour. "It's quite immaterial to me what anybody else wants. I want him and I need him and I will have him."

"So your intention is to break up their engagement?"

"Of course, how else am I to marry him?" said Milandra.

"And how do you propose to win him, Milandra?"

"How do you think?" She arched an eyebrow. "By magic."

PART 2

1916

CHAPTER 12

Milandra stood leaning against the wall at the top of the stairs, staring at the man pointing a revolver at her.

"I said – *what do you want*?"

"Is there anybody else in the house?" he demanded.

"No, but my servants are due back any minute. So just turn around and leave right now if you know what is good for you!"

She could hear more movements downstairs and a voice called up, "Downstairs and basement all clear, sir."

Suddenly she saw two young men come running up the stairs and to her horror saw they were carrying guns as well.

"Check the upstairs, make sure the building is secure," instructed the first man to the others and they marched down the landing and up the stairs that led to the next level.

Milandra realised all the men were wearing military uniforms and confusion was added to her terror.

"My goodness! Are you the Germans? Have you invaded Dublin?" she demanded.

The man lowered his revolver and swept down the landing and into the drawing room.

Milandra gathered her senses and followed him. She watched him do a quick scout around the room and then check the tall windows that lined the wall looking down into Sackville Street.

"I asked you a question?" she said. "Is this a German invasion?"

The man glanced at her before saying, "I am commandeering this building on behalf of the Irish Republic."

Milandra stared at the man in astonishment. "The Irish *what*?"

"The Irish Republic," said the man as he started to move a cabinet to stand in front of the window.

"But, my dear boy, there *is* no Irish Republic. Whatever are you talking about? And kindly stop touching my furniture!"

The man tore down curtains and pulled the shutters across two of the windows.

"How dare you! How dare you come into my home and destroy my property!" Milandra shrilled at him. As he ignored her she went marching up to him. "I insist you get out of my house now or I will have you arrested!"

He stopped what he doing and looked at her. "We are the new law. We make the arrests. The Irish Republic was declared at the General Post Office today – which is now our headquarters – and we are getting into position to defend Sackville Street if the British army strikes back. Your house is in a strategic position."

Milandra heard commotion outside and went to look out one of the windows. To her astonishment she saw groups of similarly dressed uniformed men running down Sackville Street, all carrying guns. From the buildings across the road she could see the upper windows being shuttered as well.

"What is all this nonsense?" demanded Milandra. "An Irish Republic? But the empire is at war!"

"And we are now at war with the empire," said the man as he continued to barricade the windows.

"But that's treason! You'll never get away with it! You'll all be hanged, I tell you!"

The man stopped what he doing. "I think you should leave now while you have the chance."

"I think it is *you* who should leave while *you* have the chance! You should be fighting in France along with the other men, not staging some kind of crazy uprising!"

"Is there anywhere you can go? Go and stay with family outside the city centre if that's possible."

"No, I'm not going anywhere, you fool! I am not leaving my home in the hands of some lunatic bandits!"

"Well, I cannot guarantee your safety, if you remain."

"Safety from whom? From you! You are the only threat to my safety, barging in like this," she shrilled.

"You have been warned. Stay out of our way, if you will not go."

He marched past her out of the room.

Amelia was waiting excitedly on the pier at Kingstown. The pier was crowded with soldiers returning on leave from the war in France. They had just disembarked from the boat that had docked there and were being mobbed by their loved ones.

Her eyes scanned the crowd but she could see no sign of Rupert.

"*Amelia!*" came a roar in the distance and she turned quickly to see him striding down the gangplank, waving frantically at her.

She pushed through the crowd and fought her way over to him, before throwing herself into his arms and kissing him.

She felt relief sweep through her with the absolute knowledge that he was there, safe and sound, in her arms. That he had survived so far.

"Let me look at you!" she said, pulling back and looking at his face in wonder.

"You're a sight for sore eyes!" He grinned at her before kissing her passionately again.

"Rupert, I – I –" She suddenly started to cry and soon was sobbing loudly.

"Here now!" said Rupert. "This is a fine welcome! The other chaps will think that you aren't glad to see me!"

"How wrong they would be!" she said, quickly wiping away her tears and smiling back at him. She took his hand and led him through the crowd. "I have a taxi waiting."

Milandra stood in front of the fireplace in the upstairs drawing room watching the man who had invaded her home. He was positioned at one of the tall windows, peering out. Evening was drawing in and it was becoming dark outside.

"Well, have they arrived yet?" she asked.

He glanced over at her. "Huh?"

"The forces that will be sent to put manners on you. I take it that is what you are waiting for?"

"There is no sign of the enemy yet," said the man.

"What is your name?" she asked.

"What?"

"Are you deaf as well as dumb? I asked you your name."

"You have no need to know my name," snapped the man as he continued to peer out the window.

"Well, if you're going to occupy my house until I am liberated, I would like to know the name of my captor."

"You are not a captive. I told you that you should have gone when you had the chance. The area has been barricaded now and you won't be able to leave Sackville Street."

"Then I am a captive – if not yours, then of your brothers-in-arms."

The man ignored her.

"I shan't give your name to the authorities when all this is over, if that's what you're worried about. My interest in getting involved in any politics at this time of my life is zero, I can assure you. It's just that if we are going to be sharing the same space for the foreseeable future then I should like to be able to address you as something other than 'you' or, alternatively, 'intruder'."

"Seán. Call me Seán," he said.

"I see – Seán. I doubt that's your real name, but it will do, nevertheless. Seán the Rebel. It suits you. Well, I must say, I've been hearing about Irish independence since the day I was born. Never thought it would come to anything – and here it is! In my drawing room!"

Seán glanced away from the window and looked at her. The woman didn't seem in the least scared or frightened. In the most remarkable way she didn't seem fazed in the least.

"Are you not scared?" he asked her.

"Not at my age. I have to die of something. In fact, this is the most interesting thing that has happened to me in two decades. When you have had to attend as many dull dinner parties as I have, your soul cries out for excitement, in whatever form it may come."

Seán took out a packet of cigarettes and went to light one.

"I'd rather you didn't do that in here. This has been a 'no smoking' room since 1895. I found the smoke was affecting the curtain fabric."

Seán looked up at the swish curtain he was standing beside and yanked it down off its rails with one pull, throwing it to the floor, before he continued to light up his cigarette.

"Well, seems I don't have to worry about that particular fabric any more," she said.

"It's so hard to believe you are actually here." Amelia smiled at Rupert as they sat in her parents' dining room at their house in Dalkey.

"The thought of being with you again kept me going in the trenches," said Rupert as he reached across the dining table and held her hand.

They'd had dinner with Amelia's parents, Petronella and Jordan, and were now lingering over coffee and liqueurs.

Rupert was spending the night in the Robinsons' before he and Amelia set off to spend the rest of his time off with his family in the country.

"Well, he is home, safe and sound, and let's hope you'll be home soon for good, Rupert," said Jordan, raising a glass to his future son-in-law.

"I have to say your timing was perfect, Rupert," said Petronella. "If you had arrived back yesterday you would have had to endure the company of my mother who was staying with us for the Easter break."

"Oh, I wouldn't have minded that. I'm quite fond of the old dear," said Rupert, winking at Amelia.

"Milandra is many things, but an old dear is not one of them!" remarked Jordan.

"Indeed!" said Petronella, clinking her wineglass against her husband's. "She is becoming more and more unreasonable, if that were possible."

"I'm very fond of her," said Amelia, jumping to her grandmother's defence.

"You may say that, Amelia, as you don't have to suffer her brutal comments and vicious tongue as the rest of us do!" said Jordan.

"I keep suggesting she move in here with us, but I must admit I am always relieved that she vehemently declines," said Petronella. "I think I only offer in the safe knowledge she will always decline. I don't know how we would cope living with her if she should ever accept. She would drive us out of our own home within a week!"

"Although it is totally ridiculous that an elderly woman on her own should live in such a mansion as she does," said Jordan.

"She can afford it," said Petronella.

"That's not the point – it's just silly," he responded. "And Sackville Street is now completely commercial. She must be the only private residence left. But will she listen to advice? No! Will she take heed? No!"

"Milandra will do what she wants to do, she always has – stubborn to the last!" said Petronella.

"Dear me! What must you think of us, Rupert?" said Amelia, shooting both her parents warning looks. "Being so critical of my grandmother. You must think you are marrying into a dreadful family."

Petronella looked at Rupert. "Rupert would be insulted if we didn't speak freely in front of him. He's already a member of the family as far as I'm concerned. Isn't that right, Rupert?"

Rupert started laughing and winked at Amelia. "Absolutely right, Petronella."

"So –" said Jordan, putting a cigar in his mouth and leaning forward to light it from a candle on the table before sitting back. "How long more until you bloody lick these Germans and finish this war, Rupert?"

"Still very hard to say, sir. I can't see it happening any time soon," said Rupert sadly.

"Well, what's keeping you?" demanded Jordan. "If the whole of Great Britain can't put these foreigners in their place quick sharp, then what is the world coming to? But more Irishmen need to volunteer like you did and lend a hand!"

Amelia found herself stiffening. "On the contrary, Ireland shouldn't be part of this war at all!" she said.

"Whatever do you mean, Amelia?" asked Jordan, startled.

"I mean we should be independent by now," she said.

"Independent of what?" asked Petronella, looking confused.

"Of Britain, of course, Mother!"

"Oh, nonsense!" said Petronella. "Don't be silly!"

Amelia flushed. "Don't say I'm silly. We need our freedom – not merely 'Home Rule'. There are plenty intelligent people who agree with me, and feel we should have nothing to do with this war."

"Amelia, I really cannot countenance this kind of pernicious talk at my dinner table!" spluttered Jordan.

"I'm sorry, Father," said Amelia, white-faced, "but it's not fighting for the British we should be, but fighting against them for our independence!"

"*Amelia!*" Rupert, who had been trying to stay out of the altercation, was unable to keep silence at this. "How can you say such a thing?"

"Because it's true! If the British want to get slaughtered by the million in France, then they should leave us out of it!"

"But, my dear girl, we *are* British!" said Petronella in amusement.

"For now! But hopefully not for long!" said Amelia.

Rupert sat up straight and glared at his fiancée. "Amelia, you need to be careful how you speak. It could be misconstrued as treason."

"I don't care how it's misconstrued," she said defiantly.

"You will have to forgive my daughter, Rupert," said Jordan. "Ever since she started work at that newspaper she has started to hang around with quite a bohemian crowd with some fast opinions."

"Perhaps too fast," observed Rupert, eyeing his fiancée.

"My opinions are my own, not adopted from any of my friends," Amelia said, stung by his words. "I frankly do not care who wins this war. I look forward to the day when Ireland is a republic and we are in charge of our own foreign affairs – which I hope will mean we do not slaughter our young men in some pointless foreign war!"

Jordan and Petronella exchanged worried looks as Rupert threw his napkin angrily on the table and turned to face Amelia.

"So you think that I am risking my life over a 'pointless' war?"

"Absolutely! I would love if you refused to go back to the front at the end of your leave, and stayed here with me where you belong," said Amelia.

"Desertion! You're asking me to desert? And bring disgrace on my family and myself?" Rupert was incredulous.

"Not to mention the possibility of being shot as a deserter," said Petronella under her breath.

"Rupert, there is no conscription in Ireland," said Amelia. "You had a *choice* not to go to the war. There would have been no disgrace in it as far as I am concerned. You would have been taking a stand as an Irish Nationalist, and not a sheep in the British army."

Rupert and Amelia stared at each other in anger before Rupert turned to Jordan and said, "I suspect you might be correct, sir. Amelia does indeed seem to be keeping the company of some unsuitable friends with very shocking and dangerous ideas."

"Dangerous! What is dangerous about speaking as one believes?" demanded Amelia.

Rupert stood up abruptly, his face clouded in anger. "Thank you, Jordan and Petronella for a lovely evening. I think I might retire to the gardens to have a cigar before I retire to bed."

Rupert nodded at them and, ignoring Amelia, walked over to the French window and out into the gardens.

"Amelia!" snapped Petronella. "What a dreadful way to behave on Rupert's first night back!"

"How could you say such things to him?" demanded Jordan.

"Because it's true!" cried Amelia.

"Whatever our personal opinions are of this war or of Irish independence, one shouldn't speak freely as you have in front of an army officer," cautioned Petronella.

"If I can't speak freely in front of my fiancé, then who can I speak freely in front of?" demanded Amelia. "And you yourself said earlier that he is family and we *should* speak freely in front of him!"

Jordan was exasperated. "Rupert, as he says, is risking his life daily in this war. How does he feel, hearing you ridicule everything he stands for – what he is willing to die for?"

"Oh, go to him, Amelia," pleaded Petronella. "He's only home for such a short time – don't argue with him and ruin his leave!"

Amelia thought for a moment and then quickly got up and walked out the French windows.

Rupert was standing by a fountain in the garden smoking a cigar and looking up at the moon which shone brightly over the nearby sea.

She bit her lip as she slowly approached him. "Rupert?"

He turned abruptly towards her, his face still angry.

"I apologise if I said anything to offend you," she offered.

"Offend!" He threw his cigar on the ground and stamped on it angrily. "Offend is the least of it! To hear my fiancée, the woman I love, speak so – so – disgustingly!"

"But what is disgusting about what I said?" she asked, perplexed.

"The fact you don't even know and have to ask is even more disgusting!"

"I only spoke my mind," she said.

"And that's what worries me. You were never so strident in your views – what has happened to you?"

"It's not just the men who have gone to fight that have changed – the war has changed everyone, including us at home. We all look at the world with different views now, and these are my views."

"But how can we have a future when we think so differently?" He was amazed.

"We can – because I – I love you!"

"But is that enough?" he demanded. "When you think the way you do?"

She felt herself gripped with panic on hearing his doubts about the love she held so dear.

"Excuse me, sir."

They swung around, startled.

The butler was standing there. "Sorry to disturb, but there is an attaché from the military at the door. He wishes to speak with the captain."

"For goodness' sake!" said Amelia, furious at the interruption. "Tell the attaché the captain is on leave and has no interest in what he has to say!"

"What is wrong with you? You know I can't say that," said Rupert as he turned to go.

Amelia hurried after him.

They followed the butler through another French window which led into the hallway where an agitated attaché stood.

"What's this about?" asked Rupert.

"Sorry to interrupt your leave, Captain Perkins, but all military personnel have been ordered back from leave immediately. Officers such as yourself are to report to headquarters."

"Why on earth – what's going on?" demanded Rupert.

"There is a rebellion in the city, Captain. A group of Irish rebels staged some sort of revolution in the city centre and . . ." the attaché could hardly believe the words he was about to say himself, "and declared Ireland a republic."

"Fetch my coat," said Rupert to the butler before asking the attaché, "How bad is it?"

"It's looking very bad, Captain. They have taken control of the city centre from Sackville Street and Stephen's Green and on to Northumberland Road."

"Sackville Street!" Amelia gasped.

"Bloody bastards!" cried Rupert. "Amelia, I'll be back as soon as possible, apologies to your parents."

Grabbing his coat, he raced out the door with the attaché to the waiting car. As Rupert sat into the back of the car he heard his name being called frantically and saw Amelia come rushing towards the car carrying her hat and coat.

"I'm coming with you," she said, sitting into the back of the car.

"Amelia, don't be so ridiculous – get out!" Rupert snapped impatiently at her.

"No, Rupert! I left Grandmama in her house on Sackville Street this afternoon. That means she's on her own in the middle of this rebel zone. I *have* to get to her, or find out if she safe – and you're the only way I can do that."

Rupert looked into her pleading eyes before ordering, "Drive on!"

On Sackville Street, Milandra was sitting quietly in the drawing room. It was dark outside and the rebel, who seemed to be in charge of the others, was standing guard at one of the tall windows with his gun raised. As commanded, she had stayed out of the way and sat there trying to fathom out what was happening. She had lived on Sackville Street for almost fifty years and she could never have imagined what was unfolding before her happening there. For some kind of war to break out on Dublin's main thoroughfare!

She thought back to when she had first arrived to live on Sackville Street as a young widow. She remembered Nicholas Fontenoy and her relentless pursuit of him. To everybody, including Nicholas, it looked like she was hopelessly, madly in love with him. But there was a deeper, darker motive in her pursuit of Nicholas. A dark secret buried in her past that she could not even reveal to her beloved Flancy. Only Milandra knew the truth.

PART 3

1869

CHAPTER 13

Constance was down in the kitchens in the Staffordshire house packing a lunch that their cook had made into a bag. Since Nicholas's exams had started, she had followed the same routine every day. She had a lunch prepared for Nicholas and Tom and would then go to Tom's rooms in Trinity where she would meet them and make sure they ate properly before they returned to the exam hall in the afternoon.

"I hope young Mr. Fontenoy appreciates all you are doing for him," said the cook.

"I think he's too busy trying to pass his exams to realise anything," said Constance with a smile. "I'm sure if I didn't bring the lunch and make sure he and Tom ate it every day, they would be doing their afternoon exams on empty stomachs!"

"Bless you!" said the cook. She also knew that every day, after the exams, Constance would meet Nicholas and spend the evening helping him to prepare for the following day's exams. She was such a dedicated fiancée, the cook thought, and would make Nicholas Fontenoy the best wife.

Constance took the bag and made her way up the stairs and out of the house into Mountjoy Square. It was a lovely sunny day and she felt sorry for Nicholas trapped in an exam hall. She made her way through the streets, past Rutland Square and down into Sackville Street. As had become her custom, as she passed Milandra Carter's house she stared across, looking for some sign of life. She saw a well-dressed gentleman was at the door, being shown in.

There seemed to be a steady stream of callers to the house. And Constance had heard that Milandra had now taken over the running of her late husband's business. Instead of being shocked, everyone in polite society seemed to be full of the admiration for her. Constance wondered what it was about this woman that seemed to cast a spell on everybody. It was unheard of that a woman should be in charge of a liquor business. How could she cope with the shenanigans and the cut and thrust of such a business? Was the whole thing just not utterly disreputable? Constance realised the more Milandra pushed at the boundaries that were acceptable, the more people were willing to accept her behaviour. Perhaps this was her plan all along, Constance mused as she hurried along into Lower Sackville Street and across Carlisle Bridge until she reached Trinity. Seeing she was running late, she rushed across Trinity's main square until she reached Tom's rooms and knocked on the door.

Nicholas opened the door with a tired and unhappy look on his face.

"Oh dear, was the paper that bad?" she asked, stepping in.

He closed the door behind them.

"It was very hard," he confirmed, hugging her.

She found Tom seated in the small parlour in an equally glum mood.

"You're a sight for sore eyes!" Tom managed to smile at her as she set her bag on the small round table and began to unpack it.

"I take it the exam didn't go well for you either, Tom?"

"As Nicholas said, it was very tough."

"Well, look, you have probably done better than you think. And if it was hard for you two then it was hard for everybody else." Her voice was upbeat. "Forget about this morning's paper, and concentrate on this afternoon's. Chances are it will be much easier."

Nicholas came behind her and embraced her. "It's only your encouragement that's getting me through these exams, otherwise I'd fail for sure."

"A good lunch behind you and you'll be ready for any paper this afternoon," she said. She took plates and began to lay out the sandwiches for them.

Tom came to the table and the three of them sat down. She watched happily as the two men began to devour the sandwiches.

"I suppose if we fail, we can always repeat," said Nicholas.

"Enough of that talk! You will not fail – you will pass with flying colours," insisted Constance.

Tom looked irritated as he said, "It might be an option for you to repeat, Nicholas, but it isn't for me."

"Why not?" asked Nicholas, and his innocent reaction seemed to annoy Tom further.

"Because, my dear friend, my family have barely had enough money to get me to this stage of my education. They certainly won't be able to entertain me having to re-sit exams."

Tom's family lived on a farm in County Sligo, and sending him to Trinity had been a very costly experience for them, with the added cost of renting out rooms for him while he was there.

"As soon as the exams are finished," he said, "I will have to vacate my rooms here, which means trying to find somewhere else to live. And I have no employment position offered to me yet from any law firm."

"None at all?" Constance's face creased in concern.

"No." Tom looked worried and depressed. "And I've applied to nearly everywhere."

"I'm sure something will come up for you," said Nicholas, biting into his sandwich.

"That's easy for you to say!" snapped Tom. "You have your position waiting for you at Fetherstons' even before they know your exam results!"

"I realise I've been lucky," said Nicholas.

"Yes, lucky that your father is a judge with strong influence in the legal world. My family have no contacts to give me a cushy number." Tom sounded almost bitter.

Constance tried to diffuse the situation. "You're right, Tom, Nicholas is very lucky. But you will be too. As soon as you get your exam results and you come top of the class the law firms will be queuing up for you."

"And what am I to do in the meantime? As I said, I need to leave these rooms in two weeks' time," said Tom.

"Well, you must come and live with us!" announced Nicholas happily. "We have plenty of spare bedrooms in our house and you can stay with us until you sort yourself out."

"I can't do that," said Tom.

"Of course you can! That's the answer to all your problems," insisted Nicholas.

Constance saw that Nicholas's generous offer was not having the desired effect on Tom. Instead of being grateful his face was becoming darker.

"I said – no," Tom said firmly.

"And I said yes! I think it's an excellent idea, don't you, Constance?" asked Nicholas.

"I was not telling you about my situation in order to avail of your charity!" said Tom.

"I know you weren't, but it's still the solution to all your problems," said Nicholas.

Seeing Tom's growing anger, Constance said, "Nicholas, if Tom doesn't feel comfortable with staying at your house, then don't force him."

"Of course I'll force him. If his stubborn pride is getting in the way of what's good for him!" said Nicholas.

"I am not your charity case, Nicholas!" Tom's voice was harsh. "I will stand on my own two feet and make it on my own in this world, without needing the crumbs from your table." He pushed the plate with his half-eaten sandwich away.

"Tom!" cried Constance.

"Your problem, Nicholas, is that you have been handed everything in life! You are completely unable to stand on your own two feet. You have never known hardship. You sailed through university with no financial hardship. Your father has sorted you out with your career without you even having to apply for a position. Your father's connections have landed you one of Dublin's biggest clients, Milandra Carter, without you even asking her. Your fiancée fusses over you and makes sure you don't even have to prepare your own lunch. Sometimes, Nicholas, you make me sick!"

Nicholas stared at Tom in shock and stood up slowly before saying, "I think I'd better be getting to the library to do some last-minute studying before the exams."

Nicholas turned and walked quickly from the rooms, leaving Constance and Tom alone.

"Tom! Whatever has got into you?" demanded Constance.

Tom put his face in his hands. "Oh – what have I done?" he said.

"That was very cruel of you – Nicholas was only trying to help you," Constance said with a mixture of anger and concern.

"I know. I shouldn't have said those things . . . I was taking my own troubles out on him."

"Are things really that bad?" she said, reaching out a comforting hand to him.

"I'm afraid so." He took her hand and squeezed it. "I don't know what I'll do if I don't get a position soon. I'll have to return to Sligo and I can kiss goodbye to any high-flying legal career I've ever dreamed of having."

"Something will come up for you, Tom. You just have to keep trying," Constance encouraged him. "And it won't help your situation to fall out with such a good friend as Nicholas."

"I know," he sighed loudly. "Will he ever forgive me for saying such things? The truth is, I'm just jealous of Nicholas. For all the reasons I said to him. From his job at Fetherstons', to his family – to his very lovely, kind and beautiful fiancée."

Constance blushed. "I don't know if I'm all those things, Tom. Perhaps you don't know me as well as you think you do."

"I think I know you very well, Constance."

She leaned forward earnestly to him. "We can all be guilty of jealousy at times. I myself have had to check myself recently as I allowed my own jealousies and insecurities to get the better of me. You are a wonderful man, Tom, and have the makings of being a wonderful solicitor. And I know in a short while that is exactly what you will be."

"Thank you, Constance." He took her hand again and kissed it. "How will I apologise to Nicholas? Will he ever forgive me my cruel words?"

"Of course he will. You know Nicholas adores you – are you not his best man? Don't worry about him – I'll have a word with him and explain the pressure you are under. I think exam season makes everyone go little bit daft!"

Smiling, she stood up.

"Thank you, Constance," he said, standing up and embracing her.

CHAPTER 14

That evening Constance was in the study at the Fontenoy house, setting out the papers and books for Nicholas to study, when he got back from his exams. She did this each evening, helping him as best she could with his study plan.

The door opened and Nicholas walked in, not looking in any better form than he had that lunchtime.

She left the desk she was sitting at and came over to embrace him.

"Another difficult paper?" she asked.

"I'm afraid so," he answered.

"Poor Nicholas. Well, look, today is over and you must concentrate on tomorrow. I've set out all your reading material for tomorrow's exams, ready for you to start revising."

He sat down at the desk and smiled up at her. "With the amount of work you are putting into these exams, I daresay you could sit them yourself!"

She bent down and kissed his forehead. "You get right to work and I'll go down to the kitchen and fetch you a snack to keep you going until dinner. You can eat it here at the desk and I'll test you with questions for the exams tomorrow at the same time."

"Thanks, love."

"Did you – happen to see Tom again today?" she asked.

"Yes. He came over to me this evening after the exam and apologised for his behaviour at lunchtime. He explained he was under a lot of pressure and had no right to take it out on me."

Nicholas smirked up at her. "He said you had talked sense to him!"

She shrugged. "I just gave him a shoulder to cry on, that's all. I'm glad you two have put it behind you."

"Yes, thanks to you. Tom thinks very highly of you. He listens to you and respects your opinion. I wish he would reconsider moving in here after he leaves his rooms at Trinity. Perhaps you could have another word with him?"

"I don't think that's wise, Nicholas. Tom is very proud, and it's clear he would see that as charity. I don't think he would thank us for raising the issue again."

"Perhaps you're right. I just worry about him, even more so after his outburst today," sighed Nicholas.

"I'm sure Tom will be fine. He'll find a position for himself very quickly and will be a big success. Now you get on with your study and start concentrating on our future, and I'll go fetch a snack for you."

Later that evening Constance let herself into their house on Mountjoy Square. As she walked down the hallway, she could hear talking in the parlour.

"Constance – is that you?" called her father.

"Yes, Father," answered Constance as she walked over to the parlour and entered.

To her surprise she found Milandra sitting in conversation with the Bishop.

"I thought it might be you – have you met Mrs. Carter, Constance?"

"Yes, we've met. How are you, Constance?" smiled Milandra.

"Very well, thank you."

"Take a seat and join us, Constance," said the Bishop. "My daughter often helps out with my charities and so will be interested in this."

Constance reluctantly took a seat on the couch beside her father.

"We are just discussing which charities of your father's I'm to be involved in," said Milandra.

"Very good," said Constance.

"As I was saying to you, Your Grace, I think the charities I want to contribute to most are the ones involving the city's children. And also the widows. I want to help those who weren't left in such a fortunate position as I."

"I can't think of any other better deserving causes. And it gives me pleasure that these are the ones closest to your heart, Milandra," nodded the Bishop.

"Oh, they are, Your Grace. I'll speak to Lucas Hempton tomorrow and get him to make a donation without delay. And then we can continue to discuss my contributions on an on-going basis."

"Excellent, my dear Milandra. And I will continue to give you regular reports of the good works your donations are contributing to," said the Bishop, looking delighted.

"How are your marriage plans, Constance?" Milandra asked, smiling over at her.

"They are on hold at the moment, as Nicholas is up to his eyes in his final exams," said Constance. "I just left him now, his head deep in books."

"Oh, dear! Well, at least it's only for another week. His exams are due to finish next Friday, are they not?"

"That's right. You have a good memory, Milandra."

Milandra smiled and stood up. "Well, I had better be going."

"Will you not stay and have dinner with us?" urged the Bishop, causing Constance to cringe at the thought of it.

"I'm afraid I can't. I have a meeting with one of the managers from the wine merchants this evening."

"Reeves!" called the Bishop, standing up.

The butler came in.

"Show Mrs. Carter out, Reeves."

"Yes, Your Grace."

"I will see you next week at our next meeting," said the Bishop, shaking her hand.

"I'll look forward to it. And don't forget my party in two weeks' time."

"I wouldn't miss it," said the Bishop.

Milandra turned to Constance. "Oh, you and Nicholas are invited too, Constance. Just a little soirée for my friends – the Fontenoys are coming as well. I do hope you can make it? Nicholas's exams will be finished by then."

"I – eh – will have to check with Nicholas. He will be just starting in his new position at Fetherstons' by then so his diary might not allow it," said Constance.

"Oh, please do come! Good day, Your Grace." With a smile, Milandra followed Reeves out.

"What a lovely lady she is," said the Bishop, closing the door.

"You have certainly changed your tune, Father! It wasn't long ago you were going to denounce her on the pulpit for being a scarlet woman!"

"But that was before I got to know her. It just goes to show that you should never judge a book by the cover."

"Well, you were more than happy to judge that book by the cover when she was prancing up and down Sackville Street in ruby red, and her husband – what was the expression you used – not cold in the grave!"

"Well, even I in all my wisdom may occasionally misread a person!"

"And what's all this about her throwing a party? Are you not shocked? And since when did you and Mother ever attend parties? Father! I fear Milandra Carter is turning you into a liberal!"

"At the end of the day, if Mrs. Carter feels she is able to host a party after her recent loss, then who am I to say she mustn't? And if Daniel Fontenoy has accepted the invitation, then it must be in good taste."

"I think you are being quite mercenary, Father. I think you're parking your beliefs and standards in order to ensure the funding of your charities."

"How dare you, Constance! I think it is you who needs to change your attitude. I detected a coldness in your attitude to Milandra there, and she doesn't warrant or deserve it. I won't have your bad manners risking our friendship with her. You and Nicolas will attend her party and be civil to her. Mrs. Carter may be one of the biggest benefactors this diocese has ever had and I won't have you jeopardise that."

Frowning at her, he walked out.

CHAPTER 15

By the time Nicholas's exams were over, Constance felt as exhausted by them as he did.

Her every waking moment had been dedicated to helping him through them. But, finally done, she heaved a big sigh of relief. Nicholas was at last out of university, no longer a student. He was now working in his profession. As she walked him to work on his first morning at Fetherstons', she really did feel that this was the first day of their life together. They were on the road to being independent from their families and would soon have their own home, and a family of their own. As they reached the front door of Fetherstons' law firm, an imposing Georgian building on Parliament Street, she handed him his lunch.

"I would have brought you fresh food at lunchtime, but I wasn't sure if you would even have time to leave your office to meet me."

"Yes, I'd better not be presumptuous on my first day."

She embraced him. "Work hard, make a great impression, show them they were wise in giving you this job."

"For some reason I feel a little nervous," he said, looking up at the building. "I really feel as if my youth has just ended."

"Not your youth, just a chapter. And now it's time to start the next chapter, with me," she said.

He leaned forward and kissed her cheek before going into the building.

Sanders Fetherston was seated behind his huge oak desk in his office, looking at his new client Milandra Carter who was sitting opposite him.

"I can' t tell you how delighted we are that you chose to be our client. I'm sure there were many law firms vying for your business," he said enthusiastically.

He was a man in his fifties, overweight with small round spectacles. Milandra thought that he looked like a very safe pair of hands for her business affairs.

"Well, as soon as Judge Fontenoy recommended you, I felt I could choose no other," said Milandra.

"Yes, Daniel Fontenoy is a good friend of mine. We were at university together. In fact, his boy is coming to work for us – it's his first day today."

"So I believe," she smiled.

Sanders sat forward. "Now, I have been looking through the files sent from your late husband's last solicitor. There is a considerable amount of work to be done on an on-going basis, if, as I understand it you are continuing to run the wine merchants?"

"That is correct, Mr. Sanders."

"I feel I must advise you, as your newly appointed solicitor, that Carter Wines is a very big enterprise and I hope you have secured the right management to ensure its continual running?"

"Yes, I have everything taken care of, Mr. Fetherston, no need to worry. I'm actually very well acquainted with the running of the business. Ambrose trained me himself."

"Really? Most extraordinary! However, let's face facts. Whatever could a woman really know about the wine business? And that's why I must insist you appoint a regent, a proxy . . ."

As Fetherston continued droning on in what Milandra considered a very dull and monotonous voice, she stood up and walked over to the cabinet where the decanter of wine was.

"May I help you, Mrs. Carter?" asked Fetherston as he watched her in confusion.

She took up the decanter, opened it, and poured a small amount of the wine into a glass.

Fetherston was confused and a little appalled. "I'm sorry,

perhaps I should have offered you a glass? I didn't think you would want one given your circumstances . . ."

She brought the glass of wine to her lips, and sipped it. She held it in her mouth for a while before swallowing.

"Chateau de Ville, 1856. Not a bad year, but by no means a great one. Although at least it isn't 1853 – that vintage is so bad that we refuse to stock it. I hope you didn't pay too much for this."

Fetherston stood up, walked over to the cabinet and took out the bottle of wine from which he had filled the decanter earlier.

He looked up at her in amazement. "Chateau de Ville – 1856!"

"As I said, I hope you didn't pay too much for it," she said and placed the glass back down on the cabinet.

She returned to her chair and sat down.

"I accompanied my late husband on all his wine-buying tours to the Continent. There isn't a winery in the Loire, a *champagne maison* in Champagne, a vineyard in the Rhone Valley or Italy that I have not visited and tested. My late husband trained me well."

"Evidently!" said Fetherston, returning to his own seat behind the desk.

"So I think it's wise we don't waste any more time on anything immaterial and get down to the practical," said Milandra.

"Of course," nodded Fetherston.

"First and most important is the execution of my husband's will."

"I thought you might like some more time before you tackled that?"

"More time will not ease what needs to be done. We may as well get on with it," she said.

"Of course, if that is your wish," he agreed.

"All my husband's assets need to be transferred to my name as set out in the will. Next, Lucas Hempton has found a buyer for the country estate and so we need to deal with that without delay."

He sat staring at her. He had never met a client like her before, let alone a woman client. Her reputation was not underserved.

"I have appointed my most senior solicitor to deal with your account," he said proudly.

"But I want Nicholas Fontenoy," she said.

Fetherston squinted behind his spectacles. "I beg your pardon?"

"Nicholas Fontenoy – I want him to manage my account," she repeated.

Fetherston sat back in his chair and put his hands together. "Mrs. Carter, your suggestion is quite out of the question. And shows a certain naiveté. Perhaps Judge Fontenoy did not explain his son's situation properly to you. Young Fontenoy is only starting work with us today. He has just finished his exams, and we haven't even received his results yet. He is actually not officially even a lawyer yet."

"Yes, I'm aware of all that."

"Then you must comprehend that young Fontenoy would not be able to handle work of this magnitude." Fetherston didn't know whether to laugh or cry at the woman.

"I comprehend nothing of the sort. Nicholas Fontenoy has gone through the same exams and education as you yourself did to become a lawyer, has he not?"

"Well, yes, but nothing can compensate for his lack of experience. He is just starting off, and will take years to gain the knowledge that my senior lawyers have."

"Sometimes, in my experience, it is better to deal with a less cluttered mind. Think of the bad habits and the bad ways a lawyer with much experience may have. Experience can bring tiredness, boredom and a kind of 'know it all' attitude that can lead to lack of attention to detail."

Fetherston sat forward, his face serious. "None of my lawyers have bad habits or bad ways, Mrs. Carter. I ensure they don't."

"Good! Then you can ensure that Nicholas Fontenoy will do a splendid job as well. I'm of course not suggesting he be left to his own devices, as I expect that you will be supervising and assisting him. I don't want the poor fellow to drown either."

"I'm afraid this just won't do, Mrs. Carter. I can't entrust such a large account to one so inexperienced. You may have the choice of any other of my senior solicitors if the one I have chosen is not to your liking."

Milandra's face turned frosty and she stared at Fetherston so coldly that he got goose bumps.

"Then you disappoint me, Mr. Fetherston. And Judge Fontenoy disappoints me for recommending you in the first place. He assured me you would help me and assist me in any way I wished."

"But I am trying to assist you by advising you correctly!"

"But you are not assisting me *as I wish*!" She spoke the last words so sharply and loudly that Fetherston felt a little frightened. "Surely you knew that the reason I was becoming your client was because Nicholas Fontenoy was employed here?"

"I knew the Fontenoy connection was a major factor, yes. And I expected Nicholas to be working to some extent on your account, and I give him credit for bringing you as a client. But looking through the volume of work you bring with you, he just isn't capable of taking charge of the whole account!"

"I am a stranger to this city, Mr. Fetherston, a stranger. And the Fontenoys are some of the few people I trust. If you cannot see how important it is to me in such a case to have Nicholas Fontenoy working directly for me, then I fear we have been wasting each other's time and I bid you good day." Milandra stood up abruptly.

"Wait! Please," said Fetherston, speaking coolly. "If you wish to have Nicholas Fontenoy working for you, then I will of course honour your wishes. You are the client after all."

"Thank you, Mr. Fetherston!" she said, smiling, and sat down again. "You will not throw him in at deep end though – you will help him in any way he needs?"

"Don't worry, Mrs. Carter, I will be keeping young Fetherston and your business under my own very close supervision." He sounded more worried than obliging.

"I knew Judge Fetherston would not put me wrong when he recommended you." She smiled warmly at him.

Fetherston stood up, walked to the door and opened it.

"Send Fontenoy to my office without delay," he told his secretary.

Nicholas was sitting in the office which he shared with three other solicitors.

He had found his first day so far to be informal and enjoyable. The other solicitors had been welcoming and friendly and anxious to make him feel welcome.

"If you need anything, then just shout – I'm only a desk away," said George Fetherston, the owner's son, who was in his thirties and one of the firm's rising stars. "Father will probably want to see you this afternoon. He gives all his new solicitors a talk on their first day. Letting you know what's expected of you and welcoming you to the firm. It's quite informal, all done over a nice glass of wine in his office."

"I'll look forward to it!" Nicholas had replied.

Now, as Nicholas shifted through some elementary legal work he had been given, Fetherston's clerk entered the office.

"Mr. Fetherston wants to see you, Fontenoy, straight away," said the clerk.

Nicholas stood up immediately and followed him out.

"Good luck!" called George.

Nicholas felt nervous as he followed the clerk up to the top floor. This was obviously his induction talk and, though he knew Fetherston socially through his father, he realised how important it was to make a good impression on his first day at work. As the clerk showed him into Fetherston's office he was surprised to see Milandra Carter seated there.

"Ah, there you are, Master Fontenoy!" said Fetherston. "How are you finding your first day here?"

"Very good, sir," nodded Nicholas.

"I believe you are already acquainted with Mrs. Carter?"

"Yes, of course he is. Good afternoon, Nicholas," smiled Milandra.

"Hello, Milan – eh, Mrs. Carter." Nicholas smiled back.

"Well, take a seat, boy!" ordered Fetherston and Nicholas quickly took the spare chair beside Milandra.

"Fontenoy, you will be handling Mrs. Carter's work for the firm, reporting directly to myself," Fetherston announced.

Nicholas's eyes widened and his mouth dropped open. When he found his voice, he said, "I understood I would be working on Mrs.

Carter's account, but didn't realise I would be doing all the work myself!"

"Hmmm . . ." Fetherston saw the young man's discomfort at such a responsibility and was about to voice a further concern when he saw Milandra's steely eyes. "Yes, that is Mrs. Carter's – and my own – wishes."

"I see," said Nicholas, glancing at Milandra.

"I was just explaining to Mr. Fetherston that there is so much to do – our initial tasks are the administration of my husband's will and the sale of our country estate . . . so – shall we get to work?" It was more of a command that a request as Milandra stood and walked towards the door.

"I'll have my clerk take the files down to your office, Fontenoy," said Fetherston.

Then, just as Nicholas was about to follow Milandra out the door, Fetherston called him and gestured to him to close over the door.

"Just one moment, please," Nicholas said to Milandra before closing the door, leaving her outside in reception.

He hurried back to his boss's desk.

"I am sorry to be throwing you in at the deep end with this, Fontenoy," said Fetherston earnestly. "But I have no other choice. Give me regular reports and come to me if you have any query whatsoever, no matter how small."

"Yes, Mr. Fetherston, and thank you," said Nicholas, feeling dazed at the thought of it all.

"And Nicholas," Fetherston lowered his voice, leaning forward, "be very careful with her. She may be a family friend of yours, but watch her."

Nicholas nodded, wondering what he meant.

He left the room and joined Milandra.

"Sorry about that," he apologised to her.

Milandra smiled knowingly. "Where is your office?" she said.

"If you just follow me," he said and she followed him to the end of the corridor and down the stairs.

"Isn't it a lovely day?" she said with a smile.

"Yes."

"I'm sure you're delighted to be finished those dastardly exams?"

"It's certainly a relief," he acknowledged.

"I can't tell you how delighted I am that you are handling my account – somebody I can trust."

"Yes, I hope I don't disappoint you."

"Of course you won't disappoint me! Your father says you are one of the best legal minds he has ever met."

"He may be a little prejudiced, I being his son," said Nicholas, opening the door of his office and showing her in.

Milandra walked in and her face dropped as she saw he shared an office with three others.

"What is this?" she questioned.

"My office," he said as he went and sat down behind his desk and gestured for her to sit in the vacant chair in front of him.

She looked around at the other solicitors who were all staring at her in awe.

"But this won't do at all!" she declared.

"Sorry?" asked Nicholas.

"I need to have my meetings with you in private. I can't have my private business discussed in front of these other men."

Nicholas glanced at the other solicitors in embarrassment. "These are all long-term trusted solicitors working at this firm, Mrs. Carter – there is no risk of breach of confidentiality."

"Regardless – it just won't do! For the volume of work you will be handling for me and the privacy I need, you will need your own office."

George coughed loudly. "There is a meeting room at the end of the corridor that you are welcome to use at any time."

Milandra turned around and looked at George. "But I can't have my files brought in and out of meetings rooms as if they were library books on loan! No, I'm afraid this won't do at all. I need my files in a secure permanent office. They'll just have to give Nicholas his own office."

George looked at Milandra in amusement. "I'm afraid only the very senior solicitors, with the firm over ten years, have their own offices."

At that moment Fetherston's clerk walked in carrying a load of the Carter files and plonked them down on Nicholas's desk, announcing, "That's the first of them!"

"Well, you may just pick them back up and carry them back to Fetherston," said Milandra, "and tell him he must find a private office for my solicitor Mr. Fontenoy without delay."

"I'm sorry?" asked the clerk, bewildered.

"Is it really necessary for me to repeat myself?"

George stood up. "Perhaps I should go and explain the situation to him."

"Perhaps you should!" advised Milandra.

One hour later, Nicholas, astounded, found himself ensconced in his own office, surrounded with what looked like hundreds of files from the Carter business.

He sat staring at Milandra who had positioned herself in the chair on the other side of his desk.

"Now – shall we start?" she asked, smiling sweetly.

CHAPTER 16

That evening Constance waited anxiously for Nicholas outside Fetherstons'. It was now nearly half past six and there was no sign of him. He had told her he would be finishing at six and to wait for him there. As she had seen all the other workers already leave the building, even old Mr. Fetherston, she was beginning to worry that she had missed him earlier. Perhaps they had let him leave early on his first day? But then surely Nicholas would have waited for her?

Then she saw a man come out of the building, in a finely tailored coat, and she approached him.

"Excuse me, I'm looking for Nicholas Fontenoy – is he still working?" she asked.

The man looked her up and down. "My, my! Fontenoy is in demand today, isn't he?"

"I'm sorry?"

"He's still with a client," explained the man.

"Oh, I see!" she said, relieved.

"I'm George Fetherston, a colleague of young Fontenoy's," said the man, extending his hand. "I'm Sanders Fetherston's son."

She shook his hand. "I'm Nicholas's fiancée, Constance Staffordshire."

"Oh, I see," he smiled at her. "Delighted to make your acquaintance."

"Will he be long, would you say?"

"It's really very hard to say. She's quite demanding from what I can see," smirked George.

"She?" asked Constance, confused by his smirk.

"The client – Milandra Carter."

"Oh! Milandra!"

"Anyway, I hope to see you again, Miss Staffordshire. Good evening." He smiled at her, tipped his hat, and walked on.

Constance wondered what she should do. If Nicholas was the last in the building, he might leave at the same time as Milandra, and she didn't want to be seen standing there waiting like a fool. She crossed over the street and waited in a shop doorway. As the minutes ticked by, she became more agitated. Seven o'clock came and went and she realised she had to leave or else be very late back for dinner at home. Her father would not be pleased if she was.

She waited another ten minutes and, realising Nicholas might not appear this side of eight, hurried home in time for dinner.

"You are very quiet this evening, Constance," commented the Bishop at the dinner table.

"Am I?"

"Are you feeling unwell?" asked Henrietta.

"No, I'm quite well," said Constance.

"How did Nicholas's first day at work go for him?" asked the Bishop.

"I don't know," said Constance.

"I thought you were meeting him after work?" the Bishop asked.

"I didn't actually meet him as he was delayed by a client," said Constance.

"I imagine that will be Nicholas's life from now on. His carefree university days are behind him and work now comes first," said the Bishop.

"His work and his family," Constance said quickly.

The Bishop observed his daughter. "As his wife, you will need to support Nicholas in his work. You can't demand his attention all the time. Nicholas has a very bright future ahead of him, and you can't distract him from that."

Constance flushed at the implied rebuke. "May I be excused? I'm not hungry," she said.

"Are you sure you are not unwell?" Henrietta asked, worried.

"Quite well, Mama! Will you stop fretting all the time!"

The Bishop looked at Constance sternly. "You are excused from the table, Constance. With the mood you're in, you are not very good company."

"Thank you!" she said, standing quickly and throwing her napkin on the table.

Reeves opened the door for her and she quickly left and walked up the stairs to her room. She wished she had the kind of relationship with her parents where she could confide in them, like Nicholas had with his parents. But her mother fretted so much, it was impossible to discuss anything with her. And her father was always so quick to disapprove, it was easier not to say anything to him. Quick to disapprove of everything and anyone, that was, except for Milandra Carter.

The truth was, Constance herself was feeling very fretful. Regardless of how busy Nicholas was on his first day at work, she felt depressed that she had been left in the street waiting for him and that he hadn't been able to excuse himself for a minute from his meeting with Milandra Carter to come down and tell her he couldn't walk home with her.

Nicholas wearily put his key in the door and let himself into the Fontenoy house. He walked across the hall and into the drawing room where his parents were listening to Frederick play the piano.

"The soldier returns!" said Frederick, breaking off in his playing.

"My dear boy, we thought you had forgotten your way home!" said Daniel.

"I just got delayed with a client – Milandra Carter," explained Nicholas, looking shell-shocked. He sat down heavily on a couch.

"Milandra? Excellent!" Agatha clapped her hands together. "So Mr. Fetherston did put you working on her account! Only right, considering you working there landed her as a client."

"Fetherston appreciates the business we sent him – good!" said Daniel.

"I'm not just working on her account – I'm *heading* her account!" said Nicholas.

"Heading?" Daniel looked worried.

"What a wonderful display of confidence in you by Mr. Fetherston!" Agatha was beside herself in excitement.

"Maybe Mr. Fetherston has that confidence in me, but I'm afraid I don't share it!" said Nicholas.

"Is it too much for you?" Daniel enquired anxiously.

"Of course it is! I had to keep running into Mr. Fetherston to check things – I felt a total fool!"

"And did he mind?" asked Daniel.

"No. In fact, he insisted I should do so."

Daniel sat down beside his son and placed a hand on his shoulder. "Well, I'm sure Fetherston knows what he's doing. If he didn't feel you were able then he wouldn't have appointed you."

"I'm just frightened I'm going to mess it all up!"

"You won't!" insisted Daniel. "Look, my son, this is a wonderful opportunity for you, and you have Milandra to thank for it. You could have spent years wasting your time just assisting more experienced solicitors, but now you can rise very quickly through the ranks."

"Rise through the ranks! They've already given me my own office!" exclaimed Nicholas. "At Milandra's insistence that her work be dealt with in private."

"The level of business she is bringing to Fetherstons' must be very substantial indeed," pondered Daniel.

"A few of the other chaps were fairly put out, I can tell you. They were looking at me as if to ask 'Who is this upstart taking over?'."

"Jealousy! They are only jealous of you, my sweet," said Agatha, sitting the other side of Nicholas, and putting her hand on his other shoulder.

"Your mother is right, Nicholas," said Daniel. "There will be a lot of jealousy and you must just ignore it. You can't let other people's feelings of inadequacy hold you back from your rise to the top."

"It's not the others I worry about, but myself! That I will not be up to the job," said Nicholas.

"Nonsense!" said Daniel. "You are more than able and you have Fetherston there to tell you anything you don't know. And you have a secret weapon."

"What?"

"Me!" smiled Daniel. "There is nothing about the law that I don't know. If you are having difficulty with anything you bring the file home and I'll work through it for you."

"Thanks, Papa," said Nicholas gratefully.

"With this rapid rise from the ranks, you'll become a judge within ten years!" Daniel now was as ecstatic as Agatha.

"Constance is very lucky to have you," smiled Agatha, hugging her son tightly.

"Constance!" exclaimed Nicholas, jumping up. "I completely forgot about Constance!"

CHAPTER 17

Constance was awoken by the sound of a discreet knock on her bedroom door. She struggled awake and sat up. "Who is it?"

"Reeves, Miss," came the answer from the other side of the door.

"Reeves!" she said, swinging out of the bed and into her slippers. She went to the door, opening it a crack.

"What time is it, Reeves?"

"Not yet seven, miss."

"Whatever is the matter, Reeves?"

"Sorry, miss, to disturb you, but Master Fontenoy is here to see you."

"Nicholas! What does he want?"

"He said he wished to see you, miss. He came in the back way to the kitchen. He's there waiting for you now."

She shook her head awake and said, "Tell him I'll be down in a couple of minutes."

Constance suddenly became panicked. Nicholas not meeting her yesterday evening and now arriving at the break of day must mean there was something wrong. She raced to her dressing table and tidied her appearance. Then going to her wardrobe she selected her most elaborate robe de chambre and placed a lace cap over her head.

She slipped out of her room and down the corridor quietly, past her sister's room to the stairs. She crept down the stairs to the next floor and crept past her parents' bedroom. She dreaded to think what her father would say if he found her creeping down to meet her fiancé dressed like that, but she knew it was too early for him to be awake. She hurried on down to the ground floor, over to the back stairs and down the final flight of stairs to the kitchen.

She saw Reeves waiting at the back door down the corridor and she tiptoed past the kitchen where Cook and the kitchen maids were already hard at work.

"Where is he?" she whispered.

"He's out in the back garden. I'll leave this door unbolted and you can head back upstairs after speaking with him," Reeves said.

"Thank you, Reeves." She nodded in appreciation of his discretion as she saw him head into the kitchen and close the door firmly behind him.

She walked into the garden in the early morning sunlight and saw Nicholas waiting nervously there.

"Nicholas? What's the matter?" she asked

"Oh, Constance!" he came to her and held her tightly. "I just had to come and see you and explain about yesterday evening. I was so worried I had upset you that I could not wait the day to explain."

"Oh!" She felt a great relief that it was nothing more serious, that he or one of his family were ill or that there had been an accident.

"I was stuck in the office with a client and couldn't leave. I didn't leave the office till nine!"

"I was speaking to George Fetherston outside and he explained you were with Milandra Carter?"

"That's right – I've been appointed over her business and she's very demanding. She seems to know everything, more than I do, and was putting me through my paces."

"I can imagine! But Nicholas – you knew I was waiting for you – could you not have slipped out for a moment to tell me to go home? I was standing in the street for well over an hour on my own. I felt very uncomfortable."

Nicholas looked uneasy. "If the truth be known, I forgot."

"You forgot!"

"With everything going on, on my first day at work, I forgot we had arranged to meet. It slipped my mind."

"Oh, I see," said Constance and tears sprang to her eyes. His remark felt like a slap across the face to her.

"That's why I had to come and see you straight away this morning, before I go to work. Can you forgive me?"

His face was so contrite that she felt sorry for him. "Yes, I suppose I can. I know it was a demanding day for you."

"I will never leave you standing in the street again, I promise!"

"I hope so. I hardly slept last night thinking . . . well, I didn't know what to think."

"It will never happen again," he said, reaching down and kissing her.

"You had better go, Nicholas. If Father finds us here, there will be war. In the back garden – and I in my robe de chambre!"

"And lovely you look in it too! All right, I need to go and prepare for work. I have a meeting with Milandra this morning."

"Again!"

"I'm afraid so. I'd better go. I will see you later, my love."

He kissed her again before leaving her and rushing down the garden path to the gate in the high wall at the bottom of it. She stood there, in the morning cold, watching him as he turned and waved to her before disappearing out the gate.

She turned quickly and went inside. As she hurried back to her bedroom she was a maelstrom of emotions. It had really hurt her to hear that he had merely forgotten she was waiting for him, regardless of the circumstances. And yet there he was waiting for her in the morning dew, loving her. As she closed her bedroom door behind her and began to get ready for the day, she pictured Nicholas all day at Milandra Carter's beck and call and became infuriated. Why did that damned woman have to come and live on Sackville Street?

CHAPTER 18

No matter how many times Constance visited the slums of Dublin, she never became immune to the shock. Rows and rows of rundown tenements teeming with people with so little that her heart went out to them. As part of her work with her father's charities, since she turned eighteen she would once a month go to the slums and help distribute food and clothing to the desperate and needy.

It was a Tuesday afternoon and she was in a church hall which was situated in a slum down by the river. She and other volunteers stood behind tables giving out supplies to the queues of people that formed there. She never came there by herself and her father was at another table giving out parcels of food and spiritual advice in equal measure.

"Bless you, Miss, I don't know what we would do without you," said a woman with four young children.

"How are you?" asked Constance, recognising the woman from her previous visits.

"The same, miss," said the woman, holding her baby close to her. "The young one has been sick with colic and I can't get a doctor to look at her."

"We have a nurse here today. I'll get her to look at her," said Constance.

"Oh, thank you, miss!" said the woman.

Constance looked around for the nurse and spotted her dealing with a queue of sick children. She went over to her and whispered into her ear and the nurse nodded.

Constance returned to the woman.

"Just wait over there and she'll see her shortly," she told her.

"Bless you, miss, thank you!"

Constance reached beneath the table where she kept a stack of chocolate bars and handed some to the woman's delighted children.

As she looked around the packed hall, it was nearly impossible to believe she was in the same city as that of the grand Sackville Street and its surrounding squares. As she saw her father hard at work, she understood why he pandered to the likes of Milandra Carter. Her contribution was greatly assisting these desperate people. Not that Constance could ever imagine Milandra would come down and help out herself.

"At least it's summer, Constance, and they don't have to worry about the cold," said a well-heeled woman who was distributing food at the same table as her. "In another few months it'll be fuel they will desperately need."

"Very true," sighed Constance as she thought of the worse conditions the winter would bring.

The smell in the hall was becoming overwhelming and Constance stepped over to a window to open it. As she opened it fully she got a start to see Tom walking down the rundown street outside. She was about to call out to him, but held back when she saw him enter a tenement down the road.

"Mind the fort, I'll be back shortly," Constance said to the young lady beside her and quickly made her way out of the hall and onto the teeming street outside.

She made her way down the footpath to the building she had seen Tom enter. The front door was open and a crowd of dirty-faced bedraggled children were playing around the building. She peered into the darkened hallway inside where more children were wandering around.

"Can I help you, miss?" asked a woman who was scrubbing the hallway floor.

Constance recognised the woman as another person who regularly came to the church hall down the road to avail of charity.

Constance smiled at her. "Oh, yes, I saw a young gentleman

come in here a few minutes ago. Tall, in a black overcoat." Then, to make sure there could be no doubt who she was referring to, she added, "Well dressed." Nobody else was well dressed around there.

"Ah, yes, he's in a flat on the top floor, third door down the corridor," said the woman.

"Thank you," said Constance and made her way to the rickety staircase that led to the top floor. She was becoming increasingly worried as to what Tom was doing there. She had thought he might be there on some legal venture, but the woman seemed to know what flat he had entered as if he was frequently there.

She got to the door and knocked on it timidly.

A few seconds later it opened and Tom was standing there. He went as pale as a ghost on seeing her.

"Constance! What are you doing here?"

"I was helping out in the church down the road and saw you," she said, looking past him at the small dingy room behind him.

"You should go," he said, beginning to close over the door.

"Tom?" she said, stopping the door from closing and pushing it open again. "What are you doing here?"

"It's where I live, Constance," said Tom, his face clouded in shame.

"Live?" she said, perplexed.

"Come in," he said, standing aside and allowing her to enter.

As he closed the door she looked around the room. There was a round table in the middle of the room, a couple of chairs and a small bed in the corner. In the opposite corner was a small table with a large enamel bowl on top. By its side stood an aluminium bucket. She presumed that was where he washed. She wondered how he cooked. A rickety bookcase held his law books and assorted items like a bar of soap and half a loaf of dried-up bread. There was no sign of any other food, nor was there a press or cupboard where he might be keeping any.

"I don't understand, Tom – why are you living here?" she asked, confounded.

"It's all I can afford, Constance. I told you I had to leave my rooms in Trinity – my father's funds just stretched to me doing my exams there. This was all I could find for the little money I had."

"But surely you could have found lodgings somewhere better than this?" She gestured around the room.

"No, I couldn't. I still haven't found a job. And I only have enough money to stay here until the end of the month. I'll have to return home to Sligo then if nothing turns up." He sat down on a chair at the table and offered her one. She sat down beside him.

"But that means you will never get your legal career off the ground. After all that work and study!"

"What else can I do?"

"If things were as bad as this, you could have swallowed your pride and gone and stayed with the Fontenoys as Nicholas suggested." Constance was becoming angry with him.

"My pride, dear Constance, is all I have left, and I will not let the Fontenoys take that from me."

"You sound as if you resent them, and they have only been kind and hospitable to you."

"I don't mean to sound resentful, but it's hard to be anything else when you are desperate."

"Oh, my poor Tom!" She reached out and took his hand. "Does Nicolas know about all this?"

"No, and you are not to tell him. I won't have my best friend feeling sorry for me as he climbs the ladder to success without effort. I met him a couple of nights ago and we went to a tavern."

"And what did you tell him?"

"I told him I had secured clerical work in a firm and had rented nice rooms," he said.

"I'm so sorry." Her heart went out to him.

"I don't see how our friendship can survive," he said. "I can't hope to continue to pull the wool over his eyes but I can't tell him the truth either."

"He's your best friend. Of course you should tell him!"

"Impossible. Besides, Connie, to tell you the truth it was hard for me to listen to him as he said he had been snowed under in work, and had been given Milandra Carter as a client. And that they'd given him his own office."

"He wasn't boasting," Constance defended Nicholas. "He's feeling under stress from it all."

"I know, but how I would like to have those complaints! But I doubt I ever shall now, not having his connections in the legal world."

Constance squeezed his hand. "I'm sure something will come up for you soon."

"Isn't that what you said to me last time we met?" said Tom.

"It will, I know it will. Well, I had better be getting back to the hall or Father will start to worry as to where I've got to."

They both stood up.

"Promise you won't say anything to Nicholas?" he said.

"I promise," said Constance and she reached forward and embraced him.

As she stood back she gazed into his eyes which were filling with tears.

As Constance and her father shared a carriage back to their home in Mountjoy Square that evening, her mind was filled with worry about Tom.

CHAPTER 19

Milandra reached forward, took a bonbon from a bowl on the table and placed it in her mouth. She was in the basement kitchen with Flancy and the morning sun was flooding through the windows. The back door was open. The steps outside led up into the gardens. The kitchen was dominated by a huge wooden table where Flancy was hard at work baking a cake.

Milandra had been into Fetherstons' offices practically every day to see Nicholas working on her account. And she had an appointment to see him that afternoon. Unbeknownst to Nicholas, she would not be going to meet him in his offices that day.

"Will the cake be perfect?" asked Milandra as Flancy beat the ingredients in a bowl with a whisk.

"Is my baking ever anything else but perfect?" Flancy retorted.

Milandra smiled happily and sat down at the table. She opened her purse and took out an envelope.

"Kitty!" Milandra called loudly and a few seconds later the maid came rushing down the steps from the garden outside, where she had been setting the garden table, and in through the back door.

"Kitty, I want you to take this note to Fetherstons' Solicitors on Parliament Street and deliver it to Nicholas Fontenoy," she said.

"Yes, Mrs. Carter," said Kitty as she took the envelope and rushed out of the kitchen and up the stairs.

"For a half-witted girl, at least she does what she's told," said Flancy.

"Well, I'm interviewing tomorrow for the rest of the staff for the house, so you'll have plenty of help then," said Milandra.

Flancy's face turned sour. "And you only thought to tell me this now?"

"I deliberately didn't tell you. In fact, I shouldn't be telling you now because you'll only try to interfere in the hiring."

"Of course I'll interfere! They will be under my charge, so I should get a say in who works here," said Flancy.

"Actually, the butler will be the head of the house," said Milandra.

"*The butler!* Why are you hiring a butler? I can run a house better than any butler!"

"Well, we know you don't like men, Flancy. But I need a butler! Not having one would give the impression that I can't afford one," snapped Milandra.

Frowning, Flancy continued working in silence.

Milandra reached forward and dipped her finger into the mixture Flancy was working on.

"Well?" asked Flancy.

"Perfect!" said Milandra. "It's positively seductive!"

"That's the aim, isn't it?" smirked Flancy knowingly as she started to scoop the mixture into a baking tin. "I wondered if having spent all this time with Nicholas Fontenoy, your desire for him might have diminished somewhat?"

"No, of course it hasn't! If anything it's convinced me of my feelings for him."

"I can't imagine sitting in a boring office discussing legal titles is the most romantic setting to start your relationship."

"No, that's why I'm organising for him to come to see me here this afternoon. We need to move our courtship on to the next level."

"Courtship!" Flancy guffawed derisorily. "Just to remind you, Milandra, there is no courtship! Have you got any indication from him that he holds any kind of a candle for you?"

"Well, I wouldn't say indication – but he's very attentive!"

"You're paying his firm a lot of money – of course he's going to be attentive! And have you given him any signal of your feelings towards him yet?"

"Not yet – I have to pick my moment. It's all about the timing, Flancy, all about the timing."

"Hmmm," said Flancy sceptically as she placed the cake into the oven. "Well, I can't wait to meet this man who has made such an impression on you."

Nicholas was at his desk in his office when Kitty arrived.

"Mrs. Carter asked me to deliver this to you," said Kitty, handing him the envelope.

Nicholas nodded as he took it. He opened it and read the letter it contained.

Dear Nicholas,

Unfortunately, I will not be able to visit your office today as arranged. I am anxious to have the papers we discussed yesterday signed today, however, and so I would be obliged if you could bring them to my house on Sackville Street at three o'clock this afternoon.

Yours
Milandra Carter

Nicholas's face creased with irritation on reading the note. Milandra Carter seemed to have taken over his life since she had become his client. She literally had him at her beck and call. Working through lunch, working late into the evenings and now he was to do house calls to her as well! He had hardly been able to meet Constance at all.

"Very good, tell your mistress I will see her at three this afternoon at home."

Kitty gave a little curtsy and left.

Nicholas sighed as he stood up to go tell Fetherston that he would have to leave the office for the afternoon to meet the client at her house. He knew Fetherston would not even bat an eyelid. As far as the Carter account was concerned, Fetherston would do anything to keep it. And, though working for Milandra had made him very important in the firm and to Mr. Fetherston, Nicholas also realised it was making him quite unpopular with his colleagues. And that was something Nicholas had never experienced before in his life.

CHAPTER 20

Constance waited until after lunch before she crept down to the kitchens in the Staffordshire house. She knew Cook and the kitchen maids took their break at half two every day and retired to their rooms for an hour before they were back on duty preparing the evening's dinner. She crept down the stairs and along the corridor to the kitchen door and found it, as she expected, empty. She was carrying a bag and hurried over to the pantry and began to quickly fill it with as much food as she could fit in – ham, cheese, fresh bread, butter, chicken, part of the roast leg of lamb left over from the previous night's dinner. Content with her booty, she was about to scurry back upstairs when she had a thought and dashed over to the cupboards. Opening the cupboard door, she grabbed one of the bottles of wine on a bottom shelf there. Wine was so seldom drunk in the Staffordshire household – only when there were special visitors – that she was confident Reeves would never spot it was gone.

"Can I help you, Miss Constance?" came a voice from behind her and she jumped with fright.

Turning, she saw Reeve standing behind her, looking at the bottle of wine in confusion.

"Oh, good afternoon Reeves." She tried to sound nonchalant. "I was – I was just getting Mr. Nicholas some lunch – to take to him to eat in his office."

Reeves walked towards her and glared down at the large bag of food.

"I see – Mr. Nicholas's appetite must have grown very large indeed since he started at Fetherstons'. There's enough food there to feed a small army!"

Constance bit her lower lip and realised there was no point in trying to tell another lie and say that she going to distribute the food to the city's disadvantaged. Not with a bottle of wine included. Reeves was acutely aware that alcohol could never be included in charity donations from the Staffordshire house, not with the Bishop's morals.

Constance sighed. "It's actually not for Mr. Nicholas."

"I suspected as much."

"It's for Nicholas's friend, Tom Fitzgerald. You know, he was in university with Nicholas?"

"I have heard his name mentioned. But why is Mr. Fitzgerald in need of all this food?"

"Well, he's had a bit of bad luck. He hasn't managed to find a position since he left college and I bumped into him last week while doing charity work. He's living in the most dreadful place, a tenement, and from what I can see has very little in the form of good nourishing food – or indeed any food."

"What of Mr. Fitzgerald's own family?"

"They are in County Sligo and not aware of his situation. Otherwise they would insist he returned home and that would be the end of his legal career."

"And can the Fontenoys not assist him?" asked Reeves.

"His pride is stopping him from telling others about his situation. I only happened on him by chance and he swore me to secrecy. Oh, you won't tell anybody, will you, Reeves?"

Reeves face softened and he smiled at her. "My only concern is for you, Miss Constance. I don't think His Grace would approve of all this."

"I know! That's why you mustn't say anything!"

"And why are you taking him a bottle of wine? Surely that won't help with his nourishment?"

"No, it was just an afterthought. I thought it might cheer him up."

"His Grace certainly would not approve! And are you safe going to this tenement on your own?"

"I will get a cab straight to the door. I know the women living in the tenement from the charity, so I will be quite safe. I'll leave straight away and make sure Tom sees me to a cab when I leave."

"In that case – against my better judgement," said Reeves as he stepped out of the way to let her pass.

"Thank you, Reeves!" She smiled appreciatively at him and hurried through the kitchen and out through the back door. Holding the bag tightly she went down the garden and let herself out through the gate in the bottom wall.

CHAPTER 21

Nicholas knocked loudly on the front door of Milandra's house that afternoon and waited. A minute later the door opened and a woman in her fifties dressed in a maid's uniform stood there studying him intently.

"I'm here to see Mrs. Carter – if you could tell her Nicholas –"

"I know who you are, we were expecting you," said Flancy, holding the door back for him to enter.

He stepped inside.

She closed the door and looked him up and down with curiosity.

"Is there anything the matter?" he asked, slightly unnerved by the servant's manner.

"No! Nothing at all!" said Flancy with a mischievous look on her face.

Seeing she was in no hurry to go tell her mistress he had arrived, Nicholas said, "Perhaps if you could tell Mrs. Carter I am here? And shall I wait for her in here?" He made a move towards the downstairs parlour.

"No need. She's waiting for you in the garden. Follow me!"

Nicholas walked after her down the long hallway and past the central stairs where the French windows were open. He followed her out into the garden and saw Milandra at a garden table on the lawn.

"He's here!" announced Flancy as she showed him down to the table.

"Ah, Nicholas, thank you so much for seeing me here. I hope it wasn't too much trouble for you. You see, I had a full day meeting managers from the wine merchants and thought I would have been putting too much pressure on myself going to Parliament Street this afternoon."

"It wasn't a problem," said Nicholas as he sat down on the other chair at the table, which had been all set up for afternoon tea.

"I hope Mr. Fetherston didn't mind?" said Milandra.

"Not in the least," said Nicholas.

"That's what I like about Mr. Fetherston – he is so obliging. Nothing is too much trouble for him!"

"I brought the papers for your signature," said Nicholas, opening his file.

"Oh, leave that for now, Nicholas!" she said, waving a hand in the air. "I'm absolutely famished and need to have tea first. Flancy, be a dear, and serve the tea, why don't you?"

"Very good, *madam*," smirked Flancy as she headed off to the kitchen.

"It's such a beautiful day, Nicholas – so much nicer for us to do our business here outdoors than in a stuffy office." Milandra smiled at him.

"Yes, it is a beautiful garden," he said, looking around.

"You should have seen it before. It was dreadfully overgrown, I tell you. But now it's like an oasis of paradise in the metropolis."

Flancy and Kitty emerged from the house carrying trays of sandwiches – cucumber, beef and chicken – perfectly cut with white and brown bread. Nicholas hadn't eaten since that morning, and his mouth did water at the sight of them.

"Shall I be mother?" asked Milandra, smilingly picking up the large silver teapot Kitty had just left on the table.

"Thank you," said Nicholas as she began to pour the tea into his china cup.

Kitty and Flancy went back to the kitchen and then re-emerged a couple of minutes later, Kitty holding a tray of chocolates, bonbons and éclairs, Flancy holding aloft the cake she had baked that day.

"I hope you haven't gone to all this trouble for me?" remarked Nicholas as he stared at the delicious display.

"Oh, it's no bother. We always have afternoon tea like this," said Milandra.

"Lucky you!" said Nicholas.

As Kitty headed back into the kitchen, Flancy stood there, her arms folded, looking at Nicholas.

"You may leave us, Flancy." Milandra's voice was sweet but insistent.

"If you need anything, just yell!" said Flancy as she reluctantly headed back inside.

"What an unusual servant! Wherever did you find her?" asked Nicholas.

"Oh, Flancy has been with me for years. She's slightly unconventional, but she can run a house much better than any butler and cook better food and bake better cakes than anybody I have ever met."

"You are certainly not wrong there," he said with a glance at the luscious cake.

"Ah, I always think the way to a man's heart is through his stomach." Milandra smiled as she proffered the plate of sandwiches.

He began to relax in the comfort of the delicious food and the afternoon sunshine and made good inroads into the sandwiches.

"Time for cake," said Milandra.

She carefully cut a large slice of the cake and placed it on a plate before handing it to Nicholas. It was a moist luscious Victoria Sponge, decorated lavishly with strawberries and cream swirls, with a generous layer of cream and jam inside.

"It looks too good to eat," Nicholas said.

"And I can assure you it tastes too good not to," she said, handing him a desert fork.

He slid the fork into the cake, took a scoop and placed it in his mouth. She watched as he momentarily closed his eyes in delight.

"Well?" she asked, sitting forward.

"Delicious. It's as you said – your Flancy does the best baking that I have ever tasted. You will need to be careful, or my mother will try to rob her from you."

"Oh, I have no fear on that score. Flancy would never desert me."

As Nicholas seemed lost in the moment, eating the cake in the sunshine, Milandra sat back feeling content.

"What a wonderful afternoon," she sighed after a while.

"Eh, yes, but I've taken up too much of your time. I should be getting those papers signed and explaining them to you, rather than sitting here enjoying your hospitality."

"Nonsense! You've been working so hard for me I wanted to give you afternoon tea, as a thank-you."

"Just doing my job," smiled Nicholas.

"I'm so glad I went with your father's advice and chose you to do my work. I feel I can trust you as a friend, in a way I could never trust another lawyer."

"Well, yes, of course you can trust me, Milandra. I have your best interests always at the forefront of my mind."

"Thank you. I hope – I hope Constance hasn't minded all this extra time I have caused you to spend at work?"

"Of course not – she completely understands that I need to establish my career."

"And how are the wedding plans going?"

"I'm afraid I haven't had time to catch up on Constance's plans for the last while," he said with a grimace.

"Oh dear!" said Milandra as she picked up the teapot and refilled his cup. "And what of the house-hunting?"

"Well, we have not been house-hunting. I'm afraid we won't be able to afford a house for a while after we get married."

Milandra sat up, concerned. "But where will you live?"

"We are to stay at my parents' home for the first few months of our marriage, until we can afford a place of our own."

"At your parents' house!" Milandra looked horrified. "And Constance is accepting of that?"

"What choice does she have?" laughed Nicholas.

"But that is a recipe for disaster, Nicholas. A mother-in-law and a daughter-in-law under the same roof! Two women in the same house!"

"Well, it will only be for a short time, and my parents and Constance get on extremely well."

Milandra looked sceptical. "I'm sure they do – and it's not my place to say, but I did detect a little irritation between Constance and your mother on occasions I have been in their company together."

"Really?" Nicholas looked confused and concerned.

"Probably just my imagination, but perhaps not . . . My advice to you is, once you have married Constance, do try to find your own home as quickly as you can. It would be the best for all concerned. No marriage should start off on the wrong foot, and in-laws can often be a wrong foot."

Nicholas lifted his cup to his mouth and took a sip. "The price of property is so high in any area that we want to live in, it may take some time."

"Sorry, I don't mean to be intrusive, but does Constance not have a dowry that she is bringing with her?"

"Well, yes, but it is only a small one. Her family aren't particularly rich. Outside having their own home on Mountjoy Square, I think their assets and lifestyle are quite frugal. The Bishop has dedicated his life to giving to others, not acquiring for himself."

Milandra sat back and drank her tea. "Yes, I do so admire His Grace's caring attitude in life. It is a pity though that his giving towards others has left his daughter as an unattractive commodity as a potential wife!"

"I'm sorry?" Nichols put down his cup abruptly.

Milandra sat forward quickly. "Oh, I'm not talking about Constance, dear Nicholas," she said, laughing lightly. "Of course you couldn't find a better prospect than Constance. No, I'm talking about her younger sister. Emma, isn't that her name? Let's face it, not all men will be as selfless and uncovetous as you have been in choosing Constance, when it comes to her sister Emma finding a husband."

"I – I really hadn't thought about it," said Nicholas.

"I can assure you Emma will find it very hard to find a husband of quality if her dowry is, as you say, as low as Constance's. But I think people rush too quickly into marriage these days. Fools rush in where angels fear to tread, that's what Lucas Hempton always says. Instead of taking the time to save for a nice home and surroundings, they throw themselves on the generosity of relatives, which let's face it will end in disaster!"

Nicholas was feeling uncomfortable.

"Nicholas – are you all right?"

"Yes, yes. Perhaps we can now get on with the signing of the papers?" He reached for his file.

"In a while. I think we deserve some more of that refreshing tea first, and another slice of that delicious cake. Don't you agree?"

Nicholas could only smile uncertainly.

CHAPTER 22

As Constance had promised Reeves, she took a cab to the very door of the tenement where Tom was living. As with her last visit, there were numerous children playing on the street and she walked past them and in through the front door of the building. She climbed the stairs to the top floor, heaving the heavy bag of food, and knocked on his door when she reached it.

"Constance!" said Tom, on opening the door. "What are you doing here?"

"Don't be angry with me, Tom – I brought you some supplies," she said, holding up the bag.

"Supplies?" He beckoned her in and closed the door behind them.

She walked over to the table, set the bag on it and began to unpack it.

"Where did you get all this from?" he asked in amazement, picking up a loaf of bread.

"I took it from our kitchen at home. Don't worry, I told nobody I was coming here," she lied, sure of Reeves' discretion.

"I can't take this from you, Constance," he said, putting down the loaf quickly.

"Of course you can! We have plenty. It won't even be missed," she insisted.

"But, I told you before, I will not rely on charity!" He looked flustered and angry.

"Tom!" she said, placing a hand on his shoulder. "This is not charity – it's a friend helping out another friend in need, that is all."

"You can dress it up as much as you want, but you are making me no better than the people you hand your food parcels out to in the church hall down the road!"

She glanced around and saw no sign of food. "You are really not in a position to object, Tom. Have you even enough food to feed yourself tonight?"

He glared down at the ham she had just laid out on the table.

"I even brought you a bottle of wine," she said, and tried smiling at him to coax him.

"Thank you, Constance," he finally conceded and managed to look both ashamed and grateful at the same time.

"I bet you didn't even eat today. Let me prepare you something right now."

She went to the cabinet and took a fork, knife and plate from it. Returning to the table, she cut some slices of bread and buttered them. Then she sliced some ham and cheese and put it on the plate.

She then went to him, took his arm and led him to the table to eat.

Constance was sitting in the Fontenoys' drawing room with Daniel, Agatha and Frederick as the clock on the wall struck seven thirty.

"Are you sure you won't join us for dinner, Constance?" asked Agatha.

"No, as I said I have to be home for dinner," said Constance irritably.

"Well, I'm sure His Grace wouldn't mind if you missed dinner at home just once," Agatha said. "I can send one of the servants up to explain you will be dining with us and we shall drop you back later on, if he's worried about you travelling alone at night."

"No, Agatha, Father wouldn't be happy about that," said Constance.

Agatha sighed. "Well, we are going into dinner now, dear, and I don't want to be rude but it looks like Nicholas has been delayed at work again and so there's no point in waiting for him any longer if you insist you have to get home." Agatha's patience had given out.

"Where is he?" fretted Constance. "He promised he wouldn't be delayed this evening as he only had a few papers to be signed by Milandra Carter this afternoon."

"Well, you can never tell in the legal profession, my dear – things never go as expected," said Daniel.

"You'll just have to get used to it, Constance – it's the lot of a lawyer's wife," said Agatha. "I remember, when Daniel started his career, he often didn't get home until after midnight."

The front door could be heard opening and closing.

"At last!" said Constance, jumping to her feet.

Nicholas came bounding into the drawing room, looking distressed.

"Sorry I'm late," he said.

"You're just in time – we are about to go in to dinner," said Agatha.

Constance rushed to him and embraced him. "Where were you? I've been here since five. I thought you said you would be back by six this evening."

"There was a change of plan. Milandra couldn't come to the office for our meeting, so I had to go to her house to have the papers signed."

"Her house!" Constance exclaimed.

"Yes," he said. "That's the trouble with having a client as busy as Milandra Carter – you have to fit into her schedule."

"But that's ridiculous!" snapped Constance. "She can't expect you to call to her house just because she can't be bothered going to your offices!"

"Actually, Constance, as an important client, she can choose to meet her lawyer wherever it so pleases her," said Daniel. "I have met some of my clients in the most unusual of places. Often I used to meet them on ships as they docked into the Liffey!"

Constance glared at Nicholas. "You look as if you are sunburned!" she observed.

"Yes, we had the meeting in her garden," said Nicholas.

"The garden!" Constance's voice had risen several octaves.

"Ahem, I think we shall go along in to dinner," said Agatha, standing and beckoning to Daniel and Frederick.

They rose promptly and followed her out, leaving the couple alone.

"Yes, the garden!" repeated Nicholas as soon as the door closed. "That's where she wanted to have the meeting, and so that's where we had it. I could hardly dictate to her to have the meeting indoors – and, besides, what difference does it make?"

"It sounds more like a social call than meeting, if you ask me," said Constance.

Nicholas looked at her incredulously. "Do you honestly think that Fetherstons' would allow me out of the office for a social call?"

"Well, no, but –"

"I don't understand you, Constance, I really don't. I am working every minute of every day to secure us a future so that we can live happily and all I seem to be getting from you is annoyance!"

"I fully understand your work commitments. It's just we have a wedding to plan, and you've hardly discussed anything with me since you started your job," said Constance.

"For goodness' sake! Is there anything left to be discussed about our damned wedding? I thought we had already gone through the minutest of details!"

"I didn't realise it had been such a chore for you," she said, hurt.

"Of course it's not a bloody chore! But I have to get our priorities right, Constance! Let's be honest – unless I start earning very well very soon, we are facing living under my parents' roof for the foreseeable! Is that what you want?"

"No, of course I want a home of our own as soon as possible," she said.

"Then you should be very glad that I have a good position at Fetherstons' and a good client like Milandra Carter. Let's face it, it's not as if you're bringing any kind of substantial dowry with you."

Constance's mouth dropped open and tears sprang to her eyes.

"I had better be going," she said abruptly. "I'm already late for dinner at home. Father will not be happy."

"Oh! So you're my fiancée, you're complaining about my not spending time with you, but you can't miss dinner at your father's

143

table and spend the evening here with me, having dinner with my family!"

"You know Father would not allow that without my asking permission beforehand."

"Yes, I realise everything has to be on yours and your father's terms," snapped Nicholas angrily. "I have to try and rush around to meet you at lunch or break my neck trying to get out of the office to see you for five minutes before you rush off home to be seated at your father's dinner table in time. The same father who won't even provide you with a decent dowry that would set us up in a house of our own!"

"Nicholas!" Constance was shocked. "I never realised my lack of a dowry meant so much to you."

"It didn't, it doesn't," he said, still speaking harshly. "I just want you to try to realise that we can't live under our parents' protection forever more and to try to be – understanding – about my work commitments."

"No need to worry about that, Nicholas. I have seen up close very recently an example of a law graduate who would give anything for your position. I'm sorry if I sounded selfish. I'll let you go have your dinner."

She walked out of the room quickly. He didn't follow her.

It was only when she had left the house and was making her way past Rutland Square that she allowed her tears to flow.

Constance could hardly sleep that night as she went over and over her argument with Nicholas. Yes, it had been an argument, she had to admit to herself. They had never had an argument before, not even cross words. And she was so alarmed by it. She could not forget how he had harshly called their upcoming nuptials a "*damned* wedding"! She fought back the tears at his description. Perhaps she was being selfish. Expecting Nicholas to be as free and available as he had been when a student. Maybe she was finding it hard to adapt to his new work life. It was just she was used to seeing him every day and now she wasn't and was rushing around trying to grasp an hour with him here and there. She supposed it would be different if they were married. If he was coming home to her every evening and they lived in the same house. That would make all the difference. She wished she had accepted Agatha's invitation to stay for dinner. She had put her father's demands in front of hers and Nicholas's happiness.

She could only imagine the scene with her father if she hadn't arrived back for dinner on time, but now she wished she had risked it and taken the valuable time she could with Nicholas instead of rushing off to listen to her father pontificating over a leg of lamb and mint sauce. Oh, how she wished she was already married to Nicholas!

As the dawn began to break, she got out of her bed and began to prepare herself quickly. She knew their argument would have caused Nicholas as much stress and worry as it had caused her. That she would have cost him a good night's sleep and he had a busy day ahead of him in the office. She quickly got dressed and began to do her hair. She was sure he would come to the back door of the house early that morning, like he had before, to make amends and she wanted to be ready when Reeves knocked on her door and said Nicholas was waiting to see her in the garden.

At last dressed and ready, she sat in her armchair looking out her window at Mountjoy Square, waiting for the discreet knock on the door from Reeves.

But it never came.

145

CHAPTER 23

Milandra sat in the drawing room and read through the references of the man sitting opposite her who she was interviewing for the role of butler.

"Oh, yes, these are all excellent, Mr. Barker," she said. "Have you only ever worked for members of the aristocracy previously?"

"That is correct, Mrs. Carter. You would be the first non-titled employer I have had – if I am awarded the position," said the man who was very smart-looking and in his fifties.

"Excellent!" smiled Milandra, impressed with his pedigree. "I expect to do a lot of entertaining."

"I have headed households that have entertained kings and queens, Mrs. Carter, though discretion stops me from divulging the details."

"How very exciting!" smiled Milandra.

At that moment Flancy walked in.

"Flancy, dear, I thought I asked not to be disturbed." Milandra shot her a warning look.

"Indeed you did," said Flancy as she stood her ground and glared at Barker.

"Mr. Barker, this is our cook, Flancy. She has been with my late husband and me for years. Flancy, this is our new butler, Mr. Barker."

"How do you do?" said Barker, standing up and offering his hand.

Flancy looked at it with disdain and ignored it.

"Flancy will be invaluable to you, Mr. Barker, as she is – a treasure!" Milandra smiled sweetly at Flancy, willing her to be nice.

"Amongst other things," said Flancy.

"Now, I've already hired two footmen earlier today, Mr. Barker, wonderful young men I'm sure you will approve of," said Milandra.

"I don't know what need there is of a butler and two footmen in this house when there are no men of the house to serve!" observed Flancy loudly.

"Now you are here, be a dear, Flancy, and show Mr. Barker where his room is and everything else," said Milandra.

Flancy looked up to heaven and said, "Follow me!"

Barker smiled and nodded at Milandra before following a disgruntled Flancy.

Milandra shook her head in dismay. Flancy was completely territorial and had always given other staff a hard time. She hoped she wouldn't be the same with Barker. But it wasn't looking promising.

Constance tried to keep herself busy through the day. She visited a florist's to see about flower arrangements for the wedding. She went to one of her father's church halls to help distribute charity to the underprivileged. Anything to keep her mind off Nicholas and the fact he had not come to mend their argument that morning before work. Perhaps her selfishness had truly annoyed him? Always when Nicholas and she said goodbye to each other they made an arrangement for their next meeting. But because their last meeting had ended in a row, there had been no such arrangement made. She had no plans to meet him at the Fontenoys', or at a tea room, or outside his workplace.

As the afternoon continued towards evening she began to fret. She couldn't spend another night without their argument being resolved. And she couldn't just call into the Fontenoys' and wait for him there as Agatha and Daniel would be hovering around and they wouldn't be able to speak privately. She decided she would take the bull by the horns and wait for him outside his workplace that evening. She wouldn't care how long she had to wait for him. Even if she had to miss dinner and face her father's wrath.

As Constance stood in Parliament Street that evening opposite

Fetherstons' office building, she felt a knot in her stomach. She almost dreaded seeing Nicholas. What if his anger had grown worse since yesterday evening?

It was half six and still no sign of him. As she looked up at the top floor where she knew his office was, she pictured him in there with Milandra Carter. Did this woman have no life of her own? Regardless of how much legal work that needed to be sorted after her husband's demise, was it not unhealthy to be so consumed with work? She had never met or heard of a woman like her before. She had never heard of a woman who was a merchant before. The whole thing was disreputable. Two men passed her by and looked her up and down, making her feel very uncomfortable. Whatever about meeting her fiancé at a prearranged time from his work, it wasn't right for a young lady to be standing in a street with no arrangement. She knew her dress and bearing could never have her mistaken as a prostitute, but she was sure men passing her on their way from work thought her curious.

"Come on, Nicholas!" she called under breath.

She spotted Nicholas's colleague, the one she had spoken to before outside the building when she had been kept waiting. George Fetherston – she remembered his name, Mr. Fetherston's son. She quickly turned and pretended to be peering into the shop window she was outside of, hoping he hadn't spotted her. To her horror, in the reflection in the glass she saw he was crossing the street over to her.

"Good evening, Miss Staffordshire!" said George cheerily.

Feeling herself going bright red, she turned to face him.

"Oh, hello again!" She managed to smile at him. "George, isn't it?"

"Yes, how nice of you to remember my name. Are you waiting on Nicholas again?"

"Eh, yes, will he be long, do you know?"

"I can't really say. He was still in his office when I last saw him, head deep in ledgers."

"Oh!" said Constance, looking down to the ground, relieved that at least he wasn't with Milandra.

George looked worried. "Shall I run back in and tell him you're here?"

"Oh, no, please don't! I don't want to interrupt him finishing his work."

She felt herself go beetroot red at the whole situation. What must George Fetherston think of her, hanging around streets?

"He knows you are waiting for him though?" asked George.

"Yes, of course . . . I think, unless I have mixed up the arrangement. It's not Nicholas's fault in any case." Constance didn't want Nicholas's colleague thinking badly of him.

"Well, I can't leave you a second time standing waiting for him!" declared George who managed to look both amused and puzzled by the situation.

"Oh, please, don't worry on my behalf. I'm sure he will be out any minute."

"And I'm sure by the look of the ledgers he won't be. There's a tea room a few doors down. Why don't I sit with you in the comfort inside while you wait for him? We can take a window table so you can be sure not to miss him."

"Oh, no, thank you, but no. I really couldn't possibly . . ."

"I insist! I'm sure Nicholas won't be that long and at least you can have tea and cake while you wait," said George.

Constance bit her lower lip. She really had to see Nicholas that evening no matter what. And she couldn't bear the embarrassment of standing in the street any longer.

She smiled at George and began to walk with him towards the tea room.

Inside, they sat at a window seat. As she chatted away to George, she kept one eye firmly on Fetherstons' front door across the street, on the lookout for Nicolas.

"I really do think that you and Nicholas should be more exact in making your arrangements in the future," smiled George. "Either that or you are going to be spending considerable time standing in Parliament Street!"

"What must you think of me?" said Constance as she sipped her tea.

149

"It's not what I think of you, my dear, it's what I think of Nicholas! Leaving a young lady standing in the street. Most disrespectful!"

"Oh, it's really not his fault!" Constance jumped to his defence. "He actually doesn't know that I'm here."

"I see!"

"I was surprising him, you see."

"Well, I really think you shouldn't do that in future. It just doesn't look right for a woman to be standing in the street on her own in the evening. People will get the wrong idea, if you get my meaning."

"I know, but I have to see him to discuss an urgent detail of the wedding."

"It must be very urgent indeed!" George looked at her sceptically.

She looked down at the tablecloth in embarrassment.

"Oh, you don't have to be embarrassed with me, Constance. I was engaged myself once. I know the course of true love never runs smoothly. A lovers' tiff, was it?"

Constance went bright red again, causing him to smile.

"You won't say anything, will you?" she said, alarmed.

"Of course I won't."

"Perhaps it might be better if we didn't mention to Nicholas that we went for tea. He can be quite private and would hate to think a colleague knew any of his private business."

"Don't worry – I'm the soul of discretion," he said, smiling reassuringly at her.

"Thank you, you're very kind," she smiled and took another sip of tea. She glanced out the window. "Oh, there he is now!"

George looked out the window and saw Nicholas come out of Fetherstons' and begin to walk down the street.

"I'd better go after him," she said.

"Do and good luck!" George smiled.

"Thank you for the tea and cake," she said and then hurried out of the tea room.

George watched from the window as Constance hurried across the road and down the street until she had caught up with Nicholas.

150

Then, as he took out his wallet to pay the bill, he spotted something gleaming on the table beside the cup Constance had drunk from. He reached over and, seeing it was a bracelet, picked it up and examined it. He saw the clasp had broken, no doubt causing it to fall from her wrist. It had the name *Constance* on it. He put the bracelet into his pocket and paid the bill.

"Constance! What are you doing here?" asked Nicholas as she caught up with him at the end of Parliament Street.

"I needed to see you, Nicholas. I hardly slept with worry last night after our – our – argument." She felt the word hard to say.

H studied her before saying, "I could hardly sleep myself from worry about it."

"Oh, I've been a stupid selfish girl, Nicholas. Not appreciating the pressure you've been under, trying to establish your career. You've been doing it all for us and all I've been thinking of is myself. Can you forgive me?"

Nicholas sighed. "It's not you should be apologising, but me. I said some cruel things, talking about dowries and the like. I don't know what came over me. You know that kind of thing is unimportant to me. That I only care about you."

"I know that, but it's lovely to hear it just the same," she said and tears sprang to her eyes.

"Oh, Constance!" he said, wiping away her tears and reaching out to embrace her.

They began to walk down the street, her head resting on his shoulder.

CHAPTER 24

Constance and Nicholas sat at a table in a quiet corner of the restaurant in the Shelbourne Hotel. They had chosen the hotel on Stephen's Green as it was the opposite end of the city centre from Sackville Street and they wanted to talk without risk of being interrupted by friends or neighbours. As they chatted and held hands over dinner, Constance felt a huge amount of relief. It was as if their argument had not happened and she felt they were the same as before he had gone to work at Fetherstons'. The fact that it was now nearly ten o'clock and her father would be insane with worry and anger over her non-appearance at dinner at home did not even worry her. Nicholas would soon be her husband and she had to put him first. She had lived by her father's rules all her life. She was not going to risk this opportunity of putting things right with her fiancé by rushing home for a dinner of roast beef just to appease her father.

"Have you seen Tom recently?" asked Constance.

"I met with him last week. We went to a tavern last Wednesday evening for a couple of drinks."

"How is he?"

"In excellent form. Very jovial," smiled Nicholas.

Constance nodded, realising Tom had been putting on an act for his friend.

"Has he found work yet?"

"Yes, I think so, clerical work somewhere," said Tom.

Another lie Tom had told to save his pride. And as she looked at

Nicholas's unconcerned face, Constance knew he hadn't enquired too far into Tom's circumstances. As she studied her fiancé, she wondered if he had purposefully not questioned Tom too much as he didn't want to know the real truth. She remembered Tom's explosive anger in his rooms in Trinity before their exams when the subject of employment had come up.

"Anyway, I will see him tomorrow morning," said Nicholas.

"Oh?"

"Yes, our exam results are out tomorrow," he said with a grimace.

"Oh, Nicholas! I completely forgot!" she said, reaching quickly for his hand and squeezing it. "What time?"

"Eleven, at the front square at Trinity. Father is accompanying me." Nicholas grimaced even more.

"And I shall be there too," she said, leaning forward supportively.

"Thank you, Constance."

"And what will we do to celebrate?" she asked.

"Let's see first if there is anything *to* celebrate!"

"Of course there will be. I have every faith in you."

"You are so supportive of me in everything I do. I don't think I would have even got through the exams if it weren't for you," he said.

She smiled, embarrassed but pleased.

As the clock on the wall struck she saw it was half past ten.

"Oh. Nicholas, I'd really better be getting home or else Father will have search parties out looking for me," she said, standing up abruptly.

Two waiters rushed over to them and helped them don their outdoor wear. Nicholas paid the bill and put his arm around her as they walked out of the restaurant and into the grand marble foyer. As she looked around at the other patrons coming and going, going into the restaurant or arriving in for drinks after the theatre, she felt a warm glow. This would soon be the life she and Nicholas would be having all the time, answerable to nobody but themselves.

"Oh, if I *do* pass my exams tomorrow we can always celebrate on Friday night," said Nicholas.

"Friday night?"

"Yes, it's Milandra Carter's party, remember?"

"Oh yes, how could I forget?" Constance felt her warm glow evaporate at the thought of it.

"Your parents are still going, aren't they?"

"Yes, they haven't said otherwise. I can't imagine they will stay long though."

"You never know – they might just enjoy themselves. I hope they stay till the end, because then I'll have you there for the whole night."

She smiled at him and leaned forward to kiss him as the concierge rushed out to get them a hansom cab.

Nicholas held Constance tight in the back of the hansom cab as it turned into Mountjoy Square. She felt a knot in her stomach as the cab made its way around the square and pulled up outside the Staffordshire house.

"I wish I didn't have to leave you," he said.

"It will only be for a short while." She smiled at him and they began to kiss.

The door was opened by the driver and Constance tore herself away from him.

"I'll see you in the front square at Trinity in the morning," she said as the driver helped her out.

She waved goodbye and, as she knocked on the front door, she watched the cab take off and waved again.

The front door opened and a distressed-looking Reeves let her in.

"His Grace is not well pleased," Reeves whispered to her, taking her cloak.

"*Constance – is that you?*" bellowed the Bishop from the front parlour.

Constance sighed heavily as she made her way to the parlour and, pushing the door open, walked in.

Her father was in an armchair beside the fireplace, while her mother was on a couch opposite him. She didn't know which one looked more agitated. Emma was sitting in an armchair by the front window, her eyes wide with fright.

154

"What is the meaning of this?" demanded her father, standing up.

"The meaning of what?" Constance asked, trying to sound nonchalant.

"Arriving in here at eleven o'clock!"

"I went to dinner with Nicholas," she said.

"I beg your pardon?" said her father.

Constance cleared her throat before saying, "We went to the Shelbourne for dinner."

"For what purpose?" demanded the Bishop.

"To eat!"

"Ohhh!" exclaimed Henrietta.

Her mother's expression looked so pained that Constance felt if she had answered 'To fornicate!' she could not have looked more shocked.

"But – but who gave you permission to?" asked her father.

"I didn't realise I needed to permission to eat in a public restaurant with my fiancé," Constance said, suddenly feeling very brave.

"But we waited for two hours at the dinner table for you!" said Henrietta in a shaky voice. "The beef was stone cold by the time we finally ate it!"

"Well, you shouldn't have waited for me! You should have gone ahead and eaten your dinner!" said Constance.

"Of all the ingratitude!" The Bishop was horrified.

"I'm truly sorry if I inconvenienced you, and I didn't plan it, but I really needed to spend some time with Nicholas. I can't see him during the day like I used to with his new work, and we have so much to arrange still for the wedding."

"I am disgusted beyond belief by you, Constance. That you can't even realise the error of your ways!" The Bishops voice was harsh and loud.

"There's no error of my ways – unless you count an extra helping of custard with my dessert," said Constance.

"Don't be so frivolous!" ordered the Bishop. "You know that you are expected, as long as you live in this house, to be here at the table on time for dinner!"

"But why?" demanded Constance. "Why must I?"

"*Because I say so*!" shouted the Bishop, causing Constance and the others to jump.

"Emma! Emma! Quick – a glass of water!" croaked Henrietta, gesturing to a jug of water on a nearby table.

Emma jumped from her seat and rushed to the jug and poured a glass, before sitting down beside her distraught mother and helping her to sip it.

"You are being utterly unreasonable," Constance fought back. "I will be married to Nicholas soon, and do you expect me still to be at your table then?"

"Once you are married to Nicholas, you will no longer be my responsibility or my burden. Until then I will not have a daughter of mine gaining the reputation of being a *loose woman*!" The Bishop's last two words came out as a scream.

"Oh – oh – oh!" Henrietta sank back in the couch in a faint-like position, causing Emma to grab a newspaper from a nearby table and begin to fan her frantically with it.

"Oh stop it, Mother!" snapped Constance irritably.

"I don't know what has got into you!" said the Bishop. "Do not speak to your poor scandalised mother that way!"

"Scandalised over what exactly? A serving of half a roast chicken with turnips and parsnips in the Shelbourne restaurant?"

"You little brat!" spat her father.

"You have complete double standards," said Constance. "Milandra Carter is constantly in restaurants, parties, and hotels when she should be indoors mourning and all you do is praise her!"

"You are not Milandra Carter! She is an independent woman of independent means!"

"And that is exactly it, Father! Her independent means is all you are interested in. She has bought you like she has bought everybody else!"

The Bishop shook his head solemnly. "It had passed fleetingly through my mind when you boldly announced that you had been in a hotel with Nicholas, that he was a bad influence on you. I should have known better, and known that Nicholas is faultless. It is plain

156

to me that it is *you* who are leading poor Nicholas astray. I think I shall have to pay Daniel Fontenoy a visit tomorrow and express my concerns over his son's marriage to a girl as misdirected as you."

"Don't you dare! I will never speak to you again if you do such a thing!" Constance warned, tears springing to her eyes.

Henrietta slid off the couch on to her knees on the carpeted floor and held her hands together in a pleading fashion to her husband.

"Oh please, John, I beg you! Don't do such a thing!" pleaded Henrietta. "You can't denounce your own daughter!"

"She is forcing my hand, Henrietta!" stated the Bishop.

"Oh, get up off your knees, Mother, and show some pride. Don't give him the satisfaction," demanded Constance. "You have nothing to fear. It is an idle threat to maintain his control. He has no intention of doing such a thing! He is all talk! He is too delighted with the marriage of his daughter to Nicholas Fontenoy to do anything to risk it."

"Go to your room. You've distressed your poor mother, upset your sister, and angered me. To your room, I tell you!" her father said, pointing to the door.

"With pleasure!" said Constance, turning and walking out the door.

As she walked up the stairs, despite the scene that had just unfolded, all she could think about was the joy of having mending the rift with Nicholas.

CHAPTER 25

At eleven o'clock the next morning, Nicholas and Constance were standing anxiously in the front square of Trinity College amongst the large crowd that had gathered there to receive their exam results. An austere man stood at the top of the square, calling out names. With each name he called, a young man approached him and he handed him an envelope containing his results.

"I can't see Tom," said Constance, as her eyes scoured the crowd.

"He said he would be here," said Nicholas. "They haven't called his name yet."

Nicholas didn't look too concerned about his friend's absence. He was far too preoccupied with his impending results.

A firm hand clapped Nicholas's shoulder, and he turned to see his father there.

"You haven't received them yet?" asked Daniel, who Constance thought looked even more nervous than Nicholas.

Nicholas shook his head.

"I'm sorry I'm a little late – I was delayed," said Daniel.

"No matter," said Nicholas.

As names continued to be called, Constance thought of her family. She hadn't joined them that morning for breakfast, and had Reeves deliver breakfast to her room. She couldn't face sitting at the same table as them after the previous night's explosive argument. She wasn't going to put herself through another session of disapproval and insults – although she realised that her father would now probably be cold rather than abusive towards her, until she profusely apologised. And that she was determined she would not do.

"Nicholas Fontenoy!" announced the man at the top of the square.

Nicholas gave her a nervous look and then quickly made his way up and took the envelope that was handed to him. Constance bit her lower lip as Nicholas returned to them, staring down at the envelope. When he reached them he made no effort to open it, but stood staring at the envelope.

"Well, go on, Nicholas! Put us out of our misery," coaxed Daniel.

"Wish me luck," said Nicholas as he tore the envelope open and unfolded the paper inside containing his results.

They stepped beside him and quickly read the result.

"Well done!" said Daniel excitedly, clapping his back "Well done, my dear boy!"

"I passed!" said Nicholas, more with relief than excitement.

"Oh, well done, Nicholas," said Constance, reaching up and kissing him.

"Well, that is a relief," said Daniel.

"It certainly is!" said Nicholas.

"Hello there!" said a voice from behind them, and turning around Constance saw it was Tom.

"Tom, we were looking for you earlier. Did you get your results yet?" asked Constance.

"Just got them now," said Tom proudly and handed them his exam results.

Daniel took the paper and looked at it, his eyebrows raised. "Well done indeed, Tom! This is an exceptional result."

"The Dean just told me I was second highest in our year," said Tom.

"Congratulations, Tom!" said Constance, impressed. "You deserve it."

"Thank you, Constance," smiled Tom. "And how did you do, Nicholas?"

"Very happy to say I passed," said Nicholas, smiling happily, as he discreetly put his own result into his pocket.

"Well done!" said Tom, shaking his hand.

"This calls for a celebration all round, I think," said Nicholas. "Let's celebrate this weekend."

"We have Milandra Carter's party this weekend, Nicholas," Daniel reminded him. "Perhaps Tom could come along to that and we can all celebrate together."

"That's a great idea," said Nicholas. "I'll mention it to Milandra. I'm sure she won't mind. She's inviting half of Dublin!"

"Oh, no, I don't know the woman," objected Tom.

"I think you should come, Tom," urged Constance and she looked at him earnestly. "There will be a lot of lovely food there. And a lot of important contacts for you to meet." The two things you need most at the moment, she added mentally.

Tom nodded at her, knowing what she was hinting at. "In that case – if you're sure she won't mind?"

"Well, if she does, I'll let you know," smiled Nicholas.

"Oh, there's Charles Sinclair and his son," said Daniel, waving over across the crowd. "They look quite happy – he must have passed his exams as well. Come, Nicholas, and we'll say hello."

Daniel set out in the direction of the Sinclairs.

"I'll be back in a couple of minutes," said Nicholas, following his father and leaving Constance alone with Tom.

"You must be delighted," smiled Constance. "Such a good result! You're bound to get a job now."

"I'm afraid it's too late, Constance," sighed Tom.

"I don't understand?"

"I have to return to live with my family in Sligo on Monday. I've run out of money, and if it wasn't for the food you've been bringing me I'd be pretty much starved by now."

"Oh Tom, surely you can wait another couple of weeks?"

"I'm afraid not."

"But you'll easily get a position in Dublin now, after receiving such a high result!"

"I'm afraid it's not a case of what you know, but who you know. My family just don't have any connections in the legal world. If I had known that to begin with, I'd never have done a law degree.

Well, I might be able to get something at home in Sligo."

"But you'll be stuck there forever, never achieving the high-flying career you deserve with results like that!" Constance was angry at the unfairness of it.

"There is nothing else I can do at this stage." He smiled at her. "At least we can have a good time at Milandra Carter's party on Friday. I will certainly enjoy the food on offer."

A thought struck her. "But what about the wedding? You're best man! You'll have to come back for that!"

A shadow passed over his face. "That depends. I can't guarantee it. If I do get a job, I may not be able to leave it." He looked at her with a wry smile. "Looks like Frederick may be best man after all."

CHAPTER 26

There was great festivity in the Fontenoy household for the rest of the day. Nicholas managed to get the day off work and the Fontenoys and Constance had a sumptuous lunch in the afternoon. Although Constance was delighted with Nicholas's passing his exam, and they had stepped up the next rung of the ladder of their life together, she couldn't help but feel sad for Tom. Such talent going to waste.

Daniel had excused himself after lunch to go do some work in his study and, as the rest of the family were in the drawing room, Constance watched for an opportunity to slip out of the room.

"Now, Frederick," said Agatha, "you have a lot to live up to after your brother's exam success. You are far too easily distracted from your studies. You need to buckle down if you want to be a successful lawyer like Nicholas."

"I am buckled down!" said Frederick irritably.

"Well, it doesn't look like that to me!" said Agatha. "You see how all the hard work Nicholas has put into his studies has paid off. He's a shining example to you!"

As Agatha and Frederick continued to bicker to Nicholas's amusement, Constance stood up and quietly left the room. Closing the door after her, she walked down the hallway to Daniel's study and knocked lightly on the door.

"Come in!" called Daniel from inside.

Opening the door, Constance walked into the room.

"Pardon me, Daniel, I don't mean to disturb you, but if I could have a word?"

"Of course, Constance," said Daniel warmly, but looking surprised.

Constance closed the door behind her and walked across the study and took a seat the other side of Daniel's desk.

"What is it, dear, something about the wedding arrangements?" said Daniel.

"Eh, no, it's actually about Tom."

"Tom – Nicholas's friend?"

"Yes. But I must insist that what I say is in the strictest of confidence. What I tell you can't be repeated."

"I don't like secrets, Constance," frowned Daniel. "And if there is one thing I dislike more than secrets, it's being asked to keep them."

"I don't mean to put you in a position, but if you hear me out I think you'll understand."

Daniel cleared his throat. "Go on."

Constance sat forward and spoke earnestly. "Tom is in the most terrible situation, Daniel. He has been unable to find employment, having no contacts. And he is living in the most terrible tenement. And now he has run out of funds and must return to his family in Sligo next week, giving up all hope of the legal career in Dublin that he worked so hard for and dreamed of!"

She spoke with such passion that Daniel was taken aback. "I see!"

"He's applied for jobs everywhere. Everywhere! But without contacts it's impossible to get his legal career off the ground."

"Well, yes, he is correct – the legal profession is controlled by the same families as it has been for the past hundred years, and it is very hard to get a foothold in it if you are an outsider as Tom is."

"It's just such a tragedy! You saw his results this morning – he came second in their year!"

"And I'm sure that will stand to him as he continues to apply for positions."

"But are you not listening to me?" Constance's voice rose. "He's giving up! He's run out of money and can't even afford to eat!"

"And is Nicholas aware of this? I haven't heard him say anything."

"No, Nicholas knows nothing of this and Tom would be furious and embarrassed if he or anybody else knew of his circumstances."

"And how do you know?" asked Daniel, looking at her curiously.

"It's a long story, but I bumped into him as I was doing Father's charity work and saw the appalling building he is living in."

"I see." Daniel sat back, confused. "And what do you think I could do about this?"

"Well, you being a judge with such a long legal career and all your own family connections, I was hoping, rather imploring, that you could arrange something for him?"

"Well – I always found Tom to be a very nice young fellow, I must say."

"He is!"

"Nicholas would certainly miss him greatly if he had to leave Dublin to return home." Daniel was thinking out loud.

"Nicholas would be bereft! It would be as much for Nicholas's sake if he got a job and stayed in Dublin as for Tom's!" said Constance, knowing Nicholas's happiness was Daniel's Achilles' heel in life.

"Yes, I'm sure I can ask around, and try to secure young Tom some kind of a position," said Daniel, causing Constance to clap her hands in delight.

"Oh, could you, Daniel?"

"I'm sure I could."

"But, you must do it discreetly," begged Constance. "Tom must never know that you are doing this for him. He has such pride!"

"Well, if he has applied to all the law firms in the last while then I'm sure they have his details on their files, and can approach him independently from me once I've spoken to them. I'll explain the situation to them."

"Oh, Daniel, you are an angel! An absolute angel!" sang Constance.

"Well, it would be a waste after he achieved such a high result if he doesn't get an opportunity to practise. It would be a genuine loss to the legal world."

"Thank you so much, Daniel! You've lifted a weight from my

mind!" she said, standing up.

Daniel smiled benevolently at her. "I'm glad I could be of service. And at least now Nicholas will still have his best man."

"Exactly! Thank you again, Daniel," smiled Constance as she left the room happily.

CHAPTER 27

Barker opened the front door of the house on Sackville Street to allow Milandra in.

"Oh Barker, have my shopping brought in from the cab outside, will you, and then send Flancy up to me in the parlour."

"Very good," said Barker and ordered one of the new footmen to fetch in the many bags and boxes and carry them into the parlour.

"Thank you, Albert," said Milandra, shooing the young footman out the door as soon as he had delivered the last lot of boxes.

Eagerly she began to open the largest box.

"Did you call?" asked Flancy, coming into the parlour a minute later, wiping her hands on her apron.

"Yes. What do you think of this?" asked Milandra, taking out the elaborate gown inside the box and holding it up against her.

"Very nice indeed!" said Flancy as she approached Milandra and studied the exquisite emerald-green dress that was decorated with diamantes.

"I got it in Delaneys' Store. As soon as I saw it I knew it was perfect for my party."

"Just perfect to impress all your fine guests," said Flancy, reaching out and fingering the fabric.

"Don't touch it with your dirty hands!" scolded Milandra, pulling it away from her.

"If my hands are dirty, which they aren't, it's because I'm slaving away in the kitchen preparing all the food for your damned guests!"

"And how's that coming along? Will it be a feast to impress a king?" asked Milandra excitedly.

"It's not a king you're out to impress, but Nicholas Fontenoy," smirked Flancy.

"Oh, I can't wait!" said Milandra, beginning to dance around, holding her new gown against her.

"And you're sure it's a good idea to invite his fiancée along?"

"Of course it is! I want Nicholas to see us in the same room at the same social gathering. I want him to see how plain and uninteresting she is compared to me. As I go around seducing the crème de la crème. I want him to look at his mousy little bride-to-be and realise just how mousy she is!"

"It sounds like you are ready to move in for the kill?"

"I'll have the whole thing secured by the end of the month. Nicholas will have finished with Constance Staffordshire and she will be but a distant memory by then."

Flancy's face turned sour. "Speaking of killing – I'm ready to kill that Barker!"

"Why – whatever is the matter with him?"

"What's right with him? He walks around as if there is a permanent whiff under his nose. He thinks he's too good for the rest of us!"

"Good! Then he will give the right impression to my guests at my party!"

"As for the two footmen – I can't decide which has less brains!"

"Well, we can't all have your intellect, Flancy. Now you just leave them alone! They look nice and decorative in their uniforms. And don't play any of your usual tricks – do you understand me?"

"Yes, my lady!" said Flancy with a smirk.

On the night of Milandra's party Daniel Fontenoy was fixing his bow tie in the bedroom while looking in the mirror.

"Will I do?" asked Agatha, coming in from the dressing room.

Daniel turned and looked at her.

She was dressed in a blue crinoline gown.

"Oh, yes, you do look well, Agatha," smiled Daniel.

"Well, considering it is Milandra's party, I decided I'd better try to look quite glamorous. I was going to wear my red gown, but then remembered Bishop Staffordshire will be there."

"Yes, I think the red gown might have been a little too much in Bishop Staffordshire's company," said Daniel, smiling knowingly.

"I'm very surprised he and Henrietta are going. I don't think I've ever seen them at a social occasion that wasn't connected with the church before."

"I hope he doesn't put a dampener on the party," frowned Daniel.

"I doubt anybody could put a dampener on anything that Milandra is involved in," Agatha said, crossing over the room and straightening Daniel's bow tie. She stepped back and studied her husband. "Is anything the matter. Daniel? You seem a little distracted this week."

"No – well, yes – it's just Nicholas's results," frowned Daniel.

"What about them?"

"Well, Agatha, I saw the results when they were handed to him, and he just *barely* passed."

"I see," said Agatha, looking worried.

"Between you and me, I was very shocked when I saw them. I thought Nicholas would have done far better than that. I expected him to do far better."

"You didn't say anything to him, did you?" Agatha asked, concerned.

"Of course not. I congratulated him heartily and told him what a great fellow he was."

"Good!"

"But I was very disappointed in him. Tom did far far better than him, nearly came top of the class. And Tom received none of the encouragement and support we all gave Nicholas. Not to mention all the extra tuition I gave him privately."

"But – really, what does it matter? As long as he passed."

"Well, if Fetherstons' hadn't employed him because of him being my son, I don't think he would have been able to secure any kind of a decent position in a law firm."

"I see." Agatha's brow creased.

"And but for the fact his career has taken off with such a flying start with Milandra Carter, I imagine he would have been many a year trying to prove himself, before he established his career. And the high hopes I had for him being a judge at an early age are dashed. I just don't think he will pass the next law exams to get him there."

"Poor Nicholas probably had an off-day during the exams – perhaps he wasn't feeling well?"

"An off-day wouldn't have given him such a bad grade. Every day would have to have been an off-day to achieve that!"

Agatha found herself becoming angry. "I don't know what you're getting at, Daniel. We all know how hard Nicholas worked and how dedicated he was to his studies. If his exam results don't reflect that, then the fault is entirely with the examiners!"

"I was thinking that if it weren't for the Fontenoy name, the examiners may have failed him altogether! He came dangerously close to the failure grade."

"Well, I think the Fontenoy name went against him! Half of those lecturers are jealous of your success, and they probably marked poor Nicholas extra hard just so that it could never be said that favouritism was shown towards him!"

Daniel nodded. "Yes, you may be right."

"I am!"

"I'd hate to think the poor fellow should have suffered on my account," said Daniel.

"Think nothing more of it, Daniel! Put the whole business out of your mind. Nicholas passed and that is the main thing, and as we can all see is well on his way to a glittering career."

CHAPTER 28

Milandra sat at the dressing table in her lavish bedroom fixing an emerald necklace on. It matched her emerald earrings perfectly. She stood up and walked over to the full-length mirror to inspect her appearance. She scrutinised her reflection and confirmed that the jewellery enhanced the emerald-green gown she had bought.

The door opened and Flancy walked in.

"Barker and the footmen you hired are driving me mad! You'd better get down there and tell them that I am in charge and they'd better remember that!"

Milandra turned to Flancy. "Tell them yourself! You were never shy in asserting your control before, so why should this evening be different?"

"Well!" said Flancy, looking Milandra up and down. "Aren't you the sight for the sore eyes!"

Milandra laughed excitedly. "How do I look?"

"You know very well how you look. Stunning!"

Milandra grinned and walked past Flancy out of the room. Flancy followed her.

"Other than the butler's and footmen's attitude, how is everything else?" asked Milandra as she walked down the stairs to the next level.

"Everything else is under control. The food is all ready and the house is spick and span. All ready for the young Master Fontenoy."

"He's not my only guest tonight, Flancy," said Milandra as she entered the drawing room to inspect it.

"No, but he's the only one who really matters."

Seeing the fire in the fireplace was roaring, the candles shining, the drinks waiting, Milandra continued on her journey down the next flight of stairs, followed by Flancy. The ground floor was a hive of activity as the servants rushed around carrying platters of food and trays of glasses.

Barker approached Milandra once she reached the bottom of the stairs.

"Mrs. Carter, if I could have a word?"

"Certainly," smiled Milandra.

The butler continued in his posh accent. "Mrs. – Flancy – is under the impression that she will remain upstairs orchestrating the serving of the food at tonight's event." He gave Flancy a disapproving look. "Perhaps if you could make it clear to Mrs. Flancy that a cook's place is below stairs while entertaining, and at all other times for that matter, and my footmen will be serving the food. Also it would not be proper for any women servants, her kitchen staff or Mrs. Flancy, *especially* Mrs. Flancy – to be seen above stairs tonight. They may continue to prepare the food downstairs and my footmen will bring it upstairs."

Milandra looked at Flancy in silence for a moment and then the two women burst out laughing.

The butler's face went red. "I fail to see what is amusing."

"My dear Mr. Butler –" said Milandra.

"Barker!" snapped the butler.

"Barker! Of course!" Milandra corrected her error. "My dear Mr. Barker, I don't think we have to be so precise on the etiquette tonight. Dear old Flancy will be quite an asset to you upstairs."

"I can't imagine Mrs. Flancy being an asset to me at any time," said Barker.

"I tried to tell you what he was like! Pompous and bossy," said Flancy.

"Well, really!" said Barker.

"Oh, do be quiet, Flancy!" said Milandra, still amused. "Otherwise you will make poor Mr. Barker walk out and I will be left with nobody to answer the door to my guests!"

"At least we have established the front door is the butler's job!" snapped Barker irritably.

"If you can at least do that right!" spat Flancy.

"Oh hush, the two of you," urged Milandra. "Mr. Barker, Flancy will be working as she sees fit, upstairs or down, it is of no concern to me. The two of you will just have to find a way to work around each other."

She swept past them into the dining room to continue her inspection, leaving Flancy and Barker to glare at each other.

Constance sat at the dressing table in her bedroom on Mountjoy Square and fastened a pearl necklace around her neck. Then she put on the matching earrings.

She sat back and looked at herself. Yes, the amber gown was quite becoming. She knew she should be excited about going to the party, but she wasn't feeling that. She and her father were still being cold to each other and her parents' presence that night would only put her on edge.

And whereas usually she would be delighted to be attending a party, the fact it was Milandra's dampened her excitement considerably. She could already imagine her, wearing the most outlandish frock and expensive jewels, as she effortlessly entertained her guests – all thoughts of widow's weeds long forgotten by all present.

There was a knock on the door and Emma walked in.

"Mother and Father are waiting for you in the hall," said Emma.

"Oh, I'd better not delay then," said Constance, standing up and fetching her evening bag.

"Oh, you do look gorgeous, Constance!"

"Thank you!"

"I wish I could go too. But Father says I'm too young."

"He should have allowed you to go, Emma. It would have been a lovely experience for you, and you are eighteen now."

"Well, I didn't want to push the issue," said Emma.

"You should have pushed it – it's the only way you'll ever get anywhere with Father, otherwise you'll be at his beck and call for the rest of your life."

"I'm not like you, Constance. I can't stand up for myself like you do."

Constance came and gave her little sister a hug. "You shouldn't be so frightened of offending Mother and Father, Emma. Father will disapprove and Mother will fret regardless of what you do! So you may as well begin to do what you want."

"Will you not apologise to Father for going to the Shelbourne without permission? I'm sure he would forgive you if you asked."

"I certainly will not apologise, Emma. It's he who needs to apologise to me – calling me a burden – and a brat!" Constance's eyes welled at the memory of the cruel words used.

"He only worries because he loves you so much," said Emma.

Constance sighed. "I know . . . anyway I had better go. I can't keep Milandra Carter waiting!"

CHAPTER 29

The Bishop, Henrietta and Constance climbed the steps up to the front door of Milandra's house on Sackville Street. Through the tall Georgian windows, Constance could see the house was filled with elegantly dressed people. She hoped Nicholas would already be there.

The Bishop knocked on the door loudly, and it was opened by a very smart-looking butler.

"Bishop Staffordshire and family, we're guests of Mrs. Carter's," announced the Bishop as they stepped inside.

"Good evening, Your Grace," said Barker, beginning to help him to take off his coat.

As Constance removed her cloak and handed it over, she took in the sight before her. The downstairs was filled with guests, chatting and laughing while an array of footmen mingled between them, carrying silver trays of delicacies. Other footmen attentively circulated, continuously filling up the guests' crystal glasses with wine. A quartet of musicians were positioned to the side of the staircase, playing classical music. As Constance surveyed the crowd, she recognised many as being some of the wealthiest merchant families who lived in the environs of Sackville Street. Not only that, Constance realised Milandra's guest list had gone much further than that. She recognised prominent politicians and also members of the aristocracy whose residences would be on the other side of the river in areas like Fitzwilliam Square and Merrion Row. Constance realised that Milandra had successfully ingratiated herself with all circles of Dublin society.

As Constance continued to take in the scene, she spotted Milandra herself descending the stairs in a regal manner. Constance was taken aback by how beautiful she looked in the most expensive-looking emerald dress she had ever seen. Constance was further taken aback when she realised the man walking beside her, with whom she appeared to be deep in conversation, was Nicholas. Her Nicholas!

Spotting the Staffordshires immediately, Milandra smiled brightly and made her way over to them, followed by Nicholas.

"I am so pleased you could all make it!" she said, greeting them warmly.

"Thank you for inviting us," said the Bishop before nodding at Nicholas. "Nicholas."

"Good evening, Your Grace, Mrs. Staffordshire," said Nicholas before turning to Constance and smiling happily at her. "Constance."

"Oh, Constance, you do look pretty!" said Milandra. "Doesn't she look pretty, Nicholas?"

Nicholas grinned at her. "Very!"

"Thank you, Milandra," said Constance. "Are we late? Everybody seems to have been here well before us."

"It was supposed to be starting at nine, was it not?" asked the Bishop, concerned.

"No, seven," said Nicholas.

"I distinctly heard you say nine, Milandra," said the Bishop, looking at her for clarification.

"Oh, what does it matter what time you arrive at, as long as you are here now!" said Milandra lightly.

"I just don't want you think we arrived late. I pride myself on my punctuality as a rule," said the Bishop seriously.

"Perhaps – perhaps you got the time wrong?" said Henrietta who was becoming fretful. "It's so seldom we accept invitations you became flustered?"

"I don't become flustered, Henrietta – that is your department," the Bishop defended himself.

"Oh, look, it *really* doesn't matter, does it?" Milandra's voice was sweet but firm, as she hid her irritation that the Bishop was making a scene. Yes, she had told the Bishop to arrive at nine. She had wanted the Staffordshires to arrive late, so that she could settle in with Nicholas before Constance turned up. "Now, what may we offer you to eat? We have everything the heart or the appetite could desire!"

"Yes, I can see that," said the Bishop as he looked disapprovingly at the obvious expense.

"Oh, Your Grace, I meant to ask your assistance," said Milandra. "There is bound to be so much food left over tomorrow from tonight. If we could have it distributed to the charity?"

"Oh, yes, I'm sure we can arrange that," smiled the Bishop, warming up at the suggestion.

"Excellent!" said Milandra, taking two glasses of red wine from a passing waiter and offering them to the Bishop and his wife.

"Thank you, but we rarely drink," stated the Bishop sternly.

"Come, come, Your Grace, surly you will allow yourself one on this special occasion?" Milandra urged him.

The Bishop looked hesitant before saying, "Well, perhaps, just the one."

Milandra handed him and his wife the glasses, then took another and proffered it to Constance. "Constance?"

"She doesn't drink," the Bishop answered for her.

"Surely she is allowed, like yourself, just the one?" Milandra smiled charmingly at the Bishop as she pressed the glass into Constance's hand.

"Just the one, mind you!" cautioned the Bishop as Constance took a sip.

Spotting Flancy circulating near her, Milandra called "Flancy!"

Flancy walked over to them.

"This is my Flancy, the best cook in Dublin," announced Milandra. "Flancy, this is Bishop Staffordshire and his wife Henrietta . . . and their lovely daughter Constance."

"Good evening, all!" said Flancy.

"Hello," said Constance, covering quickly for her parents who said nothing as they wondered why on earth they were being introduced to a cook.

"Pleased to meet you," said Flancy.

Constance felt uncomfortable as she felt Flancy was inspecting her closely with a strange stare.

"Flancy, be a dear and fetch the Bishop and his family some delicacies, won't you?" smiled Milandra.

Constance quickly decided she didn't want to spend any more time that night with either her parents or Milandra. She took Nicholas's arm.

"Are your parents here, Nicholas?"

"Yes, I think they're in the drawing room upstairs," he answered.

"Oh good – I must go at once and say hello," she said with a smile, drawing Nicholas away. She was gratified to see that Milandra was displeased at this.

Nicholas smiled at Milandra. "I'll talk to you later."

As Nicholas and Constance reached the stairs he said, "Wasn't that a little rude? I think we should have stayed a while to chat to your parents."

"Oh, Nicholas, I've been putting up with my parent's disapproval since we had dinner in the Shelbourne. I actually would like to enjoy myself in the company of my fiancé tonight, without looking after them the entire time."

He smiled down at her. "And I would like nothing more than having you all to myself!"

"Besides, I would very much like to enjoy this glass of wine which I won't be able to under my father's disapproving eyes!"

Constance soon began to enjoy the night. The music was wonderful, the food better and she savoured the glass of red wine she had accepted from Milandra.

In the crowded drawing room upstairs she was delighted to see that Tom had come. She wondered if Daniel had managed to do anything for him. If not, this would be the last opportunity she would have to see him for a long time as no doubt he would return to Sligo on Monday as he had intended.

"Constance! I was beginning to think you weren't going to

come!" said Tom, giving her a hug and a kiss on the cheek. "Though Nicholas assured me earlier you would."

"Seemingly my father took down the wrong time to arrive." Constance made a face.

As the three of them chatted in a corner of the drawing room, Constance felt so happy. The three of them together, it reminded her of when they used to meet in Tom's rooms in Trinity.

"She certainly knows how to entertain, your client, Nicholas," commented Tom.

"Well, let's face it, when money is no option why would she not?" said Constance.

"Now, Constance, money doesn't make one a good and gracious host," said Nicholas. "That is something one is born with."

"Indeed!" said Constance, wondering why she still became annoyed when Nicholas praised Milandra.

"May I?" asked a footman who was circulating with a bottle of red wine.

Nicholas and Tom held out their glasses to be refilled.

"Miss?" asked the footman.

Constance quickly glanced around the room to make sure her father wasn't present and then held out her glass to be refilled.

"Why not?" she said mischievously. "This reminds me of the times in your rooms at Trinity, Tom, with the two of you giving me a glass of your beer!"

"We did have some good times," smiled Tom.

"All changed now!" sighed Nicholas as he thought of his working life.

Suddenly Constance saw Milandra entering the room and looking around. On spotting them, she walked straight over to them.

"Ah, there you are, Nicholas!" she said, placing a hand on his arm. "I need you to come with me."

"Is anything the matter, Milandra?" asked Nicholas.

"Not at all. I want to introduce you to Lord and Lady Galway. They are very important clients of the wine merchants and so it's important for you to meet them."

"Oh, yes, right, I see," said Nicholas, putting down his glass on the mantelpiece beside him.

Milandra turned to Constance and smiled. "I'm sorry that I'm robbing him from you."

Constance hid her annoyance. "It's quite all right."

"Anyway, I'm sure this young gentleman will keep you entertained." Milandra looked curiously at Tom.

"Oh, ah, Milandra, this is Tom, my friend from university whom I was talking to you about earlier on in the week," said Nicholas.

"Thank you very much for inviting me tonight," said Tom courteously.

"You're very welcome. Any friend of Nicholas's is a friend of mine," said Milandra, taking Nicholas's arm and directing him away.

"Won't be long," Nicholas said to Constance.

Constance glared in irritation as Milandra escorted Nicholas to a group at the far end of the room and began to introduce him to everybody.

"So that's the famous Milandra Carter . . . Constance, are you all right?" asked Tom, seeing her angered expression.

She snapped out of her trance. "Oh, I'm sorry, Tom. I just can't believe the nerve of that woman. She seems to think she has the power to click her fingers at Nicholas any time any place just because she is his client. When we arrived late, I found him in her company walking her around. She might as well ask him to carry her purse for her!"

"Well, Constance, he is lucky to have her as a client."

Her patience snapped. "Oh, don't I know! Isn't that what everybody keeps telling me!"

She became embarrassed and tore her eyes away from Nicholas and Milandra and back to Tom. "I apologise, Tom. Here I am complaining about Nicholas's work, and you having to return to Sligo on Monday because you don't have any." She waited for his response with bated breath.

"Actually, there's been a development with that," said Tom with a grin.

"Oh really?"

"I had sent a letter into Oakleys' Solicitors some time back enquiring about employment. I had heard nothing back from them and had given up on them like all the rest. But they wrote to me this week and asked me to come in to meet them . . . and they offered me a post!"

"Tom! That's wonderful news!" Constance put her arms around him and kissed his cheek.

"I'm rather pleased myself. I'm starting Monday. It's not a great post – clerical work – but it's a post all the same. It's a chance for me."

"You deserve it," smiled Constance, touching his face.

"Thank you, Constance," said Tom, looking into her eyes. "It looks like my luck has changed."

CHAPTER 30

Later on in the night Daniel came and joined Constance.

"Did you hear Tom's good news?" Constance smiled knowingly at him.

"Yes, Constance. I believe Oakleys' have offered him a post. Excellent firm, I know them well," he responded with a wink.

Constance reached up and whispered into his ear. "Thank you."

Milandra walked down the back stairs and into the kitchen which was a hive of activity with kitchen maids and footmen rushing around. Flancy stood in the centre, giving orders. Milandra beckoned her over to a corner.

"All is going perfectly," said Milandra.

"Despite Barker's interference," said Flancy. "So *that* is Constance Staffordshire."

"Yes, what do you think of her?" asked Milandra.

"She's looks like a nice girl," commented Flancy.

"Well, you know what happens to nice girls . . ."

"What?"

"Nothing!"

The two women erupted in giggles.

"She is irritating me beyond belief," said Milandra. "Every time I have Nicholas to myself, she's scurrying around like a little mouse. It's time we laid our trap for this little mouse."

"Are you sure about all this?" cautioned Flancy.

"What do you mean?"

"Well, it's just that she and Nicholas look right together. They look perfectly suited."

Milandra tried to contain her anger. "And what would you know about such things? Keep your trap shut and you stick to your part. Just make sure you stay near her and keep that wineglass of hers full!"

Tom had left the party as he wanted to be fresh for starting his new job on the Monday. Constance wished he could have stayed longer to keep her company, as Nicholas had hardly spent any time with her during the evening. She made her way out onto the landing outside the drawing room and leaned on the banisters, looking down at the crowd in the foyer.

"Hello, dear, are you enjoying the evening?" came a woman's voice and she turned to see Flancy standing there.

"Oh, yes, thank you, it's very nice."

Flancy held out the bottle of wine she was holding and went to refill Constance's glass.

"No, thank you. I rarely drink! I'll end up squiffy!"

Flancy winked at her as she refilled the glass. "I won't tell if you don't!"

"Oh, very well then!" said Constance, smiling naughtily.

Constance was still in her position at the banisters on the first floor, looking down at the party in the foyer. The quartet had now finished playing, and had been replaced by a larger group whose elegant music filled the house. The crowd in the foyer had cleared and now there were couples dancing there. But Constance's eyes were fixed on Nicholas who was deep in conversation with Milandra on the side of the dance floor. Her anger was now boiling, as Nicholas had hardly come near her the entire night.

Flancy walked past her. "Another drop, dear?"

Constance held her glass out quickly and said irritably, "Oh – why not?"

"Why not indeed!" said Flancy as she walked on, leaving Constance to scrutinise her fiancé below her.

"Hello again!" came a male voice and she turned to see the speaker was George Fetherston.

"Oh, hello!" she smiled.

"Are you here with Nicholas?"

"Yes, eh, and my parents are here as well."

"Where is he?" asked George, looking around.

Constance felt herself going bright red. Any time she met George Fetherston she seemed to be waiting for her absent fiancé.

"He's just gone to attend to some business for Milandra."

George leaned over the banisters, surveyed the guests downstairs and spotted Nicholas speaking with Milandra.

"She *is* a very demanding client," he said, smirking at her. "I haven't seen you waiting outside the offices for Nicholas recently?"

"No, it's not a habit of mine, Mr. Fetherston."

"George," he corrected.

"George, I needed to speak to Nicholas quite urgently the evening you met me. But I thank you for keeping me company and for the tea and cake."

"Any time."

He smiled at her and they fell into an awkward silence.

Then he said, "Would you like to dance?"

Constance face registered surprise at the request. "Oh, no, thank you."

She felt herself go bright red at the suggestion. That she would go and dance with a man other than her fiancé in front of everybody! What would her parents say?

She felt somewhat light-headed as she looked again over the banisters.

"Are you all right?" asked George, noticing.

"Oh, yes, quite all right, George, it's just very warm in here," she said, smiling at him. She took another gulp of her wine and trained her eyes on Milandra and Nicholas again.

Barker came storming down into the kitchen.

"Where are those trays of food I ordered ten minutes ago?" he demanded angrily.

Flancy took one look at him and said, "They will be ready in ten minutes, Mr. Barker."

"Ten minutes! What is the delay? I need them now!"

"Oh, Mr. Barker, please relax – you've been run off your feet all night – you haven't taken one break!"

"That is my role!"

"I refuse to let you do any more until you sit down, have a nice cup of tea and a slice of this delicious cake I've made." Flancy picked up the plate of cake and held it temptingly in front of him.

"I don't have time for that!" snapped Barker.

"Just one slice and a nice cup of tea!" ordered Flancy, practically forcing him to sit at the table and putting a large slice of cake on a plate in front of him. "Kitty! Fetch a cup of tea for Mr. Barker!"

"Well, just one slice in that case," conceded Barker as he took in the sight of the luscious cake.

Downstairs, as Milandra had engaged Nicholas in conversation, she'd kept one eye on Constance who was staring anxiously at them from the banisters.

"Oh, Nicholas, dear, it's so warm, is it not?" said Milandra.

"Eh, yes, I suppose it is."

"I suddenly feel a little overcome – I need some air," said Milandra. "Would you just walk me out to the garden?"

"Of course," he said, offering her his arm.

Milandra took his arm and they walked towards the French windows at the back of the stairs. Milandra was conscious of Constance's gaze on them all the time.

They stepped out onto the terrace.

"Oh, that's much better," sighed Milandra as she led him into the garden which was bathed in moonlight. "I'm sure a few minutes out here will make me feel much better."

She stopped and faced him, making sure that he was positioned with his back to the house.

"Shall I fetch you a glass of water?" he offered as they came to a halt.

"Absolutely no need. Pray continue our conversation. You were mentioning the difference between English and American tort law? Fascinating topic."

"Yes, the main difference is . . ." Nicholas continued enthusiastically.

Milandra continued to pretend to listen, but she had one eye on the French windows, confident that she would at any moment see Constance emerge. But there was no sign of her.

Then a movement caught Milandra's eye. Through the arched window upstairs she could see Constance peering out at them in what looked like an agitated state.

"Oh, Nicholas, I feel – I feel faint!" said Milandra suddenly and she swayed on her feet. Then her knees bent and she seemed about to collapse.

"Milandra!" cried Nicholas, reaching out and grabbing her, taking her quickly into his arms.

"Nicholas!" cried Milandra as she wrapped her arms around his neck and slumped against him, putting her face right up to his.

Upstairs Constance looked on horrified as she saw Nicholas and Milandra embracing tightly, seemingly kissing.

George Fetherston had accompanied Constance to the window as she had abruptly announced that she needed some air.

He had his back to the window however and was startled when her expression became a mixture of anger and shock.

"Constance? Constance? Are you all right?"

Constance tore herself away from the window and, ignoring George, went racing down the landing and down the stairs. She pushed past the guests downstairs, causing them to look at her in confusion, as she furiously made her way to the French windows. She stormed out into the garden where she found Milandra with Nicholas's arm around her as he was escorting her back towards the house.

"*You!*" called Constance loudly at Milandra.

"Whatever is the matter with you, Constance?" asked Nicholas, seeing her anger.

"How can you ask me that," she shrieked, "when I have just seen you kissing another woman?"

"Constance! Pull yourself together!" hissed Nicholas, seeing that other guests had come onto the terrace to see what the commotion was about.

"I saw you – I saw you kiss *her* from the window upstairs!" shouted Constance, pointing at Milandra.

"Constance! How can you say such a thing?" asked Milandra whose face looked shocked, but her eyes were mocking her.

"You might have fooled everybody else here but you haven't fooled me, Milandra Carter! With your money and your charm! I can see right through you! I always knew you were after my fiancé, but to do it while I'm in the same house!" cried Constance.

"Will you shut up, Constance!" Nicholas demanded.

Daniel and Agatha emerged onto the terrace, looking horrified.

"Nicholas, what is the meaning of this?" demanded Daniel.

"I haven't a clue!" gasped Nicholas, quickly moving away from Milandra, forcing her to stand on her own two feet.

"I just can't see why the rest of you can't see what is plain to see. This woman should be indoors on her own, mourning her dead husband, dressed in black. Not seducing my fiancé before my very eyes like an old trollop!"

The crowd began to gasp and chatter in shock.

The Bishop, followed by Henrietta, marched over to their daughter.

"Has something improper occurred here?" demanded the Bishop of Nicholas and Milandra.

"Of course not!" cried Nicholas.

"On my honour – no!" said Milandra. "I was merely feeling faint and Nicholas escorted me to the garden. These accusations by Constance – as if I would! As if I could! And I in mourning!"

"I saw you from the window upstairs!" spat Constance.

"You saw nothing!" shouted Nicholas angrily. "Milandra nearly fainted and I merely saved her from falling, you stupid girl!"

Constance was about to retort when a man smoking a cigar stepped forward and spoke up.

"He's telling the truth! I was over there smoking the whole time and witnessed it all. All they were doing was discussing the difference between American and English tort law when Mrs. Carter went into a faint. This gentleman was merely saving Mrs. Carter from a fall to the ground!"

"In fact – I think I *am* now going to faint!" gasped Milandra as she went into a swoon and began to fall. Nicholas quickly reached forward and grabbed her, holding her in his arms to support her from collapsing.

"See!" said the man smoking the cigar.

"But –" cried Constance.

"Stop this nonsense at once, Constance!" demanded the Bishop sternly.

Henrietta's two hands clasped either side of her face with her mouth open as she gasped, "Whatever has got into you, Constance?"

"Alcohol!" announced a disgusted Agatha. "Alcohol has got into her!"

"My daughter doesn't drink, Mrs. Fontenoy," said the Bishop, outraged. "She had one glass this evening, and only because our hostess insisted."

"I hate to be the bearer of ill news, Your Grace, but from the state of her she has obviously consumed much more than that," said Agatha.

"I don't know what to say," said the Bishop, shaking his head in disbelief.

"That's a first!" said Agatha under her breath.

Flancy came running out with a glass of water and began fed it to Milandra who was still being held upright by Nicholas.

Daniel quickly glanced around at the spectators from the party, a great number of whom had come out to the garden to observe the spectacle. He turned to the Bishop and said quickly, "Take her home, John, immediately. Stop this circus from proceeding any further."

"Yes, yes, of course," said the Bishop as he looked at Constance but he didn't move.

Seeing the Bishop was useless in a crisis, Daniel took control and turned to a footman.

"Order a cab straight away."

Constance stood ashen-faced as everyone looked at her in silence and she realised she had made a terrible mistake. Seeing Nicholas's look of disgust, she turned and fled from the garden, pushing through the guests who were assembled there.

"I can only offer my most sincere apologies," the Bishop apologised to Milandra who was still being attended to by Flancy and Nicholas.

With that, the Bishop took Henrietta's arm and left the garden.

Nicholas gazed after them. "I should go to Constance," he said.

"Leave her!" ordered Daniel as Agatha went to attend to Milandra as well.

Outside the house the footman had hailed a cab.

Constance quickly got in, followed by the Bishop and Henrietta.

The Bishop was surprised Henrietta hadn't dissolved into hysterical tears, knowing her fretful nature. Looking at her, he realised she was in too much shock to cry.

"Drive on!" the Bishop shouted to the driver as he looked at Constance seated across from him who was dissolved in floods of tears.

Nicholas came racing out into the street but too late.

He stood and watched the cab drive off.

CHAPTER 31

Despite the scene Constance had caused, the party continued into the night. Milandra, quickly recovered from her fainting spell, entertained her guests as if nothing had happened. Nicholas sat in a corner quietly for a while and then sloped off home without saying goodbye to anybody.

At the end of the night Milandra bid farewell to Daniel and Agatha at the door.

Daniel said, "I can only apologise for Constance's behaviour. That really was so unlike her. I've never seen her so badly behaved before."

"If you say so," said Milandra.

"I can only imagine how mortified the Bishop and Henrietta are. They are pillars of respectability – her behaviour will have scandalised them," said Agatha.

"I suppose we can't always be held responsible for our children's behaviour," smiled Milandra. "The girl has a low mind, that's all I can say about her. A mind that belongs in the gutter. And I in mourning! And to attack poor Nicholas like that, when he was only being a total gentleman and so gallant!"

"Yes, we are very proud of him," Daniel said. "And please rest assured, Milandra – those things she said about you, nobody is saying those things or even thinking them."

"Oh, I am resting assured, Daniel. After tonight the only woman's name on everyone's lips will be . . . Constance Staffordshire."

189

Daniel and Agatha couldn't conceal their dismay at this, realising it to be no more than the truth. But they nodded to Milandra and took their leave.

Milandra stayed in the hallway until the last of the guests left, then quickly made her way down the foyer and down the servants' stairs into the kitchen. There she found Flancy clearing away plates.

"Recovered from your fainting fit?" asked Flancy knowingly.

"Quite recovered, thank you, Flancy."

To her surprise Milandra saw Barker sprawled in a chair by the stove, fast asleep, conked out.

"Whatever has happened to Barker?" asked Milandra as she saw the two footmen trying to revive him.

"I don't know!" said Flancy. "He had a cup of tea and some cake and didn't get up off that chair again!"

Milandra looked at her. "And what did you put in the cake?"

Flancy shrugged innocently.

"Oh really, Flancy!" Milandra whispered disapprovingly to her.

"Well, if you can have your fun, then I want to have mine!" Flancy whispered back.

"Come along, Mr. Barker, it's time to get you to your bed!" said one of the footmen.

"Just lift him out!" ordered Milandra.

The two footmen picked Barker up and pulled his arms around their shoulders. They began to half-carry him out.

As they passed Milandra, Barker opened his eyes and smiled at her. "Oh, hello, Mrs. Carter. Thank you for using my services – please call again!"

"Indeed!" said Milandra as the footmen hauled him away.

"You just can't get the staff!" sighed Flancy. "Well, that takes care of that!" She dusted her hands against each other. "And think twice next time you try to bring a butler in on my patch – they'll end up the same way!"

Milandra raised her eyes to heaven.

"Well, I saw the spectacle Miss Constance made of herself," said Flancy.

"And wasn't it a wonderful spectacle!" gloated Milandra.

"Everyone was horrified, especially Nicholas."

"Especially her parents, more like! Did you see the face of the Bishop! I don't envy her facing all that tomorrow."

"Well, it's her own fault," said Milandra.

"How on earth is it her own fault?" demanded Flancy incredulously.

"For getting in my way, of course! I can't see Daniel Fontenoy ever allowing a girl like that marrying his son now, can you?"

"It will take more than that to break that engagement, Milandra. I have a sense they are very deeply in love," warned Flancy.

"Oh, what would you know about love? That engagement is dead in the water. And after my plan for this week, I think Nicholas and I will be announcing our own engagement very soon!"

CHAPTER 32

When Constance arrived home to Mountjoy Square she rushed up to her room straight away and threw herself on her bed sobbing. She could hardly sleep that night as she replayed the events at the party.

How could she have got it so wrong? How could she have accused Nicholas of such a thing? And worst of all how could she have done it so publicly? She had disgraced herself. She realised the alcohol she had consumed played a big part in it.

There was a knock on her door and she opened her eyes to see the door crack open and Emma creep in.

"Oh, you're awake," said Emma.

Constance climbed out of her bed. "I've hardly slept. What time is it?"

"It's midday."

"Midday! But I missed breakfast – Father must be furious!"

"I think missing breakfast is the least of it, Constance," said Emma, coming towards the bed.

Constance was filled with dread. "Open the curtains, will you?"

Emma crossed over the room and pulled back the curtains, flooding the room with light.

Constance raised her hands quickly to her eyes to protect them against the sudden invasion of bright sunlight.

"You look dreadful," said Emma as she came and sat down beside her on the bed.

"I feel dreadful. I feel so . . . groggy."

"Whatever possessed you?" asked Emma carefully.

"I thought I saw Nicholas and Milandra kissing in the garden . . . I was mistaken."

"Mother says you were drunk. Blind drunk!"

"I hadn't drunk that much! But I suppose it didn't help. I don't know what came over me. I just flew into a blind jealous rage when I saw them together! They really did look as if they were embracing and kissing – but, in fact, she had fainted into his arms."

"I don't mean to make you feel worse than you do – but you must be the talk of the town!"

Constance's head now began to ache in earnest. "Where are Mother and Father?"

"Father left for work straight after breakfast. He didn't say one word. Mother has taken to her bed and said she won't be getting out of it today. I've had to bring her smelling salts to revive her."

"All I can do is apologise for my actions."

"I don't think that will be enough to redeem you, Constance. Seemingly you called Milandra Carter 'an old trollop'!"

Constance's headache escalated to a frightening level. "How will I ever make it up with Nicholas? Accusing him of being unfaithful, insulting his client, showing him up in public, disgracing his family and my own. He'll break off our engagement for sure!"

"He loves you very much, Constance. Regardless of last night, I'm sure you can work it out."

Once Emma had left, Constance got out of bed and slowly prepared herself for the day. The events of the previous night kept flashing through her mind, no matter how much she tried to blank them out. If only she could rewind time and stop herself from acting in such a fashion. If only she could rewind time and not have gone to Milandra's party at all . . . Milandra . . . Milandra had seemingly suffered the brunt of her behaviour.

She knew she had to try and mend bridges as quickly as possible. Most of all to apologise to Nicholas, and beg him to forgive her. Then she would have to deal with the Fontenoys and her own family. But before she tackled them she realised she would have to profusely apologise to Milandra and hope she forgave her. If Milandra could forgive her, then it would be a starting point with everyone else.

As she sat at her dressing table, staring at her reflection in the mirror, she desperately tried to understand her own behaviour.

With a heavy heart she stood up to begin her walk of shame.

Constance braced herself outside Milandra's house, then climbed the steps, steeling herself for whatever would come next. She knocked loudly on the door and waited.

A minute later, the door opened and the woman she was introduced to as Flancy the previous night stood there. Flancy seemed surprised see her there and Constance felt her face go beetroot red.

"Oh, good afternoon. I wonder if I would be able to see Mrs. Carter?" she said sheepishly. "If you could tell her Constance Staffordshire is here to see her?"

Flancy held the door open. "Come in."

Constance stepped gingerly into the hallway as Flancy closed the door after her.

"Wait here," said Flancy.

Constance thought she saw a slight look of sympathy on her face before she turned and walked across the foyer and up the stairs. As Constance stood there she thought how different it looked from the previous night, now empty of people and flooded with sunlight from the French windows at the back and from the tall arched window at the top of the stairs.

She seemed to be waiting an eternity there as she thought of what she should say to Milandra.

Flancy came back down the stairs and walked over to her. "Mrs. Carter is not receiving guests today."

"Oh – oh – I see," said Constance, wishing the ground would open up and swallow her.

Flancy walked over to the front door and opened it.

Constance followed her, her head bowed.

"Thank you," she said as she left the house.

Flancy firmly closed the door after her. Out on the busy

pavement Constance stood, her embarrassment and shame now acute. She turned and glanced up at the house and saw Milandra standing at one of the drawing-room windows staring down at her, her face cold and expressionless. For some reason Constance felt frightened. She quickly looked away and made her way back up Sackville Street.

Flancy came into the upstairs drawing room where Milandra was still standing at the window.

"Well?" asked Milandra.

"I sent her on her way as you said to do." Flancy sighed loudly. "Poor girl looks shattered."

"Really?" Milandra didn't sound concerned as she turned and walked towards Flancy. "Incidentally – why did you and not Barker answer the door?"

"Oh, did I forget to mention? Barker handed in his notice this morning and has left," said Flancy.

Annoyance spread over Milandra's face. "Oh, Flancy!"

"And the footmen too! They left at the same time."

"Flancy! You drove them out before they had even settled in!"

"Me?" Flancy professed innocence. "Sure I did nothing!"

"Drugged Barker's cake and did goodness knows what to the footmen! What am I to do now?"

"Don't worry your pretty little head about any of that, my dear. I've already contacted agencies this morning and they are sending over an array of staff that *I* will interview. You really have too much on your plate trying to snare young Fontenoy to be bothered with household matters. You just leave all that to me, my dear."

Milandra threw her eyes to heaven. Flancy was taking over the running of the house in Sackville Street as she had in their previous home at the country estate. She knew Flancy was extremely territorial and hated the threat of Milandra depending on any other servants but her.

"Oh, whatever you want!" she then snapped. It was true she had bigger fish to fry than the hiring of servants.

"Good!" Flancy smiled with satisfaction. "Although, as I said before, I don't think we need a big array of male servants as there is no man of the house to be valeted – yet. And we don't want an old fogey like Barker, but a young chap – who will do what he's told and not get in my way!"

Constance was mortified. So Milandra had refused to receive her. Which meant Milandra was refusing to accept any apology. It was a slap in the face and, without Milandra's forgiveness, it would be even harder to gain anybody else's understanding.

Constance wanted to just slink back to her bedroom and never venture out again, but she knew she had to face it all sometime and the longer she left it the harder it would be. And what was paramount in her mind was Nicholas. She headed to the top of Sackville Street and on to the Fontenoys' house on Rutland Square.

She knew Nicholas would be at work, but she decided it might be best to wait for him there and to tackle his parents first.

She knocked on the door and was shown into the drawing room where Agatha was sitting sewing. Agatha quickly put down her sewing and looked at her in shock.

"Hello, Agatha," said Constance meekly.

"Well – I wasn't expecting to see you today!" said Agatha, looking at her in bewilderment.

"I know – I'm sorry – I'm sorry for everything!" said Constance and she suddenly burst out crying.

"Oh Constance!" said Agatha, quickly getting up and going to her.

"I'm so sorry, Agatha," cried Constance.

Agatha led her over to a couch and sat her down, putting an arm around her.

"There – there!" soothed Agatha, handing her a handkerchief.

"I don't – don't – know – what came over me!" said Constance in between sobs.

As Agatha looked at Constance, her heart went out to her. She could only imagine the fury of the Bishop and Henrietta and imagined Constance wouldn't get a module of sympathy from her own family.

"It's not that bad," soothed Agatha, who knew her own words sounded hollow.

"Oh, it is, Agatha. Mother has taken to the bed, and Father left without saying a word this morning. And Milandra Carter won't even receive me in order for me to apologise!" Constance blew into the handkerchief.

"Oh dear!" said Agatha as she began to pat Constance's back gently.

"I don't know what I'm going to do, Agatha. I have made a show of myself!"

"Perhaps – perhaps it might be wise to avoid alcohol consumption in the future, my dear – it doesn't suit you!" was all the advice Agatha could offer.

"If that was the cause then I will never touch drink again!" declared Constance.

"Well, that's something, at least," sighed Agatha.

"I fear that, though alcohol added to the situation, it was jealousy that drove it!" Constance heaved a great sigh.

"How could you ever assume Nicholas would be dallying with Milandra Carter? And in the back garden with a full party going on? As if my Nicholas would ever not behave like the perfect gentleman he is."

"Milandra is just so beautiful, and – and, as I said, jealousy overcame me. What about Nicholas? Is he at work?"

"Yes, he went to work this morning as usual."

"How – how was he?"

"Well, I won't lie to you, Constance, he was very quiet and looked very concerned. He left the party soon after you, poor lamb."

"I ruined his night," whispered Constance.

"Well, as long as you haven't ruined his career . . ."

"Oh, don't!" Constance pleaded, grabbing Agatha's hand.

"Well, you did call Milandra Carter an 'old trollop'!"

Constance buried her head in her hands and began to sob loudly.

At that moment Daniel walked in. "Have you seen yesterday's newspaper anywhere –"

He stopped on seeing Constance there.

"Constance has come to apologise, Daniel. She is full of repentance for her actions last night." Agatha made a face at Daniel, imploring him to be lenient.

"Oh – yes – well – eh – yes." Daniel was lost for words.

"She is never going to touch a drop of alcohol again, Daniel," said Agatha.

"Wise – very wise!" said Daniel.

Constance wiped away her tears. "I want to speak to Nicholas."

"Of course. I imagine he will want to speak to you as well," said Daniel.

"Why don't we have some tea, and you can wait for him until he arrives home?" smiled Agatha.

She got up to tug the bell-pull and as she passed Daniel she made an alarmed face at him.

CHAPTER 33

Nicholas slowly made his way home from work. After he had let himself through the front door he went into the drawing room where he found his parents sitting there, looking solemn.

"How did work go for you today, Nicholas?" asked Daniel.

"I could barely concentrate on my work. Everyone was looking at me strangely."

"Did – did anyone comment?" Agatha was nearly frightened to ask.

"No. I think they were too polite to do so, but it was the talk of the place, I'm sure. I kept expecting to be summoned to Mr. Fetherston's office, but I wasn't."

"That is something, I suppose," sighed Agatha. "Did you hear from Milandra?"

"Not a word. I wasn't due to meet her today. I'm dreading meeting her after the scene Constance caused. I don't know what I shall say to her. Perhaps I will never have to see her again. I'm probably fired from her account."

"Don't say that!" Daniel was appalled. "Perhaps if I spoke to Milandra, explained –"

"No, Papa!" snapped Nicholas. "I can't have you digging me out of trouble for the rest of my life. Constance is my fiancée, and my responsibility."

"Speaking of which . . . Constance is here, Nicholas," said Agatha.

"Where?" Nicholas's eyes opened wide.

"She's in the study," said Agatha. "She arrived this afternoon in a terrible state. She was exhausted and so I sent her to the study to have a lie-down."

Nicholas sighed loudly. "I had better go and speak to her."

"I'll go with you," said Daniel, standing up.

"No, Papa! I have to handle this myself. As I said, she is my responsibility." Turning, Nicholas left the room.

"We're here if you need us!" Agatha called after him.

Nicholas walked down the hallway and steadied himself as he placed his hand on the door handle. He turned it and walked in, closing the door firmly behind him. He saw Constance lying out on the couch, her eyes closed. She sat up quickly and her pale face froze on seeing him. She quickly stood up and raced over to him, embracing him in a tight hug. He stood there, expressionless, not returning the embrace.

She pulled back and looked into his face.

"Oh, Nicholas, I'm so sorry. I really am!"

He marched across the room to the fireplace and turned to face her.

"How could you think that I would be unfaithful to you?" he demanded.

"I thought I saw it with my own eyes when I saw her in your arms!" she said, clasping her hands together.

"Have you any idea of the trouble you have caused for me?" Nicholas's voice was harsh and loud.

She hadn't ever heard that tone from him before.

She stood silently.

"*Have you?*" he shouted so loudly that she jumped with fright.

"Yes – of course I have!"

"Not only did you disgrace yourself and your parents, but you disgraced me!" He began pacing up and down in front of the fireplace, his hands clasped behind his back. "You behaved like a common street woman, shouting in public, accusing us of all sorts. I could never have expected you ever to behave in such a ridiculous fashion. How can you be taken seriously as a lawyer's wife after that show you put on? How can I be taken seriously in my career married to a woman with no self-control or breeding?"

Tears stung her eyes. "You can't say anything to me that I have not already said to myself. I would do anything – *anything* – to make amends. Just say it and I'll do it!"

"I can't imagine what Milandra thinks!"

"I called to her house today to apologise," she explained.

"And?" He stopped pacing and stared at her.

"She wouldn't receive me," said Constance, looking shamefully down at the floor.

"Oh Constance!" said Nicholas, shaking his head. "She must be furious beyond words. That's me finished on her account. Perhaps finished at Fetherstons' as well once they hear she no longer wants to work with me."

Constance rushed to him and held him, leaning her face against his chest. "Nicholas, you mean more to me than anything in the world. I would never have done anything to embarrass or damage you. You must believe me. It must have been the alcohol – that's what your mother says!"

"Plainly it must have been," said Nicholas as he looked down at her. "You've broken a trust between us, Constance. That you could think that of me, regardless of what you thought you saw. You should have known I would never do such a thing to you."

He reached his hand up and slowly stroked her hair.

"I *do* trust you. It was just the moment. I'm still your Constance," she said.

"I – think – I think you'd better go home now, Constance," he said.

She looked up at him and stopped herself from showing any emotion.

"If that is what you wish," she said.

"It is, for now," said Nicholas. "We're all tired and emotional after last night."

She nodded as she pulled back from him. She was too terrified to ask if she had lost him.

"Will I see you tomorrow?" she asked.

"We'll see. I have a lot on tomorrow."

She nodded and walked slowly to the door.

She turned and said, "I love you, Nicholas."

And then she quickly left the house.

Constance walked back home in a daze. It was almost as if the normal sights and sounds on the way to Mountjoy Square didn't exist. She had never seen Nicholas like that before. So furious and angry. And she would have much preferred that he had remained in that state with her. That he had calmed down, his face bitter with disappointment, was worse for her to bear. And that he had asked her to go home and leave him. If he had demanded her to stay to suffer the brunt of his anger it would have been more promising as regards their future together. But he had dismissed her, left her haunted with the worry that he would break their engagement. And then her life would be over. She couldn't imagine her life without Nicholas.

As Reeves opened the front door and she walked past him in a trance up to her room, she realised she might have destroyed her life.

"I felt quite sorry for her," sighed Agatha that evening at dinner.

"I have always been extremely fond of Constance, and very much approved of her as Nicholas's choice as a wife," said Daniel. "But I think in this case your sympathy is being wasted on the undeserving."

Nicholas picked at the food in front of him in silence.

"And what are you going to do, Nicholas?" asked Daniel.

"What do you mean?"

"What are your plans now with Constance?"

"I –I – don't know." Nicholas looked at his father.

"Well, it is not my business to interfere with the affairs of your heart, but have you given any thought as to whether you are doing the correct thing in still marrying Constance?"

Nicholas looked shocked. "Are you suggesting I call off the engagement?"

"I am only pointing out the questions you ought to be asking yourself," said Daniel.

"Oh goodness me, Daniel!" Agatha gasped. "Constance is already practically family. Surely you can't be suggesting –"

"I am not suggesting anything to Nicholas. But a lawyer's life is a difficult one, and is built on reputation. What is paramount is that a lawyer has a wife who he can trust – not destroy his reputation, insult his clients, and lose him business!"

"Daniel, you're being so judgemental!" cautioned Agatha.

"I am a judge by profession, my dear," replied Daniel.

"But – but I – I love Constance," Nicholas stuttered.

"Marriage is based on trust and not just love, Nicholas. Constance has demonstrated that she clearly does not trust you not to be unfaithful. And you clearly cannot trust her to conduct herself as a lady, regardless of the circumstances, in public."

Nicholas continued to toy with his food, deep in thought.

CHAPTER 34

Nicholas didn't meet Constance the next day. Or the next. He was half expecting her to be waiting outside his office building for him when he finished work, but she wasn't there. He was in a quandary. His father's warning words had sunk in. And yet he was trying to balance his anger with Constance with the deep love he had for her. The sale on Milandra Carter's country estate was due to close on the Thursday. He had heard nothing from her since the party and had wondered if he should call on her to offer his own apologies for his fiancée's behaviour. But he couldn't face the embarrassment if she refused to receive him as she had done with Constance. He knew Milandra would have to meet him on Thursday for the signature on the contract. And so he decided he would wait until then to address the situation with her.

Constance anxiously waited and hoped for Nicholas to call on her, but he didn't. She tried to stay out of her parents' way as much as possible, anxiously avoiding witnessing their disappointment and shame. She stayed away from Sackville Street for fear of bumping into Milandra. She spent her time around Grafton Street visiting the stores and tea shops, praying Nicholas would forgive her and come back to her.

Then one afternoon she was walking down Grafton Street when she came face to face with George Fetherston.

He got a start to see her there. "Constance!"

Her face went red, remembering he had been the person she was speaking to at the window before she fled downstairs and attacked

Nicholas and Milandra.

"How are you?" he asked.

"Fine," she said quietly.

He smirked at her. "That was quite a little display you put on at the party!"

"Oh, George, I'm devastated! And now Nicholas won't speak to me. Is he in trouble at work because of me?" She began to cry.

"Now, now," he said, going to her and patting her on the back.

"I don't know what I'm going to do, George!" she sobbed. "I've lost Nicholas for good."

"My dear, you need a shoulder to cry on. But this is not the place – passers-by are staring. My flat is around the corner and we can talk there out of the public eye."

He stepped down the street and beckoned for her to follow him. "Are you coming?"

She hesitated before joining him.

Then they walked around to his flat.

On Thursday morning Milandra was at the kitchen table writing a note as Flancy diligently made a cake.

"What a beautiful day!" declared Milandra.

"And this is going to be a beautiful cake!" promised Flancy.

"It had better be," said Milandra as she placed the note in an envelope, then sealed and addressed it.

"Kitty!" called Milandra.

Kitty came running down the stairs.

"Yes, Miss?"

"Kitty, you are to take this note and deliver it to Nicholas Fontenoy at Fetherstons'." Milandra handed her the envelope.

"Yes, Miss," said Kitty. Grabbing her cloak, she raced back up the stairs.

Milandra stood up and went to stand beside Flancy who was busily stirring the cake mix in a bowl.

"Well?" asked Milandra.

Flancy nodded, reached into her pocket and grabbed a handful of tiny grains.

"Is it the right amount?" asked Milandra.

"The perfect amount," confirmed Flancy as she sprinkled the grains into the cake mix.

Then, as she began to stir, she recited: "*A sprinkle of dust, and a wish from my heart, brings you further from her and right to my heart!*"

Milandra and Flancy looked at each other and nodded knowingly.

Milandra had been due to arrive at Nicholas's office that afternoon at three. Instead her maid Kitty arrived and handed him a letter. He anxiously opened the letter and read it.

> *Dear Nicholas,*
>   *I am unable to visit your office to sign the contract this afternoon as I have been delayed with business. Please bring the contract to my house for signature at five o'clock,*
>   *Yours sincerely,*
>   *Milandra Carter*

Nicholas re-read the letter. He had feared it would be Milandra informing him she would no longer be requiring his services. It was nothing unusual for Milandra to summon him to her house to conduct business. And the fact she was doing so today he took as a positive sign that she was not firing him. Perhaps it was a very good sign. It would be much better to discuss what had happened at the party in the more informal setting of her home than in his office.

At five on the dot Nicholas knocked on Milandra's door and waited.

A minute later, Flancy opened it.

"I've an appointment with Mrs. Carter," said Nicholas, stepping in.

"Oh, yes, she did mention," said Flancy. "I'm afraid she's still not back from business she had to attend to this afternoon."

"Oh?"

"You can wait for her in the upstairs drawing room," said Flancy.

Nicholas nodded and followed her to the stairs. As he passed the spot where Constance had made the scene the previous Friday, he cringed.

Upstairs, Flancy showed him into the drawing room and closed the door, leaving him alone.

CHAPTER 35

Nicholas stood at one of the tall windows in the drawing room looking out on Sackville Street. It was seven o'clock. Milandra had still not shown up and he was becoming increasingly anxious and concerned. He pondered whether he should just leave but realised that would show him in a bad light. He had come to make amends with Milandra, and not waiting for her could lose her as client for sure.

Suddenly the door swung open and Milandra walked in, in a blaze of glory, in a gorgeous primrose gown.

"I am so sorry, Nicholas, for being so late. I had a meeting that I could not leave," she said.

She looked as if she was dressed to go to a ball, he thought, instead of returning from a business meeting. However, he wasn't surprised, as Milandra's reputation as a fashion icon was now entrenched in Dublin.

"It's quite all right, Milandra – there is no need to apologise in the least. I know how busy you are."

"Still – it is unforgivable of me. You are so good to have waited for me."

"Well, the papers had to be signed today and returned in the morning," he said.

"Quite."

He deliberated whether to approach the topic of Constance, but decided it might be best to get the paperwork signed first. He reached into his briefcase and took out the contract.

"Now, perhaps if I explain –" he began.

She waved a dismissive hand through the air. "I'm afraid I am starving, Nicholas! I can't possibly look at those until I've eaten." She crossed over to the bell-pull and tugged it. "I'm sure you're hungry as well – it's almost dinner time after all. Let's have something to eat first."

Smiling, she walked over to him and, linking his arm, led him out of the room and down the stairs.

"I'm really not that hungry, Milandra."

"Nonsense. Of course you are!"

She led him into the candlelit dining room.

To his amazement Flancy and Kitty were laying out a lavish dinner of roast beef for two.

"Eh, Milandra, I couldn't possibly impose myself on your hospitality," he said, eyeing up the delicious food.

"You may as well explain the details of the contract to me while we're enjoying Flancy's cooking," said Milandra.

Flancy pulled out the chair at the top of the table and smiled at him, waiting for him to sit. Nicholas slowly walked over and sat down as Flancy pushed his chair in to the table. Milandra walked around the table and sat down to his right.

"Isn't this cosy!" she declared.

Flancy filled both their crystal glasses with red wine and left the decanter beside Milandra.

Then she beckoned to Kitty and both of them left the room, closing the doors softly behind them.

Milandra raised her glass to Nicholas. It sparkled in the candlelight.

"Now – you were saying about the contract?" she asked.

Nicholas felt uncomfortable as he tried to explain the details of the contract over dinner to Milandra. With the candlelight and the fire blazing in the fireplace, the dining room had a warm glow that seemed to accentuate Milandra's beauty. He was sure it was the most unusual setting for a business meeting that he could imagine. The thick velvet curtains were drawn, blocking out the activity outside in Sackville Street, leaving them isolated in each other's company. He explained the contract to Milandra as much as he could, but he felt she had surprisingly little interest in the details. She kept changing the conversation to other topics and continued to refill his wineglass as soon as it was empty. In fact, though she appeared to be attentive to what he was saying, he thought that as he went on her eyes began to glaze over.

"And, I suppose, that is all there is to it," concluded Nicholas. "All the terms and conditions of the contracts. Do you have any questions?"

"No! None at all!" she said promptly.

"And you are quite happy the house furniture is included in the sale?"

"Quite happy! Anything I wanted I already took, and will be glad to see the back of what's left!"

"Good," he nodded.

She raised her glass again. "May I congratulate you, Nicholas, on organising a wonderful deal for me!"

He felt himself blush. "No more than any other lawyer would have done for you."

"You are too modest, Nicholas!"

As they finished dinner he decided it was the right time to discuss Constance.

"Milandra – about last Friday night –"

"Well!" said Milandra loudly, placing down her fork and knife. "I think we are just about finished here. Shall we retire to the drawing room to have dessert?"

She stood up and waited for him.

Upstairs in the drawing room, Flancy had drawn the curtains and had a fire blazing as soft candlelight lit the room.

"I think we had better get these contracts signed," said Nicholas, reaching for his briefcase.

Milandra tugged the bell-pull. "Oh, let's not spoil a lovely evening yet by looking at those. There will be plenty of time for that after dessert." She sat down on the couch, patting the seat beside her, indicating he should sit there.

He nodded politely and went to sit on the couch. The doors

opened and in walked Flancy and Kitty. Kitty was carrying a tray with a silver teapot and china on it and put it on the low table in front of the couch. Flancy, in her usual fashion, was bearing aloft a cake-stand with a cake on it. She gently placed it on the table in front of Milandra and Nicholas.

It was another one of Flancy's wonderfully moist sponge cakes, this one even more lavishly decorated with luscious strawberries on cream swirls, and dusted with powdered sugar.

"Well, eh, Flancy, what a work of art!" said Nicholas.

"You have surpassed yourself, Flancy," smiled Milandra.

Kitty left the room while Flancy poured the tea into the cups.

"You can leave us, Flancy – I'll cut the cake," said Milandra.

"Very good," said Flancy, standing back and locking eyes with Milandra. "If there is nothing else we'll be going to bed now. We have an early start in the morning."

Milandra nodded. "We will be quite all right from here, Flancy."

"Goodnight, Mr. Nicholas," said Flancy.

"Goodnight, Flancy."

Flancy backed out of the room and closed the doors, leaving them alone.

Milandra smiled and, taking the cake knife, cut a large wedge of it and placed it on a plate.

As Nicholas took the plate he saw it was as delicious-looking inside as outside, with a thick layer of cream and strawberry jam running through the middle.

"Enjoy!" encouraged Milandra, sitting back into the couch.

Nicholas took a fork and scooped up a large chunk and placed it in his mouth. His eyes closed at the taste.

"Well?" asked Milandra.

"Scrumptious!" he declared.

As he continued to eat, savouring every morsel, he noticed Milandra wasn't having any.

"Are you not having a slice?" he asked.

"Not for now, perhaps a little later. I'm trying to watch my figure."

He gave a small laugh. "You have no need to watch your figure,

Milandra – rest assured."

"Oh?" She raised an eyebrow at him. "You *have* noticed my figure then, have you?"

He was slightly taken aback and said nothing but continued to eat.

She smiled demurely.

He finished the cake and placed the plate back on the table.

"Milandra – I really need to speak to you about what happened here at your party last Friday," he said.

"Oh?"

"You have been far too much of a lady to bring the subject up, but I really feel I need to clear the air with you and apologise on Constance's behalf," Nicholas looked at her seriously.

Milandra's smile dropped and she sat back into the couch.

"There is no reason for you to apologise, Nicholas. It was not you who behaved in such an appalling manner."

"She did try to apologise to you directly, but I understand you would not receive her?"

"I was not at home when she called," lied Milandra.

"Oh, I see," said Nicholas. "Then if she called to you again, you would receive her and listen to her apology?"

Milandra's expression tightened. "I really have no interest in seeing the girl ever again, Nicholas."

"I see," sighed Nicholas, very disappointed. "Then you won't accept her apology or mine, on her behalf?"

"As I said, Nicholas, there is no need for *you* to feel sorry about anything. She made a disgrace of you as much as me!"

"But of course I have to apologise! She is my fiancée."

Milandra's eyes narrowed in surprise. "Still your fiancée?"

"Well, yes, of course."

Milandra sat forward urgently. "But how on earth could you still be engaged to her after the way she acted?"

Nicholas was taken aback and his mouth opened but closed quickly again.

"Are you trying to tell me that you and Constance are going on in your usual fashion, as if nothing happened last Friday?"

"Well – of course not. Constance is very ashamed –"

"Good!"

"And I have only met her once since then, as I am so angry and disappointed in her –"

"Good!"

"Of course her actions have caused serious consequences for us –"

"Good! I mean – as should be expected! A woman, a supposed lady, can't act in that fashion and not be ostracised from society. And to accuse us publicly and try to ruin my good name! Well, it backfired on her, and it's her name that is ruined!"

"But –"

"Have you any idea of the things people have been saying about Constance? They are calling her crude, rude and delusional! They are suggesting she is suffering from hysteria and has an unstable mind. Her reputation is seriously damaged. And, I suggest, if you want to salvage your own reputation you will have nothing more to do with the girl."

"I don't think you understand, Milandra. Constance and I have committed to each other for the rest of our lives. I can't just abandon her – or think to desert her – because of one silly incident."

"One silly incident!" Milandra's voice rose to a level he had never heard her use before. "Nicholas! I believe you are in shock from her behaviour and have not realised, for your own sake, that this marriage you were contemplating cannot go ahead! What does your father say about it all?"

"Papa – my father – has –" Nicholas looked down at the floor. "My father has urged me to reconsider my commitment to Constance."

"Exactly!" snapped Milandra. "Your father is a wise man. And you would be a fool not to listen to him!"

Nicholas put his hands to his face and closed his eyes. He began to feel upset and bewildered.

Milandra moved closer to him and tentatively put an arm around him. She spoke soothingly. "There, there, Nicholas. I understand how painful this must be for you. To discover that the woman you thought you loved and thought you were going to marry, is not the woman you believed her to be. How could you ever trust a woman who doesn't trust you? A terrible setback for you, I'm sure. But Nicholas – and I'm not speaking as a client, but as a close friend of your family's – and a close friend of yours – you simply must realise to continue your relationship with this girl would be folly of the highest degree. You are young, handsome, talented and destined to reach the very top. Marriage to Constance Staffordshire will destroy all that. She will drag you down into the gutter she is destined for. She doesn't even have a dowry to soften the blow! Isn't it time for you to ask yourself sincerely – what use is she? What good do you actually get from this relationship?"

He removed his hands from his face and looked at her, feeling rather lightheaded.

"I know what you are saying makes sense on some level –"

"Perfect sense, Nicholas." Her voice was a whisper.

She moved her hand from his back and began to stroke his hair.

"It's just –" he began, but he couldn't remember what he was going to say. He began to feel dizzy. As he looked around, the room seemed to swim in front of his eyes.

"Nicholas – are you all right?" she whispered.

He turned and looked at her and realised how close she was sitting to him, how close her face was to his.

"Nicholas?" she said gently.

"I feel funny," he said.

"Funny?"

"Kind of strange," he said and he shook his head a couple of times and blinked his eyes.

"It's fine, Nicholas," she whispered. "You're here with me, completely safe. Let's not even mention that silly girl Constance again. She's in the past."

He lay back on the couch as he let the strange feeling sweep over him. After a while the dizziness passed and he began to feel good.

"Yes, she can be very silly, can't she?" said Nicholas and suddenly he was giggling.

"Yes, the silliest girl in the world!" And Milandra joined him in

214

his laughter as she lay back into the couch herself, with her arms around him.

He pulled back and looked at her. She seemed to have a glow around her, and he wondered if he had realised how beautiful she was before.

He blinked a few times, trying to focus, but found it impossible to. And then he felt he must be dreaming because Milandra's lips brushed against his.

"Milandra, I don't understand what's happening to me. I feel very strange," he muttered.

"You are perfectly well, Nicholas. Don't fight it, go with the feeling," she said and she stood up.

And, as he watched, Milandra was like a vision floating across the room to the door. And then he realised he was holding Milandra's hand and she was leading him out of the drawing room and onto the landing outside. She let go his hand and he watched as she climbed the stairs up to the next floor. He waited there, not knowing what to do. He gripped the banisters to give him support as the dizzy feeling overwhelmed him again.

"Nicholas!"

He heard his name being called from upstairs. Gripping the banisters, he slowly made his way up the stairs to the next floor.

He looked around but couldn't see Milandra.

"In here!" called her soft voice and looking around he saw it came from an open door at the end of the corridor with light spilling through it. He moved slowly down the corridor and walked through the open door. As he looked around the softly lit room, he realised it was a luxurious bedroom, with a wonderful chandelier.

A luxurious four-poster bed invited him to lie down.

Try as he might, he could not think straight.

"Where am I?" he whispered.

"My room," said a voice behind him, as the door he had just came in through slammed shut.

Milandra was standing there against the back of the door. And, as he looked at her, he realised she had changed from the elegant gown she had been wearing and was now wearing a light, flimsy robe de chambre. And her hair . . . he stared at her hair. She usually wore her hair up, but her long blonde tresses were now flowing freely down over her shoulders.

She walked towards him, and he seemed incapable of moving. She put her arms around him and, as she held him tightly and kissed him, he didn't want to move.

"Oh, Nicholas, how I've dreamed of this moment!" she said.

Taking his hand, she led him over to the bed and lay down on it, bringing him with her.

PART 4

1916

CHAPTER 36

As night began to fall, there was the sound of gunshots in the distance. Seán remained positioned at the window, his revolver in his hand.

Milandra never took her eyes off him.

"What are you staring at me all the time for?" he demanded.

"Don't I have a right to? If you have a right to break into my house and take it over, then surely I have a right to stare at the person who is doing it?"

There was the sound of smashing glass and shouting and screaming from the street outside.

"What's all that noise?" asked Milandra, getting up and crossing to a window and looking out. Along Sackville Street she could see crowds of people fighting and brawling as they smashed shop windows and began looting the premises. "Ah, I see. The marauding mob have come to take advantage of your rebellion. Is this your idea of the new republic you have declared? A breakdown of law and order that allows the people from the slums to come and steal?"

"They have no permission to steal," said Seán.

"They might have no permission to steal, but stealing is what they're doing!"

As Milandra watched, people carried looted goods away from the stores, shops and boutiques.

"Disgusting! They're just walking into premises and taking what they want!" she said. "No police – no law and order! I hope you're proud of what you're achieving?"

"I am proud! Proud that we are finally standing up to tyranny!"

"Oh, please!" chided Milandra. "If you wanted to achieve change then this is not the way to do it. The world appears to have gone stark raving mad! Everyone seems to think the bullet and the gun is the way to achieve things these days. All that needless killing on the continent, and now it seems to have reached our shores. Who would ever have thought?"

"It's very easy for you to attack and criticise these peoples. I don't approve of them robbing – it's not part of our plan. But I don't blame them either! They are desperate people living in the worst slums in Europe. Of course they will try to take advantage of what's going on!"

"No excuse," said Milandra.

"Plenty of excuses! You have no idea what it's like for these people, living on nothing in squalid tenements. If they get a pair of new shoes out of the rebellion, good for them!"

"Perhaps good for them, but not for the poor shop-owner who had to buy the shoes to sell them in the first place!"

"I'm wasting my time talking to you – you'll never understand. Living here in your mansion, with the best of everything."

"I actually have worked very hard all my life, I'll have you know. I suggest some of these people try it," she snapped.

"How can they work when they don't have opportunity? The only opportunity they have is to sign up to the army and go get their heads blown off in France!"

"And do *you* know what it feels like?" she asked. "To live in the tenements and struggle?"

"Oh, I know all right – all my life," said Seán bitterly.

"Yes, I guessed you did. There are many reasons, I imagine, why people have joined this rebellion. In fact, I know of many in my aristocratic circle who have been proclaiming the joys of nationalism this many a year. They are driven by a sense of cultural pride, national pride. But others I'm sure are driven to change the order of how things are. The people from the slums, people like you."

"I make no apology for wanting – demanding – social justice and equality," said Seán.

"But, my dear boy, whatever comes out of this revolution, successful or unsuccessful, it won't change anything. All it will do is replace one set of elite with another, and perhaps a worse one than there already is."

"We'll see," snapped Seán.

"Yes, we shall," said Milandra. "Now, I'm going to my bed for the night. I hope I will be able to sleep with all the racket that is out there. It's almost reassuring that you are here. You'll be able to keep the marauding masses from breaking in, I hope."

He watched dumbfounded as Milandra walked out of the room.

As she walked across the landing and up the stairs to her bedroom, she saw one of the other rebels positioned with a rifle at the window on the landing, facing down onto the back garden.

"Tut tut, so young," she said as she passed him and made her way to her bedroom.

Amelia held on to Rupert's arm as they hurried through the military headquarters following the attaché. They were shown into a room where a group of men in uniform were bent over a map of Dublin spread out on a table.

"Hello, Captain Perkins, apologies for disturbing your leave," said one of them, shaking his hand.

"What the blazes is happening, Captain Hollingsworth?" demanded Rupert.

Hollingsworth looked curiously at the concerned young woman at Rupert's side.

"This my fiancée, Amelia Robinson," said Rupert.

"This is really no place for a civilian woman," said Hollingsworth.

Amelia leaned forward and earnestly said, "Please, Captain Hollingsworth, I am frantic with worry about my grandmother – she lives on Sackville Street. I just want news of her."

Rupert saw Hollingsworth's dubious expression.

"Her grandmother is Lady Milandra Havington. She could be quite a prize if she falls into the hands of the rebels."

"Very well," nodded Hollingsworth. "Come and see." He returned to the table and began to point to the map. "The rebels

221

have taken charge of most of the city centre, occupying key positions. They have now barricaded large sections of the streets, making it more difficult to gain access. They have occupied buildings throughout the city, and snipers are positioned at upper windows everywhere. We sent the cavalry into Sackville Street earlier – they were immediately fired on, and three shot dead."

Amelia gasped and blurted out, "They've done it! They've actually finally done it!"

Rupert looked at his fiancée. Shaken by her words, he quickly distracted Hollingsworth by asking, "Sackville Street then is impregnable, sir?"

"Yes," said Hollingsworth.

"But my grandmother is on Sackville Street!" said Amelia. "Is there any way she can be rescued from her house?"

"I'm afraid not," said Hollingsworth. "The city has little defence in place as nobody expected this. We are awaiting instructions from London."

Amelia gripped Rupert's arm and looked at him desperately, thinking of her grandmother hopelessly trapped.

"Captain Hollingsworth, a word?" said an official as he popped his head through the door and Hollingsworth quickly left the room, leaving Amelia and Rupert alone.

Rupert studied his fiancée intently.

"What did you mean when you said *'They've finally done it'*?" he demanded.

Amelia looked up from the map guiltily.

"Oh, Amelia! Did you know of this rebellion?"

"No! Of course I didn't! Do you think I would have left my grandmother in Sackville Street today if I had known? What do you take me for?"

"I don't know what I take you for any more, Amelia! But you *did* know something?"

"I – I – I knew a rebellion was being planned sometime in the future," she stuttered. "But I had no idea when!"

"How did you know this?" demanded Rupert.

"From the people I know, my friends. I've got to know many

new people through my work at the newspaper."

Rupert was incredulous. "So these opinions you expressed earlier about Irish independence – they are not just opinions? You have become involved politically?"

"Not in any meaningful way, but yes, I've attended meetings and –"

"Subversive meetings! What have you got yourself involved in, your stupid girl?"

"I'm not stupid!" she became angry. "I have a right to my beliefs."

"Don't you realise you have allowed yourself to be used!" Rupert's face was red with anger. "They never saw you as one of them, not when you are engaged to an officer in the army! Don't you see that? They were using you to get information from the letters I wrote to you about the war – private letters meant only for you!"

"That's not true!" Amelia cried.

"But you don't deny discussing information from my letters with them?"

Amelia looked guiltily at the floor.

"Amelia!" demanded Rupert.

"Yes! I did! The public are not being told the truth about the war in Europe, because of the Defence of the Realm Act and censorship. Through the newspapers we're being fed a series of lies, not reporting British blunders and losses and not reporting German victories. Your letters spoke the truth. The casualties, how weak the British really are. So I did talk about these facts . . . I had to do something."

"How could you betray me like that, Amelia? In your naiveté you have assisted this rebellion. You showed them how weak we actually are, and they took advantage of it by hitting us when we are down. Of course they didn't tell you the details of the rebellion – they didn't trust you in case you carried the information back to me and their plans were discovered. You have allowed yourself to be used, and put your grandmother's life in danger."

Rupert turned and marched out the door.

"Rupert!" Amelia cried after him, but he ignored her.

It was seven the next morning and Milandra was dressing herself. As she thought back on the previous day, it seemed like a strange dream. Had this man Seán with his accomplices really broken into her house? Was there really a rebellion taking place? But as she looked out her window she realised it was all very real. Sackville Street was a mess, with broken windows all down its smart avenue. Barricades had been erected along the street and there were still crowds of looters taking whatever they could. She carefully unlocked her bedroom door and walked down the landing. The young rebel who had been there the previous night was still there, except he was fast asleep.

"There lies the hopes of a nation!" she whispered to herself as she passed his snoring form and walked down the stairs to the next floor.

"Good morning to you, Seán," she said as she entered the drawing room and found him wide awake in his position at the window.

He ignored her.

"I was just going to go down to make myself a breakfast. Can I get you anything?" she asked.

"No, thank you," he said.

"Do avail of my hospitality. I like to keep a full larder. One never knows when one might get unexpected guests . . . and they don't come more unexpected than you!" She smiled as she walked out.

Rupert had insisted that Amelia return home to Dalkey in the early hours and she had managed to get some sleep. That afternoon she drove herself back to the military headquarters and found Rupert looking exhausted. The day had passed there in tense confusion.

"My poor darling," she said, embracing him. "This is supposed to be your leave and you have found yourself caught up in another war zone."

"You shouldn't have come back here, Amelia. There's nothing that you can do," he said curtly.

He was obviously still angry with her.

"I have spent the past year yearning to be in your company for just five minutes, so if my only opportunity is standing in a corridor with you, then I'll take it," she said softly. "What news is there?"

"The rebels still have a strong hold on the city. Our troops managed to get into the tall buildings surrounding Stephen's Green today and shoot down at them in the park and drive them away. But that's the only advance we've made."

"And what of Sackville Street?" She was almost frightened to ask.

"It's still impregnable. We can't get anywhere near it. We're getting reports that a mob is rioting in the area, destroying everything in their path."

Amelia thought of her grandmother and began to fear the worse.

PART 5

1869

CHAPTER 37

Nicholas woke up and blinked several times. There was bright sunlight around him and he lay for a while trying to focus. Then he sat up quickly and looked around, not knowing where he. He was in a large four-poster bed in a beautiful bedroom, the curtains drawn back. He had a thumping headache and he began to massage his temples as he tried to decipher where he was and what he was doing there. Suddenly, memories from the previous night began to seep back to him. Coming to Milandra Carter's house, having dinner, talking to her, her comforting him as they discussed Constance, and then him following up to her bedroom . . .

His eyes opened wide in horror as he recalled what had happened. He was in Milandra's bedroom! His head spun around, looking for her, but he could see no sign of her. As he saw his clothes strewn across the room he realised he was still naked. He threw the covers off and went to jump out of the bed, but as he tried to do so he was overcome with dizziness and grabbed a bedside locker for support. He sat down on the side of the bed and tried to concentrate on the night's events. Could he have been dreaming that he had been with Milandra? But, as hazy and distorted his memories were, he knew that his being with Milandra was no dream. Him waking up in her bed was evidence enough, even if he still doubted his memory. More slowly, he got up again and made his way over to his clothes and dressed himself.

He went and looked at himself in the mirror at her dressing table and got a fright at the sight. He looked ghastly and his eyes were red. As he took another look around the room he wondered where she was. Her flimsy robe de chambre still lay cast on the floor beside the bed where he had flung it after he had removed it from her body.

He stumbled to the bedroom door and, opening it, walked out onto the landing. He carefully made his way down to the second floor and sheepishly looked into the drawing room, but there was no sign of her there. He continued his journey down to the ground floor.

As he saw the front door he wondered should he just hastily leave the house? Quickly remove himself from this bizarre and dreadful situation before he had to face anybody and simply pretend it had not happened?

He had stepped forward to make his way to the door when he suddenly heard a voice call from the dining room, "Nicholas!"

He turned and through the open door he saw Milandra sitting at the dining-room table. He stood like a statue, not knowing what to do or say.

Milandra stood up from the table and walked out to him, smiling warmly.

"Oh, you're up, are you? You were sleeping so soundly I didn't want to disturb you." And, to his dismay, she put her hands around the back of his neck, drew him to her, and kissed him passionately on the lips. She then drew back and smiled at him, took his hand and led him into the dining room.

"Now, Flancy has made us the loveliest lunch," she said as she sat down and gestured for him to sit down beside her.

"Lunch!" he gasped. "What time is it?"

"It's after one, my darling. Sit down, you must be starving as you missed breakfast."

He felt panicked. "After one! But I should have been in the office hours ago! Mr. Fetherston will be insane with anger! And the contract! You never signed the contract! And it had to be back in the buyer's lawyer's office this morning or the deal will be off!"

Milandra stood up and smilingly came over to him and placed a finger on his lips.

"Hush, sweetie! It's all been taken care of. I signed the contract first thing this morning and had Kitty deliver it back to Mr. Fetherston for execution himself. I also delivered a note to Fetherstons' to say I needed you to attend work for me today and not to expect you in to the office. As I said, no need to worry about a thing – I've taken care of everything. Now sit down, and enjoy your lunch."

He stared at her in amazement, wondering if he was still trapped in a bizarre dream. She pushed him to the chair and gently forced him to sit down.

At that moment Flancy walked in.

"Good afternoon, Mr. Nicholas, how are you today?" she asked brightly as she picked up a teapot and poured him a cup of tea.

Nicholas said nothing but looked at Milandra in horror. Milandra didn't seem to care that her servants knew he had spent the night there.

"He's feeling very good, aren't you, Nicholas?" said Milandra as she reached forward and began to fill his plate with chicken and salad.

As he looked down at the food, he felt queasy, and pushed the plate away.

"Perhaps some orange juice for Nicholas, Flancy," suggested Milandra.

Flancy nodded and, grinning, left the room.

Nicholas stood up abruptly. "I'm sorry, but I have to go!"

"Go – go where?" asked a surprised Milandra.

"To work!"

"But I've already told you I explained to Fetherstons' –"

"I have clients other than you – I have to go in to work," he said, backing to the door.

"Oh, I see," she said uncertainly. She stood up and followed him out to the hallway.

He quickly headed for the door and turned to her.

"I'll talk to you later," he mumbled.

Her arms went around his neck and she kissed him tenderly.

"I'll look forward to it, my love. I'll be counting the minutes," she whispered.

He nodded, undid the bolts and quickly left the house. As he stumbled onto the street the sunlight blinded him.

As quickly as he could he made his way up to Rutland Square. Reaching the house, he let himself in with his key and began to tiptoe across the hall to the stairs, hoping nobody would see him.

"Nicholas – is that you?" came his mother's voice from the drawing room. She appeared at the door. "Nicholas? You never came home last night – we were worried sick about you!"

She quickly walked over to him.

"Yes – I went out with Tom. I ended up staying at his flat," he said.

"Well, I wish you had told us of your plans, Nicholas. I have been out of my mind with worry about you, especially with everything that has been going on with Constance." Her face was creased with worry.

"Yes, I know, thoughtless of me."

"Are you all right? You don't look very well," she said, placing a hand on his forehead.

"Just a little under the weather. I'm going for a lie-down."

"But what about work?"

"Oh, I've told them I'm not well."

She took in his appearance. "You've been drinking, Nicholas. Perfectly understandable with what you are going through with Constance. But you won't find any answers at the bottom of a whiskey bottle!"

"I know. It won't happen again," said Nicholas as he manoeuvred his way to the staircase and up the steps.

"Call me if you want anything!" Agatha said as she watched him gingerly climb the stairs.

Flancy walked into the dining room with a jug of orange juice for Nicholas.

"Where's he gone?" she asked.

"Oh, he was tired, so he went home."

Milandra hugged herself tightly, smiling in glee.

Flancy put the orange juice on the table. "Well, you certainly look like the cat that got the cream!"

"Oh, I feel like that cat!" laughed Milandra. "It's all worked out perfectly, Flancy."

"Well, I have to hand it to you, Milandra, you always get what you want – by whatever means."

Milandra stopped smiling and her eyes became intent. "I've haven't secured him yet. He raced out of this house a little too quickly. But we can build from here."

CHAPTER 38

Nicholas lay on his bed, staring at the ceiling. As he continually replayed the previous night's events, he wondered what on earth had come over him. That he had ended up in bed with his client, a family friend, Milandra Carter. It was like he didn't know his own mind and all the normal rules and inhibitions had vanished. He was overcome with a sense of deep shame that he had betrayed Constance in such a vile way. Whatever problems he had been having with his Constance, how could he ever forgive himself for doing what he had done? And Constance would never forgive him if she ever found out. He would lose her for sure, forever. Her behaviour at the party was insignificant compared to the ultimate betrayal he was guilty of. And at that moment he had never loved Constance more. The thought of losing her was too hard to even contemplate. If only he hadn't gone to Milandra's house the previous day! As he thought about it he wondered what kind of a woman Milandra Carter was? That she would just have sexual relations with him and not even appear to be worried about it?

What did she want? Who was she? It was like she had cast a spell on him and he was unable to resist, to even think straight or normally. He had a dreadful feeling in the pit of his stomach. And he never wanted to see Milandra Carter again. After he had behaved so dispassionately to Constance, he now feared he might have lost her for good.

He would have to win her back as soon as possible.

The next morning Nicholas sent one of the servants to Fetherstons' with a note to say he was ill and would not be in work that day. He didn't care what they thought. He had put work before Constance for too long. He now had to put her first and fix their relationship if possible before it was too late. His head still felt hazy but he felt better than the day before. He had obviously consumed too much wine at Milandra's dinner table, but that was no excuse for his behaviour. But he still couldn't understand it. He was well used to drinking and had consumed quite a lot during his student days. But alcohol had never made him feel like that or brought him to act in such a reckless manner. He couldn't even bring himself to think about Milandra Carter as that afternoon he hastily made his way up to Mountjoy Square. He knocked on the door and Reeves answered it.

"Is Constance home?" he asked urgently.

"Good afternoon, Mr. Nicholas. Yes, she is," said Reeves, stepping out of the way to allow him in. "She is in her room. His Grace, Mrs. Staffordshire and Miss Emma are away in the country. I will tell her you are here."

On hearing the rest of the Staffordshires were away, Nicholas was delighted. He would be able to speak to Constance without any fear of interruption.

"No need. I will tell her I'm here myself," he said as he bounded up the stairs, leaving a shocked Reeves looking after him.

Nicholas reached the landing of the first floor. He had never been upstairs and had no idea where Constance's room was. He hurried down the landing to the base of the stairs leading to the third floor.

"*Constance!*" he called loudly.

In her bedroom, Constance was sitting at her window, looking out at the nannies walking their charges in the park in the centre of Mountjoy Square. On hearing her name being called, she got up and went to the door and opened it.

"*Constance!*" called the voice again.

Constance looked down the stairs and saw Nicholas standing at the bottom of it.

They stared at each other. Then Nicholas slowly walked up the stairs to her.

When he reached her they stood, gazing into each other's eyes.

"Nicholas – I didn't think I'd ever see you again," she whispered.

"We need to talk."

She nodded and they walked into her bedroom and closed the door.

Downstairs Reeves was still standing like a statue, completely at a loss as to what it was his duty to do.

Tears stung Constance's eyes at the very sight of Nicholas standing in front of her. As each day had passed by and she heard nothing from him, a little more hope that their relationship would survive died. She had prepared herself for losing Nicholas for good. Now he was standing there in front of her.

"Constance –" he began, but was lost for words, as he kept remembering himself and Milandra in bed together.

"It's all right, Nicholas, there is no need to explain. I understand, I really do." She forced herself not to cry.

"Understand what?" he said, fearing she might know something of his night with Milandra.

"I understand that you have to end our engagement. I'd probably do the same if I was in your situation. The last thing you need is a liability as a wife."

"No – no, that's not what I was going to say to you at all." He rushed over to her. "It's I who needs to apologise to you."

"But – for what?"

"For not being supportive of you all week. For judging you. For not loving you the way I should have. For not showing you that I love you regardless of anything. Regardless of anything you did."

"You – forgive me?" She could hardly bear to ask the question.

"Of course I forgive you. There's nothing to forgive. I've missed you so much this week, I can hardly explain to you how much I missed you. The idea of you not being in my life, well, I don't know how I'd cope."

Tears sprang to her eyes as she put her arms around him and held him tightly. "Oh, Nicholas. Thank you so much."

"There's no need to thank me for anything. It's I who need to thank you. I only realised what I have in you, when I feared I might lose you."

"I only acted the way I did because I love you so much I feared I was losing you to Milandra. I've had the worst week of my life, Nicholas. Thinking I'd lost you over my silly jealousy. Then my family are hardly speaking to me!" She went and sat on the edge of the bed.

"Where are they? Reeves said they were away."

"Father has a seminar in Limerick. Mother and Emma went with him – I think to get away from me."

He went and sat beside her. "My poor darling, left all alone. I blame myself entirely. I put everything else before you. You wouldn't have felt jealous that night if I had given you the attention you deserved."

"You had to concentrate on your new job." She was tempted to rant against Milandra's role in it all but knew she must restrain herself.

"But I knew about your father's curfew," he said. "So I shouldn't have expected you to run around after me. I should have come here for dinner with you and your family each evening, just so I could see you." He smirked at her. "Regardless of how solemn dinner in your father's company is."

She smiled back at him but quickly became serious again and asked anxiously, "But, Nicholas – your family, and your work colleagues. There could be consequences for you if you forgive me."

"I don't care! Besides, I think you have an ally in Mama. She's always had a soft spot for the underdog."

"I don't want to marry into your family as an underdog, Nicholas," she said, slightly offended.

He reached out and grabbed her hands. "Don't you understand? I don't care about any of them!"

"But you have probably lost Fetherstons' main client, Milandra, because of me," she said.

Nicholas went red at the mention of Milandra's name and blinked a couple of times.

"*Please* let's not talk about any of them any more," he said. "I just want to talk about you and me. We are the only ones that matter."

"But Milandra Carter will not forgive me, and she has such power and money that –"

"*Constance – please stop!*" His voice was shrill.

He reached forward and held her face in his hands. Moving forward, he kissed her passionately and continued to kiss her in an almost desperate fashion. Almost as if he was attempting to eliminate all thoughts of Milandra Carter from his memory.

"Nicholas, stop!" she muttered as he kissed her neck and started to unbutton the back of her dress.

"Nicholas – what are you doing?" she said was she felt her dress slip from around her shoulders.

He got up and went to lock the door before returning to her and sitting down. He gently pushed her back on the bed and looked at her, as she placed her hand around the back of his neck, pulling him close.

CHAPTER 39

Constance lay in Nicholas's arms on her bed.

"We shouldn't have," she said. "We promised after last time it wouldn't happen again until we were married."

"Do you regret it?" he anxiously enquired.

She thought back to a lazy afternoon in the spring when she had been with Nicholas at Tom's room in Trinity. Tom had been called away unexpectedly, leaving them alone. She remembered how they had embraced and, as one thing led to another, they had ended up in bed. Although at the time she hadn't regretted being with the man she loved and was engaged to, it had troubled her a little in retrospect as it went against all the conventions and her stern religious upbringing. But now, as she lay in his arms, she had no regrets about being with Nicholas again. She felt it confirmed their love for each other and their future together.

"No, my darling, of course I don't regret it," she reassured Nicholas.

"Well, we'll be married soon – so what does it matter?"

"I don't think anybody else would look at it that way!" she said wryly. "My parents would disown me if they found out."

As he held her he felt an incredible sense of relief that they were still together. Being with Constance made what had happened with Milandra seem less important. It was a misdemeanour, a mistake, that he now needed to forgive himself for and get on with the rest of his life with Constance.

He smiled at her. "I don't want to be apart from you for a

moment any more. We've been letting everything get in the way of our wedding – my exams, then my work. Let's just set the date. As soon as possible."

She sat up and looked down at him. "Really, Nicholas?"

"Yes. There's no point waiting around any more. You have all the arrangements already made! We just need to set a date. How about the end of next month?"

"Oh, Nicholas – yes!" She bent down and kissed him. "Will your parents be happy with that?"

"It's my life, they have no say . . . Besides, maybe it's not such a good idea that we live with my parents after we're married."

"But where would we live?"

"We could rent something small. It wouldn't be like the houses we are used to, but at least it would be ours."

"I think that would be wonderful!" said Constance, getting more excited.

"I think it would be good to get away from Sackville Street, and all the airs and graces of the people that live there, don't you?"

"Well, since I am being judged so harshly by them now – yes, I do!"

"I've been giving things a lot of thought this past week. I don't think I'm happy at Fetherstons' either."

"Not happy at Fetherstons'? But I thought you loved it there?"

"Did I ever say that? No – what I said was I was lucky to be there. But I now realise I'm not happy there at all. They have given me too much work for my limited experience. I want to enjoy my life and I don't think I can do that at Fetherstons'. Look how it's taken me away from you since I started there."

"But what would you do? Where would you go?"

"To another law firm. Fetherston is an old friend of Papa's so will be give me a good reference regardless of how short a time I've been there. In fact, maybe I will apply for a position in London."

"London! For us to move to London?" she said, her eyes wide with amazement.

"Yes, why not? It would be good for us to get away, live away from our families and everyone we know for a while. To stand on our own feet. Would you like that?"

Constance thought it the most thrilling thing she had ever heard. She knew that, even with her marriage to Nicholas, it would take the gossip about her crisis at Milandra's party a very long time to die down. To just get away from all that and start anew where nobody knew of it was a wonderful idea. And as she looked down at Nicholas, she was sure that was why he was suggesting a move to London. To save her from suffering any more embarrassment. It made her love him all the more.

"Yes, I'd like that very much," she said, bending down and kissing him.

He closed his eyes and heaved a sigh of relief. A year or two in London was just what they needed. To get away from Sackville Street and Milandra Carter. He would do anything to get away from Milandra and the memory of what had happened. And if that meant leaving his job and the city, then so be it. He felt sure that Milandra would not divulge to anybody what had happened between them as it would ruin her own reputation. But, still, he did not want her anywhere near his life from now on.

Reeves opened the front door that evening and in walked the Bishop, Henrietta and Emma.

"Did you have a good journey, Your Grace?"

"Adequate, Reeves. Where is Miss Constance?"

"She's in the drawing room, Your Grace."

"Ah – so she can actually leave her room occasionally, can she?" said the Bishop.

"Mr. Nicholas is with her, Your Grace."

Henrietta and the Bishop exchanged worried looks.

"Oh, what's he here for?" said Henrietta in panic. "To break the engagement?"

"Well, there is only one way to find out," said the Bishop. "Emma, run along to your room – this is not for your ears."

The Bishop and Henrietta went to the drawing-room door and, opening it, walked in to find Constance sitting on the couch beside Nicholas.

"Ah, good evening, Your Grace, Mrs. Staffordshire," Nicholas greeted them cheerily.

"Nicholas, we weren't expecting to see you," said the Bishop, "but I understand there are things that need to be sorted after my daughter's eruption at Mrs. Carter's party. There is a reason why I am so against the consumption of alcohol. But I never expected that a daughter of mine would be living proof of it. I, for one, can only offer my apologies and sincere –"

"Your Grace!" interrupted Nicholas. "I am here to make the final arrangements for my marriage to Constance. We have settled on the date – the 28th of next month."

Both the Bishop's and Henrietta's mouths dropped open.

Nicholas smiled at Constance and reached out and took her hand.

"I – I – don't know what to say!" said the Bishop.

"Then say nothing!" pleaded Henrietta who clasped her hands together in joy.

"Although I am naturally happy that you are continuing with your intentions to marry my daughter, Nicholas," said the Bishop, "I still think that what occurred cannot be simply ignored. We must set a good example for people, not a bad one. Constance has left us with no option but to examine her behaviour to ensure that such an event can never happen –"

"*John!*" Henrietta spoke so loudly that everybody jumped.

Constance had never thought it possible her mother's vocals could hit so high a note.

"What?" said an amazed Bishop.

"Shut up!" Henrietta said, before marching over to Nicholas and Constance and giving each of them a kiss. "Wonderful news! Just wonderful!"

Henrietta flew over to the door and, opening it, called "Emma! Quick, get down here. The wedding is fixed for next month! All is well!"

Nicholas looked at Henrietta's relieved reaction in bemusement and, as he squeezed Constance's hand, all thoughts of Milandra were swept from his mind.

CHAPTER 40

Milandra stood at a tall window in her upstairs drawing room, looking through a pair of binoculars that she had trained on the Fontenoys' house.

Flancy came in and said, "What do you want for tonight's dinner?"

Milandra ignored her as she continued to look through her binoculars.

"Milandra?"

"*What*?" snapped Milandra, swinging around.

"Tonight's dinner? What do you want?" said an exasperated Flancy.

"Anything. Nothing. I'm not hungry," she answered in an irritated voice.

"Well, you have to eat something!"

"Will you stop bothering me, you silly old bitch!" snapped Milandra, lifting up the binoculars again and peering through them.

Flancy walked over and grabbed the binoculars from her.

"Give them back to me!" demanded Milandra.

"No!"

"Give them back to me this instance, or I'll fire you!"

"Sure you will!" mocked Flancy. "If you spend any more time looking through this thing, you'll develop a squint! It's just not healthy."

"Oh, shut up and leave me alone!" Milandra stormed past her and threw herself down onto the couch.

Flancy walked over to her. "No word from him yet?

"Not yet!" said Milandra grumpily. "Where is he? Why hasn't he come and seen me? After what happened between us, he should at least be calling to me. Not just disappear without a backward glance."

"Have you any legal business to conduct with him?"

"Not at the moment. Ambrose's will has been administered and the country estate is now sold, so there is nothing pressing that he would *have* to see me about."

Pondering, Flancy sat down beside her. "Well, in that case, make something up! I'm sure there's loads of work pending with the wine merchants."

"But nothing urgent. I don't want him to think I'm looking for an excuse to pursue him. I do have some pride!" said Milandra.

"Really? Your pride never stopped you before."

"That was different!"

After a few moments of silence Flancy said, "Perhaps . . ."

"Perhaps what?" demanded Milandra.

"Perhaps . . . you frightened him off?"

"Oh, for goodness' sake, how could I frighten him off! I handed myself on a plate to him!"

"Well, some men don't like that, you know," cautioned Flancy. "They like the chase, and to be the ones in charge."

"Oh shut up, Flancy! Stop nagging me! If I waited around for him to make the move, I'd have been waiting forever. With that mousy little creature Constance lurking around, and him continuing to change the subject back to legal work when I tried to move the conversation to us. No! I had to act decisively to move our relationship to the next level."

CHAPTER 41

Nicholas and Constance sat on the couch, holding hands, in the Fontenoys' drawing room as Daniel and Agatha sat opposite them.

"So," continued Nicholas, turning to Constance and smiling. "We have set the date for the end of next month."

"I see!" said Daniel.

"I know you must have had some misgivings after my atrocious conduct at Mrs. Carter's party. But I *swear* to you that I will never let Nicholas or you down again," said Constance earnestly. "And I *promise* that I will make Nicholas the very best wife he could ever possibly hope to have."

"It was certainly out of character for you, Constance. Not the girl we have come to know," said Agatha who managed to look pleased that the young couple appeared to have sorted out their problems. Nicholas certainly looked much happier than he had been recently.

"Nicholas's happiness is our utmost concern," said Daniel. "And if you are happy to go ahead with this marriage, Nicholas –"

"Oh, I am, Papa!" cried Nicholas. "I couldn't be happier. Constance means everything to me."

"Then who are we to raise objections?" concluded Daniel.

Constance saw he wasn't managing to look pleased at all. She realised it would take some time to gain Daniel Fontenoy's respect and trust again. Which made it a good reason that they would not be moving in with the Fontenoys after the marriage.

Nicholas cleared his throat before continuing. "Also, we have made another decision. After the marriage, Constance and I have decided to move to London for a while."

"*What?*" shouted Daniel.

"My Nicholas – in London!" Agatha was dismayed.

"But that is out of the question," said Daniel. "Nicholas, what of your career? Your position at Fetherstons'?"

"I have given it serious thought, Papa. And I think it would do my career the world of good to work for a law firm in London for a couple of years. You did it yourself after graduating as a lawyer. You always said the experience was invaluable to you."

"But, Nicholas! I don't understand why you should do such a thing? When you have everything here," said Daniel.

"The most important thing in my life is Constance, Papa. And over the last few months I have lost sight of that. I put clients and work and everything else before her, when I should have been putting her first. I have no doubt that it was I that caused Constance's outburst, by not being the attentive and good fiancé that I should have been."

"Has Milandra Carter fired you? Is it, as I thought, that your job at Fetherstons' is in jeopardy because of Constance? And this harebrain plan to go to London is just a cover for this?"

Nicholas went bright red at the mention of Milandra's name and he said angrily, "No, it has nothing to do with it! Please don't insinuate it has again! We just want to experience another life for a while, nothing more, nothing less."

"But what will I do without my Nicholas?" wailed Agatha.

"This is exactly it, Mama! I will be a married man, and Constance must be my priority. I can't be living under my parents' or anybody else's shadow any more."

"I can see you've made up your mind," Daniel said, his lips tight.

"We have," said Nicholas.

"And where will you work in London?" asked Daniel.

"I don't know yet. I'll have to apply for positions. Hopefully I will get something soon."

"And it will only be for a year or two?" asked Agatha anxiously.

"That's all," said Constance.

"In that case, I have plenty of contacts in London," said Daniel. "I will write to them and organise a position in a law firm for you."

"Oh, Papa!" smiled Nicholas. "Was there ever a better papa?"

"Well, I have to make sure that you are comfortable while living in London," said Daniel.

"Thank you, Daniel, for your kindness and your support," said Constance.

Daniel nodded, but he didn't smile back.

CHAPTER 42

Milandra stood at the drawing-room window, peering through the binoculars. She suddenly lowered them before quickly raising them and squinting through them again.

"*Flancy*!" she suddenly screamed at the top of her voice.

Seconds later Flancy came running in.

"Whatever is the matter?" cried Flancy.

"Come here! Quick!"

Flancy raced over to her and Milandra handed her the binoculars. Flancy took them and looked through them, pointing them in the direction Milandra was indicating across the street.

There she saw Nicholas and Constance walking down the street arm in arm.

"What on earth?" asked Flancy, dropping the binoculars.

"He's b-back – with – h-her," stuttered Milandra.

"But how could he be? After all that's happened?"

"Well, you can see with your own eyes, can't you?" said Milandra as she slowly walked over to the couch and sank down into it. "What does he think he's doing?" she whispered.

Flancy sighed. "Looks like your plans didn't work, Milandra."

Nicholas sat in his office and with trepidation he opened the letter that Milandra's servant Kitty had handed to him.

Dear Nicholas,
 I wish to discuss a pressing legal matter with you. Please

call to my house tomorrow at three in the afternoon to discuss.
   Yours sincerely,
   Milandra

As Nicholas reread the letter, he broke out in a cold sweat.

Kitty handed Milandra a letter.
   "Mr. Fontenoy asked for me to deliver this back to you, ma'am."
   "Very well, you may go," said Milandra and Kitty hurried off.
   With a sense of excitement Milandra hastily broke the seal on the envelope and unfolded the letter.

Dear Mrs. Carter,
   Unfortunately, I shall not be able to make a house call tomorrow as my schedule is full. However, you can meet me at three, as you suggest, at Fetherstons'.
   Yours sincerely,
   Nicholas Fontenoy

Devastated, Milandra flopped down into a chair.

CHAPTER 43

Milandra swept into Fetherstons' the next day at three precisely.

"I am here to see Nicholas Fontenoy," she announced to the clerk on the front desk.

"Certainly, Mrs. Carter, please follow me," said the clerk.

Milandra followed him up the stairs but, instead of going in the usual direction to Nicholas's office, the clerk continued up the stairs to the next floor.

"Where are you going? That's not the way to Nicholas's office," Milandra pointed out.

"No, I'm to bring you to Mr. Fetherston's office," said the clerk.

"But why? My appointment is with Mr. Fontenoy, not Mr. Fetherston," said Milandra.

The clerk shrugged. "Those were my instructions."

"I don't have time to meet Mr. Fetherston – my appointment is for three with Nicholas Fontenoy," snapped Milandra but the clerk ignored her and continued up the stairs.

Confused and irritated, she followed him up to the top floor.

The clerk opened the door of Sanders Fetherston's office to show her in.

Milandra marched inside and was very surprised to see Nicholas sitting there beside Fetherston behind the desk.

"Ah, Mrs. Carter, good day to you. Please take a seat," said Fetherston, directing her with his hand to the empty chair on the other side of the desk.

Milandra stared at Nicholas, whose face was bright red, but he was avoiding any eye contact with her.

Slowly Milandra crossed the room and sat down.

"There is no need to bother you with the matter I have to discuss, Mr. Fetherston. It is Nicholas I wish to speak to," she said.

She looked at Nicholas who was staring at the floor, steadfastly avoiding her gaze.

"Yes, indeed, Mrs. Carter," smiled Fetherston. "However, I felt I should meet you personally with Nicholas to discuss the change of circumstances."

"What change of circumstances?" demanded Milandra, staring at Nicholas, challenging him to look at her.

But he didn't raise his eyes, as his face went even redder.

"Young Nicholas is leaving us unfortunately, Mrs. Carter," announced Fetherston.

"Leaving us? Leaving who?" demanded Milandra.

"Leaving Fetherstons', I'm afraid to say. He has only been with us a short time, but we will miss him, as I'm sure you will," said Fetherston, who didn't look too perturbed by Nicholas's leaving in the least.

"But I don't understand! Why is he leaving? Where is he going?" Milandra's voice was high with anxiety.

"He's off to London," said Fetherston.

"*London*!" shrieked Milandra, causing the two men to jump.

"That's correct," said Fetherston.

Milandra leaned towards Nicholas "What are you doing going to London?"

"He's going –" began Fetherston.

"Can the man not speak for himself?" demanded Milandra angrily. "Has he lost his power of speech? Gone mute? Why are you going to London, Nicholas?"

Now, with both Milandra and Fetherston looking at him to answer, Nicholas forced himself to look up from the floor.

"I'm taking up a position in a new firm in London," he replied.

Milandra stared at him in shock. "Are you indeed?"

"I know this must come as an inconvenience for you, Mrs. Carter," said Fetherston.

"That is putting it very lightly, Mr. Fetherston!"

"And may come as quite a surprise."

"Another understatement, Mr. Fetherston!"

"So, as you can see, that is why I am meeting with you today. To organise your account to be moved from Nicholas to another of our solicitors in the firm. I was thinking that, in the meantime, I myself will handle your affairs."

"I don't think you understand the magnitude of what is happening!" Milandra's voice was dark with anger. "The reason why I came to Fetherstons' in the first place was because Nicholas's father recommended you, and that was because his son Nicholas was working here. I have come to entirely trust and rely on Nicholas for all my legal work. And now you expect me to just change lawyers at the drop of the hat, as if – as if I am choosing a new frock to wear to a ball!"

Fetherston was taken aback by her furious reaction.

"Well, I don't know what you suggest I can do?" he said with a slightly bemused expression which hid the concern he felt. "Young Fontenoy is off to London, and we shall just all have to make do without him."

"It's not good enough! It's just not good enough!" Milandra slammed her hand down on the desk.

"But, Mrs. Carter, are you suggesting we chain Nicholas to his desk here and stop him from leaving for London? Because other than that drastic measure, I can't think of anything else we can do!"

"You can start by telling me the reasons why he is going to London?" demanded Milandra.

"Because, after he gets married next month, he and his new wife want to live for a while in London. I believe that is his privilege in life – to decide which city he wishes to reside in," said Fetherston, who was losing patience with Milandra Carter's demanding nature, regardless of how wealthy she was.

"Married?" Milandra said the word as a whisper.

Nicholas held his head up and looked her straight in the eye. "Yes, myself and Constance have fixed our wedding date. Next month. We'll be leaving for London straight after the wedding."

Milandra's eyes narrowed as she glared at him. "You are still marrying Constance?"

"Yes, of course I am. Why would I not?" said Nicholas.

"I thought you would have cancelled your wedding after –" Milandra nearly forgot for a moment that Fetherston was present and almost divulged what had happened between them, "after she made a fool of herself and attacked me, your client, at my party. Did you hear of that serious incident, Mr. Fetherston?"

"Unfortunately I did, from my son who was present," sighed Fetherston.

"And what do you propose to do about it, Mr. Fetherston?" demanded Milandra, realising she was clutching at straws.

"Well, I think the question is, Mrs. Carter – what do *you* expect me to do about it? If you are suggesting that I fire Nicholas because of his fiancée's conduct, then it is quite a fruitless exercise, as he has already given his notice and is leaving. In any case, even if I did fire him it would be pointless, because by your reaction it seems you are annoyed that Nicholas *is* leaving. In short – Mrs. Carter – what the blazes do you want me to do?" Fetherston was a patient man, but even his patience had snapped. He had bent over backwards for Milandra Carter since she had become a client. Always a difficult client, she was now becoming an impossible one.

"I wish to speak to Nicholas alone," demanded Milandra, causing Nicholas to shiver.

"Quite impossible, Mrs. Carter," said Fetherston. He'd had enough of this woman. He had appeased her too much since she had become a client and now she thought the firm were at her beck and call. He had a feeling that she had made up her mind to leave Fetherstons' anyway.

"Why so?" asked Milandra.

"Because he has other clients, Mrs. Carter! And he must tidy up their affairs before he leaves. He has an afternoon of appointments. I am quite happy to discuss your pressing matter myself. In the meantime – Fontenoy, return to your office!"

"Yes, sir," said Nicholas, quickly standing.

As he hurried past Milandra, he gave her a glance.

Her eyes were cold with fury.

Milandra stormed into the drawing room at home, quickly followed by Flancy.

"*Ahhh!*" Milandra screamed at the top of her voice, picking up an ornament and firing it against a wall.

"What happened?" asked Flancy.

"He's leaving for London with that mouse! He's marrying her next month!"

"Oh dear!" sighed Flancy.

"How dare he! How dare he treat me like this? He spent the night fornicating with me and then runs up the aisle with that unimportant girl!"

"He's obviously in love with that unimportant girl," said Flancy.

Milandra was storming up and down the room in a temper.

"Does he not know who he's messing with? Does he not realise what I can do?"

"I'd say he does, Milandra. That's why he's running away to London."

"He won't get away with this, not for one moment. He can't just bed me and run from me as if I was a common – prostitute!"

"If the cap fits!" said Flancy under her breath.

"I will expose him! I will go to his parents and his mouse of a fiancée tonight and tell them all about us."

"You can't, Milandra. If you go and tell them you slept with Nicholas, then you will only be ruining yourself! Yes, you will destroy Nicholas, but you will destroy yourself first! You *will* be seen as a common prostitute, and the role you have created for yourself in society and put so much work into will be destroyed. You will be ostracized and never be received in a drawing room or a parlour again."

Milandra threw herself down on the couch in desperation.

"Then what can I do, Flancy?"

Flancy sat down beside her and put her arm around her.

"You will just have to let him go. There's plenty more men in Dublin. Plenty of suitors who would be delighted to be with you.

And suitors who are not promised or in love with another woman."

"I can't, Flancy. I can't even look at another man. I'm completely head over heels in love with Nicholas. I have to have him!"

"Then you will destroy yourself if you continue with this folly," warned Flancy.

CHAPTER 44

Constance stood in her bedroom in her wedding dress as two of the fitters attended to her. Henrietta and Emma looked on with pride.

"I think we need to just take the waistline out a tiny bit," said one of the fitters.

"And just puff up the shoulders a little more," suggested the other.

The dress fitting had taken up much of the afternoon. But Constance didn't care. She would have stood there all day and all night to make sure she looked perfect on her wedding day for Nicholas.

"I think you will be the most beautiful bride this year," sighed Henrietta.

"I'm sure I won't!" said Constance.

"Well – take a look at yourself in the mirror!" urged Emma excitedly.

The fitters stepped away and Constance gathered her long train and walked over to the full-length mirror.

"I hardly recognise myself," she whispered.

"You've done a wonderful job," Henrietta congratulated the fitters.

As Constance continued to study herself, she realised that the fact she had nearly broken up with Nicholas had made her appreciate her marriage to him even more.

As Nicholas hurried down Sackville Street on his way home one evening, he glanced across at Milandra's house. With a shiver he quickly walked on. Since her meeting with Fetherston and himself, Milandra had sent her servant Kitty to his office several times with notes requesting him to come to her house. The tone of some of the notes were charming, others pleading, others demanding. He had treated them all in the same fashion by tearing them up and ignoring them. What did the woman want to see him for? If she had envisaged any hope that she and he had some kind of a future, it must now be plainly clear, on learning of his wedding to Constance and their moving to London, that this was out of the question. So why would she want to see him?

The woman was beginning to frighten him, and he was certain that he would never be in her company again if he could help it.

He let himself into the Fontenoy home. He could hear chatter in the drawing room so he walked over and into the room.

His mouth dropped open when he saw Milandra sitting there in conversation with his parents.

"Good evening, Nicholas. How are you?" she said, smiling sweetly over to him.

"Milandra just dropped in for tea, and I've invited her to stay for dinner," said Agatha.

"I feel I have been neglecting my good friends the Fontenoys recently and not visiting as often as I should be," said Milandra.

"You are always welcome in our home, Milandra," smiled Daniel.

"We've just been telling Milandra all about the wedding plans," said Agatha.

"It all sounds very exciting!" exclaimed Milandra.

"I told her that you had decided to have the reception in the Gresham and have everything booked," said Agatha.

"Well, if they do weddings as well as funerals then you couldn't have a better venue," said Milandra.

As Nicholas stood there speechless, he tried to gauge Milandra's mood. There didn't seem to be any animosity emanating from her or negative feelings. But he knew by now that Milandra was very good at acting.

"You must check with Constance and her parents, Nicholas –

Milandra hasn't received her wedding invitation yet," said Daniel.

"Wedding invitation!" said Nicholas, appalled at the thought of her being there.

"I'm sure it is merely an oversight," sighed Milandra. "Weddings can be such fussy affairs, so much to organise and arrange."

"Well, do remind Constance to post Milandra her invite," ordered Daniel.

Nicholas mouth closed and his lips became tight at this intrusion.

"I would say Constance will make a stunning bride," said Milandra. "It's amazing how a wedding dress can transform even the most ordinary-looking of girls."

"Ah – I think I hear them serving dinner," said Agatha, rising. "Shall we go into the dining room?"

"Oh, yes!" said Milandra, standing up.

"I'm afraid I won't be here for dinner this evening!" Nicholas blurted out.

"You didn't say before?" said Agatha.

"I have to go to the Staffordshires for dinner. I told them I would be there." If Milandra was determined to trap him in her company, he was just as determined not to be trapped.

"Well, I wish you would give Cook some notice!" Agatha chastised him.

Nicholas backed out into the hall as his parents and Milandra followed him out.

"Well – cheerio! See you later!" said Nicholas, rushing to the front door.

As Agatha and Daniel continued to the dining room Milandra called, "Nicholas! If I could have a quick word? A query on my country estate sale?"

Frustrated at her tactic, Nicholas paused at the front door as Milandra walked towards him. She waited until Daniel and Agatha were safely in the dining room before speaking.

"You have been avoiding me!" she hissed.

"Mr. Fetherston explained I'm no longer working on your account."

"I'm not talking about my account. You received seven letters from me, all of which were ignored!"

"I've been very busy," he excused himself.

"Well, you had better un-busy yourself. Come to my house tomorrow evening at six sharp!"

"Out of the question!" Nicholas became annoyed. "We have no reason to meet. Nothing to discuss!"

"That is where you are completely wrong, my dear Nicholas. If you are not at my house tomorrow evening at six, then I will be paying your parents another visit. And the Staffordshires, and your Constance. I will blow the lid off our affair and tell them just what a cheating low-life you are! Do we understand each other?"

As he glared at her angrily, he couldn't help feeling fearful. She spoke with such venom, her eyes filled with such malice.

He nodded quickly and then rushed out the door.

CHAPTER 45

As ordered, the next evening at six sharp Nicholas knocked on Milandra's front door. He had a dreadful feeling in the pit of his stomach. He had steadfastly avoided being in her company since their night together. Even organised moving to London with Constance to avoid having any interaction with her in the future. And now here he was because she had threatened him.

Flancy opened the door.

"Mr. Nicholas! So good to see you again!"

He nodded at her coldly and stepped inside.

"She's in the drawing room upstairs," said Flancy.

He followed her down the lobby and up the stairs. He entered the drawing room awkwardly and Flancy closed the door behind him, leaving him alone with Milandra. She was perched on a Queen Anne chair, with a happy smiling face. All traces of the cold malice she had flashed at him the previous evening were gone.

"Alone at last!" she declared, throwing her hands into the air.

He said nothing but cautiously walked further into the room.

"Please – have a seat!" She gestured for him to sit in a chair beside her.

"There's no need. I won't be staying –"

"Sit down!" she ordered.

Holding back his anger, he sat down.

"You wanted to speak with me?" he said.

"Yes, very much so. And you've been extremely hard to get an audience with."

"Well – I'm here now!"

"Indeed you are. I'll get Flancy to bring us some tea." She made to get up.

"No need! I don't have that much time. I have to be at the Staffordshires in an hour."

"I see," she said, reclining back in her chair. "To arrange more of your wedding day, I presume?"

"Exactly. What do you want, Milandra?"

"Well, I thought that was perfectly obvious by now – *you*!"

Nicholas became exasperated. "In what way?"

"In every way I can. I want a future with you, Nicholas. And I think you want one with me. You are just too afraid to admit it. To admit it to yourself, to your family, to Constance."

Nicholas spoke angrily and urgently. "Let me make myself very clear – I am in love with Constance. I have always been in love with her and I always will be. We are going to get married shortly and we will be very happy together for the rest of our lives. Have I made myself clear enough?"

"But what about you and me?"

"*There is no you and me!*" he shouted.

"You weren't saying that the night you were frolicking around my bed!"

"That –" he looked down at the ground, "that was a mistake."

"*A mistake!*"

"Yes – an unfortunate mistake."

"You don't just end up in a woman's bed by mistake, Nicholas!"

"I don't know what happened that night. I think I shall never understand what possessed me. I deeply regret it and feel shame –"

"*Shame!*" She was incredulous.

"Yes – shame! I just now want to forget about the whole episode and be allowed to get on with my life. My life with Constance."

She sat back and studied him intently.

"If only everything was as simple as that, Nicholas. Do you really think you can come here, bed me, profess undying love for me –"

"I don't remember ever saying that!"

"– and then just swan off without a backward glance. No, Nicholas, I don't think so!"

"What are you proposing in that case?" Nicholas cried out.

"I want you, for a start, to cancel this ridiculous wedding with Constance. It's just not right that you marry the girl when she has no idea of our relationship."

"Our relationship! We spent one night together!"

"In all honesty I can't just stand idly by and watch you make any more of a fool of that unfortunate girl. If you don't break off the engagement and cancel your wedding day, you are giving me no option but to tell her about us. I will also have to tell your parents, and her parents."

"You wouldn't dare!"

"Try me!" she challenged.

"No – actually you really wouldn't dare! As you well know, if you did such a thing, you might very well destroy me and Constance and my character, but you would destroy yourself much more. You would be showing yourself as nothing more than a whore. A cheap nasty whore, regardless of how much money you have!"

"Don't you dare speak to me like that!"

"I will speak like that because it's the truth. You would be ruined in society to such an extent that you would have to leave Sackville Street and Dublin forever. Yes, you might temporarily cause myself and Constance to break up. But do you think, after your actions, that I would have anything to do with you? I can't stand you. Even now I can't bear being in the same room as you."

Her eyes filled with hurt.

"I despise you, and I despise myself for having anything to do with you!" spat Nicholas. "If you tell Constance what happened between us, all I will do is spend every day of the rest of my life trying to win her back. And I *will* win her back. Because she loves me as much as I love her. And that is something you will never have. Not with a mean heart like yours." He stood up abruptly. "I think we are finished here now."

She said nothing as he walked over to the door.

He turned and looked at her.

"In their naiveté, not knowing what kind of a woman you are, my parents are insisting you be invited to our wedding. I think it would be in the absolute worst taste that you should show yourself on our wedding day, so I expect you to decline any invitation you receive. Goodbye, Milandra, I wish you the very best."

Nicholas walked out the door.

As he made his way to the top of the stairs he began to feel liberated and as he rushed down the stairs he couldn't wait to be out of the house and away from Milandra.

Once out on Sackville Street, he felt free.

Milandra lay sobbing in Flancy's arms.

"He called me a whore!" she cried between her sobs.

"The bastard!" said Flancy.

"A cheap nasty whore!"

"The cheek of him!"

"I never thought he would be able – be capable of speaking like that! Of speaking like that to me!"

"Isn't it as well you found out what he's like now, rather than further on?" soothed Flancy, stroking Milandra's hair.

"He wasn't my sweet kind Nicholas. I hardly recognised him!"

"I never thought you were suited, to be honest."

"What do you know about anything!"

"Well, you'll have to get over it as quickly as possible. That ship has sailed, my darling. And it's not carrying you as a passenger. As I told you before there's plenty of men who would fight to be your husband. I'm hearing a rumour that that nice Lord Galway is in need of a wife, a rich wife, as he had a bit of a gambling problem in the past. A title would be nice for you, wouldn't it? Lady Milandra Galway?"

"But you don't understand, Flancy! I just can't let him go!"

"Oh, my poor darling," Flancy said as she held her closer and continued to stroke her hair.

CHAPTER 46

Constance couldn't have been happier as she counted the days down to her wedding. She and Nicholas were blissfully happy and all she could do was dream of their bright future together. Even her father looked happy and was smiling.

But, with all the excitement of the wedding, she had been neglecting her charity duties. It was two weeks before her wedding and, as they were going to live in London straight after their honeymoon, she decided to make a trip around her usual charity runs to say goodbye to the other volunteers and some of the mothers who came for food parcels whom she had got to know well over the years.

She soon found herself in a packed church hall, standing behind a stall handing out food parcels to the women queuing there.

"We'll miss you, Miss Constance," said one of the women as she took the food parcel from her.

"Oh, and I'll miss you, Mrs. Darcy," smiled Constance. "But I won't be gone forever, and I'll be back helping out here again when we return from London."

"Ah, well, you'll make a beautiful bride, and a lovely wife. He's a lucky fella, the lad that's got you."

"Thank you, Mrs. Darcy. You look after yourself and your children."

As Mrs. Darcy moved on, Constance smiled at the next woman who stepped forward. She reached down for a food parcel for her. As she did she suddenly felt dizzy. She stood up quickly and reached out for the table in front of her to steady herself. But she missed her grip, and suddenly she was falling. As she hit the ground she blacked out.

"How very stupid of me," said Constance. She was lying on a bed in a back room of the church hall.

A doctor had been called and he was examining her.

"They shouldn't have bothered calling you – wasting your time," said Constance, puzzled at the thoroughness of the examination.

"Always better to be safe than sorry," said the doctor good-naturedly.

"I missed my grip when I went to hold the table and ended up falling."

"I believe you actually fainted, Constance," said the doctor.

"Fainted?"

"Yes, you didn't fall, you fainted . . . how have you been feeling recently?"

"Absolutely wonderful, Doctor."

"No other dizzy spells. Feelings of being sick?"

"Not really. I've been rushing around a lot recently with my wedding arrangements, so I have been a bit exhausted – that's what probably led me to faint, if that's what I did."

The doctor studied her and then, pulling up a chair, sat down beside her as she sat up.

"Constance, you are pregnant."

Constance stared at the doctor as if she couldn't comprehend what he had said.

"Constance?"

"Yes – sorry?"

"Did you hear what I said – you are with child."

"Well, there must be some mistake –"

"No mistake, Constance. You are definitely pregnant."

"I – I – don't understand."

"Now, now!" The doctor smiled and put his hand reassuringly on her arm. "I don't want you to fret – it's neither good for you or the baby."

"Fret! But, Doctor –" Constance was in shock.

"I understand you are to be married in a couple of weeks?"

"Yes – but," Constance was as white as a ghost and was shivering uncontrollably, "I think I'm going to be sick."

The doctor quickly reached for a bowl and held it as Constance retched.

After she sat up, tears were streaming down her face.

"What will I do?" She was terrified. "Nicholas – my father!"

"If you take my advice – nothing!"

"Sorry?"

"Look, you'll be married in a couple of weeks, so I think once you are married this won't be a problem for you. In fact, it's good news."

"Good news – how?"

"A baby is always good news, Constance. So – you put the cart a little in front of the horse – so what? Nobody will ever know."

"But, Doctor, the timing?"

"I wouldn't worry about it. The amount of 'premature' babies I have delivered to the most prim and proper young ladies, you would not believe. You won't be the first and you won't be last. Now – if you were pregnant and not due to be married in a couple of weeks, then of course it would be your ruination."

Constance was now shaking uncontrollably. "What must you think of me?"

"I've learned to think nothing of anybody's situation, Constance. The things I have been called to attend to behind the velvet curtains of some of Dublin's finest houses and families would shock you beyond compare."

"You are very kind." She tried to stop herself from sobbing loudly.

"Take my advice and say nothing to anybody – even your fiancé. Announce the pregnancy after you are safely married. All will be well, you'll see. And in the meantime, get on with your wedding plans. In a couple of weeks you'll be safely wed."

PART 6

1916

CHAPTER 47

Inside the house on Sackville Street, a knife could cut the tense atmosphere as the hours wore on throughout Tuesday.

Milandra was down in the kitchen.

She prepared herself a sandwich and ate it at the kitchen table.

The rebels were still in position, their rifles ready to defend the area from any onslaught from the British troops. Seán remained in the drawing room, constantly alert behind the shuttered windows.

Milandra took some cheese from the larder, made a big sandwich and poured milk into a large glass. Placing the sandwich and milk on a tray, she carried it up the servants' stairs and then up the main staircase to the first-floor drawing room. She walked in and found Seán asleep at his post. She gently put the tray down beside him, stirring him from his sleep. With a jolt he jumped up with his pistol and peered out the window.

"You're quite all right, Seán. Nothing has happened since you fell asleep. Everything is the same," she said.

Outside, the rioting mob could be heard and much gunfire in the distance.

Seán looked at her suspiciously.

"I thought you must be hungry, and so I made you a sandwich," she said, pointing at the tray. "I'll make some for your men too in a while. You all need to keep your strength up if you're to liberate the country!"

"I'm not hungry," he snapped, confused as to why she was giving him food.

"Eat it, Seán," she ordered as she went over to the drinks cabinet. Taking a decanter, she filled a glass with sherry. "Would you like one?"

He shook his head vehemently.

"Well, I hope you don't mind if I do. I always find a glass of sherry solves every problem." She took a taste and closed her eyes in delight. "Excellent vintage . . . I worked in the wine trade for years, you know. I would consider myself to have the best knowledge of wine of anybody in Dublin."

He gingerly reached out for the sandwich and began to eat it.

"Are all your sort like you?" he said.

"My sort?"

"Your class."

"Like me?"

"Flouncing around drinking sherry when there are gunmen in your house," he scoffed.

"Ah, I see . . . yes, I guess a lot are. We old buzzards are made of tough stuff, you know. I've seen it all, and I doubt anything you do could shock me," she said, sitting down close to him. "Are you married?"

He shook his head.

"It's probably just as well, because you would be leaving a widow behind by the time all this is finished, you know."

He stared at her as he ate his sandwich.

"You do realise that, don't you? You will most likely be killed, either in the fighting or by being hanged afterwards. I would like to make that very plain to you."

"So what of it? If I die for my cause, I can be proud," he said.

"But, Seán, how can you be proud if you're dead? It's not too late for you, you know." She bent earnestly towards him. "You can just walk out the back door and try and get away from all of this as quickly as possible."

"What do you care, sitting here in your fancy house, if I live or die?"

"I don't care – but I don't think you have thought this through. There's something in your eyes that is . . . uncertain. And I know what it's like to act on impulse and then live with a lifetime of regrets. What's done is done, and you can't undo it."

He became angry. "I am committed to this revolution. I will not stop until we have achieved our aims."

"But is it worth your death, Seán?"

"Why don't you go back to your room and leave me alone to do my job," he said in a raised voice.

She sat back and sipped her sherry. "If you are not married, do you have a sweetheart? Imagine how she will feel when you are killed."

His eyes betrayed a longing feeling and he looked anxiously out the window.

"Oh, I see," she said, nodding her head in acknowledgement. "She's a rebel too, is she?"

"As you said before, we all have our reasons for being part of this rising," he answered. "Mine is to stop social injustice, hers is the suffragette movement. A liberated country where men and women are equal."

"Well, she sounds like a most interesting girl. What's her name?"

"You know I'm not going to tell you that," said Seán as he finished the sandwich.

"I'm going to take a wild guess here," mused Milandra. "Is the reason you have joined the rebellion . . . her? Did she lead you into all this?"

"Nobody led me into it. I'm here because of my free will," he snapped.

"Some women are very good at letting men think they are doing something of their own free will. I imagine this is the case with your young woman. If she wants to go to an early grave, then let her! But why should you go along with her?"

He stood up abruptly. "I'm going to check on the other soldiers. I can't listen to you any more with your stupid rantings!" He marched out of the room.

Milandra shrugged and got up to go back down to the kitchen to make more sandwiches. As she came out of the drawing room, she could hear Seán talking to the other rebels downstairs.

"Word from the GPO, we have managed to maintain our positions throughout the city," said one of the young men. "We are to hold our positions, and can expect British re-enforcements to enter the city in the morning to try to regain control. We are to shoot to kill to stop positions being retaken."

Amelia sat on a bench that evening in a corridor at military headquarters as she watched officials rush backwards and forwards. She was mired in the most terrible internal conflict. Rupert was right in what he had said. She had betrayed him. She had become involved in the Irish independence movement the previous year through her work in the newspaper. She was opposed to the war in Europe and Ireland's involvement in it and wanted a strong independent Ireland, free of that bloody war.

And as she attended meetings – subversive, as Rupert had called them – she had revealed the true information from the front that Rupert had written in his letters. As a high-ranking officer, his letters hadn't been censored and he knew the full extent of the war and how badly it was going for the British. This information had prompted the rebels to act, realising that the British were too weak to defend against an uprising. And Rupert was correct: her comrades had not trusted her to have any involvement or knowledge of the rebellion. They probably realised that if she could carry information from her fiancé, then she could not be trusted with any details of the rising. And now she had betrayed the man she loved, and put Milandra's life in danger.

She was trying to stay out of the way as much as possible, but at the same time get any news of developments.

She saw a door open at the end of the corridor and officers come rushing out.

Spotting Rupert, she got up and quickly went to him.

"Amelia, why are you still here?"

"Tell me what's going on?" she demanded.

"I will get an army attaché to drive you home. You need to get back to Dalkey without delay – and it isn't safe for you to travel alone."

"Why not? The drive to Dalkey isn't anywhere near the trouble spots," she said.

"The whole country has just been put under martial law, Amelia," he said gravely.

"*What*?"

"There is simply no other solution! The looting and rioting is out of control, there are rebel snipers everywhere shooting at any troops. I'll try and find an attaché to take you home. And *stay* there until all this is over."

He began to walk off but she grabbed his arm.

"But you shouldn't be involved in any of this, Rupert! You're supposed to be on leave!" She became panicked that he was about to be in more danger in the leafy streets of their city than in the trenches at the front.

He looked angrily at her. "Do you never give up? Do you understand nothing of duty? We have to quell this rising before it begins to spread. Who knows where it might lead? We will march on the city centre to recapture it."

"*We*?" she repeated.

"I will be marching with them."

"Rupert!" She put her arms around his neck and pulled him close to her.

He took her arms and forced them and her away from him.

"Don't you realise that you have played a part in all this? With your crazy political ideas?"

"They are not crazy!"

"No? Well, then, maybe it's just you that's crazy . . . I hadn't realised, or ever dreamed, how far this war has driven us apart."

"Captain Perkins – *if you please*!" came a harsh voice from the end of the corridor.

"I have to go. I'll try and find an attaché to take you home," said Rupert.

She watched him rush away down the corridor and into the room he had been summoned to. She sat down on the bench again and fidgeted with her hands. Two officers were passing by and she heard them speaking.

"A gunship will set sail up the River Liffey in the morning and will start bombarding the city centre to drive out the rebels. It will start with Sackville Street."

"But they can't do that! They can't bombard the second city of the empire!"

"There's no choice. Reinforcements are arriving in Kingstown Harbour tomorrow and will march on the city centre."

Amelia became gripped with fear as she realised Rupert would be marching with those troops. Gripped with fear that Sackville Street, where her grandmother was, would be shelled and bombed. It all seemed so different when she attended the secret meetings with the Irish Nationalists and they discussed a utopian future as an independent nation – something she fervently believed in. But she hadn't envisaged this as the means to get there.

PART 7

1869

CHAPTER 48

Despite the doctor's kind words, Constance was gripped with terror. She didn't know who to turn to and yet she had a burning desire to talk to someone. Certainly nobody in her family. It was unthinkable that they should find out. She wanted to run to Nicholas and be comforted and reassured by him. And yet she remembered the doctor's advice not to tell anyone, not even her fiancé. The doctor was a wise man who understood people's emotions and reactions.

She couldn't face being at the same table as her father that evening and so excused herself from dinner. As she sat in her room, deep in thought, the doctor's words kept going through her mind. His reassuring words that everything would be fine, as long as she said nothing to anybody. It did make sense, complete sense. She would be married in a couple of weeks, and then she would be a respectably married woman: Mrs. Nicholas Fontenoy. She must act as normally as possible until then. In case the truth ever came out.

Constance nursed her secret to herself in the following days. She kept telling herself there was nothing to worry about. A baby always was good news and Nicholas would be delighted when he found out. He would make a wonderful father. And the very best thing was that they would be living in London in a short while, away from prying eyes. She should be happy, she kept telling herself. But as much as she was looking forward to her wedding day before, now there was an added urgency and she was counting down the hours and minutes.

A week before the wedding the Fontenoys were throwing a party at their house for close friends and family. It was a pre-wedding celebration and Constance decided it was just what she needed to help take her mind off the situation.

"Do stay away from having any alcohol, dear," advised Henrietta as they arrived at the Fontenoys' the night of the party. "We don't want to have a repeat performance of your behaviour at Mrs. Carter's."

"Yes, Mother," agreed Constance.

Nicholas came out into the hallway to greet them.

"The future Mrs. Fontenoy," laughed Nicholas as he put his arm around her and led her into the drawing room which was already filled with people, most of whom were familiar faces she knew.

"We won't be staying long," warned the Bishop as he and Henrietta followed them in.

"Indeed, Your Grace. We are very pleased that you and Mrs. Staffordshire managed to come at all," said Nicholas, smirking down at Constance.

As Constance and Nicholas circled the room, greeting everybody and thanking them for coming, she was surprised to see Milandra Carter wasn't present. It was not like her to miss any social event. Even more surprising was a decline to her wedding invitation which had arrived in the post that morning. Agatha had insisted Milandra be invited. Obviously, Milandra was still very offended by her insulting accusations.

Constance was secretly happy Milandra now seemed safely out of their lives. Nicholas wasn't even working on her account any more, and he never even mentioned her name. How silly she had been to let that stranger come between them! As time went on she would look back and laugh at how insecure Milandra had made her. If she ever even gave her a thought after the wedding.

"Tom!" said Constance as she suddenly came face to face with him.

"Hello, Constance, you look lovely." He bent forward and kissed her cheek.

"Thank you. How's the new job going?"

"Quite well. They have stuck me with a lot of filing to do, not much actual legal work. But I shouldn't complain."

"No, you shouldn't. You could be back on the farm in Sligo!" she laughed.

"True!"

There was an awkward moment between them as they looked at each other.

"Constance!" Nicholas suddenly called from the other end of the drawing room.

"My fiancé beckons! I'll talk to you later," she said with a smile.

Tom stood in the corner sipping his wine as his eyes followed Constance and Nicholas moving among their guests, making light conversation.

Agatha came and stood beside him. "Are you enjoying yourself, Tom?" she asked.

"Oh, yes, thank you, Mrs. Fontenoy." He smiled back at her.

"They make such a lovely couple, don't they?"

"Eh, yes, they do," agreed Tom.

"How is your new job going at Oakleys' Solicitors?"

"So far so good. I'm still there anyway, Mrs. Fontenoy!"

"Good," smiled Agatha.

Daniel had confided in Agatha that Constance had come to him and divulged the dire situation Tom had been in. It slightly irked her that Tom had no knowledge that his getting a job at Oakleys' had been down to Daniel pulling strings to arrange it. She felt Tom should be very grateful to them, and yet Daniel had sworn her to secrecy. Agatha believed that there was no point in doing a good turn for somebody if they never found out about it! If she were truthful with herself, the real reason she was irked by Tom was because he had achieved a higher result in his law exams than Nicholas. She remembered Tom arriving from Sligo when he first became Nicholas's friend. He was a nobody from nowhere. It didn't seem right that he should have done so much better than Nicholas

279

at Trinity. He seemed to always ride on Nicholas's coat-tails at university, and even now he owed his work position to them.

"Are you all ready for your best man duties next week?" she asked.

"As ready as I ever will be!"

"I'm so glad that Nicholas chose you as his best man."

"Really?"

"Yes. I always think that a bridesmaid should not be prettier than the bride, and a best man should never be better-looking than the bridegroom!"

Tom's eyes widened at her comment.

"Anyway, Tom dear, I must circulate. Do avail yourself of our hospitality . . . you know where everything is by now."

Tom stared after her as she left.

"Ladies and gentlemen!" Daniel Fontenoy clinked a fork against a glass, bringing a hush to the party.

The servants were going around quickly giving everyone a glass of champagne.

"I just want to say a few words on behalf of the family. Thank you all for coming. It is so good to see you and to be here to enjoy what is the happiest time for our family: the coming nuptials between our doted-upon Nicholas and his beautiful Constance! This time next week we shall be celebrating their wedding day. And so I ask you all to join me in a toast to – Nicholas and Constance!"

"To Nicholas and Constance!" the guests called back in unison.

As the guests began to talk loudly amongst themselves again, Tom still stood in a corner on his own, his eyes still trained on Nicholas and Constance as they happily accepted good wishes from everybody. As he watched them, he found himself becoming increasingly agitated. Realising his hand was shaking, he placed the glass he was holding on a nearby table and wiped away the light film of sweat that had gathered on his brow. As he watched Constance separate from her fiancé and go to speak to a maiden aunt, he tried to steady himself for what he had to do next. He had an overwhelming desire to turn and run from the house.

But he knew what he had to do and, trembling, he slowly

walked up to Nicholas who was speaking to some of his cousins by the fireplace.

"Hello, Tom! Apologies – I haven't had a chance to speak to you all night," said Nicholas, smiling warmly at him.

Tom stepped closer to him, faltered for a moment in uncertainty and then gently placed a hand on his shoulder, leaning in to him.

Nicholas leaned towards Tom to listen as he started whispering in his ear.

As Tom continued whispering, Nicholas's expression changed from jovial to concerned to anger.

Nicholas pulled back from Tom and stared at him.

Suddenly out of the blue Nicholas struck Tom hard across the face.

There were gasps and cries from the surrounding guests as Nicholas flew at Tom and knocked him to the ground and then jumped on top of him and started to repeatedly strike him.

"*Oh – oh – oh!*" squealed Henrietta as she dropped her glass on the floor at the sight of the two young men fighting ferociously in front of her.

"*Daniel – Daniel!*" screamed Agatha at the top of her voice.

Daniel came racing over to the fight.

"What on earth is going on – *Nicholas – Tom!*" roared Daniel, appalled, as he and some of the male guests reached down and pulled Nicholas away from Tom.

As the guests held Nicholas tightly, Tom managed to stand up and wipe the blood from his mouth with the back of his hand.

"What is the meaning of this?" demanded Daniel.

"*Get out! Get out of my house!*" Nicholas screamed at Tom.

Constance came rushing over to Nicholas. "Whatever has got into you?"

"Get him out of my sight, or I swear I will kill him with my bare hands!" roared Nicholas.

Constance looked fearfully at Tom, who now looked to be shaking uncontrollably and had gone as pale as a ghost.

"I'll bloody well kill him!" shouted Nicholas as he struggled to break free from the hold of the others.

"I think you had better just go, Tom!" begged Constance.

"Constance!" uttered Tom, with a look of guilt and sorrow in his eyes.

Agatha stepped forward. "Please show him to the door," she said to one of the servants.

Tom seemed to become smaller as he backed guiltily to the door.

With one last look of regret at Constance, he turned and quickly left.

"Let him go," Daniel ordered the other guests who were still restraining Nicholas.

They released him.

"Nicholas – whatever happened?" cried Constance, rushing to him and embracing him.

"I think we'd all like to know that!" demanded Daniel.

"Just leave me alone!" shouted Nicholas as he pushed Constance away and stormed out of the room.

The guests erupted in loud chatter and talk.

"I think there is a reason why I never attend parties – somebody always seems to make a disgrace of themselves at them," said the Bishop. "Constance, let us go home!"

"No, I have to speak to Nicholas and find out what is going on," she said as she went to rush out of the room.

The Bishop grabbed her hand. "We are leaving now. Your mother cannot take any more of the drama and we are not leaving you here on your own after that little debacle! You can find out tomorrow the cause of such disgraceful behaviour – in the meantime we are leaving."

Daniel nodded at Constance. "I'll go speak to him. He'll be all right."

"But I –" objected Constance.

"We are going now!" commanded the Bishop, marching Constance to the front door, followed quickly by Henrietta.

"Well, if I hadn't seen it with my own eyes I would never have believed it!" said the Bishop.

The Staffordshires were in the back of a hansom cab on the way back to their home.

"I still don't believe it, and I witnessed it with my own eyes!" said Henrietta.

"I'd never in my wildest dreams have thought that Nicholas has a violent temper," said the Bishop.

"He doesn't!" Constance defended him.

"His actions tonight say otherwise. That is his best man he attacked, isn't it?" said the Bishop.

"Yes – Tom." Constance uttered the words in a low voice.

"But why would he do such a thing?"

"If you had let me stay then perhaps I might have found out!" she snapped.

"I'm afraid, Constance dear, Nicholas had no desire to talk to you tonight, the way he pushed you away and rushed off," said the Bishop.

Constance stared out the cab window, consumed with worry. What had Tom said to provoke Nicholas?

"As soon as I get home, I'm going straight to my bed," said Henrietta. "And I don't think I'll be getting out of it tomorrow!"

Nicholas did not come back downstairs. After the incident, the party had become subdued and people began to leave quickly. After all the guests had safely departed, Daniel knocked on Nicholas's bedroom door and entered. He found his son standing at the window, staring out blankly.

"Would you care to explain to me what on earth all that was about?" asked Daniel as he closed the bedroom door behind him.

"No, I don't wish to discuss it, or anything. Leave me alone," said Nicholas, not turning around.

Daniel became annoyed. "Well, I'm not giving you any choice in the matter! I want an explanation. I did not raise you to brawl in public. In our drawing room in front of your mother! Why did you hit Tom?"

"I had my reasons."

"Then give them to me! I am not leaving until you do! I will stay here all night if necessary!"

Nicholas turned slowly to face his father and Daniel thought he had never seen his son so upset.

"Nicholas – what is it?" Daniel's tone was now soft as he placed a hand on his son's shoulder.

"He – he said – the most awful things," Nicholas said, his voice breaking.

"Go on."

"He – he – *he said he's been having an affair with Constance!*" Nicholas rushed the words out in horror.

"He said what?" Daniel's face was confused, as if he hadn't heard correctly.

"He said he's slept with Constance. That she visited his flat and they ended up in bed."

Daniel heard the words, but he could hardly comprehend them. "But why would Tom say such a thing?"

"How the hell would I know?" snapped Nicholas.

"Well – we must – we must –" Daniel prided himself in always having a quick and proper solution to any dilemma. But he had to admit he didn't know what to suggest on this occasion. "And do you believe there is any truth to this?" he asked at last.

"No! Of course not! How can you even ask?"

"Because to understand how we must proceed in any given situation, it is first necessary to establish the facts beyond doubt," stated Daniel.

"Oh, Papa! You are not presiding over one of your courts now!"

"That's as it may be, but a serious accusation has been levelled against Constance. She must be told of this accusation and be allowed to act as she sees fit. This is her honour at stake, after all."

"I am not ever going to repeat what Tom said tonight, to anybody other than you. Especially not to Constance!"

"Well, I'm afraid you will have to. Constance has an absolute right to know what has been said about her. And you, due to be her husband in one week, have an absolute right to hear her deny it."

"I'll speak to her tomorrow," conceded Nicholas.

"I shall go with you, and we shall talk to Constance and her father together and inform them of the spurious allegation that has been made by Tom."

"Her father! Have you lost your mind? The Bishop would have a heart attack on the spot if he heard what Tom had said. And, as for her mother, she would be hospitalised for the rest of her life at the very suggestion!"

Daniel shook his head in despair. "I do get your point."

"She is my fiancée. I must talk to her alone," said Nicholas.

"I'm afraid I need to be there as well, Nicholas. It's far too serious for you to handle by yourself. If there is any truth in what Tom said, then you are about to make the biggest mistake of your life."

"There isn't a grain of truth in it. Don't ever say that again!" Nicholas screamed at the top of his voice, giving Daniel a fright.

"Good," said Daniel in a relaxed voice. "And we can establish that without question when we talk to Constance tomorrow." He was determined to be present when Constance was informed of the allegation. His son was a young man very much in love with his fiancée and, as such, prone to believe anything she would say. She wouldn't be able to pull the wool over Daniel's eyes, if that was her intention.

CHAPTER 49

The next day Reeves showed Daniel and Nicholas into the drawing room at the Staffordshire home.

"I'm afraid His Grace is not at home," said Reeves.

"That is fine. We are here to see Miss Constance, if you could let her know," said Daniel.

"Very well, sir."

Daniel sat down in an armchair while Nicholas just stood in the centre of the room in the greatest agitation.

A minute later Constance came rushing through the door.

"Nicholas!" she gasped as she ran into his arms and they held each other tightly. "Are you all right? I've been worried sick about you! I didn't sleep a wink last night." The words came tumbling out of her mouth. "Why on earth did you hit Tom? What did he say?"

"That is what we are here to discuss with you, Constance. If you could take a seat?" said Daniel.

Constance got a start to see Nicholas's father present.

"What's all this about?" she demanded.

"Sit down, dear," urged Daniel.

Nicholas took Constance's hand and they both went and sat on the couch.

"Nicholas certainly did have cause to react as he did last night at the party, although I never condone violence," said Daniel.

"Tom is such a bastard, Constance. It's the only word I can think of to describe him," said Nicholas, gripping her hand tightly.

"Why? What has he said?" asked Constance, fear gripping her.

286

"Tom has made a serious allegation, Constance," said Daniel. "There's no easy way to say this, so I'll just come out and say it . . . he has suggested, nay stated, that you and he have had sexual relations."

Daniel studied her intently for her reaction.

Constance went pale as a ghost and her eyes began to water. She then gave a nervous high-pitched giggle.

"Is this some kind of joke?" she demanded.

"Unfortunately, it is not," said Daniel. "He approached Nicholas last night and told him that you have visited him at his flat, that you brought him food and wine when he was not in employment. That one thing led to another and you ended up – being intimate."

Constance was gripped with panic. She thought of the baby she was carrying. She thought of her wedding day the following week. She thought of her love for Nicholas.

"All lies! Complete and utter lies!" she declared.

Nicholas seemed to heave with relief.

"My darling Constance, I didn't believe it for a moment, you must believe me," he said as he put his arm around her. "Papa said you had to be told though, as it was your right to know what he said."

"I have no idea why he would say those things. Apart from jealousy – he must be jealous of our happiness," said Constance.

"I thought the same thing," said Nicholas. "He's always been jealous of me."

"Yes, he has! It all makes sense now," said Constance.

"What makes sense exactly?" asked Daniel.

"Just his reaction to things. He's never happy when good things happen for Nicholas."

"How do you know this?" asked Daniel.

"From talking to him," said Constance.

"And when have you been talking to him, Constance? Are you alone for these conversations?" queried Daniel.

"No – well, not exactly. If we were at a party at your house, or when Nicholas and I used to visit his rooms at Trinity – I did on occasion speak to him one to one."

"But you've never visited him on your own? At his rooms in Trinity, or at his flat?" Daniel cross-examined her.

"No! Of course not! I don't even know where his flat is since he left Trinity! Let alone visit him there. My father would kill me if I visited a man other than my fiancé on my own."

"I have a question for you, Constance," said Daniel.

"Yes?"

"When you came to me and pleaded for help for Tom to secure a position in a law firm because otherwise he was going to be forced to return to Sligo and give up any dream of a legal career, how did you know this?" Daniel's eyes on her were as steady as his voice as he posed the question.

Constance felt the wind was knocked out of her with this question.

"What's all this about?" asked Nicholas, confused, as he looked from one to the other.

"Constance came to me a while back and said Tom was returning to Sligo and could I do anything to help him. I did, in fact, help him, unknown even to himself, and arranged a position for him at Oakleys' law firm."

"And why did nobody think to tell me of this?" demanded Nicholas.

"To answer your question, Daniel," Constance spoke evenly, "I found out about Tom's predicament the morning of the law-exam results in the front square at Trinity. You and Nicholas went off to speak to an acquaintance, leaving Tom and me alone for – I would say – no longer than five minutes. In a square full of people, with you less than twenty feet away. Hardly a situation to have sexual relations, I would think."

Her voice did not falter as she spoke, and she returned Daniel's stare without flinching. She realised from Daniel's questioning that he was not automatically on her side, contrary to what she would have hoped and expected.

"I wish both of you could have told me of this when it happened!" Nicholas was angry now. "Why didn't you tell me, Constance?"

"I felt sorry for Tom, and was just trying to help him. I didn't

288

think he would return my kindness with such cruel lies!"

"And I always liked Tom, and felt it was no harm if I could assist him," said Daniel, defending himself in turn.

"Oh, Constance, sometimes I think you are too good for your own sake!" chided Nicholas. "You should have let him go back to Sligo and bugger his career!"

"With hindsight, that is exactly what I should have done," said Constance.

"Well, I never want to see him again. He is no longer my friend, let alone my best man next week," said Nicholas bitterly. "He's just a nasty jealous pig. I would never have thought he could be capable of telling such dreadful lies and trying to destroy our happiness."

Daniel said nothing as he looked at the couple tightly holding hands.

"He can't get away with what he's done!" said Nicholas.

"And what do you suggest we do?" asked Daniel.

"I'll – I'll challenge him to a duel!"

"Don't be so ridiculous, Nicholas. This is not the eighteenth century. Duelling is an illegal activity – and besides, you are a dreadful shot!" said Daniel. "What do you suggest be done, Constance?"

"Nothing!" she said. "Nothing at all. As Nicholas says, he is no longer our friend, and will be excluded from our circle. This will be his loss, not ours."

"You are happy to let it rest?" asked Daniel.

"What else can I do?" she asked. "By making any more of it, then we are risking others hearing of his shameless lies. I just don't want to hear any more about it or any more about him."

"Taking everything into consideration, I imagine that is a wise course of action," agreed Daniel.

A double door lay between the front drawing room and the dining room to its rear. Behind the closed door stood Reeves, who had been listening to every word.

That night in their bedroom Daniel and Agatha were preparing for bed.

"I will tell you one thing – that girl is not telling the truth," said Daniel.

"How do you know?" demanded Agatha.

"I have not been a judge for twenty years sitting on the bench without being able to spot a liar in an instant," said Daniel. "And she was lying today. Nicholas believed every word, but I didn't."

"Goodness gracious me!" said Agatha, sitting down on the side of the bed in shock. "So she was with Tom?"

"I can't fathom the situation, but she was covering up – lying. Her whole body demeanour, her answers . . . she's hiding something. And something very serious, that I am sure of."

"But then we must tell Nicholas and stop this wedding!"

"There is no point. He will not believe me. I fear he will turn against us if we try to push it. In fact, I believe he would," sighed Daniel.

"But we can't just let him ruin his life," cried Agatha.

"There is no evidence of this affair between Tom and Constance. It is his word against hers. And Nicholas will always believe her. And she is correct in one thing she says. If we try to bring this any further, than it will become common gossip, and her reputation will be ruined and, as her husband, Nicholas's reputation along with it."

CHAPTER 50

The next day Daniel was in his office in his chambers, having just come back from presiding at court. There was a knock on the door and in walked Henry Shrimpton, a fellow judge who had been a friend for many years.

"Good day to you, Daniel, how are you?"

"Very good, Henry. I'm finishing work today for two weeks. It's my son's wedding next week and so I am taking some time off to spend with the family."

"Yes, so I had heard. An exciting time for you," Henry said, sitting down opposite him.

"Yes, indeed."

"And how is Agatha?"

"Very well. Flapping about, as can be expected of the Mother of the Groom," said Daniel.

"Yes . . . it's Bishop Staffordshire's daughter Nicholas is marrying, is it not?"

"That's right – Constance."

Henry's kindly smile began to drop and his face took on a concerned expression.

"I wanted to have a word with you about Constance Staffordshire," said Henry.

"Constance? Why?" Daniel was perplexed.

"I really had to delve into my conscience as to whether I should come and speak to you at all. I wasn't sure if it was the right thing to do . . . but if it were me, I would want to know."

"Whatever are you talking about, Henry?"

"It's just there's a rumour doing the rounds of the law circles – about her."

"What kind of a rumour?" Daniel began to fill with dread.

"I mean, I don't know the girl at all. I know Bishop Staffordshire vaguely – and what I know of him, I find it very hard to believe what everyone is saying about his daughter."

Daniel sat up straight. "What are people saying?"

"Well, they are saying that she has been sleeping with another man behind Nicholas's back," stated Henry.

Daniel momentarily closed his eyes in dread. His worst fears had quickly been realised. Tom had not been content in just saying what he had said to Nicholas but had also told others and, by the sound of it, many others. In Dublin's tight-knit legal world rumours spread like wildfire. That was why it was so important to keep one's reputation squeaky clean. The vultures began to circulate very quickly and they fed on scandal.

"I see, thank you for telling me," said Daniel.

"I thought it best you know. If it were my son . . ."

"Indeed."

"I mean, I'm sure there's no truth in the rumour," continued Henry. "George Fetherston doesn't strike me as the type who would take another man's fiancée."

"*George Fetherston!*" cried Daniel.

"Yes, you know, from Fetherstons' Solicitors?"

"But – who is spreading these rumours?" asked Daniel, now completely confounded.

"Well, I suppose that's the point it all, and why I felt you should know – it's George Fetherston himself who says he slept with Constance Staffordshire."

Agatha looked at Daniel in horror as he retold the conversation he had with Henry Shrimpton.

"George Fetherston! Nicholas's colleague?"

They were in Daniel's study at home. He had brought her in there to discuss the situation without fear of being disturbed.

"Yes, the son of the firm's owner."

"But – but I don't think George Fetherston is even a friend of Nicholas. I have never heard Nicholas say they socialised together, so how on earth could Constance even have got to know him?"

"I don't know . . . but . . ."

"But what?"

"At Milandra Carter's party, I did see Constance talking to George Fetherston for a quite a while. In fact, I remember it was George she was speaking to just before she had her episode and started shouting and screaming at Nicholas and Milandra in the garden. Perhaps somehow he was the cause of her display that night?"

"Oh, my goodness, you are right! I saw them too." Agatha closed her eyes in despair. "They are clearly acquainted with each other! Daniel! What are we going to do? It's a few days to the wedding and first Tom, and now George Fetherston – there is obviously another side to Constance that none of us have ever been aware of, although we did get a glimpse of it the night of Milandra Carter's party. We can't let Nicholas marry her!"

"I will go and see George Fetherston tomorrow and confront him on what Henry told me."

"Are you not going to tell Nicholas?" asked Agatha.

"No! You saw how he reacted when Tom said what he did. If he heard what George Fetherston was saying, he'd be likely to commit murder."

"Daniel!"

"Well, he said he was going to challenge Tom to a duel."

"Oh my! That little hussy Constance! She's going to end up ruining him!"

"Where is Nicholas now?"

"He's gone out to meet some friends."

Nicholas walked down by the river, deep in thought. He hadn't seen or spoken to Tom since their fight. He never wanted to speak to him or see him again. How could his dear friend Tom say such terrible things? Was he so jealous of his happiness that he didn't care what he said or did?

Nicholas had arranged to meet some of his other college friends that night to take his mind off everything. His brother was now going to be his best man. He should have never asked Tom in the first place.

Nicholas reached the tavern. There was loud music and laughter coming from inside. He pushed open the door and entered. The tavern was packed with people and he spotted the table where six of his friends were already there enjoying beer. They were laughing and seemed in good spirits. As he walked across the tavern and they saw him, their laughter and talk abruptly stopped and they all looked at him.

"Hello, everyone!" he said as he took a spare seat and sat down, wondering why they were staring at him.

"Hello, Fontenoy," a couple of them answered back.

A barmaid brought him over a large tankard of beer and he took a big gulp from it.

Nobody was saying anything as they all stared at Nicholas.

"So – what's been happening?" he asked.

"Eh – nothing – nothing at all!" answered one.

As Nicholas smiled at them, waiting to engage in banter, he realised something was definitely wrong. His friends were looking embarrassed, and giving each other sly looks.

"Is something the matter?" he asked.

"No – nothing – nothing at all! Anything new with you?"

"Just getting ready for the big day next week! I hope you'll all be at my wedding?"

The young men looked incredulously at each other.

"Yes, eh, of course. Wouldn't dream of missing it," answered one.

"How – is – Constance?" asked another.

"Excellent!"

"Really?"

Nicholas stared at him in surprise. "Why should she not be?"

"No reason!" he answered and then burst into giggles.

"Is something the matter? Has anybody got something to say?" demanded Nicholas.

"No!" they all cried in unison.

"Good!" said Nicholas, taking another swig of beer.

"I have to say, Fontenoy, you're taking it all very well," said one brave chap, sitting forward.

"Taking what well?" demanded Nicholas.

"The fact that your fiancée slept with your best man Tom!" he answered, his face full of mirth.

Nicholas felt like somebody had punched him in the stomach.

"Still – perhaps it may be a good thing for you! At least your wife will already know what to do on your wedding night!"

Three of the young men erupted in laughter while the other three looked embarrassed.

Nicholas jumped to his feet and, reaching forward, swiped all the tankards of beer from the table onto the floor in a rage.

"Fontenoy!"

But Nicholas had already turned and was running out of the tavern.

As he ran down the street, he was consumed with anger and disbelief. What had happened to his life? What had happened to Constance and himself?

CHAPTER 51

Daniel did not want to discuss the situation with George Fetherston at his work. So he made enquiries as to where the man lived. His flat was in a handsome Georgian building at the bottom of Parliament Street.

The following evening Daniel made his way to the top floor and knocked on the door of the flat. A moment later, George stood there.

"Judge Fontenoy," said George, not looking as surprised to see him as Daniel would have expected.

"May I come in?"

"Of course," said George, standing aside.

Daniel entered and looked around at the flat which was plush and glamorous. He didn't know too much of George Fetherston but, since he had made his enquiries, he had discovered that George was quite the ladies' man with a penchant for rich living.

"Please, take a seat," urged George.

"You don't seem that surprised to see me," said Daniel, sitting down.

"How can I help you, sir?"

"It has come to my attention that you have been spreading malicious and vicious lies about my son's fiancée, Miss Constance Staffordshire."

"Really?"

"Don't play with me, boy – have you or haven't you?"

"Anything I have said about my relationship with Constance is not a lie," said George evenly.

"Your *relationship*? How do you even know her? You're not a friend of my son's?"

"I met her on the street," George said.

"The *street*!"

"Yes, she was hanging around Parliament Street in the evenings where our offices are. I began to talking to her . . . to be honest, when I saw her first I thought she was a prostitute looking for trade."

"For pity's sake!"

"But she didn't seem dressed like the ones that I've usually seen hanging around street corners looking for trade, and her manner didn't indicate she was one. And so my interest was piqued and I went to speak to her."

"And – and do you make a habit of speaking to women you do not know in the street?" asked Daniel.

"If they are attractive – then yes."

Daniel shook his head in disgusted disapproval. "And what happened between you?"

"Do you really want to hear all this?" asked George.

"Since you have already told enough people about your alleged affair with my future daughter-in-law and it is the talk of the legal world, then I suggest it is too late to feign discretion now!"

George shrugged, took out a cigar and lit it before sitting down. "Very well, if you insist. I struck up a conversation with her. I learned she was waiting for Nicholas who had been delayed in work, and she asked me if I knew how long he would be. I met her again on another occasion while she was waiting in Parliament Street and, I suppose, we struck up a friendship. She told me she was having problems with Nicholas at the time . . . she appeared distressed so I invited her back here to talk . . . I suppose she confided in me. One thing led to another, and we ended up in bed together. It was only the once – it wasn't 'an affair' as you called it."

"And – you did this knowing she was my son's fiancée?" Daniel was trying to understand him.

"Yes, it was she who was engaged, not I. It was for her

297

conscience, not mine," said George.

"Young man, I urge you to examine whatever conscience you have. I have had a great deal of respect for your father over the years, but you are not like him in any way. You have no moral compass, if what you are saying is right. And are no gentleman."

"I never pretended to be a gentleman," George shrugged. "And what I am saying is correct. I don't know why Constance cheated on Nicholas with me. It was obvious she was in love with him. Perhaps to teach him a lesson? They were having difficulties and I believe she thought the relationship was over. I was a shoulder to cry on, amongst other things."

"I have no wish to hear your opinion of why she did what she did, if I can believe what you are saying is true," said Daniel.

"Oh, it's true all right," he said, extinguishing his cigar in an ashtray.

He got up and walked over to a sideboard. Pulling out a drawer, he took out a bracelet.

He walked over to Daniel and handed it to him.

Daniel examined it. It was a silver bracelet with the engraving *Constance* on it.

"She left this behind. You might return it to her when you see her next," said George.

Daniel stood up.

"Thank you for your honesty, if nothing else," said Daniel. "My son has ceased employment at Fetherstons', for which I am very glad, as I hope none of my family ever have occasion to meet you again."

CHAPTER 52

After leaving the tavern Nicholas walked aimlessly through the streets of Dublin for what seemed like hours. All manner of thoughts were racing through his mind. Now all his friends knew the lies that Tom had made up about Constance. And from the comments in the tavern, his friends were believing the lies. He was becoming a laughing stock. If it was older times he would challenge Tom to a duel; now, he didn't know what to do. The woman who would be his wife in less than a week had a reputation that was severely tarnished. And once a woman's reputation was tarnished, it was near impossible to repair the damage. He suddenly found himself becoming angry with Constance. Why had she allowed herself to become even friendly with Tom? As the thoughts went racing through his mind, he remembered how she always seemed to enjoy being in Tom's company. How fond she was of him. How she would bring lunch to Tom as well as Nicholas during exam times. He remembered the day he was choosing his best man – whether it should be Tom or Frederick. He remembered how he had left the decision to Constance and she had opted for Tom. "I choose Tom" were the words she had used.

"Nicholas!" came the call from the drawing room late that night as he let himself in through his front door.

He walked to the drawing room and inside he found his parents waiting for him.

"How were your friends tonight?" asked Daniel.

"I didn't stay long in the tavern . . . I couldn't."

"Why ever not?" asked Agatha.

Nicholas looked distressed as he went to sit down the couch. "Tom has told all my friends that he has been with Constance. He's spread the lies. Why would he do something like that? I've been his best friend for years. Supported him, helped him. We were like brothers."

Daniel and Agatha exchanged distraught looks.

"Nicholas – did you ever – has it occurred to you that what Tom is saying – might be true?" asked Daniel softly.

Nicholas stared at his father in disbelief. "Of course not! Why would you say such a thing?"

"I want you to brace yourself for what I'm about to tell you, son . . . I visited George Fetherston this evening."

"George? Whatever for?"

"It had been brought to my attention that a rumour was circulating concerning George Fetherston and Constance," said Daniel.

Nicholas's expression darkened. "What kind of a rumour?"

"A rumour that young Fetherston had shared intimate relations with Constance . . . I confronted him and he confirmed it was the truth. And I believe him," said Daniel gravely.

Nicholas jumped to his feet. "What the hell is going on here? Why would Fetherston claim such a thing? And why would you believe him?"

Daniel reached into his pocket and took out Constance's bracelet and handed it to Nicholas. "Do you recognise it? I believe it belongs to Constance. She left it behind at Fetherston's flat."

Nicholas scrutinised the bracelet in horror. "How did he get this? There's a simple explanation . . . he must have stolen it . . . he took it from her when he was helping me take her to the carriage the night of Milandra's party!"

It was Daniel's turn to jump up as he became angry. "Will you see sense, boy! First Tom, now Fetherston! And both your mother and I saw Fetherston and her speaking quite intimately at Milandra's party. How was she acquainted with him? Did you know they knew each other?"

"No!"

"Look at her behaviour that night of Milandra's party," said Daniel. "She's clearly a most unstable girl! Something has obviously happened to Constance this past while. She has become somebody different from the girl we knew and all loved. And with her reputation now in tatters, you have no option but to call off the wedding!"

"I will not call off my wedding to Constance! I simply can't believe all this rubbish!"

"For pity's sake!" exclaimed Agatha, feeling traumatised by the scandal that was flooding to their door. "There must be a simple way to disprove all this dreadfulness. A medical examination! Constance can have a medical examination to prove that she has not been with these men."

"*What*?" yelled Nicholas. "You are asking for my fiancée to submit to such humiliation?"

"I believe it is standard practice for girls marrying into the Russian Royal family!" Agatha defended her suggestion.

"And what do you propose we do with the results of this medical examination to retrieve Constance's lost reputation?" asked Daniel. "Print the results in the *Irish Times* to confirm her virginity!"

"Well, at least it would satisfy us!" retorted Agatha.

"And what would the Bishop say if we requested his daughter should undergo such an examination? What could we give as our reasons?" asked Daniel.

"We could try the truth!" said Agatha.

"And give the man an early heart attack? And his wife one as well while we're at it?" said Daniel.

Nicholas sank down on the couch, ashen-faced, as his parents continued to argue.

"Stop!" he muttered, head in hands. "There would be no point."

"What did you say?" asked his father.

Nicholas was silent.

"Nicholas?"

"There would be no point in such an examination," whispered Nicholas.

"Why ever not?"

Nicholas sighed loudly before saying, "Because she would not pass it."

Daniel and Agatha stared at Nicholas in confusion before realisation dawned on each of them at the same time.

"Oh Nicholas – say it isn't so!" pleaded Daniel.

"You have bedded her?" asked Agatha.

"She is my fiancée! We are to be wed shortly. Are we not entitled to?"

"No! Of course you aren't!" exclaimed Agatha in horror. "Not till your wedding night!"

Daniel face was full of disappointment. "For the first time in my life, Nicholas, I am ashamed of you."

"Well – that's that then!" Agatha sat back and threw her arms in the air. "If she's bedded you, then she has obviously bedded Tom and George Fetherston as well – and probably half of Dublin while she was at it. Thank goodness we discovered it before the wedding rather than after when it would be too late and she would have destroyed our family. Who would ever have thought it of her, a Bishop's daughter? It reminds me of when I was growing up in Mayo. One of my contemporaries was a young woman who looked as if butter wouldn't melt in her mouth. It turned out she had slept with half of the hunt!"

"I will visit the Bishop tomorrow and inform him the wedding is off," said Daniel. "I will try to refrain from repeating the gorier details of the whole debacle, though I daresay he will hear about it all soon enough from other sources."

"I feel sorry for her. What will become of her now?" sighed Agatha.

"She has made her own bed – nay, many beds! And she must live with the consequences," said Daniel. "It is Nicholas we must concern ourselves with now, and try to limit any of the scandal that will follow his name from being attached to her."

Suddenly, Nicholas jumped up from the couch and ran out of the room.

"*Nicholas!*" Daniel shouted after him.

As they heard the front door open and slam shut, Agatha cried, "Oh, go after him, Daniel! There's no knowing what he might do in his condition."

Daniel went racing out into the night.

CHAPTER 53

"*Nicholas! Nicholas!*" cried Daniel as he tried to race up the street after his son. But Nicholas was going so fast that Daniel was many paces behind him.

Daniel followed him up to the top of Rutland Square and through the maze of gaslight-lit streets that led to Mountjoy Square.

"*Nicholas! Don't do anything stupid!*" Daniel shouted after him.

But Nicholas had reached the Staffordshire front door and was hammering on it heavily.

It took a couple of minutes for Reeves to answer the door.

"Who is it?" demanded Reeves from inside, seeing from the clock on the wall that it had just turned midnight.

"Nicholas Fontenoy! Open up! I want to see Constance!"

Reeves hastily opened the door and Nicholas went rushing in.

"Where is she?" he demanded.

"Miss Constance has retired to bed, Mr. Nicholas!" said a shocked Reeves.

"Well, get her up! I want to see her!"

The Bishop had fallen asleep on an armchair in the drawing room while reading a book. With the commotion he woke up.

"What is all this racket?" he demanded as he came stumbling into the hallway.

Daniel reached the front door and hurried in to find Nicholas there shouting to see Constance. A shocked Bishop and Reeves

304

stood beside him, while at the top of the stairs Daniel could see Henrietta and Emma cowering.

Upstairs in her bedroom on the third floor, Constance was standing in her wedding dress, looking at herself in the full-length mirror. The dressmakers had visited that afternoon, adding the final touches and now it was perfect. As Constance stood admiring the fabulous ivory-white creation, she heard a commotion downstairs. She went to her door and opened it and could hear Nicholas's voice. She gathered her train up and headed down the landing and down the stairs to the second floor. At the end of that landing she found her mother and sister, looking confused and scared.

"Whatever is the matter?" demanded Constance.

"It's Nicholas. He's demanding to see you," said Emma.

Henrietta and Emma was so preoccupied with the commotion downstairs that they barely registered that Constance was in her wedding gown.

Constance looked downstairs and saw Nicholas ranting at the top of his voice while Daniel tried to calm him down.

Constance pushed Emma out of the way and hurried down to the hallway.

"Nicholas! What's wrong with you?" she pleaded.

Nicholas was taken aback at the sight of Constance in her full wedding gown, and was stunned into silence by the sight of her.

"Nicholas? What is the meaning of this?" she insisted.

"I know all about you! I know everything about you!" accused Nicholas.

Constance paled at his words but put on a brave face.

"You are making no sense, Nicholas!" she cried.

"You lied to me when you said you didn't sleep with Tom!" His voice was harsh and loud.

"*What*?" cried the Bishop.

"I know you lied now! And I know about you and George Fetherston!"

"What about George Fetherston?" cried the Bishop.

Nicholas turned and looked witheringly at him. "Your precious daughter slept with him, Your Grace. In case you don't understand what I'm saying, she had sexual relations with my best friend Tom Fitzgerald and my work colleague George Fetherston. Your daughter is a whore, Your Grace."

"*Mother!*" squealed Emma at the top of the stairs as Henrietta collapsed on the landing.

Constance stared at Nicholas in disbelief. This wasn't her kind, loving Nicholas. This was a stranger, with hate and venom pouring out of his eyes at her.

"*You –!*" she screamed as she lurched at him, her arms flailing in anger. As she lurched, the train of her wedding dress caught on the stair railing and ripped viciously.

She began to strike him anywhere she could. "*Get out! Get out of my home! Out of my life!*" she yelled at him as her clenched fists rained down on him.

"To think I was once thinking that you should move into my parents' home!" he hissed at her as he managed to restrain her by the wrists. "You're not good enough to walk past their house!"

"*I never want to see you again!*" Constance screamed.

"Don't worry – you never will!" Nicholas promised.

"Nicholas! That's enough!" commanded Daniel as he stepped forward and separated the couple. "We must leave immediately, Nicholas."

Daniel pushed Nicholas out the front door then looked back before closing it.

Constance stood like a statue in the centre of the hall, in her ruined wedding dress, her face covered in angry tears. Reeves was helping the Bishop to a chair to sit down, the Bishop looking incapable of being able to walk unassisted. While at the top of the stairs, Emma was kneeling as she frantically tried to revive her mother.

Daniel closed the door on the scene of chaos.

As Constance watched the front door close she saw her future close with it. She slowly turned and began to climb the stairs. The house was in an eerie silence after all of Nicholas's filthy screaming.

On reaching the first floor, she stepped over her mother's groaning form.

"What have you done?" demanded Emma, but Constance ignored her and continued almost in a trance up to the third floor and into her bedroom. She slowly closed the door behind her and locked it. Moving slowly to the bed, she sat down on the side in shock.

CHAPTER 54

"I'll sue!" declared the Bishop. "I'll sue every last one of them! I'll sue this Tom Fitzgerald and this George Fetherston for slander, for trying to ruin my daughter's good name! And I'll sue Nicholas Fontenoy for making up the most dreadful lies . . . and for breach of contract! He can't just end his engagement to Constance over these unscrupulous and vicious lies he has made up! By the time I'm finished with them Daniel Fontenoy and his precious son will be crawling on their hands and knees up to my front door, begging for my forgiveness!"

It was the next morning and only Emma and the Bishop were at the table being served breakfast by Reeves.

Emma tried not to stare at her father in his extremely agitated state. The Bishop had spent the night in the drawing room, unable to sleep. He had paced up and down after he had managed to regain the strength to stand again after Nicholas's outburst.

"How is your mother?" asked the Bishop.

"She's still in bed. Barely able to talk," said Emma.

"Traumatised! The poor woman is traumatised after experiencing such a – a – a horrendous scene."

"Perhaps I should fetch the doctor?" ventured Emma.

"No! We want no more strangers in the house for now! Just keep her in a darkened room and keep feeding her water. And – and how is Constance?" He was almost afraid to ask.

"I don't know. Her door is locked and she won't answer me when I call to her."

The Bishop nodded and looked lost in thought before he spouted again, "I'll sue them! I'll make them pay! They'll be sorry!"

"I think I'll go and check on Mother," said Emma as she quietly rose from the table and left the room.

As Reeves cleared away the breakfast plates, he covertly watched the Bishop who looked completely lost and in another world.

"Your Grace, may I have a word?"

"Not now, Reeves."

"It's very pertinent, Your Grace."

"Pertinent? What do you mean?"

"I feel compelled to tell you the truth. Daniel Fontenoy and Nicholas Fontenoy visited the house here to see Miss Constance recently. I stayed in the dining room here, and could hear their conversation through the double doors to the drawing room."

"Why was I not told of this visit?"

"I didn't think it my place to say anything at the time, Your Grace . . . I overheard Mr. Nicholas tell Miss Constance that this Tom Fitzgerald had bragged about having sexual intercourse with her."

"*What*? And what did Miss Constance say to this disgusting accusation?"

"She denied it."

"Well, then!" said the Bishop, managing to look comforted.

"The fact is, Your Grace, I know Miss Constance was lying to them," said Reeves.

"What do you mean?"

"This Tom Fitzgerald had said that Miss Constance had visited him at his flat and that she had brought him food and *wine*. She denied to the Fontenoys that she had ever visited his flat or brought him groceries. But I caught Miss Constance previously in the kitchen with a bag of groceries and *wine* and, when I questioned her, she told me she was taking them to Tom Fitzgerald's flat for him."

The Bishop managed to grow even paler as he stared ahead.

"I'm sorry, Your Grace, to be the one to inform you of this. She told me Mr. Fitzgerald was down on his luck and that was why she was bringing him supplies. But I can't let you sue as you say you intend to without telling you this, for I fear Miss Constance is in the wrong and you will be shamed publicly and destroyed if you try to bring this to a court. Forgive me for saying this, but I have begun to question Miss Constance's character recently. While you and the rest of the family were at the conference in Limerick, Mr. Nicholas paid a visit to the house here and went straight up to Miss Constance's room, where they spent the afternoon. I heard strange sounds coming from the room, Your Grace. I fear Mr. Nicholas was telling the truth last night."

The Bishop stood up silently from the table and walked out of the dining room.

CHAPTER 55

Later that morning, the Bishop left the house and made his way to his office. When he arrived there he found Lady Vrayford in his reception waiting for him.

"I apologise, Lady Vrayford, I forgot about our appointment," he said, showing her into his office.

"We didn't have an appointment, Your Grace, but I had to come and see you," she said as she walked across his office and plonked her ample behind on a chair.

Lady Vrayford was one of the Bishop's biggest benefactors for his charities and had been donating to his causes for many years.

"How can I help you, Lady Vrayford?"

"I've come to inform you, Your Grace, that I will cease from having any involvement in your charities from now on."

"I see," said the Bishop, sitting back in his chair. "May I ask why?"

"You most certainly can, Your Grace, and I can certainly answer. It is because of your daughter. I just can't allow myself to be associated with the family of a girl of such low moral character. I mean the whole point of the work of your charities is to try to direct the young women from deprived areas to live good, moral, respectable lives. And how can we do that when Constance is setting such a dreadful example? I mean, there are so many rumours circulating about the girl at this stage that she is little better than a harlot!"

"Get out," the Bishop said lowly.

"I beg your pardon?"

"Get out! Get out of my office now!" the Bishop shouted, jumping to his feet.

"Well, really!" said Lady Vrayford, standing up.

The Bishop marched over the door and held it open for her as she marched out. Then he slammed the door shut and sank to his knees, sobbing loudly into his hands.

"F-l-a-a-n-c-y!" called Milandra loudly as she came flying through the front door of her house.

"What is it, Milandra?" called Flancy from the top of the stairs.

"Oh, Flancy, the most wonderful news!" Milandra gathered her skirts and climbed quickly up the stairs.

"What?" demanded Flancy as she followed her into the drawing room.

"The engagement is off! Nicholas has broken off his engagement with Constance!" Milandra took off her bonnet and cape and flung them on a couch.

"I don't believe it!"

"It's true, I tell you! It's the talk of Sackville Street! Seemingly Constance was unfaithful to him! Can you believe that! She's been with his best man, and one of Nicholas's work colleagues, and half of Dublin from what I'm hearing!"

"Surely not!" Flancy was shocked.

"Surely so! I know! I could hardly believe it of that little mouse myself. Still waters run deep!"

"And you should never judge a book by its cover," concurred Flancy.

"But isn't it wonderful news? I mean, now Nicholas and I stand a chance! With her not around, we can move our relationship on!"

"Yes – but you ended on very bad terms with Nicholas," Flancy pointed out.

"It wasn't *that* bad!"

"He called you a whore!"

"*Pah!* People say all sorts when they're upset. And the course of true love never runs smooth. We are just friends who had a bit of a spat. I'm sure he has forgotten all about it, with everything he has had to put up with regarding this Constance scandal. The poor man!"

"Hmmm . . ."

"I think I'll pay the Fontenoys a visit," said Milandra.

"For goodness' sake, Milandra, give it a little time!"

"But why?"

"For decency's sake!" snapped Flancy.

"There wasn't much decent about Constance Staffordshire, from what I hear. He needs a shoulder to cry on. And I'm very good at listening to other people's problems."

"You are all heart," smirked Flancy.

"It's an awful pity one cannot announce the ending of an engagement in the *Times* in the same manner as one announces the beginning of one," mused Agatha as she sat with Nicholas and Daniel in their drawing room.

"I think there is no need for such an announcement," said Daniel. "With all those rumours circulating about Constance, I imagine people have guessed, nay, expected Nicholas to have broken off the engagement."

"Well, I've made sure everyone we know is aware the engagement is off! The scandal of it all!" cried Agatha. "Who would have ever thought it of her? Constance Staffordshire, the Bishop's daughter!"

"She has broken my heart," whispered Nicholas.

"A broken heart can be mended, a broken reputation cannot. And Constance will never be able to recover from her broken reputation. She is destroyed. It is her parents I feel sorry for," said Daniel.

"Utterly destroyed!" concurred Agatha.

"Perhaps her parents are to blame," mused Daniel. "Perhaps she rebelled after being brought up in such a strict environment."

"Maybe she had a nervous breakdown, that could explain her actions," offered Agatha.

"Or she took to the drink!" said Daniel. "I mean, she was drunk at Milandra's party – the writing was on the wall when one thinks of her behaviour that night. She must have been drinking heavily and secretly and that led her to do what she did. I see it all the time in my court – drink is the ruination of many a man and woman."

"Who cares why she did it?" muttered Nicholas. "She did it, that's the point! And ruined my life."

"You are not whiter than white in this whole unfortunate episode yourself, Nicholas," said Daniel sternly. "There is a reason the wedding vows are there, and you flaunted them by bedding your fiancée before the wedding night! I would never have thought it of you. I have never been ashamed of you before, but I am now! You're as much a part of that girl's downfall as anybody else."

"Well, I think she is primarily the cause of her own downfall," said Agatha.

"But – what am I do now?" asked Nicholas forlornly.

"I know exactly what you are to do. I have written to the law firm in London this morning, informing them that you will not be taking up your position with them. As you will now not be getting married, you will not be going to London. I have arranged a new position for you at Gilligans' law firm, starting Monday morning eight sharp. Do you understand?"

"Yes, Papa," answered Nicholas meekly.

CHAPTER 56

Constance stared out her bedroom window at the park that occupied the centre of Mountjoy Square. It was the same view she had seen all her life. The nannies from the fine Georgian houses that surrounded the park were out with their charges, the children playing happily. And yet it all looked different. It looked completely different from the day before. But then everything looked different. It was as if what happened the previous night had been a bad dream. That she would wake up and find it didn't happen. That she was still blissfully engaged to Nicholas and they would be man and wife the following week. But one look at her wedding gown in a crumpled heap in the corner of the room made her realise it was all terrifyingly real. She didn't know what to do. And, as she thought of the baby she was carrying, that nobody knew about, she knew that no matter how bad things were now, they would truly erupt when her pregnancy became apparent.

Emma had come to her door sporadically during the day, begging to be allowed in. But Constance couldn't face her, or her parents. She needed to get out of the house, to go for a walk, to clear her head. She grabbed a cape from her wardrobe and quietly unlocked her bedroom door. She sneaked down the landing and, seeing the coast was clear, made her way down the stairs to the ground floor. She flew across the hall and let herself out the front door.

She quickly raced across to the park and made her way through it to the other side of Mountjoy Square and began to walk down

315

the streets that led to Rutland Square and Sackville Street.

When she came to the Fontenoys' house, she paused and looked up at it. There was no sign of activity, and she could see nobody through the windows. She hurried on, in case she was spotted, and was relieved when she got to busy Sackville Street.

She was lost in thought as she made her way down the street. So much so that she was oblivious to the stares and glances she was getting from people passing her by. But when she got to Delaneys' Monster store, she couldn't help but notice a group of young girls that she knew gathered at the doorway. When they saw her, the girls huddled together and began to whisper and giggle and she noticed a couple of them pointing to her. Ignoring them, she continued down the street.

She saw two young women she knew well walk in her direction. They were out shopping and carried hat boxes. On seeing her, one started whispering in the other's ear, which caused the other young woman to gasp, her hand flying to cover her open mouth. Constance quickened her pace past them.

As she continued to the end of the street, she became more aware of the stares she was getting. Some young men were coming in her direction that she vaguely recognised as Trinity students.

They all became excited at the sight of her and, as she passed them, they started jeering and calling after her.

"*Constance! Constance!*" they catcalled, in a way she had never heard young men of their breeding speak to a young lady in public before.

She didn't know what to do as she frantically hurried on away from them, their catcalling becoming obscene in her wake.

As she reached Carlisle Bridge at the bottom of the street, she saw Mrs. Vickers walking across the same side of the bridge as her. Mrs. Vickers, that paragon of virtue in Dublin society, who was a good friend of the family.

"Hello, Mrs. Vickers," greeted Constance.

Mrs. Vickers stopped abruptly. "I was not going to acknowledge you, Constance, but intended to walk past you with my head in the air. However, I think I should take this opportunity to let you know that you are a disgrace! You are a disgrace to your parents and to yourself! There's only one place where young women like you end up, but I'm too much of a lady to even say the word. Good day!"

Constance stared after her in shock. As she stood there on Carlisle Bridge, a man in his thirties who she did not even recognise walked straight up to her. He was well dressed and smart. He was smiling and he took his hat off to her.

"Miss Staffordshire, I believe?"

"Yes, what do you want?"

"I would like to invite you to have a drink with me," he said, and his smile turned to a leer.

"I beg your pardon?"

He leaned towards her and whispered, "There's a tavern nearby, and it has hotel rooms upstairs. I'll make it worth your while, whatever you charge."

"Oh!" cried Constance as she backed away in horror from the man.

She ran out into the street and frantically flagged down a hansom cab.

"Mountjoy Square!" she commanded the driver as she climbed into the back of the cab. "As quick as you can!"

When the cab reached her home, she paid the driver and ran up the steps to the front door. Letting herself in, she flew up the stairs to her room, where she threw herself on her bed and sobbed her heart out.

CHAPTER 57

That night Emma knocked on Constance's door.

"Constance?" she called but there was no answer. She reached down and tried the handle on the door and to her surprise found the door unlocked. She pushed the door open and entered and saw Constance lying face down on her bed.

"Constance, are you awake?" she asked as she moved over to the bed and, sitting down, placed a hand on her sister's shoulder.

Constance raised her head and, turning around, sat up.

"Oh, Constance!" whispered Emma as she witnessed her sister's tear-stained, anguished face.

Constance said nothing, but her eyes said everything.

"Father and Mother are in the drawing room – they want to speak with you. They have to speak with you."

Constance nodded and sighed loudly as she climbed off the bed.

"Are you up to speaking to them?" asked Emma.

"As you said, I have to," said Constance and she went to the mirror and wiped her face with a handkerchief. "Lead the way."

She followed Emma out of the room and down the stairs, preparing herself for what was to come.

As they reached the drawing-room door, Emma gave Constance a brief supportive smile.

In the drawing room the Bishop was sitting in an armchair while Henrietta was on the couch. Constance got a fright when she saw them. Both of them looked as if they had aged ten years overnight.

As Emma sat beside her mother and took her hand, Constance

walked over to an armchair to sit down, nearly stumbling and falling.

She took her seat and could not look either of her parents in the eye.

"Well?" asked the Bishop eventually. "I think we deserve some kind of an explanation from you. I think you owe us at least that."

Constance cleared her throat. "I'm afraid it is far too late to offer any explanation, Father . . . for I am with child. I am pregnant."

PART 8

1916

CHAPTER 58

Milandra found it hard to sleep on the Tuesday night. The gunfire seemed to be more intense and not as distant, the looters louder and more riotous. She lay on her bed for a while, but sleep didn't come. As she lay there, the years of her life began to play before her. Thinking back over everything. Thinking that if she should be killed in the carnage of this revolution, it would be a very strange way to die after all she had done and been through. And yet she was not scared. Perhaps it was as she had said to Seán: an old buzzard like her had seen everything already.

She made her way down to the kitchen in the basement as the sun came up and, taking out a baking bowl and ingredients, got to work. Time passed as she became engrossed in the task and her mind drifted from the situation she was in.

With the two baking tins of sponge cake at last in the oven, she turned to making some sandwiches for Seán and his men, and boiled a kettle for tea.

She then checked on the cake and smiled in satisfaction when she saw that both layers had risen beautifully. Just as she was taking the tins from the oven, Seán entered the kitchen.

"What are you doing now?" he asked in surprise.

"What does it look like? I'm making a cake."

"*A cake!*" he guffawed. "Why?"

"Because I find baking very therapeutic. I always have." She ran a knife around the edges of the cake layers to loosen them from their tins, then gently turned them out onto a wire baking rack to cool.

"I never thought the likes of you would be in a kitchen baking. Didn't think you would know how – you must have a load of servants to do that for you."

"I used to have the best cook in Dublin. Her name was Flancy, and she taught me to bake. She taught me very well. It's a form of art, I've always thought. Making a cake just perfect."

"I see!"

"Oh, I made sandwiches for you and your friends," she said, nodding to the plates waiting for him at the bottom of the table, each laden with several large sandwiches. "Can't let you starve."

Seán shook his head in bewilderment and went to pick up the plates for his companions.

"No," said Milandra. "Sit and eat. I'll make a pot of tea and you can take some up to them with the sandwiches."

Seán sat down to eat. "Thanks."

"See. I knew we could become old friends," she said with a wink as she scalded a teapot. "In fact, I might be much more sympathetic to your cause than you think. I just don't approve of your methods."

He munched away on a sandwich as she made the tea and poured some for him.

She placed a sugar bowl and a jug of milk in front of him then went to the refrigerator and brought back a big jug of cream.

"Where did you get that?" asked Seán, pointing to the refrigerator. He had never seen one before.

"I imported it from America. Everyone has one on Fifth Avenue, I understand."

He watched as she poured the cream into a bowl and began to beat it with a wire whisk.

"Do you bake for your family?" he asked.

"No, not any more. I used to a little when my granddaughter Amelia was a child."

"Do you have many grandchildren?"

"Just Amelia. And I have only one child – Petronella. Dreadful girl." She looked at him and smiled. "We don't get on."

"Right!" He smirked back at her.

"I don't blame her, it's all my fault. I didn't give her a very good basis. I was too wrapped up in other things to be a dedicated mother. That's why I don't think this suffragette woman you are with would be very good for you. People who are too wrapped up in causes and other things don't make very good spouses or parents."

"I'll bear that in mind!" He shook his head and laughed.

She pointed the whisk, dripping in cream, at him and fixed him with her eyes. "Do! You could learn a lot from an old buzzard like me."

"I'm sure!"

"What you should do is take yourself off to America, if you don't get killed this week. Start anew. Build a new life for yourself. After all this I don't think Ireland is going to be a good place to be for a long time. America – that's where you should go."

"I'll be staying here to build the new republic," he said as he pushed his empty plate away.

She raised her eyes to heaven. "Indeed!"

He watched, nearly mesmerised, as she spread strawberry jam on one of the cake halves and topped the jam with a generous layer of thickly whipped cream. She then gently placed the other half of the cake on top and dusted it with powdered sugar. Finally, she brought some strawberries from the refrigerator and decorated the top of the cake with cut strawberries nestled in swirls of cream.

"Now, what do you think?" she asked, stepping back from the finished cake and admiring it.

"Not bad!" he said with a smirk. "Not bad at –"

Suddenly a gigantic explosion rocked the house, causing Milandra to stumble. Seán jumped to his feet.

"*What the fuck was that?*" he roared.

Milandra steadied herself. She saw Seán fly across the kitchen and up the stairs. She followed him and found Seán with the two others hunkered at the dining-room window, peering out.

"What was that?" she asked, just as a second explosion erupted, causing the building to shake.

"*Fuck!*" shouted Seán as he cowered.

Getting up, he saw a rebel running down the street outside the house. With his pistol handle, Seán smashed one of the window panes.

"*What's happening?*" he roared at the rebel.

The rebel stopped momentarily and shouted back. "*They're shelling us! They've sent a gunship up the river and its guns are aimed on Sackville Street!*" Then he raced off again.

Milandra watched as Seán and the others in the house began whispering frantically to each other.

A third blast detonated somewhere in Sackville Street.

Milandra quickly turned and made her way across the hallway and up the stairs to her bedroom. She took out a leather bag and quickly started taking out her jewellery and shoving it into the bag. She scurried across the room and began to unlock drawers, grabbing any valuables she could lay her hands on and throwing them into the bag. As she was doing so, there was a fourth blast, this time much nearer, shattering the glass in two of the windows in the room. Milandra was thrown to the ground.

"What the fuck do think you're doing?" barked Seán as he came into the room and found her pulling herself off the floor, using the bedpost.

"I came to get my valuables," she said, sitting down on the bed. "If they're going to bring my house down, I want my valuables!"

"Will you come down to the basement *now*!" he ordered, grabbing her and pulling her towards the door.

"Wait! My bag!" she pleaded, pointing to the bag on the bed.

"Quickly then!" he said, grabbing the bag.

"And my album!" she pleaded. "It's in the top drawer – it's got all my memories in it!"

"For fuck's sake!" shouted Seán as he rushed to the drawer and grabbed the album before pushing her out the door.

As they quickly made their way to the stairs an explosion shattered the windows. Seán pushed Milandra to the ground and covered her from the falling glass.

Amelia had not gone home to Dalkey the previous night as Rupert had requested. The attaché did come and find her, but she easily persuaded him that there had been some mistake and she was to remain at the military headquarters. The attaché was quickly distracted with everything going on and didn't come near her again.

Amelia couldn't go home. Whatever news there was of Sackville Street and her grandmother, she would only find it out by staying at the headquarters. And now with Rupert due to march into the city centre with the newly arrived reinforcements, she needed to be close to make sure he was safe as well.

She kept out of the way, sitting in corridors, trying to eavesdrop for information as much as she could. Little did the passing military know, she thought, that in fact she was a rebel, due to her past actions, sitting amongst them.

Reinforcements had arrived at Kingston Harbour and quickly had been assembled to march on the city centre. As Rupert took command of a platoon, he realised that some of these soldiers had not realised they were being sent to Ireland. They were due to go to France to fight the war there, and were perplexed that they would be fighting on the streets of a United Kingdom city. Rupert was clear in his mission. They must suppress the rising as quickly as possible, in order to stop the need for any more resources being diverted from the war in Europe. He was convinced that the rebellion had only been as successful as it had been because the rebels had the element of surprise and Dublin had been largely left undefended. As there had been no perceived threat, there had been no reason for a strong military presence there. Now that the army had organised themselves, they would march on the city and recapture it with little effort.

As Rupert led the lines of troops through the affluent leafy streets of the suburbs of south Dublin, he found it all unreal. He knew those streets like the back of his hand. They were the most genteel streets imaginable. Large redbrick houses, the homes of dentists and doctors and businessmen. He never imagined in his lifetime the army would be marching down these streets to defend them.

As they marched down Northumberland Road to cross the bridge at the canal, the area seemed not to have seen any occupation by the rebels. Then suddenly, as they reached the bridge, gunshots rang out. Rupert quickly looked around to establish where they were coming from. As he did so, the soldier to his right let out a scream and fell to the ground. Then the same thing happened to the soldier to his left.

"*Take cover*!" yelled Rupert at the top of his voice as he realised they were being shot at from snipers stationed in the buildings around them. The snipers were safely protected in the buildings, but the British troops were sitting ducks as they marched down the middle of the road.

As Rupert ducked to the ground, he saw more soldiers falling around him as they were struck by the rebels' fire. He saw a large tree on the side of the road, and made a dash to it to get some cover. As he ran towards the tree, the gunshots rang out again, and Rupert was hit. He had blacked out by the time he hit the ground.

PART 9

1869

CHAPTER 59

The days and weeks that followed were like a blur to Constance. She hardly left her bedroom, with Emma bringing her food to eat there.

Henrietta stayed in her own bedroom most of the time. Her loud continual sobs which ascended into wailing echoed through the house. Her wailing seemed to come from some empty pit in her very soul and cut through Constance, compounding her guilt, compounding her desperation. It was true what she had told her parents. It was too late for an explanation, too late for any begging of forgiveness. Her fate was sealed and she had also sealed the fate of her whole family.

The Bishop seemed to be away from the house a lot. Constance would watch from her window each morning, watching the Bishop slope off, hunched, the weight of the world on his shoulders. She often didn't hear him returning until after midnight. She wondered what he was doing, where he was going. But, as her pregnancy developed, she was gripped with a terror of what was to come. How would her family react, how would they cope? She wouldn't have been surprised if they had thrown her out, leaving her to her fate. But this was not mentioned nor did they suggest she leave. She imagined they couldn't bear to do such a thing, no matter how much she had ruined them. Or perhaps they couldn't face being *seen* to do such an uncharitable thing? Or perhaps they just didn't know what to do?

Only Emma, her young sister, who was always a studious serious girl, seemed to sustain any kind of normality. Emma took over the running of the house, in the absence of her parents' ability to do so.

It was Emma who insisted that Constance went to see the doctor.

"You have to!" Emma insisted. "You have to check everything is all right!"

Reluctantly Constance made an appointment to see the same doctor who had attended to her the day she had fainted and informed her she was pregnant. He had been kind and reassuring, she remembered. Now, as she sat in his surgery, he didn't look as reassuring as that day in the church hall. He, like everyone else, had heard of the Bishop's daughter's broken engagement with Nicholas Fontenoy. But he, unlike everyone else in Dublin, was aware she was also pregnant, and now in a perilous position.

"The pregnancy is progressing very well, Constance – everything appears normal," he said after examining her.

"Thank you, Doctor," she whispered as she sat up.

"You look very pale. Are you eating?"

"I find I'm not that hungry."

"You must eat, Constance – you need to keep up your strength."

"Yes, Doctor."

"I – understand – that your marriage to Nicholas Fontenoy has been called off?"

"Yes, Doctor."

"And what are your plans now?"

"I have none, Doctor."

His face creased in concern. "Is Nicholas Fontenoy aware that you are in the family way?"

"No, Doctor."

The doctor saw a glimmer of hope for her salvation. "Well, then, I think this changes everything for you. You must tell him you are pregnant without further delay. He must marry you under these circumstances."

"I can't, Doctor."

"Well, if you can't do it yourself, then your father must visit his father without delay and explain that you are pregnant and young Fontenoy must do the decent thing and marry you."

"I can't, Doctor."

The doctor lost his patience. "But why ever not, you stupid girl? I think you are in denial of what a terrible situation you are in now. You will be an unwed mother, coping with a child and all that will embrace. The child itself will suffer the stigma of your sins. Is that fair?"

"You don't understand, Doctor. There are – other men involved. Nicholas will not marry me as he cannot be sure that he is the father. Now, do you understand?"

The doctor's eyes widened. He didn't mix in the same circles as the wealthy Fontenoys, but he had heard some rumours about Constance. Apparently they were true.

"I see," he said. "In that case, what plans has your father made for you?"

"Plans?"

"Yes – are you to go to a convent for the duration of the pregnancy, and arrange a family for the child after its birth?"

"Nothing has been discussed, Doctor."

"I think you or your family need to face up to this situation and stop pretending it is not happening!" he said in exasperation.

"It is utterly pointless to send me to a convent to save my reputation, Doctor, as it is gone – gone forever!" She suddenly broke down in tears.

The doctor looked at the sobbing girl in pity. He came and sat beside her and put his arm around her.

It was the first moment of tenderness Constance could remember for a long time and she sank into his arms in bitter tears.

After arriving back from the doctor, Constance let herself through the front door and slowly walked towards the stairs.

The drawing-room door opened and Emma appeared.

"I need to speak to you, Constance."

Constance looked about her fearfully.

"Don't worry, Constance. Father is not at home, and Mother is in bed."

Constance nodded and walked into the drawing room.

Emma sat down on the couch and beckoned Constance to take the seat beside her.

Sitting down, Constance looked at her sister. It was a strange feeling that her little sister now seemed in control.

"There have been some decisions made," began Emma.

"What decisions?"

"Father has resigned his post as Bishop," said Emma.

"Oh!" cried Constance, guilt sweeping over her that she was the cause of forcing him to leave the position he loved so much. "But what is he going to do?"

"He has accepted a post as a missionary in the outback of Australia," said Emma.

"*Australia!*"

"We are to leave at the end of the month. Father, Mother and I. We are all moving to Australia, to the outback. Where at least there, it is hoped, nobody will know us and we can start again, away from this scandal you have caused which has engulfed us, and rendered our lives in Dublin unliveable."

Emma sounded cold and there was an edge of anger in her voice. But Constance understood the reasons why.

"I see," said Constance. Digesting the whole plan, she eventually asked, "And what about me?"

"Well, you cannot accompany us, for obvious reasons. We can't have an unmarried daughter with a screaming infant accompany us as we try to rebuild a life of respectability in our new home."

"So – where am I to go?"

"You will remain here, for now. Reeves and the other staff have been given their notice and will leave when we set off for Australia."

It was all too much for Constance to take in. "So, I am to stay in the house here by myself?"

"Yes, until it is decided what to do with the house in the future. It won't be until after your baby is born – you can rest assured about that."

Constance felt panicked at the thought of being all alone. "Please don't leave me, Emma!" she begged.

"You've given me no choice, Constance. You've given none of us any choice. How can I remain living here in Dublin, where I will be always known as your sister? I will be tarred with the same brush. I will never find a man to marry me in Ireland, with a sister with your reputation."

Constance put her hand to her mouth to stifle her sobs. "I'm frightened, Emma," she gasped.

Emma sighed as she took her into her arms. "I know, Constance. And there's a lot to be frightened of now. I'm truly sorry, truly sorry for all of us."

CHAPTER 60

Milandra swung around in a glitzy new lilac frock in front of the mirror in her bedroom. She was due to attend a ball that evening, being hosted by the Lord Lieutenant at the Viceregal Lodge. She knew that Daniel Fontenoy was being given an award at the ball and all the Fontenoys would be present, including Nicholas. Because of Flancy's insistence, she had not visited the Fontenoys since Nicholas had broken his engagement with Constance. Flancy said it would make her look far too keen to do such a thing, and her forwardness would put Nicholas off. Flancy was a wise old bird, and Milandra decided to take her advice, as much as it frustrated her not to rush to Nicholas now he was free. But she would see him that night. It was her first opportunity. She began to waltz around her bedroom in glee.

"Well, you look in good form," said Flancy, appearing at the doorway.

"Oh, I am, Flancy! I can't wait to see Nicholas again."

"Lucas Hempton has just arrived and wants to see you," said Flancy.

Milandra stopped waltzing and her face turned sour. "Well, tell him I can't see him. I'm off to a ball."

"I told him, but he won't take no for an answer. He's waiting for you in the drawing room."

Milandra raised her eyes to heaven. "What does he want *now*?" She marched past Flancy and towards the stairs. "You should have shown him into the parlour, not the drawing room – it's nearer the front door!"

Milandra went down the stairs to the second floor and walked briskly into the drawing room where, to her annoyance, Lucas had made himself comfortable on the couch.

"Dear Lucas!" She smiled at him. "I wasn't expecting you! I'm afraid I can't offer you anything to drink as I'm about to go out to a ball."

"Yes, you do look stunning for it, Milandra."

"Thank you."

"Where is the ball?"

"At the Viceregal Lodge in the Phoenix Park," she said.

"I do know where the Viceregal Lodge is, Milandra. I have lived in Dublin all my life. Unlike you, who are a newcomer."

"Yes, of course."

"My, my! How far you have come so quickly since you came to Sackville Street. You knew nobody when you arrived here and now invitations from the Lord Lieutenant!"

"Yes, I make friends easily, luckily," Milandra said with a smile.

"With my help in introducing you to everybody," Lucas pointed out.

"Yes, I will be forever grateful, Lucas. Now, how can I help you? As I said, I don't have much time."

"How can *you* help *me*! My goodness, Milandra, you have come such a long way. I thought the nature of our relationship was that I was here to help you."

"As I said, Lucas, I don't have much time . . ."

"I wanted to discuss your business with you."

"What about it?" Milandra's face showed her impatience.

"I have left countless messages for you and called to your door here and you never seem to be in."

"I'm a busy woman," she said. Over the recent months, she had slowly isolated Lucas from Carter Wines, making sure he had no further involvement with decisions or the bookkeeping.

"I understand that you have changed all the management at the wine merchants."

"Yes, what of it?"

337

"But, Milandra, my dear, that management has been with Carter Wines for decades! You can't just sweep them all out with a sweeping brush as if they don't matter! They *are* the business! Without their expertise, what is Carter Wines?"

"Carter Wines is the best wine merchants in Dublin, with the best prices," she retorted. "It does not rely on a few old fogeys to keep it going. They were dragging it down, stopping it from moving on. I needed fresh new younger staff who can keep up with the times."

"So says you!"

"Yes, so says I! It is my business and I feel I should be allowed to run it in the best way I can." Milandra's voice was on edge.

"But what of Mr. Wilkinson?"

"What of him?"

"He has been with Carter Wines for thirty-five years! Running the main store on Sackville Street. And you just sent him packing!"

Milandra was becoming increasingly annoyed. "I didn't 'send him packing'! He left of his own accord and he handed in his notice."

"That's a lie, Milandra!"

"I beg your pardon?"

"I tracked down Mr. Wilkinson and he said you just fired him without any explanation. A cruel thing to do, Milandra. He dedicated his life to Carter Wines. And Ambrose would be outraged you did such a thing to him!"

"As I have told you a hundred times before, Lucas, Ambrose is gone and not here to be happy or outraged about anything!"

"And what is all this I hear about you opening a new store on Grafton Street?"

"Yes, I plan to! I'm opening it next month."

"But I think this is a foolish move! Why open a new store on the south side of the river when you already have such a large one on the north side, on Sackville Street?"

"Because I believe the south side is going to get richer, and the north side is going to get poorer," she declared. "Have you not seen some of the houses that are going for sale in the squares like

338

Mountjoy Square to the north of Sackville Street? There seems to be a desire for the wealthy families there to sell up and move to the south of the city. I predict this a trend that is going to continue."

"So now you are an expert on Dublin's future!" Lucas mocked.

"Lucas!" Milandra lost her patience. "I have told you before that I have been grateful for your help, but now this – interference – really must stop!"

"Interference!" Lucas was horrified.

"Yes, you are interfering with my business, Lucas, when it is really no business of yours!"

"But, Milandra, I promised Ambrose –"

"I don't care what you promised Ambrose!" she said loudly and harshly. "I now really must insist that you cease to have any more to do with Carter Wines."

"But I have always been involved in Ambrose's business! Advising, helping and guiding."

"Well, I no longer want your advice, help or guidance! I want you to stop meddling! Stop annoying me with your suggestions and your disapproval. You are no longer required."

Lucas stared at her in shock. "I see!"

"Good! At last!"

"Well, I shall not stay where I am not wanted," he said, standing up.

"Best not! And also, Lucas, I would much appreciate it if you returned the keys you have for my house here and for my business premises. *All* of them."

As he walked past her he stopped and turned his head to look sideways at her. "As you wish, Milandra. Enjoy your ball tonight."

As Lucas continued out of the room, Milandra rolled her eyes in annoyance with the man, but glad to be finally rid of him.

CHAPTER 61

Nicholas was standing in the corner of the great ballroom in the Viceregal Lodge, holding a glass of champagne. As he looked around at the great and the good of Dublin, he didn't feel like joining in the fun. His father had been given an award earlier and his parents were busy circulating with their friends and associates. He felt more comfortable in the darkened corner he was occupying. In the four weeks since he had broken his engagement with Constance, he had hardly gone anywhere. He knew that what Constance had done was the talk of Dublin and he didn't want to face people. Constance had made a joke of him. All his friends were laughing at him: the man who had been cheated on by his fiancée with his best man and work colleague. He felt embarrassed and ashamed. He felt so angry when he thought of Constance and what she had done. And yet he missed her too – the girl he had once known, not the girl she had become. He was mortified by it all. Would he ever recover his pride? Would people always be sniggering behind his back? Could he ever hold his head up with pride like he used to? Constance might be disgraced, but he was seen as a fool. He had never experienced his parents' disapproval before, but now he felt it all the time, since he had divulged that he had slept with Constance too. Usually they would be the first he would run to, and receive their sympathy and understanding. But even that was now out of the question.

Suddenly, he saw Milandra across the dance floor. She looked spectacular as she greeted people. A woman full of pride, confident

340

of her position in society. He looked on as she spoke amicably with the Lord Lieutenant, feeling almost envious of her, full of admiration of how she was conducting herself. A pillar of the community, a woman whom everyone respected and admired. As an hour passed, he didn't take his eyes off her, following her around the ballroom as she effortlessly socialised. With everything that had happened with Constance, he had nearly forgotten his own encounter with Milandra. He went red when he thought about it. He remembered when he had met her last, and the unpleasant confrontation they'd had. He had not acted like a gentleman, that he was sure of. As Milandra moved to the corner of the ballroom he was in, he stepped further back into the shadows behind a large plant so she wouldn't see him.

But suddenly Milandra spotted him and, to his surprise, smiled at him. He managed to smile back. She excused herself from the company she was in and walked straight over to him.

"Hello, Nicholas," she said with a warm smile.

"Milandra," he nodded at her, taken aback.

"You do look smart in your black tie," she complimented him.

"And you look very beautiful tonight, Milandra."

"Thank you – you were always such a charmer."

"Not always," he said, looking down at the marble floor, embarrassed.

She stepped a little closer to him and looked at him earnestly. "I was so sorry to hear about you and Constance. It took me by surprise to hear."

He nodded. "You, like everyone else, probably know everything?"

She nodded sadly.

"You must think me a terrible fool," he said.

"It is no crime to be a fool occasionally, Nicholas. We have all been fools in love."

He looked into her face. It was the first time anyone had shown him any sympathy or understanding.

"My, the band is so loud, isn't it?" she said. "Hard to hear oneself think!"

"Yes, it is, certainly."

"Shall we – shall we step out for a second? To get some fresh air? And hear ourselves think?" she suggested as she indicated the French window near them.

"Eh – yes," he said. "Let's do that."

They stepped out on to the terrace. Down either side of it were couples chatting, and some were walking through the extensive lawns before them.

"That's a bit better, isn't it?" she smiled at him.

"Yes, it certainly is – less loud," he said awkwardly.

"Have you – have you spoken to Constance since the break-up?" she asked.

"No," he said and his face darkened. "I never want to speak to her or see her again. "

She nodded, understanding. "She hurt you very much, didn't she, Nicholas?"

He nodded and looked out across the lawns.

"You will recover, Nicholas. It will just take a little time."

"Will I?"

"Of course you will . . . with the help of your friends."

He turned and faced her. "Are you still a friend of mine, Milandra? After all the things I said about you?"

"Of course I am!" She put a reassuring hand on his shoulder. "Friends fall out all the time, but true friends always come back to each other."

He nodded and bit his lip. "I- I- I'm v-v-very sorry for the things I said to you, Milandra," he stuttered. "You didn't deserve that, and I am truly sorry. Can you ever forgive me?"

"Oh, Nicholas!" Her eyes twinkled sympathy. "Of course I can! I already have! It's forgotten, it's as if it never happened as far as I'm concerned."

"Thank you," he whispered and he tightened his face muscles to try to stop the emotion he was feeling from pouring out.

"Well – now," she said a little cheerily, "I think we've had enough fresh air! Why don't we rejoin the ball? I haven't danced all night. Shall we have a dance?"

"I don't – I don't dance any more," he said quietly.

"Nonsense! Of course you do! Now, come along!" she said, taking his arm and leading him inside.

She led him to the centre of the ballroom. He felt people's eyes stare at him as they went. But somehow, being with Milandra, it didn't seem to matter. It was as if she was so strong and important that her dancing with him was making him able to hold his head high again. He took her in his arms and they began to twirl around the dance floor with the other couples.

CHAPTER 62

Flancy was busy cooking in the kitchen and instructing the rest of the staff when the young butler she had hired came down.

"Pardon, Mrs. Flancy, but Mr. Lucas Hempton is here to see you," said the butler.

"*Me?* What does he want to see me for?"

"He didn't say. I showed him into the downstairs parlour."

"Goodness me," Flancy said, wiping her hands on her apron.

She went upstairs and headed into the parlour where she found Lucas standing.

"Mrs. Carter isn't at home," said Flancy.

"I shouldn't think it would matter if she was – she has expressed no desire to see me again. I just came by to give these back." He held out a bunch of keys.

"Oh, I see, I'll make sure she gets them," said Flancy, taking the keys.

Lucas made no move to leave. Flancy waited curiously, wondering what else he had to say. She noticed that he looked depressed and rejected.

"Milandra is not the woman I thought she was," he suddenly said.

"Are any of us?"

"A great disappointment to me. I feel very used."

"Well . . . that's life!" Flancy shrugged.

"I've a good mind to inform all the people to whom I introduced her as to her true nature," sighed Lucas.

Flancy's eyes narrowed. "Now, look here, Mr. Hempton – you say anything about Milandra and you'll have me to answer to!"

"Don't worry – I don't really mean that. I have no intention of bothering Milandra again. I know when I'm not wanted." Now he looked even more depressed.

"Probably for the best. Now if you don't mind – I'm in the middle of a some baking."

She showed him to the front door, then stood there and watched him walking down the street, a dejected depressed figure.

As precious heirlooms and articles were removed from the Staffordshire house, Constance realised that when her parents left for Australia they never intended to return to Dublin or to their home again. She understood that most items were being taken to sell at Dublin auction houses and a modest number were to be transported to Australia with the family.

On the day her family were due to leave, Constance stood at her bedroom window and watched the hansom cab outside being packed with their personal luggage.

She turned as there was a knock on her door and got a fright to see her father walk in. They had steadfastly avoided each other since the scandal had erupted and, now, as he entered the room she got a shock to see how physically he had aged in such a short period of time. He looked smaller, older, broken. The once indomitable presence was gone, replaced by a shadow. Even when he spoke his voice was weak.

"I came to say goodbye – and to give you this," he said holding out a small cloth bag. "It's all the money I can spare as I had to pay for our travel to Australia and will need enough to set us up there, and have some as an insurance in case anything goes wrong. It's not that much, but should get you through the – the – *pregnancy* –" On saying the last word, the Bishop broke down in tears.

"Oh, Father!" gasped Constance as she rushed to him and threw her arms around him. It was one of the few times in her life she had ever embraced him.

He tried to stifle his sobs. "I let you down. I wasn't a good father to you. I thought I was showing you the way to lead a good righteous life, but clearly I wasn't."

Holding back her tears, Constance pulled back and said, "You must not blame yourself for any of my actions, Father. It is nobody's fault but my own."

"Perhaps I spent too much time trying to save other people's daughters, and not enough on my own daughters." It was as if he was speaking to his own soul and not to Constance.

"You mustn't blame yourself," she insisted.

He wiped away his tears. "We can't stay here, you understand? I just can't face the shame of it all."

"I understand," she nodded.

"And you understand we can't take you with us?"

Constance held back her tears and nodded.

"We have to start a new life for Emma's sake, to try and forget all of this – but, apart from that, I have to dedicate the rest of my life to trying to atone for what has happened to my family. And the only way I can do that is by working tirelessly for the poor and disadvantaged as a missionary."

The door opened and Emma walked in. "Father, the driver is waiting. Mother is already in the carriage."

The Bishop then quickly turned away, as he looked in danger of collapsing in tears again, and hurried out of the room.

Emma and Constance looked at each other and then rushed to each other and embraced.

"You will be fine," said Emma. "The doctor is kind and will organise a good family to adopt the child when it's born."

Constance nodded and held her tightly.

Emma tore herself away and raced out of the room without saying another word, leaving Constance at the window, watching the carriage outside begin her family's journey to the other side of the world.

Milandra and Nicholas were sitting at the best table in the restaurant at the Shelbourne Hotel. With Christmas approaching the restaurant was filled with jovial diners.

"And how are you this evening, Mrs Carter?" asked the waiter with a friendly smile.

"I'm very good, Joe. What's on the menu this evening?"

"The lobster is very good, Mrs Carter."

"Oh, that sounds nice. What do you think, Nicholas?" asked Milandra, smiling across the table at him.

"Whatever you are having is fine by me," he said, smiling back at her.

"Lobster it is then, Joe," said Milandra, handing him back the menu. "And what of the wine?"

"We just got a delivery of a crate of the best Beaujolais from your store on Grafton Street this morning," he told her.

"I know the vintage well. We'll have a bottle of that," said Milandra.

She looked across at Nicholas and thought he was looking rather downcast.

"Are you all right?" she asked.

"Yes, it's just, I haven't been out to a restaurant since – since –"

She leaned across, smiling at him. "Well, I'm glad I twisted your arm to come out. You can't stay indoors forever, Nicholas. You have to try and get on with your life now."

"I know you are right," he said.

"Then smile!"

He forced himself to smile, but his eyes were still sad.

The waiter came over and opened the bottle of wine and filled both their glasses.

"To the future!" toasted Milandra as she raised her glass to him.

Nicholas took up his glass of wine, clinked it against hers and repeated, "To the future."

CHAPTER 63

Christmas Day at the Fontenoys' was always a joyous affair. They always invited close family friends to spend the day with them and the long table in the dining room was always filled to capacity. And that year was no different from the rest. Except that Milandra sat in the place at the dinner table that had been reserved for Constance for the past three years.

Daniel carved the huge goose, and the table was filled with delicious food and treats. Milandra had had a crate of wine delivered from Carter Wines the previous evening, and it flowed freely during dinner and throughout the rest of the evening. As the evening crept into night, the snow began to fall again and Nicholas and Milandra stood watching it beside the Christmas tree in the drawing room, as the rest of the party enjoyed parlour games including charades.

"A penny for your thoughts," said Milandra.

"Oh – nothing. I was just hoping that next year will be better than this has been," he said.

"It has been such a tough time for you," conceded Milandra, placing a hand on his arm.

He turned and faced her. "I don't know how I would have got through it without you."

"I'll always be here for you, Nicholas, you know that."

"I do – and I love you for it –" He stopped abruptly as he realised what he had said.

"Do you – love me?" she asked.

"Yes – I do!" he suddenly said, as if only realising it himself.

"That makes me so happy to hear – because I love you too, Nicholas. More than you'll ever know."

"Then – then – why wait any longer?"

"What do you mean?"

"Why don't we get married?"

Milandra's heart started racing. "What . . . are you asking me to marry you?"

"Yes! Yes, I am! Milandra – will you marry me?"

"Yes! Of course I will!" she exclaimed and threw herself into his arms and kissed him.

Nicholas swung around to face the room.

"Everybody! Everybody!" he called, bringing a hush to the room.

When he had everyone's attention, he took Milandra's hand and spoke loudly.

"We would like to announce something important. I have asked Milandra to marry me – and she has consented!"

There was silence in the room as everyone took in the announcement.

Agatha was completely taken aback. She knew her son had been courting Milandra of late, but she hadn't expected this. Now, as she looked at the happy couple holding hands, she realised the surprise of the announcement had left them all not knowing how to react. She took control of the situation and stood up.

"Well, congratulations!" she declared and quickly moved to Nicholas and Milandra. She embraced both of them and kissed them. "What wonderful news! Daniel, isn't that wonderful news?"

Daniel had nearly dropped his glass of eggnog when he heard Nicholas's announcement, but now he too was spurred into action.

"Truly wonderful news!" he confirmed and he went to the couple and embraced them. "Congratulations!"

Suddenly all the other people in the room erupted in joy and came quickly over to congratulate the happy couple as well.

It was nearly midnight and Nicholas was on his own in the dining room, looking out at the snow falling. Milandra was still in the drawing room, participating in the party games. Daniel came in and walked up to his son.

"Are you all right, Nicholas?" asked Daniel.

Nicholas smiled happily. "Of course I am! Am I not getting married to the most beautiful and exceptional woman in Dublin?"

"And one of the richest," said Daniel.

"What has that got to do with it?"

"Nothing, I'm sure. It's just that I hope marrying Milandra is not some attempt to exonerate yourself from the mess of your engagement with Constance?"

"Of course it's not!"

"I'm glad to hear it. Though you are going through a rough time now because of Constance's scandal, marriage is forever, and not a quick fix to get yourself out of an uncomfortable situation."

"I don't even know what you're talking about, Papa. Milandra is wonderful. If it wasn't for her, I'd don't know what I'd have done after my marriage to Constance was called off. She saved me."

"That is my point – I hope this is not a rebound?"

"I love her, and she loves me – is there anything more to be said?"

"No, not in that case . . . but Milandra is a different kind of woman from the ones you have been used to, do you realise that?"

"In what way?"

"Well, she has been married before. She has experience and is worldly wise. She is independent of mind and independent financially. She's not like the young ladies you grew up with."

"If you mean by 'the young ladies I grew up with' girls like Constance Staffordshire, then I am very much glad she is not like them!" Nicholas spoke angrily and bitterly. "I don't want to marry a girl who on the surface is a proper young lady but is something very different underneath. Milandra has never pretended to be anything else than what she is, and makes no apologies for it. I know where I am with her, and that is what I want!"

"Well, in that case, I wish you all the luck in the world," conceded Daniel, hiding all the doubts he harboured.

"Thank you, Papa."

Constance sat with a blanket around her, huddled near the fireplace in her bedroom. She only lit the fireplace in her bedroom and not in the drawing room, in order to preserve the supply of logs and turf that had been left at the back of the house when her family left for Australia. She was grateful that there had been a good supply as she was trying to preserve the money her father had left her as best she could. She had become acutely aware that she needed to budget the money to last through the pregnancy and beyond. After the initial shock of being left alone in the large house with no support, she quickly had to get over what seemed now like small problems – like being frightened of being alone in the house. She had never been alone before in her whole life.

She also had to solve pressing practicalities like how to feed herself. She had never gone shopping for food before. She strictly avoided any of the stores around Sackville Street where she might have to face the shame of bumping into somebody who she knew. Also the prices in those stores were now too high for her. Instead, she would head in the opposite direction towards the tenements, where the small shops there were much cheaper and there was no risk of meeting anyone she knew. She frugally bought what she needed there. She would be all right financially until the baby was born and for some time after that, but she didn't know what she would do when the money eventually ran out.

As much as she thought, she couldn't find a way forward. Her doctor kept urging her to allow him to find a family for the baby, but she couldn't bear to do that, even though the doctor advised it was the best thing for the baby in the dire circumstances she was in.

She had received no communication from her family, not even a letter from Emma. Constance supposed she was such a painful memory for them that they were probably trying their hardest to forget her. She was lost, she knew.

As she thought of Nicholas, she wondered what he was doing.

As the festivities of Christmas week continued into the New Year,

Milandra seemed to spend almost all of her time at the Fontenoys'.

They were all in the drawing room one afternoon playing a card game when Daniel came in holding that day's newspaper.

"Has anybody seen today's news?" he asked, all concerned. "Lucas Hempton has seemingly gone missing."

"What?" asked Agatha. "However can that be?"

"It says here –" Daniel began to read from the newspaper, "*Concerns are rising over the unexplained disappearance of prominent Dublin businessman Lucas Hempton. Mr Hempton was last seen leaving his house by a neighbour the night before Christmas Eve. Police have asked anybody with information to come forward.*"

"But wherever could he be?" said Milandra, looking perplexed.

"I hope he hasn't been a victim of foul play," said Daniel.

"Foul play!" cried Agatha.

"Perhaps he was a victim of a robbery, or an assault in the course of a mugging," said Daniel.

"Milandra? When did you see him last?" asked Agatha.

"Not for a while. He ceased to have any involvement in my business a while back. And we had not as much reason to see each other after that."

"Perhaps he went away for the Christmas, on holiday," suggested Agatha.

"Holiday!" scoffed Daniel. "Lucas Hempton never went on a holiday in all the time I've known him."

"I do hope he comes back soon, wherever he is, to put our minds at rest," said Agatha.

As Lucas did not reappear people became more and more concerned about him. The newspapers began to carry the story with greater coverage as the mystery deepened. The police conducted their enquiries and called on everybody he knew.

A constable called to Milandra and interviewed her in the drawing room.

"You are well acquainted with Mr Hempton, Mrs Carter?"

"I am. He was a good friend of my late husband's. And advised our business. But his role at Carter Wines had ceased over the past months."

"Any reason for that?"

"Not really. I suppose my management style and his differed. I must admit I side-lined him, and he didn't take it well."

"What mood was he in when you saw him last?"

"Somewhat down, I suppose," said Milandra. "Perhaps I didn't realise how down he was."

"Perhaps. You are suggesting suicide?"

"I really couldn't speculate. I sincerely hope not though," said Milandra. "The guilt would be too much for me to bear."

CHAPTER 64

1870

Everyone in the congregation was in agreement that Milandra made a stunning bride as she walked up the aisle to be married to Nicholas Fontenoy.

As the couple exchanged their vows, it was clear to everyone that they were a couple very much in love. Privately, people thought what a lucky escape Nicholas had in not marrying Constance Staffordshire. His whole life could have been utterly ruined. Now he faced a bright and happy future with Milandra by his side.

On the morning of Nicholas's marriage to Milandra, Constance gave birth to a boy. She was tended to by the doctor and, as she cradled her new-born close to her in her bedroom, the doctor became concerned.

"Don't get too attached, Constance. The new family that I have arranged is waiting for him."

"I'm sorry, Doctor. But I've changed my mind. I'm keeping my child," said Constance, holding the baby close.

"But you haven't thought this through, Constance! You have no support, you have nothing. How could you cope?"

"It's precisely because I have nothing that I must keep him. He's is all I have in the world."

The doctor scratched his head in bewilderment and all he could think to say was, "What are you going to name him?"

"John," answered Constance as she held her baby close to her. "After my father."

PART 10

1916

CHAPTER 65

The shelling had continued through the day and into the night –
continual blastings from the British gunship *Helga* which had sailed
right up the River Liffey and aimed its big guns at Sackville Street
and the rest of the city centre. As Milandra's house was at the
furthest end from the river it had avoided any direct hit. But that
didn't stop the constant shaking of the building from the continual
bombardment.

Milandra sat in an armchair by the stove, watching Seán and the
other two rebels becoming increasingly anxious. From their
conversation she realised they had not expected this. They had not
expected the British to send in a gunship to shell the city.

They had expected troops to be sent in and that there would be
a street battle where the rebels would have the advantage from their
vantage points, hidden in the buildings they occupied. But the
shelling from the gunship meant the British were going to blast the
rebels out of those buildings – bring the buildings down around
them before sweeping in to destroy them.

Milandra observed that Seán as the group's leader was trying to
maintain morale and confidence for the other two men. She also
saw that he was failing to do so.

Milandra ducked as a shell seemed to explode directly over the
house, causing a crashing sound upstairs and knocking over the
dresser full of china in the kitchen.

The youngest rebel jumped up from the floor and shouted,
"Right, I'm out of here!"

Seán stood up abruptly and faced him. "What are you talking about?"

"I'm getting the fuck out of here before the whole fucking building collapses down on top of us!" He was covered in sweat.

"You cannot abandon your post!" Seán stated.

"What fucking post? Our post is supposed to be upstairs at the windows firing down on the fucking British soldiers! They're not here! They're in that gunship bombing the shite out of us! It's over – I'm out of here!"

"You can't abandon the cause!" roared Seán.

"I'm not going to be buried under this building – that's no hero's death, to be sure!"

"Where will you go?" demanded Seán. "You'll be shot by the British as soon as you go outside!"

"I'll take my chances out there on the street with a gun in my hand, instead of waiting here for certain death." The young man turned his back on Seán and spoke to the other one. "Are ya coming or are ya staying?"

The other rebel looked at Seán but the sound of another shell exploding made his mind up quickly. "Come on, let's get the fuck out of here!"

The two rebels ran towards the basement back door. One of them stopped abruptly and pointed at Milandra. "What about her?"

The other rebel shoved him forward. "What *about* her? Come on, let's get the fuck out of here. Republic, my arse!"

Milandra watched as the two young rebels sprinted to the kitchen back door and ran up the steps into the garden.

"Well – that's a turn-up for the books!" she said. "I would never have imagined he would have that amount of intelligence! He looks rather dumb! Self-preservation kicked in for him – he should go far in life!"

"He won't get far at all. He'll be shot as soon as he meets the first British soldiers," said Seán who looked despairing.

"Well, as he says, at least he'll have a fighting chance out on the streets. And I imagine he will know every little back alleyway to try

358

and get to safety. If you had any sense you would run too, Seán, before you get killed."

"*I'm not going anywhere*!" he roared. "I'm staying here at my post to defend this building. And when the British arrive, they'll have to shoot me dead before they take me captive."

Milandra sighed heavily. "Oh dear, you must love this suffragette very much – too much! She might have done a runner herself by now, abandoned whatever post she is at."

"She would never do that," said Seán.

"The blindness of love!" said Milandra as she sat back in her chair, eyeing him. "And then there was one."

At military headquarters, Amelia sat trembling on a bench in the corridor. There were officers flying up and down constantly in a state of panic. From what she could overhear, the *Helga* was destroying the city centre, with many buildings just shells at this stage. Where was Milandra? Had she survived and got to safety? And then she heard that there had been a massacre on Northumberland Street. The rebels had massacred the British troops that had arrived in Kingstown as they marched into the city.

Fear gripped her as she knew Rupert was among those troops marching in to recapture the city. She vigilantly watched every passing officer's face in the hope it would be Rupert. But there was no sign of him.

Her mind was plagued with guilt. She racked her brain, thinking of all the information she had freely given the republicans courtesy of Rupert. How the war on the Continent was going badly for the British, how troop morale was bad, how they were strained to breaking point. And all the time that information was being noted and used to plan the timing for the rebellion. She couldn't regret that it would all lead to her dream of independence from the British. But what if her actions caused the death of her fiancé and grandmother? Could she live with herself? She began to realise that her position of being on both sides was untenable and dangerous.

She saw Captain Hollingsworth rush into an office down the corridor. She got up and walked down and into the office.

He was bent over a map spread across his desk.

"Captain Hollingsworth –" she began.

"What are *you* still doing here?" he said, confounded to see her.

"I never left. I was waiting for Rupert to return. I heard that there was a massacre on Northumberland Road. Have you any news of Rupert?"

"No, I haven't. Will you please leave! I can't have some hysterical woman around here," snapped Hollingsworth.

"Captain Hollingsworth, *please,* have you any idea where my fiancé is?" she begged.

He sighed. "No, I don't know where Rupert is. I don't know if he is alive or dead . . . the streets were awash with blood. Go home and pray."

"I can't! Where were the injured taken to?"

"To Kilmainham Hospital."

"Can you get an attaché to take me there?"

"No, I can't! In case you haven't realised, the city is at war now. I can't spare a man to take you anywhere."

"Well, then, give me a military pass. I have my automobile outside and I'll drive myself."

"The city is under martial law – you won't be allowed anywhere except back to the suburbs."

"That's why I need the military pass."

"No! Go home!"

She slammed her hands on his desk. *"Give me the pass!"*

He shook his head and quickly reached into a drawer and handed her a military pass.

"This is on your head!" he warned.

"Thank you!" She grabbed the pass and quickly ran out.

Milandra woke with a jolt. She saw it was bright outside and she was still in the armchair by the stove. The sound of the shelling was still roaring outside.

Seán was at the sink, drinking a glass of water.

"Well, if I can sleep through that I can sleep through anything!" she said, sitting up and yawning. "What time is it?"

"Four in the afternoon," he said.

There was shouting in the distance.

"What's that?" Seán rushed to the basement door, opened it and strained to listen.

"*Retreat! Retreat – retreat to Moore Street!*" called the distant voice.

"The troops must be advancing into Sackville Street," he said.

"I imagine there's very little left of Sackville Street to advance into!" said Milandra.

"That's what they wanted. Shell the area so badly that we can't defend it. Where does that garden gate at the back of the garden lead to?"

"To the back lanes," she said. "Why?"

"I'll be able to find my way to Moore Street through them."

Milandra stood up quickly. "But you're abandoning your post!"

"We're under order to retreat," said Seán.

"But – but how do you know it's not a trap?" asked Milandra.

"What?"

"It could be a trap laid by the army! It could be them shouting retreat to flush you all out and then shoot you as soon as you leave your posts!"

Seán's mouth dropped open in bewilderment.

"I should think you would be very foolish to run out into the lanes just because you hear some voice shouting to do so," she said.

Milandra could see from Seán's face that his mind was swirling in confusion.

"If I were you I would wait for some solid confirmation that the order is coming from your boys, and not the enemy."

"I'll wait till the next lull in the shelling and go upstairs to try to see what's happening from the front windows," he said.

"That's what I would do," she said.

Going over to him, she took him by the arm, led him to the table and sat him down.

"What are you doing?" he asked.

"You haven't eaten since yesterday. You look exhausted. If you're going to fight a street battle, best to do it on a full stomach."

He watched her as she went to the pantry and brought back a loaf of bread, then took a cooked chicken from the refrigerator. She set about making a chicken sandwich.

"Why are you doing this?" he said eventually. "Why do you care if I live or die? I would have thought you'd be delighted to see the back of me."

"I have my reasons," she said as she put the sandwich in front of him and smiled.

Then she went back to the pantry and took out the cake she had baked and placed it on the table before him.

"Cake too?" he said with a smirk.

"Oh yes – cake too," she said, cutting a large slice and putting it on a plate in front of him.

It took an eternity for Amelia to get to Kilmainham Hospital. She could see now that Dublin was under complete military occupation. Roadblocks were everywhere, armed soldiers on every corner. She used her knowledge of what she had heard at the headquarters to avoid areas that were battle zones. She avoided anywhere near the city centre, instead navigating the residential suburbs to get to her destination. But even here she was stopped at every turn by the army, interrogating her. Every citizen in the city now was under suspicion by the authorities of being a rebel. As she drove through the usually quiet sedate districts, she witnessed the army ruthlessly carrying out house searches, trying to flush out any rebels who might be hiding there. Amelia had overheard back at the headquarters that any man found suspected of being a rebel would be shot. She found this order incomprehensible. Why should the main population, who had nothing to do with this rebellion, be tarred with the same brush?

As Amelia was constantly stopped by the military on her way to Kilmainham, she realised being a woman of clear upper-class bearing did not make her any less of a suspect. Only the military pass allowed her to continue her journey.

Her automobile was pulled over by yet another army patrol.

"Who are you – where are you going?" asked the soldier aggressively.

Amelia said confidently, "I am Amelia Robinson, and I'm on the way to Kilmainham Hospital with the authority of Captain Hollingsworth to try and find my fiancé Captain Rupert Perkins."

She quickly handed over the pass and the solider scrutinised it before nodding and waving her on. Amelia put down her foot and sped on.

Seán carefully climbed the servants' stairs up from the basement to the ground floor of the house, his pistol ready in his hand. Upstairs he found the house was still intact as it had not received a direct hit. But all windows were smashed, and the furniture in disarray from the continual pounding. He made his way to the front of the house and stooped by a window in the dining room, spying out. He could see that the once glorious Sackville Street was now in ruins. He saw two rebels running past outside and they were shouting *"Retreat! Retreat to Moore Street!"*

Seán then knew the old lady had been wrong. It was not a trick by the British. With a heavy heart he understood the rising was now in jeopardy and they were retreating from the key position they had held in Sackville Street. He turned and made his way back down to the basement.

"Well?" asked Milandra.

"It's our order all right. We're retreating," he said.

"I see! I wonder what it was all for?" She shook her head in dismay.

"It's not over yet! The fiercest of the fighting has yet to come."

"That's what I'm afraid of," she said as she watched him gather his coat and make his way to the back door.

"Where are you going?" she asked.

"To Moore Street."

"But what about me?"

"What about you?"

"Well, you can't just leave me here!"

"Well, I can't take you to Moore Street, if that's what you're saying. Looks like the British army will be here soon – they will liberate you, make sure you're all right."

As he looked at the old woman, her face became hazy and he suddenly got a strange sensation, like nothing he had ever felt before. The kitchen seemed to waver in front of his eyes.

As he tried to get his bearings, the room began to spin and swirl before him.

"Seán – are you all right?" asked Milandra.

But he wasn't all right, as the room kept spinning.

"Seán?"

He tried to focus on the old woman who was speaking to him, but he was unable. He began to sway and he quickly reached forward and grabbed the table-top to stop himself from falling.

"I – I – I – don't feel – g-g-ood," he managed to whisper.

"What on earth is wrong with you, Seán?"

He was swaying backwards and forwards. Only the fact he was holding on to the table stopped him from falling flat on the ground.

As he looked up at the old woman's face, now beside him, it seemed to contort and change colour. She was speaking, but her words seemed to echo as if from down a tunnel and he couldn't hear what she was saying.

"Something – is happening – to me," he said and he gripped his head with both his hands.

"Yes, something is happening to you, Seán," Milandra said and he saw her smile unpleasantly. "Best not to fight it."

She took him by the arm and began to lead him across the kitchen. He was getting weaker by the minute and she knew he wouldn't be able to move at all shortly.

"Let me go," he muttered.

"No, Seán, don't try and fight it, I tell you!" she said as she moved him down a small corridor and into the footman's bedroom.

He sank down on the small single bed, trying to maintain his balance.

"What have you done to me?" he pleaded as he fell back in the bed.

She took his feet and raised them up on the bed so he was lying completely flat on his back.

"You've poisoned me!" he accused her as the memory of the

delicious cake she had fed him flashed through his mind.

"Yes, the cake, Seán," she gloated as she sat down on a chair beside the bed and studied him. "The delicious cake. Isn't it amazing, Seán, that what we cannot resist leads us to our downfall?"

"You're a witch, a sorcerer," he gasped.

"No, I'm not a witch or a sorcerer. Flancy, the cook I told you about before, who taught me to bake, was the most amazing woman. When she was young, growing up in the west of Ireland, she learned from her mother all about the herbs and wild mushrooms and flora that grew wild in the forests. She learned all about how giving them to people gave you power over people. We used to call it magic. But it wasn't magic really. It was just understanding the power these wild herbs had. She taught me the power they had and I've used them throughout my life to get what I want with people – to seduce or to destroy them."

Seán was panting now and he was finding it hard to keep his eyes open.

"Why are you doing this to me?" he gasped. "Why are you killing me? I wasn't going to harm you – you knew that."

Milandra reached forward and reached into his inside pockets until she found a wallet and took it out. She began to look through the wallet and nodded, satisfied.

"Staffordshire," she confirmed aloud.

PART 11

1881

CHAPTER 66

It was a bright sunny day as Nicholas Fontenoy, now Lord Havington, walked down Sackville Street to his home.

"Good afternoon, Lord Havington," greeted a woman as she passed him.

"Good afternoon, Mrs Green," he said, smiling back at her.

In the eleven years since Nicholas had married Milandra, much had changed – apart from the fact they still lived in her house on Sackville Street. The year after they married they had a daughter, Petronella, a beautiful girl, who was the mirror image of her mother.

A few years later, to the family's great astonishment, Daniel unexpectedly inherited a title and became Lord Havington. Daniel's distant cousin in England had been an earl, as Agatha liked to boast. Daniel had hardly known the man. When he died, his son had inherited the title. By all accounts the young man was a somewhat wayward character, with gambling and drinking addictions, who one night drove his carriage off a bridge while coming home from a tavern and drowned. He had died without heir. As he had also left a series of gambling debts, whatever was left of the estate went to pay them off. But as Daniel was the next in line, being the nearest male relative, the title of Lord Havington had passed to him. Sadly, Daniel's time as Lord Havington was short-lived as he had died from a heart attack a couple of years later and the family had been left devastated. Nicholas in particular had always relied on his father for so much guidance. On Daniel's death, Nicholas had inherited his father's newly acquired title. And Milandra, much to her delight, became Lady Havington.

Nicholas's brother Frederick had gone to live in India, where he occupied a prominent role in government. Agatha had retired to live by the sea after Daniel's death, had backed out of society and rarely came to Dublin any more. Their house had been sold and was now the offices of an insurance company. For it wasn't just in the Fontenoy family that there had been such dramatic changes. Sackville Street too had changed. As Daniel Fontenoy had always feared, the commercial end of Lower Sackville Street spread to Upper Sackville Street, with new stores opening. A lot of the well-heeled families had moved away from this northern end of Sackville Street to the south side of Dublin, and their former homes were now offices.

But the streets and squares further north had seen a rapid deterioration. As the families who had lived in those townhouses around the fine parks had moved to the south side, property speculators had moved in and bought them and turned them into flats. Nicholas thought it generous to use the term *flats* to describe what these buildings had become. They were tenements, owned by greedy speculators which resulted in them becoming slums. If it was left to Nicholas, he would have moved the family from their house in Sackville Street to the south side as well, but Milandra would hear none of it. She loved the new lively commercial element that was now more pronounced in Upper Sackville Street, and she had no intention of ever moving from their mansion townhouse.

Milandra, Lady Havington. As he approached the front door of their home, his mind became heavy thinking about her. The new Lady Havington was now one of the most prominent business people in Dublin. Carter Wines had continued to expand at a rapid pace. Milandra was always in charge, thriving on her success. She was rarely home – she was always either at a business meeting or out socialising with her wide range of friends, who all occupied the top positions in society. As for his own career, Nicholas still worked at Gilligans', the position his father had set up for him all those years ago after he had left Fetherstons' Solicitors. He did well there and was respected, but everyone knew by now, including Nicholas himself, that his career would not go much higher. He would not reach the dizzy heights of success his father had, and that had been expected of him when he was starting off in his career. He would never make judge, as his father had.

As for his marriage with Milandra, they had enjoyed a honeymoon period for a couple of years after the marriage. Then, after Petronella was born, Milandra announced that she had no intention or desire to have any more children. So that was the end of that. They argued, if Milandra could be bothered to row with him. Often she wouldn't waste her time even arguing with him, as she did exactly what she wanted to do and ignored him. He was used to being ignored in his own home by everybody, including his ten-year-old daughter Petronella. As much as he had tried, he had not been able to build a loving relationship with his daughter, like the one he had with his own parents. She seemed to view him as an irrelevance, as Milandra indulged her and spoilt her dreadfully. As did Flancy. The dread Flancy he had to share his home with these past years. Flancy, the bane of his life.

Nicholas thought of all this as he let himself into his home. They had no butler, regardless of how much he insisted a house of that size and a family of their importance needed one. Flancy refused to have a butler in the house, and Milandra had sided with her, not even listening to his objections. Flancy didn't want anyone in the house who would threaten her position of power. And so Petronella had not had a nanny when she was younger, her care being left to Flancy. And now she had no governess. Flancy didn't want one in the house. Instead a teacher was employed to come in and instruct Petronella for a few hours each day. Nicholas had never heard anything so bizarre. He knew of no other family where such a situation existed. But he had been overruled on the matter. As he had with everything else.

That morning Nicholas had a meeting near Sackville Street and, as he hadn't anything else on in the office that afternoon, he had decided to come home early. As he walked up the stairs, he knew Milandra wouldn't be home but, as usual, would be out at one thing or another. He continued up the stairs past the second and third floors, up to the schoolroom which was in thc attic of the house. He would sit in on Petronella's lessons and see how she was getting on with her teacher. He opened the schoolroom door, smiling, but was surprised to see that it was empty. Confused, he looked at his watch and saw it was only two in the afternoon and Petronella and her teacher should be there. He searched the other rooms on the floor, but they were empty. Scratching his head, he came down to the other floors but there was no sign of anybody. On the ground floor, he went to the back of the stairs and peered out the French windows into the garden but Petronella wasn't there either.

He turned and walked down the stairs that led to the kitchens and the servants' quarters. He stopped on reaching the kitchen door as he saw his daughter Petronella standing at the large kitchen table baking with Flancy.

He watched them for a while, unnoticed, as Flancy instructed her on how to make a Victoria Sponge in great detail. Petronella, for her part, seemed engrossed in the whole process.

Nicholas walked abruptly into the kitchen, demanding, "What is going on here?"

"Oh, Your Lordship, we weren't expecting you!" said Flancy, startled.

"Clearly! Petronella, what are you doing down here in the servants' quarters?"

"Baking! What else does it look like?" she replied cheekily, not even bothering to look at him as she continued to beat the mixture in the baking bowl.

"But you should be in the schoolroom, with your teacher. Where is your teacher? Where is Miss Giddings?"

"Miss Giddings ate something that didn't agree with her, and had to go home," explained Flancy, focusing on the baking and not paying him much attention.

"You didn't send her home then, Flancy?" asked Nicholas, who had learned all of Flancy's tricks years ago. She made it impossible for anybody to work in the house other than the kitchen maids and parlour maids who were under her direct supervision.

"Of course I didn't! Why should I do such a thing?" she said unconvincingly.

"This is the third teacher of Petronella's who has had food poisoning!" Nicholas said.

"Perhaps they need to choose the restaurants they eat in better," said Flancy.

Nicholas, becoming madder, addressed his daughter. "Petronella, I've told you a million times before, you are not to come down to the servants' quarters! You are to stay out of the kitchens!"

"Well, she's doing no harm, Your Lordship – I don't mind her being here with me," said Flancy.

"But *I* mind!" snapped Nicholas.

"But why do you mind?" asked Flancy, as she and Petronella continued to bake as if he wasn't there.

"Because the kitchen is not the place for a young lady of Petronella's breeding! And besides, I don't have to answer to you as regards my decisions for my daughter!"

"Somebody's not in a good mood today, pet," Flancy muttered to Petronella, causing the girl to giggle loudly.

"How many times have I told you before, Flancy? Petronella is *not* to be addressed as *pet*!" ranted Nicholas, but they both continued to ignore him. "Is anybody listening to me?"

He fought an overwhelming desire to stamp his feet on the ground, like a small boy, in order to get their attention.

"Petronella! Return at once to the schoolroom where you can study your geography for the rest of the afternoon *without* Miss Giddings!" he ordered.

"Have I beaten this enough, Flancy?" asked Petronella.

"Yes, pet," said Flancy.

"*Petronella*!" yelled Nicholas.

"*What do you want*?" Petronella suddenly shouted back, looking at him for the first time, her eyes blazing with defiance.

"Did you not hear me? I said go to the schoolroom!"

"No!" Petronella snapped back. "I'm staying here baking with Flancy until the cake is done. If you have any problem with it – then tell Mama when she gets home!"

Nicholas stared at the two of them, bottling up the rage inside him which was in danger of exploding.

He quickly turned and stormed out of the kitchen and back up the stairs.

"I'm getting truly sick and tired of that fellow," Flancy said to Petronella, placing two greased baking tins on the table.

"He's such a nuisance, Flancy!" said Petronella, as she started to spoon the mixture into the tins.

Nicholas was in the drawing room nursing a glass of whiskey. Milandra had not arrived home yet.

Flancy walked into the room.

"Your dinner is waiting for you in the dining room, Your Lordship," she informed him.

"I will wait until my wife arrives home, and I will eat with her," said Nicholas.

"But, sure, Milandra is attending a function at the Lord Mayor's – she won't be home until after midnight."

"The Lord Mayor's! It's the first I've heard it," said Nicholas, who really wasn't surprised, as Milandra was out at one thing or another most nights.

"Well, that's where Milandra is!"

"You are not to address my wife by her first name, Flancy. She is Lady Havington to you. How many times do I have to tell you?"

"She'll always be Milandra to me, and she hasn't told me to call her anything else," Flancy said dismissively.

Nicholas could not believe the woman's cheek. He thought of what the consequences would have been in his own home if a servant had ever dared to address his parents in such a manner.

"As I said, your dinner is waiting for you – it will be cold if you leave it much longer," said Flancy.

"I am not hungry. I do not want it. I had lunch at my Club," said Nicholas.

"But that was hours ago! You must be hungry by now . . . I'll send you up a sandwich."

"I said I wasn't hungry! Will you listen to my wishes and stop contradicting me!"

Flancy shrugged, walked over to the windows and began to draw the curtains.

"Leave them!" Nicholas called over to her abruptly.

"You don't want the curtains drawn? But it's getting dark."

"I said – leave them!"

"Very well, Your Lordship." She walked over to the table in front of him and took up his nearly empty whiskey glass.

"Where are you taking that?" he asked.

"To refill it for you," said Flancy.

"Put it back at once! If I wanted you to refill it, I'd have asked for you to do so. I am not my wife, Flancy – I do not need you to do everything for me!"

"As you wish, Your Lordship." Flancy pursed her lips and walked out.

CHAPTER 67

It was way past midnight and Milandra still hadn't come home. Nicholas looked out the window to see if he could see his wife. At that moment a carriage pulled up outside. He peered down and saw Milandra step out – but instead of coming straight in, she was talking to a man in the carriage. He peered further and recognised the man as Philip Bunton, a man with an unscrupulous reputation as a property speculator who was ruthless with his tenants in the slums.

As Nicholas continued to peer, he saw Milandra laughing and joking with Bunton, sharing an intimate joke.

As Milandra came through the front door, Flancy greeted her and took her shawl.

"Did you have a nice night?" asked Flancy.

"Superb, Flancy. The Lord Mayor certainly knows how to entertain. Is Petronella in bed?"

"Yes, Milandra."

"I'll look in on her. Is Nicholas in bed?"

"No, His *Lordship* is in the drawing room. I think he's waiting up to speak with you."

"Oh, what a bore!"

"He's been drinking," warned Flancy.

"Even more boring!"

"And he's been in a dreadful mood all day."

Milandra sighed and raised her eyes to heaven. "I'd better go and face the music."

Milandra walked up the stairs, down the landing and into the drawing room where she found Nicholas standing by the fireplace.

"Oh, you're back, are you?"

"Yes, the Lord Mayor's function went on longer than I expected," she said.

"You didn't mention this morning that you were going to the Lord Mayor's?"

"Didn't I? It must have slipped my mind." She crossed over to a cabinet, opened her cigarette box, took one and lit it with a match.

"I really wish you wouldn't smoke, Milandra! It's such a disgusting habit in a woman!"

"Oh, for goodness sake, it's hardly a habit. I have one in the evening!"

"Still, it's so unbecoming."

Milandra ignored him and continued to smoke.

"Was that Philip Bunton I saw you in a carriage with?" he asked.

"Yes, he was coming my way, so kindly offered me a lift."

"Why are you consorting with that man? He has an atrocious reputation. He treats people like dirt. Hardly a suitable connection for Lady Havington."

"He also happens to be one of Carters Wines' best customers," said Milandra. "His tastes are wide and expensive. I don't care what his reputation is – he puts a lot of money in my tills."

"Well, I think it's a disgrace. Being seen with a man like that in public. I forbid it in future, as your husband."

"Indeed, I shall try to avoid him in future in that case, I'm sure." Her voice dripped sarcasm. She pointed down to the empty glass on the table. "I'm in no mood to speak to you when you've been drinking."

"I've only had two drinks all night," he said truthfully.

"Yes, I'm sure," she said sarcastically. "Well, I'm going to bed."

"Not before I've spoken to you about Petronella."

"What about her?"

"I came home early and found her down in the kitchens baking with Flancy," he said.

"What of it?"

"*What of it*? Our daughter should not be baking in the kitchen with the cook – she should be receiving her proper education. I received a note from Miss Giddings this evening saying she would not be returning to teach Petronella."

"So? Teachers are two a penny – we'll just hire a new one."

Nicholas went to the table and picked up Miss Giddings' note. "She says she cannot continue to work here as Flancy has been hostile to her."

"I didn't like the look of that Miss Giddings in any case," said Milandra.

"Milandra! This is the third teacher Flancy has driven out in six months! If this continues, we will have an illiterate and uneducated daughter! She has no clue of history or geography!"

"Petronella is far from illiterate or uneducated. She receives most of the education she needs in life from me. I teach her maths and business, the essentials of life. Geography! What is the point in knowing where Borneo is, if you are not equipped to make money enough to ever get there! History! What is the point of learning about things that are already done and dusted!"

Nicholas looked at her incredulously. "So you are part of this conspiracy to get rid of the teachers along with Flancy! Well, no more! From now on, I forbid Petronella to enter the servants' quarters. She is to stay out of the kitchen!"

"Oh, you are so funny when you try to be all manly!" laughed Milandra as she drew on her cigarette.

Nicholas's face went red with rage. "I am the head of this house! The husband, father and master of this house!"

"Of course you are all those things." Milandra's voice was thick with sarcasm.

"And as the head of this house, I demand, nay, *command* there will be changes around here from now on!"

"Do tell! Pray, do tell!" Milandra stifled a giggle.

"First of all – Flancy must leave!" Nicholas said.

"I beg your pardon?"

"Flancy! I want her out of this house. She's a bad influence on everything and everyone. She doesn't act like a cook, but as if she owns the house. We can't get a butler, or even a footman in the house because she forbids it. I'm not even allowed a valet! Most of all, I will not allow her to continue this unhealthy influence she has over Petronella."

Milandra walked to the fireplace and flung her cigarette into it before turning to face him. "That suggestion, my dear Nicholas, is quite out of the question."

"I'm not giving in this time, Milandra. I mean it. Either she goes – or I go!"

Her eyes narrowed as she focused on him. "Nicholas, *never* give me an ultimatum again if you know what is good for you. I'm going to make myself very clear here. In the pecking order of things in this house, you are at the very bottom! Below me, below Petronella, below Flancy – why, even below Sally the scullery maid! Because at least Sally the scullery maid clears the fireplaces out every morning, which is more useful than anything that you ever do! So if you any notion that you are the head of this house, simply remove it from your mind. I will never, *ever* get rid of Flancy, and I never want to hear you say a bad word about or against her again."

"How dare you speak to me, your husband, like that!" Nicholas was enraged.

"I speak it because it's true. What have you ever achieved for yourself? Nothing! You only have your title because you inherited it from your father, who only got that by chance when his drunken relative killed himself. You only have your position at Gilligans' Solicitors because your father organised it for you years ago, and you have never moved on. And you have only managed to retain your position there because of the amount of work I give them! You owe everything to your father and to me. I hate to use the word, but the only word that aptly describes you is – useless! Useless beyond compare!"

Nicholas was so wounded by the cruelty of her words that he was stunned into silence.

"Now, I don't want to hear any more of this nonsense. I am going to bed." Milandra walked to the door, then turned around and looked at him.

"Are you coming to bed?" she asked.

"No! I am not!" he muttered.

"Fine. Let us be honest – you were always useless in that department as well," she said and she swept out of the room.

CHAPTER 68

Constance inspected her work and, content with the sewing, took the dress she had been working on and walked over to the supervisor Mrs. Cleary.

"All finished, Constance?" she asked.

"Yes," said Constance as she handed over the gown.

Mrs. Cleary made a quick inspection of the work.

"Very good, as always."

"Is there anything else?" asked Constance.

"No, you get yourself off for the night. See you in the morning, eight sharp."

"Thank you, Mrs. Cleary," nodded Constance and she walked across the draper's workshop to get her hat and coat from the coat-stand and put them on.

As Mrs. Cleary watched her go, she wondered why she always bothered to inspect Constance's work or say the words 'eight sharp' each evening to her. She was so used to doing it with the other women in the workshop that it was just force of habit. In the five years that Constance had worked as a seamstress for Mrs. Cleary, her work had always been perfect, and she had never been late. She was a perfect employee.

The first day Constance had stepped into her workshop looking for employment, Mrs. Cleary knew by her manner and accent that this young woman was different from the usual ones who came her way. She liked the look of her and took a chance on her, and had never regretted it. And she was glad she could offer the hardworking girl decent employment – she knew that previously Constance had worked as a seamstress in a notorious sweatshop, whose workers were exploited, with awful working conditions and appalling pay.

Mrs. Cleary had heard the rumours about a bishop's daughter who years ago had disgraced herself by acting like a common whore, and quickly realised by Constance's surname that this was her. She knew Constance had a son, and that there was no sign of a husband. But if Mrs. Cleary paid heed to every misdoing a potential employee had attached to her, she wouldn't have any employees. She had learned to ignore such things. They were plentiful in the slums of Dublin. Constance kept to herself, didn't chatter to the other women and her work was always faultless. And that, as far as Mrs. Cleary was concerned, was all that mattered.

As Constance stepped out of Mrs. Cleary's workshop onto the narrow street outside, she was engulfed with that familiar feeling. That familiar feeling of freedom. Freedom for just a few short hours each night to be rid of that place, to go home, and spend time with the love of her life, her eleven-year-old son John.

Constance knew she should never complain about Mrs. Cleary's – it was bliss compared to the sweatshop she had toiled in for five years before that. At least at Mrs. Cleary's she was allowed to sit for her ten-hour working day. And they opened windows during the summer to let in air – the last place didn't even have windows. And they lit a fire in the winter to warm the place – the last place didn't even have a fireplace. Yes, Mrs. Cleary's was bliss compared to that dreadful place.

But as Constance quickened her pace through the streets of the tenements and slums that evening, it wasn't just to see John that she hurried along. Something out of the ordinary had happened the previous night.

When Constance had arrived home the day before, she found she had received an envelope in the post. She got a shock when she saw it. Because she immediately recognised the writing on it as her sister

Emma's, and it had been posted from Australia. In the years since her family had emigrated to Australia, she had received only sporadic letters from them. They had all been from Emma and just to inform her that they were well and working hard in the outback where life was harsh. In the letters Emma had never asked how Constance was, or how her circumstances were. The only thing she seemed interested in was the condition of the house. Deeply hurt, Constance responded only a few times in kind – assuring them that she was surviving, as was the house. She didn't mention John, realising that Emma didn't want to know anything about the fate of her baby.

The previous night Constance's hands had started to shake as she held the envelope. Some instinct made her feel that this letter was not the usual perfunctory few lines. Had something happened? Were her parents all right? Recently she had become full of worry about them – they were getting older now.

Standing there, holding the letter, all the dreadful memories from the past had come flooding in on her. Remembering her family leaving her abandoned to her fate. How she had eked out the money her father had left her. How it had eventually dried up. How she had then sold anything she could find of value in the house to feed herself and her child. She wondered how she hadn't gone mad when she thought back to those times. Alone with an infant with no way of supporting herself, and no support from anybody. Soon she realised she would have to rely on charity to survive.

To her great shame, one morning she had taken her infant son and gone to one of the church halls to line up with the other mothers and wait to be given a food parcel. She had made sure to avoid any of the church halls her father had run. The idea of being handed a food parcel by one of the volunteers that she used to work alongside was just too shaming to bear. So she went to one where she was sure she wouldn't meet anybody she knew and stood alongside the mothers from the tenements and gratefully received her small bundle that was to last her a week. As she fed herself and her baby that week, she realised she was probably the recipient of donations from somebody like Lady Vrayford, or Milandra Carter, or the Fontenoys.

She'd had to put all thoughts of Nicholas Fontenoy from her head, otherwise she definitely would have gone mad. Her Nicholas, now married to Milandra Carter. She had been overcome by bitter feelings at first. Dreadful all-consuming bitter feelings, as she read in the newspaper of their lavish wedding and then of the birth of their daughter. She remembered the girl's name – Petronella. How that name suited Milandra Carter's daughter! She had read in the newspapers over the years of Daniel Fontenoy inheriting a title from a cousin, and how he had died. She had seen how Nicholas had inherited his father's recently acquired title. And she had thought bitterly how everything had always come so easy to Nicholas. And now Nicholas and Milandra were Lord and Lady Havington of Sackville Street, the world at their feet. Constance had forced herself out of her bitterness over time, and had to realise that she was responsible for her own path of ruin in life. She couldn't blame other people for ever. She had to get on with her life as best she could. She had a son to raise. Once he was old enough, she had come to an arrangement with a woman called Máire, who lived in a tenement to the back of Mountjoy Square, to mind him during the time she tried to find work. Eventually she had found work in the sweatshop, which led to her working at Mrs. Cleary's. She earned enough to put food on the table and an occasional treat. John went to school during the day and then went to stay with Máire and her own brood of six children until Constance came home from work.

Constance hardly ever thought of Nicholas any more, or even her own family, or that other destiny she could have had where she would have been Lady Havington by now. Now her life was about working to give John the best life she could give him under the circumstances they lived in.

As her mind was flooded with all these memories, Constance found she could not face opening the letter from Australia. She placed it on the mantelpiece in the drawing room and went to spend precious time with her son.

As Constance approached the tenement where John's child-minder lived, she saw John already waiting on the doorstep for her.

"Mam!" he shouted and came running down the street into her arms.

She hugged him tightly. This was what it was all for, she reminded herself.

The window of the downstairs flat was opened and Máire stuck out her head, surrounded by three of her own children's heads.

"Will ya come in for a cup of tea, Constance?" asked Máire.

"Not this evening, thank you, Máire. There's something I have to do."

"That's fine. Drop him back to me in the morning as usual and I'll make sure he gets to school with the rest of mine!"

"I will, and thank you, Máire, thank you so very much," said Constance, who never tired of thanking her. Even though she paid her to mind John, she didn't know how she would have coped without her kindness throughout the years. It was really the only kindness she ever received.

Máire's greatest kindness was that she never asked or enquired about John's father or what circumstances had brought Constance to where she was in life. Constance knew that Máire and the other women in the tenements must have realised that she had come from a good family – and they must have wondered how she came to live in a big townhouse on her own. But instead of judging her or questioning her, they had closed rank around her, offering her the only support she had received. These women struggled in their own lives – every day was a challenge. Widowhood, desertion and illegitimacy was widespread amongst them. To these women, Constance, despite her education and manner, was one of them.

Constance took John's hand and he cheerily told her his stories from his day at school and playing with Máire's children after school. She listened intently.

They turned the corner into Mountjoy Square. She thought if her parents came back to see it now they wouldn't recognise it. She passed the once fine Georgian townhouses – the vast majority of them, having been bought up by speculators, were now turned into tenements. The houses had been subdivided and turned into one-room flats where large families lived. Washing hung out of windows, and the park in the centre of the Square where once nannies minded their precious charges, was now overrun with grubby and neglected children. The Staffordshire house was nearly the last house that had not been taken over and turned into tenements on the Square.

Constance and John walked up the steps to the front door and, taking her key, she let them in.

The house was much barer now than it had been when the Bishop lived there. They had taken all the personal things to Australia with them and had sold off anything of value. Then Constance had sold much of what remained during the lean times. But she had made the house as homely as she could, and she realised how lucky they were to have it, even though it was much too big for the two of them, and was a house that was designed to have a full staff of servants.

Constance and John spent the evening as they always did – talking, doing his homework and playing games. As an only child, she was delighted he had the company of Máire's children during the day. Children needed company, though she had never thought a child of hers would be friends with children from the tenements.

She put John to bed and kissed him goodnight, and then she came back downstairs and into the drawing room. She looked at the letter from Emma that was still standing on the mantelpiece where she had put it the previous night, and immediately felt anxious again.

She stood up and went to get it. Sitting down, she opened it and saw it was a very short letter. She read it quickly and then looked up, confused and afraid. Emma had written to inform her she would be arriving in Dublin from Australia the next week and would be visiting her on the Wednesday evening. There was no explanation, no message about her parents, no indication of why she was coming back to Dublin. Constance began to panic at the thought of seeing her sister again after all the years.

"Am I really going to meet my aunt?" asked John the following Wednesday evening.

"Yes, she's coming all the way from Australia to see you," said Constance.

She had scrubbed him up and put on his best clothes. Now she took a final look at him before leading him downstairs to the drawing room.

She knew John was over-excited. He had been brought up with no relatives but her, and she knew he would have desperately liked a large family. Growing up spending so much time with Máire's family had given him a longing for the same.

She had spent all her week's wages on food as fancy as she could get her hands on and tea was all set out in the drawing room, ready for Emma. And her old bedroom was prepared for her upstairs.

She was really excited at the thought of seeing her sister again, even though she was a bundle of nerves. She went to the mirror and inspected her own appearance and smoothed down her hair.

"Now, remember, you are to be on your best behaviour when Aunt Emma arrives," she said as she kissed his forehead.

"Yes, Mam," he promised.

She cringed to hear him call her 'Mam'. He used to call her 'Mama' as she would have preferred. But all the other children made fun of him when they heard him say it. It was completely out of place in the environment that Mountjoy Square had become. But she wondered what Emma would think if she heard him use such a working-class word.

There was a knock on the door, and her heart began to beat fast.

"You stay here," she said to John.

She steadied herself and went to the front door and opened it.

"Hello, Constance," said Emma.

Constance was speechless for a moment as she looked at her sister. Emma had grown from a girl to a woman. The girl's serious expression had now become a stern look. With her hair tightly pulled back in a bun, she was wearing the severe black dress, the starched white-collared uniform of a colonial teacher and missionary.

"Emma!" gasped Constance and embraced her.

Emma stood still for a while before awkwardly placing her arms around her sister and hugging her back.

Constance pulled back and looked at her. "It's so wonderful to see you!" she said.

Emma didn't respond in kind.

"Come in, come in!"

As Emma stepped in, Constance looked at the steps outside, expecting to see some luggage. But there was nothing.

"You don't have any luggage?" she asked.

"Oh – no," said Emma.

Constance wondered where she had left it but didn't ask, closing the front door behind them.

"It's so good to see you! I can't tell you how good it is!" Constance wiped tears from her eyes.

"Yes, you too," said Emma, looking around the hall and up the stairs.

"Come! There's somebody who cannot wait to meet you!" said Constance, leading her sister by the hand into the drawing room.

Emma stood stock still as a little boy came rushing over to her and threw his arms around her in a tight hug.

"Oh, Aunt Emma!" John cried happily.

Emma was clearly stunned as she held her hands in the air and looked down at the child smiling up at her.

"Emma, this is your nephew, John," said Constance.

"I see!" said Emma eventually and managed to bring one of her hands down and pat him on the head.

"John! Let Aunt Emma alone now, and let her sit down," urged Constance and he finally released her.

Emma walked past the child and sat down on the couch. He followed her and sat beside her, with a hand on her arm.

"You must be starving! We prepared tea for you," said Constance, sitting down on a nearby armchair.

"You shouldn't have. I've already eaten."

"Oh!" said Constance as she thought of the money wasted on all the food she had bought. "Well – perhaps later?"

"I can't stay that long, Constance. I'm only staying in Dublin a few days and I've a lot to do."

"I see . . . you gave so few details in your letter . . . I prepared a room for you . . . I assumed you would stay here."

"There is no need. I have booked into a hotel for my visit."

"I see," said Constance, nodding.

John began to babble on, telling his Aunt Emma all about his life, his school and his friends. But Constance soon saw that Emma had little interest in what he was saying and was becoming impatient.

"John, why don't you go and play in the garden for a while and let Emma and me have a grown-up talk," urged Constance.

"But –" John began to object.

"Just for a while," insisted his mother.

"All right then," he agreed and smiled at Emma.

He ran out, leaving them alone.

Constance couldn't restrain herself. "You could have been kinder to him – he's only a child, Emma."

"Forgive me if I appeared unkind. It was just such a shock seeing him . . . I didn't realise you had kept him."

"Of course I did!"

"I thought the doctor at the time was arranging something?"

"I didn't agree to the doctor's arrangements. And I've never regretted it. We are quite happy."

"Why didn't you tell us?" cried Emma.

"Why didn't you ask? Even once! You obviously didn't want to know!"

"Father and Mother didn't want me to refer to the matter," said Emma.

"And you've always done what Father and Mother required of you," said Constance cynically.

"Unlike you!" Emma shot back.

They sat in silence for a while before Constance said, almost afraid to ask, "How are Mother and Father?"

"They are as fine as they can be. They never really got over . . . They have been very busy these years, dedicating their lives to the less fortunate."

"They couldn't have found somebody less fortunate then I when they walked out on me!" Constance's bitterness came tumbling out.

"All of your own making!" Emma retorted.

Constance blinked back her tears. "Why are you being so cruel? You were never cruel! What has happened to you?"

Emma's own eyes filled with tears and she quickly wiped them away. "Years in the outback of Australia, that's what happened to me!"

"Has it been – very hard?" asked Constance.

Emma wiped away a tear that spilled down her face. "More than you can imagine. Father and Mother never recovered from what happened to you. Father seemed to think he was fully responsible and has worked himself ragged working in the outback trying to atone. Mother too. And the conditions are awful – miles and miles of dust and sweltering heat with only the very basics of any kind of comfort."

"I brought a lot of pain to your door," whispered Constance.

"You did. So you must forgive me if I appear bitter. When you did what you did, and we had to leave for Australia, you consigned me to a life of spinsterhood."

"Hardly!" objected Constance.

"Yes! What respectable man would ever have looked at me in Dublin with you as a sister? And in the outback there is absolutely no suitable marriage prospects, I can assure you. Your actions cost me a good life as a wife and mother." Emma wiped away another tear.

Constance looked at the floor, ashamed.

"Well, look, I haven't come all this way to drag over ancient history," said Emma. "I've come on other business."

Constance felt vaguely alarmed. "Oh? What other business?"

"I need to inform you that Father and Mother are now getting older –"

"That I already know!"

"If you could let me finish? They don't wish to continue to work as relentlessly as they have been all these years. They wish to open a school for the disadvantaged that I will help them run."

"It sounds like a good plan."

"It is. But in order to fund the school we need to sell the house here."

"*What?*"

"Well, it's the only way forward. You must have known that you couldn't occupy the house indefinitely. That it would be sold eventually. You are fortunate that you have had it for as long as you had."

"But it's impossible. This is our home!"

"It's far too big for one woman and a little boy. And, naturally, its condition is deteriorating by the year. We can't let it crumble around your ears until it loses all value."

"But you can't sell it from under us!"

"It's already done, Constance. You're wasting your breath. The contract is being finalised today. It has been bought by a property investor who will turn it into flats, as I understand it."

"But you're leaving us with nowhere to live!" cried Constance.

"Of course we're not. It has been agreed with the buyer that you can stay on in one of the flats here – there will be no rent," said Emma.

"But – but – but I've seen the flats the other houses on the Square have been turned into and they are just one room! And they are appalling places to live!" Constance was becoming a quivering wreck.

"That is what has been agreed with the buyer, that you and the child may remain in your own room after the house is sold."

"Just one room!"

"I am sorry, Constance, but you can't continue to keep this big house here while Father and Mother see out their days in a basic missionary house in Australia. There is no money to be made as missionaries and they simply have to sell here."

"I understand that but –"

"You had decisions in life, and you made them. Even after you got yourself pregnant by God knows who, and destroyed our family and our reputation, you had options. You could have done as the doctor advised and arranged a family for the child, and gone away, as we did, and tried to live a respectable life where nobody knew you. That is what we expected you to do. What else? You could have found a position as a companion to a wealthy widow. You might have even managed to get somebody else to marry you, given your colourful history with men."

Constance got to her feet. "I think it's best you leave now, Emma," she said.

"Very well," said Emma, standing up. "I probably won't see you again before I leave for Australia."

Constance walked her to the front door and opened it. Then she faced her sister and said, "Regardless of everything, if I hadn't done what I had done, then I wouldn't have John. He is my life."

"Well, then, something good has come out of it, Constance," said Emma awkwardly, "and that I am glad of."

Emma leaned forward and kissed Constance's cheek before leaving quickly.

CHAPTER 69

Milandra looked at Nicholas across the dining-room table as she ate her breakfast. It had been a week since their vicious argument and he had barely spoken two words to her since. He had kept out of her way and tried to avoid her as best he could.

"More tea, Your Lordship?" Flancy smiled happily at him as she hovered beside him with the teapot.

"No," answered a surly Nicholas.

Flancy ignored him and to his irritation filled his teacup to the brim.

"Busy day ahead of you at the office?" Milandra smiled at him across the table.

"Very," he answered.

"Well, a good hearty breakfast is what you need inside you then," said Flancy as she shovelled more bacon on his plate, causing Nicholas to glare at her.

"I didn't want any more bacon!" he objected.

"Whatever you don't want you can leave," said Flancy, throwing more sausages on his plate while she was at it.

He heaved a sigh of exasperation.

"What are Petronella's plans for the day?" he then asked.

"Oh, I'm sure she'll be busy – brushing up on her history and geography," said Milandra and she and Flancy exchanged smirks.

Nicholas stood up and threw his napkin on the table. "I'm going to work."

"But you haven't finished your breakfast," Milandra pointed out.

Flancy grabbed his shoulders and forced him back down into his chair.

"You're not leaving this table till you have a hearty breakfast inside you, Your Lordship!" she said.

As Nicholas looked at the two of them he felt suffocated, trapped.

"I do not need you to tell me when I am full, Flancy!" he snapped.

"Of course you don't," agreed Flancy as she cut a slice of bacon from his plate and held it up to his mouth on a fork for him to eat.

"For goodness' sake!" He jumped to his feet again.

"Whatever is the matter with you, Nicholas? Flancy is only trying to help you," said Milandra.

"I don't need her help! I don't need anything from her – or you!"

He marched out of the dining room and they heard the front door open and slam.

Milandra sighed as she continued to eat her breakfast. "His loss!"

"He's such a contrary fellow," sighed Flancy.

"Isn't he just?"

"You could have had anybody . . . do you ever regret marrying him?" asked Flancy.

Milandra stopped eating and looked up at her. "Of course not! I never regret anything."

CHAPTER 70

Nicholas was in his office at Gilligans' Solicitors, deep in thought. He felt so low. He had never expected his life to turn out like it had. With no control or power over anything. Having to put up with Milandra, her vicious tongue and devious ways. How different she was from the wonderful, kind woman he had married. The woman who treated him like the most important man in the world. Now, he felt like just an accessory in her life. And as for the dread Flancy! The control the woman had was breath-taking. How his father would be disappointed in him! He had expected him to go so far in life.

There was a knock on the door and his clerk walked in with a stack of contracts.

"Pardon me, Lord Havington, I've looked through these contracts and all are in order – they just require a signature from you." The clerk placed the contracts on his desk in front of him.

"Just a signature, eh?" sighed Nicholas. He was even surplus to requirement in his job. His clerk did everything, and all he had to do was sign it off.

"Sorry, Your Lordship?" The clerk was confused.

"It's nothing, ignore me. Leave them with me and I'll sign them," said Nicholas and the clerk nodded and left.

Sighing, Nicholas took up the first contact, glanced through it and scribbled his signature on it. He did the same for the second and third contract. As he was doing the same for the fourth, something caught his eye. It was for a house in Mountjoy Square.

Always when he heard or saw a mention of Mountjoy Square, the memories came flooding back to him. Constance. Whatever had happened to her? He had heard the family had emigrated to Australia after all the scandal and never been heard from again. He wondered what Constance was doing in Australia – had she managed to escape her past? Had she managed to start anew? Had she met somebody? Had she married? Was she happy? He flicked through the contract and stopped abruptly when he saw the name on the contract: *John Staffordshire.* He sat up quickly and began to study the contract and saw it was for the sale of the Staffordshire house in Mountjoy Square. He could not believe that they had owned it all this time. He imagined that it would have been sold when they emigrated to Australia. Curiosity overcame him as he wondered if it had been lying idle all that time. Or perhaps it had been rented out. He knew that over the years the slums had crept nearer to Mountjoy Square and it was now full of tenements. He saw the buyer of the property was Milandra's acquaintance, Philip Bunton. Nicholas wasn't surprised by that. Bunton was always looking for an opportunity to open a new tenement. Nicholas remembered all the happy times he'd had in that house with Constance. It saddened him to see it would fall into Bunton's hands and be turned in a tenement. A lot saddened him when he thought of Constance.

Nicholas walked up Sackville Street after work and on to Rutland Square. But, instead of stopping at his old home, he walked on. He passed the house and glanced through the window into the room that used to be their drawing-room, seeing it was converted to an office. He always felt saddened when he passed his family home, thinking of the happy times he had there. It seemed to make his life now all the more unhappy. Nicholas did not know himself what he was doing that evening as he continued on his journey through the streets that led to Mountjoy Square. He hadn't been to Mountjoy Square in years. All the families he used to know in the area had moved. And as he neared Mountjoy Square, he quickly realised why. He became increasingly shocked at how the area had deteriorated, as he observed laundry hanging out of windows and an air of dereliction. It only got worse as he entered Mountjoy Square. The park was still in the centre of the Square and as he walked through it he was besieged by children asking for money. He threw some coins away from him to get rid of the children as they scurried after them. Reaching the other end of the park, he stopped and looked up at the Staffordshire house through the park railings. All the memories of the house came crashing back in on top of him – the good times – and the bad times as he thought of that dreadful night when he had charged in and broken off his engagement with Constance. In a way that night had altered the course of his life, and set him on the path to his marriage to Milandra and the misery he now lived under. The Staffordshire house seemed the only house on that row that had not already been turned into tenements. And soon that would change too, when Philip Bunton converted it. He was glad he had come to take one final look at the house that evening.

He was about to turn away when he noticed a woman walking down the other side of the road.

He squinted as he stared. She reminded him so much of . . .

"Constance!" he whispered disbelievingly.

As she came nearer, he quickly hid behind a tree and continued to observe. She was holding the hand of a child, a young boy. He stood like a statue behind the tree as they reached the Staffordshire house and began to climb the steps to the front door. As he strained to hear, he could hear the boy excitedly telling his mother about his day in school.

He stared at the child in disbelief as Constance opened the door and let them in. And then they were out of view as she closed the door behind them.

He leaned against the tree as he tried to catch his breath. Constance had never gone to Australia with her family! She had been in Dublin all along. And she was a mother. He began to wipe his hand across his mouth in disbelief and excitement. Just seeing her again had filled him with excitement. But the child! There was no mistaking the child! The boy was the image of him. His heart began to palpitate and he bent over and threw up. It was all too much for him and he didn't know what to do. His head was telling him to walk away as quickly as possible and never return to Mountjoy Square. Not to bring this trouble on himself. Constance was obviously living her life and he should return to living his. His empty life with Milandra.

But just seeing Constance again had awakened something that he never thought he would feel again. And – and – the child! His head began to throb as realisation dawned on him that Constance must have been pregnant with his child when he broke off the engagement.

Before he could think further, he found himself running out of the park and across the road to the Staffordshire front door.

He knocked loudly.

There was no answer for a minute and he knocked even louder. Then the door opened and Constance was standing before him. She was shocked momentarily and then she burst into tears at the sight of him.

She quickly backed away from the door and then turned her back and began to wipe her tears away with her hands.

"What do you want? Why are you here?" she demanded through her tears.

"I've come to speak to you," he said, coming through the door.

At that moment John came rushing in from the back.

"What's wrong, Mam, why are you crying? Who is that man?"

Nicholas stared down at the boy in astonishment.

Coming to her senses, Constance quickly rushed to John.

"Everything's fine, John. Just go back into the garden and play," she urged.

"But, Mam –" began John.

"Now!" she snapped.

Regaining her composure, she turned to face Nicholas.

"I don't know what you have to talk to me about, but I have no desire to talk to you. Please leave. My husband will be home shortly." She spoke evenly, trying to hide the tremor in her voice.

He looked down at her fingers and saw no wedding ring.

"You have no husband," he said.

"*Now! Please go!*"

"Not till I've found out what has been going on," he said, closing the door behind him and walking forward.

"Get out of my house now!" she demanded.

Nicholas nodded towards the back garden. "Where is the boy's father?"

"I told you! He'll be home any minute and if he finds a strange man in his house he will punch you! And throw you out!"

"The only man this house belongs to is Bishop Staffordshire, your father. I saw the contract in my office that he is selling it."

"Oh, just go, Nicholas! I don't want to ever speak to you again. You can't just barge in here like you did all those years ago to create the terrible scene that tore my family apart forever. Haven't you done enough damage?"

"I didn't realise, that night I barged in here and called off our engagement, that you were already pregnant," he said.

"I wasn't. The child came later!"

"What age is he, Constance? Don't lie to me, I can find out on the birth records."

"And even if I was pregnant at the time, you most assuredly are not his father! He's Tom Fitzgerald's child, or George Fetherston's! I've always believed he is Tom's."

"He might have been either of theirs, but he's not. He's my child, Constance. It's like looking into a mirror when I look at him."

She put her hand to her mouth. "Oh, just go, Nicholas. For pity's sake, leave me in peace. You have no right to just arrive in like this, no right at all."

"I have every right if the boy is mine," said Nicholas.

"He's not yours! He has nothing to do with you! He's mine! You have your own wife and family – go back to them. Does Milandra know you are here?"

"No, she doesn't," said Nicholas.

"Well, I think she would have something to say if she knew you were! Go back to your wife, Nicholas. I have no wish to talk to you. Leave us alone, please!"

"Five minutes! Just give me five minutes! That's all I ask, and then you will never have to see me again," he pleaded.

She stood and sighed before conceding. "Five minutes."

He followed her into the drawing room.

"I thought you had gone to Australia with the rest of your family," he said.

She realised there was no use in lying. John was the image of his father, and Nicholas would check the birth records for him and see it was possible that he was the father.

"They didn't want me to go with them . . . after everything," she said.

"Did they know you were pregnant?"

"Oh, they knew all right. It hastened their departure," she said bitterly.

"Why didn't you come to me – tell me?" He was incredulous.

"Because you had no way of knowing if you were the father."

"But how have you survived all these years? On your own?"

"I've survived very well. I work as a seamstress and am very happy," she replied.

"A seamstress!"

"Yes." She looked at him defiantly.

"And lived here all this time?"

She waved her hand in the air. "Clearly!"

"But you won't for long more?"

"What do you mean?" she asked.

"As I told you, I know from my work that your father has sold the house. Where are you to go?"

"That is none of your business!" she snapped.

"It is now! I want to know what will happen to my son!"

"He has been perfectly well cared for all these years without you, and will continue to be without you!"

"I want to see him, speak to him."

"No!"

"Please!"

"Out of the question! Now your five minutes are up. Please leave."

"I want to provide for him, financially. He's my responsibility."

"He is not and never has been and never will be your responsibility. Go back to your family now, Nicholas! I insist!"

"But –"

"You promised – five minutes and you would be gone!" she insisted.

He stood there thinking, before saying, "Very well. But I will be back."

"Do not come back ever!" she cried.

"I will be back," Nicholas promised and turned and walked away.

Only when she heard the front door close behind him did she fall to her knees on the floor, running her hands through her hair in desperation.

She never wanted to see him again.

CHAPTER 71

Over the following days, Nicholas could not concentrate on anything. He was totally preoccupied with Constance and her son, their son. It was a shock to him to discover he had a son. Everything was a shock. Everything else seemed unimportant as he went around in a daze. He could barely even pretend to listen when Milandra was talking, he was oblivious to Flancy's constant diatribes, couldn't care less that Petronella's schooling was still being neglected. At work, he stared out of the window and just signed anything his clerk put in front of him without even looking at it. His life had been turned upside down. After work, instead of going straight home, he began to go to Mountjoy Square where he would hide in the park, anxious to get a glimpse of Constance and his son. He began to learn their timing. They came home each evening at the same time and he watched them, content it was only for a minute as they walked down the street. He began to do the same in the mornings. Waiting across from the house and watching them. After a while he began to discreetly follow them and saw which school his son was attending. He was shocked that he was attending such a low-calibre school: it was school for children from the slums. He followed Constance and saw where she worked, as a seamstress at Mrs. Cleary's. He desperately wanted to reach out to them, but Constance had made it very clear how unwelcome he was. And he understood why she felt that.

He was in her past, and had no place in her present. As Constance preoccupied his mind, he became increasingly resentful of Milandra as he watched her extravagance and lavish lifestyle. He became annoyed with Petronella's ingratitude and indifference to the educational and other opportunities that were on offer to her. It broke his heart to think of his son in such disadvantaged circumstances while Petronella was so spoilt. How Petronella was not interested in spending one minute with him while John had never known what having a father was like. As he thought of Constance, his admiration grew and grew, thinking of what she had gone through, with no support from anybody. He always remembered her as having a quiet pride. And that pride had got her through everything. There was a difference between pride and vanity, Nicholas thought. Constance had pride, but Milandra had vanity. And vanity was very hard to live with. He resolved to do something so that John would know what it was like to be spoilt, for just once in his short life.

Meeting Nicholas had thrown Constance so much that she had barely given thought to her approaching circumstances, to the fact that the house would soon be sold. It had shaken her to her very core for him to just show up like that. For one brief moment when she had opened the door, it was like nothing had happened. That he was just showing up to visit her like when they had been courting, or engaged. And that was why she had burst into tears. Because for one brief moment she remembered how much she had been in love with him. And it frightened her. She hoped he would abide by his promise and never make contact with her again. Because it was too hard on her to see him again. Too much of a reminder of the destiny that she was deprived of. Too much of a reminder of how different her life could have been. But she knew she had to put all that aside and start realising that the house she had lived in all her life would soon be teeming with strangers. She had been in the tenement buildings around there before, in Máire's and other people's. She knew what they would do. The drawing room would be one flat or perhaps even two, the dining room another, all the bedrooms turned into one-room flats filled with large families. She didn't know if she could bear it as she started moving anything precious of hers from the other rooms into her bedroom on the top floor, which under Emma's arrangement with the buyer was to be Constance's and John's room in the building. How would she cope living in such a small place and all these strangers packed into the same building as her? She would break if she thought about it, so she put it to one side and concentrated on preparing her bedroom as the place where she and John would live from now on. She tried to present it to John as a big adventure. That there were lots of other children who would be living in their house soon and he would have so many new friends to choose from. The whole idea confused him, but he didn't seem too perturbed. He would be when he saw the result of the house being turned into a tenement, she knew.

One evening as she was moving china up to her bedroom, there was a knock on the door. She went down and opened it and was surprised to see a young man dressed in livery from Delaneys' Monster Store on Sackville Street, holding a huge hamper of food.

"Yes?" she asked.

"Delivery for Constance Staffordshire," said the man as he nodded back to another man in the Delaneys' horse-drawn van parked out the front. The other man got out of the van, took out another hamper from it and marched up to the house.

"There must be a mistake! I didn't order this," she objected, panicking, as the men walked in and placed the hampers in the hallway.

"No mistake," said the man as he went back out to the van.

She watched as the men carried in more hampers and other items. As she looked at the boxes she realised that many of the contents were toys.

"But who ordered all this?" she demanded. "I can't pay for it. You will have to turn around and take it all back."

"It's already been paid for," said the man.

John came running from the back garden. "What is it, Mam?"

"Nothing, go back and play in the garden," she ordered.

"Oh, look!" cried John as he sank to his knees and picked up a spectacular toy sailing boat.

"Will you please take all this stuff away!" repeated Constance to the men.

"We can't do that. Strict orders not to allow for return. And don't worry about the tip, it's already taken care of." The young man winked as he skipped out and closed the front door behind him.

"Mam, come and look at all this!" squealed John as he rummaged through the hampers and tore open the presents.

"John! Stop, will you! We can't keep all this!"

"Why not?"

"Because we don't know who sent it! We can't accept gifts from strangers," she insisted.

"It wouldn't be a stranger who gave us all this, Mam!" said John, his child's common sense prevailing over Constance's.

"Yes . . . it must be Emma. She must have ordered it before she left for Australia," said Constance. So she has some kind of a conscience, she thought.

"Here's an envelope!" cried John excitedly, holding it out to her.

"Oh!" said Constance. Ripping open the envelope, she pulled out a card and read aloud: "*To John and Constance, love from Nicholas.*"

"Who's Nicholas?" demanded John.

Constance stared at the card in amazement.

"Mam – who is Nicholas?" asked John again, snapping her out of her trance.

"Just an old friend," she whispered.

"Well, he's a very nice old friend to give us all this," laughed John as he kept tearing the wrapping off the boxes.

CHAPTER 72

Nicholas checked with Delaneys' Monster store the next day to make sure the delivery had been made. He was relieved to find it had. He had visions of Constance throwing all the hampers and presents out onto the street after the delivery men. But he was counting on the fact that they were so needy she couldn't deny the child such a feast and presents.

He'd leave it a few days before he called to the house again. If she slammed the door in his face, as he expected her to do, then he would just keep calling back until she left him in.

Nervously Nicholas knocked on the door after watching them coming home, from the park across the road. The door opened and there stood Constance.

As he expected, she went to close the door as soon as she saw him, but he quickly blocked it with his foot and pushed it open.

"Why are you here? I told you not to come back!" Her face was blazing with anger.

Suddenly he saw John come running down the hallway to the door.

"Hello!" said the boy. "Are you Nicholas?"

Nicholas stared down at him in wonder before finally answering, "Yes, I am."

John threw himself at Nicholas and wrapped his arms around his waist, hugging him tightly.

"Thank you! Thank you for all my presents!" he said happily.

Nicholas stood, not knowing what to do, his hands awkwardly in the air as he looked down at the happy child.

"You're very welcome, John. Did you like them?" asked Nicholas.

"Oh, I loved them! Come and I'll show you the sailing boat – it's in the pond in the garden!" John released his grip of Nicholas's waist, grabbed his hand and began to pull him into the house.

"John!" shouted Constance. "Nicholas can't stay! He has to go home to his family – right now!" She shot Nicholas a warning look.

"Just five minutes!" pleaded John, leading Nicholas down the corridor towards the garden. "We'll only be five minutes!"

"No!" commanded Constance.

"Looks like you have no choice in the matter!" said Nicholas, smiling as he was pulled through the house to the back garden.

Panicked, Constance ran into the dining room and looked through the French windows there. She watched as Nicholas got down on in his knees and paid attention to John as he showed him how the sailing boat worked and sailed it across the pond. As she studied them, tears came to her eyes.

John was so excited and Nicholas was just staring at him, almost in awe. As the five minutes passed, Constance couldn't bring herself to go out and interrupt them, they seemed so engrossed in each other's company. Hours seemed to pass by as she didn't move from the window and they made no attempt to come in. Finally, she realised they would be out there all night if she didn't do something and John had to be up early in the morning to be dropped over to Máire's before school.

She opened the French windows and walked out.

"John, it's way past your bedtime," she said.

"Just five minutes more!" John pleaded.

"Absolutely not!" she said.

"We had better do as your mother says." Nicholas smiled at John and led him inside.

"Go up to bed, John, and I'll check in on you in a little while," said Constance.

"Thank you again, Nicholas," said John, enveloping him in another hug.

This time Nicholas hugged him tightly back.

"John!" snapped Constance.

Nicholas reluctantly let him go and watched as the child went to kiss Constance goodnight, gathered up a few scattered toys, and then went off happily upstairs to bed.

"Thank you," said Nicholas to Constance.

"For what?"

"For letting me spend some time with him . . . he's wonderful!"

"I know," said Constance, looking down to the floor.

She turned and walked through the double doors into the drawing room.

"You shouldn't have sent all that stuff from Delaneys'," she said.

"I wasn't sure you'd accept them."

"What choice did I have? Once John had seen them?"

"That's what I was banking on," smiled Nicholas.

"Well, we've managed very well so far without such luxuries, and I daresay we will again. So please do not do it again!"

"I just wanted him to be spoiled for once," he explained.

"Well, it's not fair on him. We can't get such things normally, so he shouldn't get used to them."

"But I told you the last time, I want to financially provide for him, now that I know. I owe him that."

"And I told you – no!"

"But I can help you so much," said Nicholas.

"I haven't gone through all this to rely on your charity now. Have you discussed this with Milandra?" She already knew the answer to the question.

He shook his head and looked down at the floor. "No."

"No, and I daresay she would not agree to this plan of yours, even if I ever would. You didn't even tell her you came and met us, did you?"

"No."

"Of course not – how could you?" she said, sitting down on an armchair.

"I don't discuss anything with Milandra, Constance. It's not a marriage fit for discussing things. It's not a marriage fit for anything."

Despite herself, she became curious. "How do you mean?"

"We don't *talk* about anything – she speaks – but I don't even listen any more."

"But you must have things to talk about – is that not what marriage is about? Your daughter?" Constance knew she was probing but couldn't resist.

"Petronella? We especially don't talk about her. I am excluded from her upbringing, as she is completely taken over by Milandra and that dreadful cook of hers, Flancy."

"I remember her," said Constance, remembering her reputation as the best baker in Dublin. "I'm surprised she is still with you."

"Flancy will *always* be with us! Wretched woman! She and Milandra have left me with no relationship with my daughter, and at this stage I have no relationship with my wife either."

Constance saw the great sadness in his face. "Well, perhaps it should, but hearing this gives no pleasure to me, Nicholas. No pleasure at all."

"You were always very kind," said Nicholas.

"Not kind at this stage, just not spiteful either. I think you should go now, Nicholas, and concentrate on trying to build your relationship with Petronella, and reviving your marriage with Milandra." She stood up. "There's nothing for you here, if you are searching for another outlet. It's not fair on John, to be popping in and out to see him, if that's what you're planning on doing. He doesn't know you, and it's best left that way."

He nodded very sadly and followed her out into the hallway.

She opened the door for him.

"And what about providing financially for him?" he said again. "Can I at least do that?"

Constance shook her head sadly and went to close the door.

Before she closed it she said, "Petronella? What an unusual name – I take it the name choice was Milandra's?"

Nicholas nodded. "Yes."

Constance sighed and smiled "I thought so. Milandra was never going to pick anything ordinary."

Despite Constance's warning, Nicholas could not keep away. The next day, as he thought of the evening he had spent playing with John in the garden, it mesmerised him.

He had never experienced such a time with Petronella, such a connection. It reminded him of his relationships with his own family, who he missed so much. Meeting Constance again had brought him back to those feelings that he thought were long dead. The feelings he had when he was young. Before he ever met Milandra.

That evening, Constance was astounded when she answered the knock at the front door and found Nicholas there again, holding a smaller hamper of food and a toy solider.

"You!" she gasped. "Stop coming here!" She went to close the door, but John had come rushing into the hallway and seen him.

"Nicholas!" he cried as he pushed Constance away and pulled him into the house.

"John, go to your room at once! Nicholas is not staying!" Constance was angry.

"Just for five minutes!" pleaded John as he joyfully took the toy soldier from Nicholas.

"The famous five minutes!" exclaimed Constance.

Nicholas smiled as he thrust the hamper at her and was happily led by the hand out the back to play with John.

The next evening Nicholas was at the door again, knocking loudly and banging, but there was no answer.

Constance sat in the drawing room, ignoring the banging.

"He won't go away until you let him in," warned John who was kneeling up at the window peering out at Nicholas on the doorstep.

"Well, he can stay there all night then for all I care!" answered Constance.

Outside Nicholas stepped back from the unanswered door and looked up at the house

As he did so he saw John waving to him from the drawing-room window. Nicholas grinned at him and waved. John was signalling to him. Nicholas stared and realised he was signalling him around

410

the back of the house.

Nicholas nodded happily and set off.

As the knocking and banging stopped Constance sighed with relief.

"He must have given up," said a relieved Constance.

"He must have!" agreed John as he skipped out of the room.

Nicholas remembered the route that led to the back of the houses and a few minutes later he was at the gate that led through a wall into the back garden. He opened the wooden gate and saw John standing there waiting for him.

"I didn't tell her I was meeting you here," said John.

Nicholas laughed as he took his hand and they went to play with the boat in the pond.

Constance was fraught with worry in the drawing room. She should have never have let Nicholas in that first evening. She should have known he wouldn't give up. At least he had gone this time and left her in peace.

She could hear laughing and talking in the distance, and didn't give it much thought. She got up to make dinner. The hampers that Nicholas had brought made dinner each night a joy. She had forgotten what good food tasted like.

As she moved through the house, she became aware the laughing and talking was coming from the back garden. She hurried out and was aghast to see Nicolas at the pond with John.

"How on earth . . .?" she demanded.

"Just five minutes!" Nicholas winked over at her.

CHAPTER 73

Nicholas continued to show up every evening at the house. Constance soon realised it was pointless trying to stop him from coming in. John persisted in thinking up ingenious ways for Nicholas to get into the house. It the end it was easier not to fight them.

She knew it wouldn't or couldn't last forever and decided that maybe she should let John enjoy this time, with his father. It might be the only time he ever had with him. But she swore Nicholas to secrecy that he would not reveal to John he was his father. She figured it was a safe promise, as Nicholas had so much more to lose if the truth ever got out. Soon, Nicholas was joining them for dinner.

One evening Nicholas was standing at the French windows in the dining room looking out at John playing in the garden.

Constance studied Nicholas as he stood there.

"It was all lies, you know," she said.

"What was?" he asked, turning quickly to face her.

"What they said about me. Tom Fitzgerald and George Fetherston. I never went to bed with them," she said.

He studied her face intently and saw she was not lying. He was overcome with confusion, his feelings see-sawing between joyful relief and a kind of horror.

At last he managed to say, "Constance, you don't have to explain yourself to me at this stage."

"I know. But I would like you to know that I did not cheat on you with them," she said.

"But why – why would they say such things?" he asked in bewilderment.

"I have never known the answer to that," she said. "Tom, I know, was always very jealous of you. He was jealous of the privileges you were handed and took for granted. Perhaps George Fetherston was jealous too. I think he might have been jealous of our love."

"And they ruined our lives, why? Why did the bastards do such a thing?" He stared at the floor, his anger and confusion growing.

"We ruined our lives, not them," said Constance.

"But why didn't you defend yourself back then? Why didn't you tell me the truth?" he demanded.

She became angry. "You never gave me a chance to defend myself. You came storming in here and accused me of everything. You had already made up your mind, as had your parents. And there was enough circumstantial evidence to lead people to find me guilty, as I brought food to Tom's flat and had been alone with George Fetherston. I knew it would be pointless to defend myself. Especially as, if we hadn't broken up, when my pregnancy became apparent it would make me guilty in your parents' eyes. They would have definitely seen me as a slut."

"But I knew *I* had been with you!" Nicholas cried. "I would have known the baby could be *mine*!"

"And what good would that have been, since you believed Tom and George had also been with me?" Constance countered passionately. "You would not have married me on the chance the baby was yours! Nor would *I* have married you on that basis!"

"I wouldn't have left you, if I'd know the truth," he insisted.

"But you didn't know the truth, that's the point, and you had left me already, Nicholas," she said and, opening the French windows, she went out to play with John.

Nicholas was whistling as he came through the house on Sackville street after returning from an evening visit with Constance and John. It was just after eleven and he bounced up the stairs and into the drawing room where he was surprised to find Milandra.

She was out so much it was rare for her to be home before midnight.

"Where have you been?" she asked.

"At my Club," he answered.

"Have you been drinking?" It was an accusation.

He walked over to her sitting on the couch and, bending down, breathed on her. "As you can smell, I have not! I thought you were at a bash being held in the Mansion House?"

"Yes, I was. I left early, as the food didn't agree with me . . . Flancy said you have been out a lot of evenings recently?"

"Have I?" He looked innocent.

"That's what Flancy says."

"Well, if Flancy says it, it must be true! I suppose I have been at my Club more than usual recently."

"Well, it's best you don't spend as much time there in future. A husband who spends too much time at his Club is giving a clear sign to the world that he is not happy in his marriage!"

"But is a wife who is at social occasions all the time without her husband not giving the same signal?" he asked cynically.

"I've invited you to many of the social occasions I go to – you decline to attend!"

"That is because, my dear, it becomes tiresome to be at those events with you, as I spend my time fetching and carrying for you. 'Get me a drink – take this glass away – introduce me to that person – hold my shawl' – it becomes quite tiresome, I tell you!"

"Well, I thought it gave the impression that you are actually useful!" she said. "Anyway, you must attend one of those functions tomorrow night – at Lady Vrayford's – it's a husband-and-wife-only invitation, so you must attend with me. I always think Lady Vrayford insists on husband-and-wife invitations because she fears a woman on her own there may seduce her husband! As if!"

Nicholas was filled with dread at the thought of missing a night with Nicholas and Constance.

"But I can't!" he objected.

"Why can't you?"

"Because I'm meeting Jack Henderson for dinner tomorrow night, at my Club," he lied.

"Well, you'll have to cancel it," she said.

"I can't, I tell you!"

"Of course you can! If you consider attending a function with me as tiresome, then I can't imagine how you can get through a dinner with Jack Henderson! He's the most boring man I have ever met – all he talks about is cricket!"

"I actually like to talk about cricket."

"Not for four hours solid! I'm afraid you have to accompany me tomorrow, Nicholas. Lady Vrayford has become of one of my most important clients, and so I can't let her down. And, as I said, in her world, where a wife goes the husband goes too!"

"I said I can't!"

He was becoming angry, causing her to look at him curiously. He realised he had to be careful, otherwise he would arouse her suspicions.

"What time does it start?" he asked.

Milandra smiled. "Seven o'clock sharp. And we can't be late. Lady Vrayford detests lateness."

Milandra walked over to the mirror and began to fix her hair as she studied her reflection.

Nicholas poured himself a whiskey. "Do you know who I was thinking about the other day?" he said, his eyes becoming distant.

"Enlighten me."

"Lucas Hempton."

"Lucas? That's a name I haven't heard in a long time. Whatever made you think of him?" asked Milandra, surprised.

"Just thinking how Lucas just disappeared that time, and nobody ever saw or heard from him again."

"I always maintained he fell into the river and drowned, and was washed out to sea," said Milandra.

"Or he might have just had enough. Took off and has been living in the south of France all these years. Tempting, isn't it?"

"What is?"

"Just to go away and start a new life," said Nicholas.

"And I don't know which is worse – to be married to a fool or a dreamer!"

CHAPTER 74

The next evening at Lady Vrayfords', all Nicholas could do was think of Constance and John. He wished he was with them instead of at the boring function. It was the first evening in a month that he had not called to them. He spent the night as ever at Milandra's beck and call. She really treated him like her footman when they were out. As he watched her swan around the party speaking to everybody, he tried to fight the feelings of hate he felt towards her.

It was after ten and Constance was in the armchair in the drawing room looking at John, who had been positioned at the window all evening, his face perched on his two hands, staring out expectantly.

"Nicholas won't be coming tonight," she said.

"He will! He comes every evening. He's just running late."

"It's after ten, John, he's not coming! Now go to bed – it's way past your bedtime."

John tore himself away from the window. "But why isn't he coming?"

"Nicholas has – a lot of other responsibilities. We can't expect him to be visiting us all the time."

"You said something to drive him away!" John accused her. "You told him not to come back! You never like him being here! You're always telling him to go!"

"That's not why he isn't here tonight, John! I told you – he has other things to do!"

"It's all your fault!"

John ran away upset, leaving Constance crying.

The next evening, Nicholas made his way to Mountjoy Square by hansom cab – he had bought a tricycle for John. He had got something extra special for him to make up for not visiting the previous evening.

He carried the tricycle up the steps and knocked on the door.

Constance answered with a cold look on her face.

"I'm so sorry about last night. Something came up and I couldn't get out of it," he said, lifting the tricycle and carrying it inside where he placed it down on the floor.

"You don't have to explain yourself to me, Nicholas," she said coolly as she closed the door.

"Where is he?" asked Nicholas excitedly, dying to show John his new toy.

John came out of the drawing room, but didn't look his normal happy self.

"Hello, John! Look what I got you! It's the latest tricycle. All your friends will be jealous of you when they see you with this!"

To Nicholas's surprise, John didn't come rushing excitedly like he normally did and barely cast a glance at the tricycle.

"John?" asked Nicholas.

"I can't play this evening, Nicholas – I have extra school work to do," said the boy as he turned and walked up the stairs.

Nicholas turned to Constance, confused. "What's the matter with him?"

Constance walked past him briskly into the drawing room and he followed her.

"Constance?"

"What is the matter with him? What is the matter with *you*?" she blazed.

"Sorry? I thought he would be happy with the tricycle."

"Don't you get it? It's not the toys you bring him he wants! It's you! He loves being with you, he wants to be with you! The toys are only an excuse so he can play with them with you!" Constance's voice was raised.

Nicholas's heart sank at the thought he had let John down. But he felt elated at hearing this at the same time.

"I'm sorry! I'll go and apologise to him now. Explain –"

"Don't!" snapped Constance. "This is what I was afraid of all along! That he would become attached to you, and you can't give him what he really wants. And what he wants is you! I'm not simple enough to think that a father can spend every minute of his time with his child. But that is my point! This situation with you coming here every evening cannot last, and it is unfair on John to give him so much attention only for it to be cruelly snatched away. Because you are somebody else's father, somebody else's husband – you can never put John first. So just go, Nicholas, before you cause any more damage."

"But I can't go, not now . . . because I love him too much, and I love you too much," he whispered.

She blinked several times and moved away from him. "You don't even know what you're saying."

"I do. I've never been more sure of anything I've said. These past few weeks have been the happiest of my life. I didn't realise how unhappy I was before, until I met you again." He kept stepping towards her as she stepped back.

"Go, Nicholas, just go!"

"No! I'm going to leave Milandra."

"Stop!"

"And come and live with you. And when I'm free of her, I'm going to marry you and we can be a family together, as we always should have been."

"You've lost your mind!"

"Yes, I have! Lost it completely! And I'm so happy to have! I've never felt happier. I love you and am going to marry you."

"Of all the cruel things you said to me in the past, this is the cruellest ever. To lie to me like this, and offer false happiness – to tease me and torment me, when you know how much I've always loved you."

He grabbed her and stared into her eyes. "It's not lies, it's the truth."

"How can you leave Milandra? She will never allow it. And you would be destroyed! Destroyed socially – you could never hold your head up in society again –"

He planted his mouth down on hers and kissed her and she swung her arms around him, never wanting to let him go again.

"I don't just want to leave her – I'll divorce her as well."

"But what grounds for divorce, Nicholas?"

"Leave all that to me."

Through her tears, she stared to laugh.

"What's so funny?" he asked, confused.

"A divorce!" she said. "After everything that happened before – what would father say?"

And he joined her in her laughter.

It was two o'clock in the morning when Constance let him out the front door. They stood for a while, holding each other in silence.

"Are you sure about all this, Nicholas?" she asked for the hundredth time that night.

"Yes!" he exclaimed. "Now please don't ask me again!"

"I just don't know if you have thought of the consequences for your name, for your life."

"I'm fully aware of the consequences as you have persisted in telling me all night. The consequence I cannot live with is not having you and John permanently in my life."

"How do you think Milandra will take it?"

"I imagine not very well. Oh, I'm sure if she thought about it, it is not me she will be unwilling to lose. But she will not want to lose the prestige, she will not want the ensuing scandal. She will not want her place in society in any way damaged."

"I almost feel sorry for her, but I am too happy for myself to feel sorry for her very long," said Constance, kissing him again. "When will you tell her?"

"Not just yet. I need to prepare, to see where I stand legally. She is ruthless, and will do everything in her power to stop me from leaving her, so I need to have the ball rolling before she even suspects anything. I suspect she will use every dirty trick she can to smear my name."

"Would she do that?" Constance was fearful.

"As the father I have the first rights to our daughter. But Milandra has huge wealth and will use it against me to try to take my daughter away from me. And that I cannot bear. I can't abandon Petronella to be brought up by Milandra and Flancy. She may not know it now, but it will be the ruin of her. I'd better go! Milandra will be wondering where I am."

"All right, my love, until tomorrow?" she said, kissing him.

"Until tomorrow!" He smiled at her and walked away.

It was nearly three in the morning when Nicholas put his key in the front door and let himself in. He listened intently but couldn't hear anything. But he knew Milandra would be awake and want to know where he had been until such an unearthly hour.

He quickly walked into the downstairs parlour and, picking up a decanter of whiskey, took a couple of gulps from it. He then took another gulp and washed his mouth out with it before spitting it into the fire. Then he poured an amount down the front of his suit and rubbed it in. Then he left the parlour and pretended to stumble across the hallway and up the stairs, humming to himself.

The gaslights came on upstairs and there stood Milandra at the top of the landing in her robe de chambre.

"Where have you been until now?" she demanded furiously.

"*If I could find words to tell you I love you!*" Nicholas sang at the top of his voice as he stumbled up the steps.

"I said – where have you been till now?" Milandra repeated.

"Ah, my darling wife!" he said, grinning as he reached the top of the stairs.

At that moment, Flancy came rushing down from her bedroom upstairs in her nightdress and nightcap and stood beside Milandra.

"He's drunk!" declared Flancy.

"The powers of your observation have always amazed me, Flancy!" said Nicholas as he swayed from one foot to the other.

"The stench of whiskey off him!" Flancy pulled a face in disgust.

"What time of night is this to arrive home at?" demanded Milandra.

Nicholas took out his watch and looked at it before saying, "Three in the morning?"

"Where have you been until now?" she asked.

"At my Club, and then on to a couple of taverns with the chaps."

"Cheap nasty taverns for cheap nasty men!" snapped Flancy.

"Isn't that the fact of it, Flancy!" said Milandra, her lips pursing.

"Ah, you're gorgeous, come here to me, my beauty!" said Nicholas, lunging at Milandra and going to kiss her.

"*Ahhh!*" cried Milandra as she pushed him off her.

"Get away from her!" cried Flancy, giving Nicholas a push that caused him to stumble to the ground.

He lay out flat on his back, laughing loudly.

"You're just a cheap drunken filthy nasty disgusting tramp!" Flancy spat down at him.

"I couldn't have put it better myself, Flancy!" said Milandra.

Flancy put her arm around Milandra and began to lead her down the landing.

"Come on, my darling. Leave him there to wallow in his own filth!"

"Don't you dare come anywhere near the bedroom tonight, Nicholas Fontenoy!" warned Milandra. "I don't care where you sleep as long as it is nowhere near me."

As Nicholas heard them go up the stairs to the next floor, he sat up, grinning to himself.

"I told you his drinking was getting out of hand!" he heard Flancy tell Milandra, which made him grin even more as he happily headed off to one of the guest bedrooms.

CHAPTER 75

As Nicholas sat in his office the next day, he realised he hadn't felt as happy or as purposeful for years. He knew what he wanted and he was going to get it. Constance was still as much in love with him as he was with her. He had forgotten what that feeling was like. But, as he said to Constance, he had to tread carefully with Milandra. He knew what she was capable of, and if she even got a whiff of him and Constance, it was unthinkable what she might do. The element of surprise was what he had to use with Milandra.

He could leave Milandra in the morning and set up home with Constance and John. But he wanted a divorce from Milandra. He wanted to sever his ties from her and marry Constance and give her and John his name. But divorces were so difficult to achieve. They were only granted on the grounds of adultery or cruelty. Although his marriage to Milandra had become cruel, his wife's mental torture and vicious tongue would not be entertained by a court as true grounds for cruelty, and were also impossible to prove. The adultery was on his part, and so he couldn't apply for a divorce on those grounds.

It would have to Milandra who did this. And he was certain, even if Milandra was aware of his adultery, however enraged she was, she still would not agree to a divorce – out of sheer spite and because of the ensuing scandal. And there was also the question of money and Petronella – the two things Milandra cared about most. As her husband he could claim control over her wealth and property and, if they divorced, as Petronella's father he had premier

422

guardianship and could deny her access to Petronella. These factors would also make her refuse a divorce.

Somehow he needed to barter with Milandra. Use access to her daughter and control over her own money in exchange for consent to a divorce.

Before he broached the subject with Milandra, he needed to be prepared and understand, as a lawyer himself, the strength of his position and understand fully divorce procedure.

He met with a trusted lawyer friend who specialised in divorce cases, to discuss the situation. After much fruitful discussion, the lawyer told him to begin by obtaining copies of their marriage certificate and birth certificates.

He had copies of the marriage certificate and his own birth certificate. He just needed a copy of Milandra's birth certificate.

She was married to him under her legal name at the time, Milandra Carter. Milandra was from a 'landed gentry' family in the west of the Ireland of the name Smith, and that had been her maiden name before marrying Ambrose Carter.

He called his clerk into his office.

"Go to the records office and get me a birth certificate for my wife, Milandra. Her maiden name was Smith and she was born in Galway in 1841."

"Yes, Your Lordship," said the clerk and he headed off on his mission.

Nicholas spent the rest of the day engrossed in divorce law. By six o'clock, his clerk still hadn't returned and Nicholas was getting impatient as he didn't want to be late for his visit to Constance and John.

Finally, his clerk came rushing into his office at half past six.

"Whatever took you so long?" asked Nicholas.

"Truly sorry, Your Lordship, but it was not an easy task!"

"Since when has getting a birth certificate not been an easy task?" asked Nicholas, surprised by his clerk's inefficiency. He had learned that you could send this clerk to do anything, and his diligence was exceptional.

"Because I could not find a record of your wife's birth," said the clerk.

"I'm sorry?"

"There was no Milandra Smith born in Galway or anywhere else in Ireland in 1841, or any other year around then. I searched enough."

"I don't understand. There has to be a birth certificate for the woman!" Nicholas was irritated by the delay.

"As your wife's Christian name is so unusual, I then started to search for *any* Milandras born at that time."

"And?" asked Nicholas.

"This is all I found, but it's the wrong year and the wrong surname," said the clerk, handing over a birth certificate.

In irritation, Nicholas grabbed that birth certificate and studied it.

His eyes opened wide in amazement as he read it.

16th *of April 1839, the County of Kerry, Ireland*
Christian Name: Milandra
Surname: Flancy
Mother: Noleen Flancy
Occupation: Scullery maid
Father: Unknown

"Is everything all right, Your Lordship?" asked the clerk as he saw Nicholas go pale as a ghost.

"Yes – yes, you can go home," Nicholas managed to say and the clerk left.

Nicholas sat there staring at the birth certificate and all he could do was whimper one word to himself: "Flancy."

As Nicholas walked up to Mountjoy Square that evening, his head was spinning as he thought of what he had just discovered. Milandra, his wife, Lady Havington, the mother of his daughter, was not the offspring of the gentry in Galway as she had always maintained. She was the illegitimate daughter of their cook. She wasn't even the age she had always pretended to be, but two years older! She was a fraud beyond compare. Her life was one long lie, and he was biggest fool she had lied to. It all made sense to him now. The unnatural closeness between Milandra and Flancy. Flancy's assurance that Milandra would never contradict her. She was her mother! Instead of living with their cook all these years, he had been living with his mother-in-law! He felt sick to his stomach. But as Constance opened the door and rushed into his arms, he decided to say nothing of all this to her. Not until he had got to the bottom of it.

CHAPTER 76

The next morning Nicholas sat in the office of Richard Dolans. Dolans was a private investigator who their law firm had used in the past. A man of diligence and discretion, he had got to the bottom of many cases they had handled. If anyone could get to the bottom of who or what Nicholas's wife was, then Dolans could.

Dolans listened intently as Nicholas told him about the birth certificate.

"So you're telling me that you believe Lady Havington is the daughter of your cook, this Flancy woman?" asked Dolans, who had heard many a story before, but none as shocking as this.

"That is my belief. She clearly is. Our cook's name is Flancy, and I believe her first name is Noleen," said Nicholas.

"Are you certain you want me to investigate this, Nicholas? I think whatever you might learn might only bring you pain. In fact, I think stumbling across this has already brought you enough pain."

"I am certain. I want to know who I am married to," insisted Nicholas.

The next few days went by in a haze for Nicholas. When at home he pretended that everything was normal. He watched Milandra, with her airs and graces, interacting with her rich and famous friends, hardly believing that she had been able to propel herself to the top of society from such humble origins. He watched Flancy and her together, their intimacy obvious, but never any sign they were mother and daughter. It was now obvious why Flancy doted on Petronella, and Milandra was content with the fact their daughter had been practically brought up by her. Petronella was Flancy's granddaughter.

Milandra was due to go on one of her regular wine-buying tours of the Loire Valley. He waved her off as she left for France, as he had done countless times before, giving her no suspicion that anything was wrong.

He burned with curiosity to hear back from Dolans and a week later Dolans showed up at his workplace and firmly closed the door behind him.

He took a seat opposite Nicholas.

"Well?" Nicholas's impatience had reached fever point.

"I can confirm that your wife was born in a small village in Kerry in 1846 and that she is the daughter of the woman that is in your employ as your cook, Noleen Flancy," said Dolans.

"And what did you find out?" said Nicholas, who did not need to hear something he already knew.

"It was exceptionally hard to find out anything, as many people from there either died or emigrated during the Famine. The Famine acted as a very good reason why your wife has managed to hide her past, as there were very few people left after the Famine who would have known Flancy."

"Go on!" demanded Nicholas.

"I could not find out who the father was. But Flancy was working as scullery maid in a manor house at the time. Flancy managed to put her daughter into a good school that was subsidised by charity. As I understand it, Flancy had an exceptional talent as a cook. And this led her to get very good positions in Big Houses that paid more than usual for her talents. She used this extra money she earned to contribute to Milandra's school fees at the school in Galway."

"The deception started early," whispered Nicholas.

"In the meantime, Flancy obtained a position working at the country estate of one Ambrose Carter."

"Ambrose Carter! Milandra's first husband!"

"Indeed. And I believe Flancy infiltrated Mr Carter's household, ending up running his house for him. When Milandra graduated from school, she became a visitor to Ambrose Carter's estate, and she eventually married him."

"But – but did anyone who knew Ambrose and Milandra realise she was the cook's daughter?"

"No. Milandra was introduced as a young woman Ambrose had met during the course of his work as a wine merchant, the daughter of Galway gentry," said Dolans.

"But did Ambrose Carter know the truth, before he married Milandra?" asked Nicholas.

"That I can't answer, as only he can answer and he is dead these many years. But I suspect he did know, given his closeness to Flancy and the fact that Flancy introduced them. As Milandra's first husband, before she married him she wouldn't have had the means or money to disguise her past. Also her legal name at the time on the marriage certificate would have been Milandra Flancy, which had been changed to Carter by the time she married you."

"It is hard to believe the level of deception." Nicholas shook his head.

"In a way, it is hard not to admire her," said Dolans.

"It is easy for you to say – as you are not married to her!"

"I understand this has all come as a terrible shock for you."

"I married a lie. My marriage is a lie," said Nicholas.

CHAPTER 77

Nicolas lay on John's bed at the Staffordshire house, with his arm around him as he read from a book of fairy tales he had bought him.

Constance sat at the end of the bed, smiling at the sight of them.

"... *and they all lived happily ever after!*" Nicholas concluded the story and closed over the book.

"One more!" pleaded John.

"No, that's quite enough for tonight," said Constance, standing up.

"Your mother is right, time you went to sleep," said Nicholas as he gave John a hug and stood up.

"Goodnight!" called John as he watched them leave the room and close the door.

Nicholas smiled at Constance and took her hand as they walked downstairs and into the drawing room.

"Constance, I won't be coming tomorrow evening," he said solemnly, sitting down on the couch.

"Oh?" She was concerned as she sat beside him and took his hand.

"I'm going to tell Milandra everything. She's due back from France tomorrow and it's time to tell her that I'm leaving her. I've now prepared all the papers for the divorce and I'm going to tell her I want one. I'm going to leave her tomorrow night."

Constance was gripped with fear and panic, now that her dream was about to become reality.

"But why tomorrow night?" she asked.

"Because Flancy is taking Petronella away tomorrow, down the country to see some show and they won't be back until very late. I don't want Petronella in the house when I tell Milandra – and tell her about you."

"Oh, Nicholas, she won't be able to believe it! I doubt I've even crossed her mind in years."

"Well, she will believe it when I walk out the door after I've told her everything. I'll be coming to stay here tomorrow night, if that's all right? I won't be able to stay in the same house as her after she knows."

"Of course it is. It's what I wish for more than anything." She leaned forward and kissed him.

"After tomorrow we will be together for the rest of our lives," he promised.

Nicholas did not go into work the next day. He felt very nervous but strangely euphoric at the thought of telling Milandra he was going. That morning, once Flancy and Petronella had left for the country, he gave the other staff the night off and told them they could go home and stay with their families for the night. Perhaps he was also being mean, but he wanted Milandra to feel isolated once he walked out. For once in her life she wouldn't have Flancy or Petronella or anyone else in the house. She would not have anybody to fill the void and would have to spend time alone, thinking of her life and what she had lost. Maybe it was small piece of revenge for him, after the years of being treated the way he had by her.

In the afternoon he packed two suitcases and left them downstairs behind the stairs to collect as he made his exit. Once he told her he was going, he wanted to go quickly.

As the evening began to descend he waited in the upstairs drawing room for Milandra's return. He poured himself a glass of whiskey and then another one and sat down and waited patiently for her.

CHAPTER 78

The hansom cab swept up to the front of the house on Sackville
Street just after seven that evening. Milandra quickly got out and
hurried up the steps and into the house as the driver carried in her
trunk for her.

"You can leave it there," she instructed the driver.

She tipped him well and closed the door after him.

"Hello!" she called loudly, but there was no answer. "Flancy!"

There was still no answer. She shrugged and took off her cape
and gloves, flung them on a side table and walked across the lobby
and up the stairs.

"Can anybody hear me?" she called loudly, becoming annoyed
there was nobody there to greet her.

She swept into the drawing room and saw Nicholas in an armchair
nursing a glass of whiskey.

"Have you gone deaf? I was calling!" she snapped.

"Oh, I heard you all right," he said.

"Drinking again! Does it ever stop?" She raised her eyes to
heaven and walked over to the bell-pull and tugged it. "Where is
everybody? Or have they all gone deaf as well? I had the most
dreadful time in France! Dreadful, I tell you! The price of Merlot
has shot through the roof! I had to negotiate hard to get any kind
of a good deal from the vineyards."

"I'm sure you managed it just fine," he said.

"And then the crossing back on the boat! I'm sure the crossing
from France is getting worse! The waves! I was glad to arrive in one

431

piece, I tell you!"

"But you did," he said.

"And I literally just have to change, turn around and go back out tonight!"

"Where to?"

"A dinner dance in Merrion Square. I'm going to be late if I don't hurry . . . where *is* everybody?" she demanded, becoming angry and tugging the bell-pull again.

"There's nobody else here."

"What are you talking about? Where's Flancy?"

"She's taken Petronella to some show down the country. They won't be back till after midnight."

"Oh, I see. Well, where is everyone else?"

"I gave them all the night off," he said.

"Why ever did you do such a stupid thing?" She was horrified. "How am I supposed to manage a night without my servants?"

He shrugged disinterestedly.

"Honestly, Nicholas, I swear you're getting worse! Do not *ever* let all the servants take off together like that again! I've told you a thousand times before not to interfere with the running of the house, but to leave it to Flancy! Stop interfering, Nicholas!" She began to unpin her hat. "Where did you say Flancy had taken Petronella?"

"Your mother didn't say exactly," he said.

Milandra was thrusting her hatpins back into the hat.

"Did you hear what I said?" he asked.

"Yes! She didn't say! What of it?" she snapped, placing the hat on a side table.

"You don't look like her, I must say."

"Look like who, you fool?" she snapped even louder.

"Your mother."

She turned around to face him. "Have you lost your mind altogether? How on earth would you know what my mother looks like, as she was dead and buried many years before I ever met you."

"But that's just it, your mother isn't dead and buried. She's very much alive and kicking, pretending to be our cook!"

Milandra's mouth dropped as she was stunned into silence.

Nicholas rose and, reaching into his pocket, took out a copy of Milandra's birth certificate. He handed it to her.

She stared at the birth certificate.

"It took digging, but I found it," he said.

She quickly tried to regain her composure but he could see she had gone as white as a sheet.

"I don't know what you're talking about," she said, but there was a strong quiver in her voice.

"I know all about you, Milandra Flancy!" he said.

Milandra gripped the back of the chair beside her. "How dare you! How dare you go looking for birth certificates without my permission!"

"And how dare you marry me pretending to be somebody else. From a distinguished landed gentry family! Ha! Orphaned at a young age! Ha bloody ha!" His face neared hers and it was full of venom and vicious joy. "You are a fraud, Milandra! Nothing but a fraud! Your whole life is a concoction of lies. Gentry! You're not even a Protestant!" He waved her birth certificate in front of her face. "But a Catholic peasant, the bastard child of a scullery maid!"

Milandra blinked back tears before whispering, "So now you know."

"So, now I bloody well do!" he shouted.

"I can't see that it makes any difference at this stage," she said, pretending nonchalance.

"It makes every difference!" He shook his head in disbelief.

"Why would it? I am still who I am, regardless of where I came from. And I am your wife Milandra Fontenoy, Lady Havington."

"Lady! My dear woman, you are a peasant! An illegitimate daughter of a peasant. And who was your father? Did Flancy even know his name when she took a roll in the hay with him?"

"Don't, Nicholas, please!" she begged.

"Was he a rich man, poor man, beggarman or thief?" His joy was intensifying. "If I was a betting man I would wager – thief!"

"Nicholas!" she implored.

"Or perhaps – tinker, tailor, soldier or spy? I would wager he

433

was a tinker! A passing itinerant who Flancy fucked in a hayshed!"

"I'm not listening to any more of this!" She turned quickly to walk away, putting her hands over her ears.

But Nicholas grabbed her and turned her to him, placing his hands on her shoulders.

"*Let me go, you bastard!*" she roared.

"But it is you that is the bastard, not I!" He hooted with laughter as he held her tightly by the shoulders. "Did your first husband know? Did Ambrose Carter know you were his cook's illegitimate daughter?"

She struggled to free herself from his grip.

"*Answer me!*" he said, shaking her violently.

"Yes!" she cried. "Yes, Ambrose knew! How could he not? Flancy brought me to stay at his estate once I left school, and he fell in love with me. They cooked the marriage up between them, Ambrose and Flancy, so that nobody would ever know who I really was, who he was really marrying."

"And you went along with it?"

"Happily. It gave me a name, his name. A name that made me important, and made me his heir. What was there not to be happy about?" she fumed. "Now, you know everything – release me!"

He suddenly dropped his hands from her and she stepped back, clutching her arms where he had held her.

They stood in silence for a while, eyeing each other.

"The truth is, Nicholas –"

"Truth! You don't know the meaning of the word."

"The truth is, Nicholas, that now you know everything there is to know about me, it does not matter a tinker's damn! There is nothing you can do. I am married to you. I am the mother of your daughter. I am now Milandra, Lady Havington. So now you know I was not to the manor born, with a silver spoon in my mouth. So enjoy your moment of triumph in my humiliation, but there is nothing you can do about it. You must keep the secret as closely guarded as I have. Or else you will risk your own ruin. If it ever got out about my true background, your name will be destroyed too. And you would ruin Petronella forever too, if the truth came out.

And I know, whatever you think of me, you would never destroy your daughter."

He sighed and shook his head. "You are right, of course. I can and never will divulge your dirty secrets. Your secret remains safe."

Milandra visibly relaxed. She had never seen him in such a frightening temper before, and hadn't been sure what he would do.

"I won't even bring it into the divorce," he said.

Milandra's face tensed with confusion. "*Divorce*!"

"I am divorcing you."

"On what grounds?" She was petrified.

"On the grounds that I do not love you and you do not love me, and it is out of the question that we remain living as man and wife."

"You are not divorcing me, that I can tell you now!" she snarled. "I will not be a divorced woman! I will not have to put up with whispers and rumours and being a laughing stock. I've come too far and worked too hard for you to piss on it now!"

"You have no choice in the matter, Milandra. You might be able to control everything else in your life, but you can't control my heart."

"Heart?" Realisation dawned on her. "You've been seeing another woman!"

"I won't deny it," he shrugged.

Her eyes widened as everything became clear. "All those nights at your Club! You were in bed with some tart!"

"Think what you may, it is of no consequence to me any more."

"Who is she?" demanded Milandra and it was her turn to become vicious with joy. "Who is the tart! I will finish the little tart off before she thinks she can take my position in life!"

Nicholas stepped back from her and prepared himself for the onslaught. "It's Constance . . . Constance Staffordshire."

"Constance?"

As Milandra repeated the name, Nicholas wasn't sure from her expression if she even remembered who Constance was.

"Constance Staffordshire! The Bishop's daughter!" she then exclaimed in disbelief.

"Yes," nodded Nicholas.

"And where on earth has she been all these years?"

"Just getting on living her life," said Nicholas.

"Well, you can tell that little whore from me that she can go and climb back into the grubby little hole she crawled out of! Constance Staffordshire! The woman who slept with half of Dublin! And I see time has not improved her character – as now she is bedding married men!"

"Just one married man – me," said Nicholas.

"*Ohhh!*" Milandra cried in frustration. "Damn you!"

"I want a divorce, Milandra."

"*Ha!*"

"I'm going to marry the woman I always should have, and be happy. And it's not too late for you – I suggest you meet somebody who can make you happy too, as I clearly do not."

Milandra's expression suddenly turned to sorrow and she threw herself into his arms.

"But that's not true, Nicholas. You do make me happy! I love you, you're the only man I've ever loved! The only man I've ever wanted!"

He pushed her away from him. "Come on, Milandra, please don't insult my intelligence at this late stage with your act. I can see through you easier than glass. It's over – best you just accept it. There's a child, you see, as well."

Milandra's eyes narrowed. "What child?"

"Constance was pregnant when I broke off my engagement. She had a son by me. He deserves a father."

"But he could be anyone's child . . . she was up more alleys than an alley-cat!"

His face changed and she had never seen the expression on his face before: a look of pride, joy and assurance.

He said, "He's my child."

She stepped away slowly and sat down on the couch, her head falling into her hands to steady herself.

"I'm sure this has all come as a shock. My intention was to cause you hurt tonight, but perhaps not as much as I see you are in."

"You actually want a divorce?" she managed.

"I want to marry Constance," he said. "I want you to divorce me on the grounds of adultery. I won't take any of your money, if you cooperate. Naturally we will keep Constance's name out of it. First I will leave this house and fulfil the legal definition of 'deserting' you. That will be the first requirement. Later, I will go to a hotel room and pretend to be with some lady of the night and you arrive and swear you found me fornicating. That is the way, I believe, these things are handled according to a friend of mine who deals in these cases. It's distasteful but I see no other way."

"My god! You've got the whole thing done and dusted! Seen a lawyer and everything!" Milandra was aghast.

"If you do this I won't claim any of your fortune or property. I have more than enough to set myself up anew and give Constance and John a good life."

"John . . ." she whispered.

"You can keep the house, your money, everything. I'll allow you generous access to Petronella as well."

She looked up. "Access? *Access!* You're not taking my daughter!"

"As the father, I am entitled to full custody. But I will let her visit and stay with you as much as possible. I don't want to be cruel."

"You will not take Petronella! You will not! Are you forgetting how powerful and wealthy I am. You won't stand a chance!"

"Force my hand and I'll take Petronella away from you altogether! The law is on my side with this one."

"Please, Nicholas, please – I'm begging you!"

"But I have no choice, Milandra. Can't you see I have to take her away from you to save her from you. If I leave her with you and Flancy, she will end up just the same as you. And I can't allow that."

As he looked down at her he couldn't help but feel sorry her. She looked broken. He had never seen her like that before. He knew he had to leave now before he faltered.

"I'm leaving now, Milandra," he said.

"Leaving – for where?"

"For Constance. She's expecting me. I told her I would be leaving you tonight."

"But we need to talk!"

"There's nothing left to talk about. I already packed my suitcases – they're waiting downstairs. I'll be touch about the divorce and about Petronella. Goodbye, Milandra."

He walked out of the drawing room and down the landing. With each step he took away from her, he felt more free. Like a burden was being lifted from him.

He had reached the top of the stairs when a screech came from behind him.

"You're not taking my daughter!"

Turning quickly, he saw Milandra standing right behind him, having followed his every step. Her beautiful face was contorted in fury.

She lunged towards him, and with her two hands pushed him backwards towards the stairs. He fell back from the top step, and seemed to hover there, as he desperately flailed in the air trying to find his balance. As he teetered, he tried to reach out for the banisters but they were beyond his reach. Gravity won out and suddenly he toppled backwards down the stairs.

Milandra watched him rotating through the air, head over heels, bouncing off every third or fourth step, before finally crashing to the ground of the lobby below, causing a loud thud to echo through the house. She stood at the top of the stairs for a long while, watching his motionless body splayed out below. Finally, she carefully descended the stairs and stood by him. His eyes were flickering open and shut.

"Get – someone," he whimpered and tried to reach his hand out to her, which she ignored.

She bent down beside him. "My poor darling Nicholas," she said and, reaching forward, stroked his hair.

Then she stood and went and bolted the front door before going to a nearby chair and taking a cushion from it. She could feel his eyes try to follow her as she moved towards him. Kneeling down close to his head, she put the cushion on her lap and moved his head so it rested on it. She began to stroke his hair as his eyes glared up at her.

"D-octor . . ." he managed to whisper.

"But I can't get you a doctor, Nicholas. I can't risk anyone finding you now. Can't you see? You gave me no choice. I couldn't have you running off with that Staffordshire girl, not after all these years, not after how I fought so intensely to get you away from her. I knew we were destined to be together before I ever met you that day at Ambrose's funeral. I had read in the newspaper your engagement announcement to Constance Staffordshire. Constance Staffordshire, Bishop Staffordshire's daughter. And all the memories, the painful memories came flooding back from when I was at Hillsdale Abbey boarding school where the Bishop was the governor."

PART 12

Hillsdale Abbey

1853

CHAPTER 79

Hillsdale Abbey was a large imposing grey building situated near the cliffs which the wild Atlantic Ocean crashed relentlessly against on the west coast of Ireland. It was a boarding school for girls, or 'young ladies' as the Headmistress Mrs. Kellings preferred to state. It was where Milandra was brought up, where she spent the most part of her younger years. All the girls, or young ladies, at Hillsdale had something in common. It was not so much that they were unwanted, though many of them were, but there was no other place for them. The girls were not from loving families with means. If they had been they would not be at Hillsdale. Partly funded by charity, partly by the girls' benefactors, its pure and simple goal was to give their young charges a start in life that would enable them to have respectable lives. These girls were from families who could not afford a dowry or hadn't the social means to ensure they made good marriages. Some were orphans whose relatives paid a small contribution for their charges to stay there. Occasionally, as in Milandra's case, they were illegitimate and Hillsdale offered them the only chance to receive an education and to gain meaningful and respectable employment. All the girls had somebody in their background who had arranged for them to be there and felt Hillsdale was the girl's best opportunity in life. Somebody who wanted more for the girl than just to be in domestic service or work in a factory. Somebody who hoped the girl could receive enough education to go on to become a governess, a teacher, a nurse or join the growing number of women who worked in bookkeeping. In

Milandra's case it was Flancy who arranged for Milandra to be at Hillsdale. Due to her excellent cooking skills, Flancy could earn more than the average cook and every penny she earned went to pay the fees at Hillsdale. Even at that, the girls could not be at Hillsdale and the school could not survive without great contributions from charity. A board of directors worked tirelessly to raise funds for Hillsdale, and the head of the board, the governor of the school, was one Bishop Staffordshire.

Hillsdale Abbey was a loveless place which joy had by-passed, a place dedicated to discipline, classes with the girls constantly reminded that they were only there due to the generosity of the board of directors' fundraising.

"May I remind you, girls," said Mrs. Kellings each morning at assembly in the hall, in more or less the same words, "that you are only here due to the tireless work of Bishop Staffordshire and his colleagues. Your guardians' contributions alone would not allow the continuation of Hillsdale. As such, you owe it to Bishop Staffordshire to work to your very best ability and make decent respectable lives that can make Hillsdale proud."

There was no laughter at Hillsdale, no recreation. The girls were allowed to walk in the gardens and along the cliffs for an hour a day.

As Milandra surveyed the schoolgirls gathered in assembly, she realised she had rarely seen any of them smile, let alone laugh. But Milandra knew she was different from most of the other girls. Because she was loved. She knew her mother loved her dearly and was working every hour she could to give her the best start in life through Hillsdale. But she rarely saw her mother, because of this. Flancy only managed to visit Milandra twice a year. Although Flancy could not hide that she worked in domestic service, she had told the school that she was widowed and Milandra's father had died when she was a baby. Thus deception had started early in Milandra's life. Milandra realised survival depended on deceit.

"I have high hopes for you, Milandra," Mrs. Kellings informed her as she sat in the principal's office to hear her monthly report. "I am told you excel at mathematics and bookkeeping."

"Thank you, Mrs. Kellings."

"I think, when it comes to your time to leave, we can find a position as a teacher or governess for you. Only our best pupils are recommended for those positions. I hope you are grateful."

"Yes, Mrs. Kellings."

As Mrs. Kellings studied the girl, she thought how unfortunate it was that she was so pretty. Milandra was in danger of turning into a beautiful woman, which was not an advantage for a girl in her position. Beauty was for the daughters of well-to-do families, to help them make suitable and good matches. For a girl from Milandra's background it would only get in the way of her dedicating her life to a respectable job. Male attention was not something a spinster teacher needed. However, thankfully, the girl did not seem aware of her looks. If there was any sign of vanity in her, Mrs. Kellings would have been concerned. Still, she decided it was wise to keep Milandra away from the burgeoning profession of bookkeeping which would bring her too much into the company of male colleagues. Her destiny firmly lay as a teacher in an all-girls school, she decided.

CHAPTER 80

Milandra's friend at school was Katie who, due to her hopeless grammar and spelling Mrs. Kellings had decided was destined for a nursing career after Hillsdale.

"But I can't stand the sight of blood!" objected Katie as she and Milandra walked through the gardens at Hillsdale during their hour of recreation.

"Then work harder and get better results!" urged Milandra. "Then she might organise a teaching job for you."

"I can't work any harder! I study as hard as I can. But it's in one ear and out the other with me! I'm not bright like you."

"Anybody can be bright – it just takes dedication," said Milandra, remembering what Flancy had said to her once during one of her visits.

"That's easy for you to say," sighed Katie.

"What does your uncle say?"

"He couldn't care less as long as I'm not a burden to him!"

Katie had been orphaned when she was a child and her uncle had become her guardian but had no interest in her.

"He looks forward to the day when I graduate from here and he no longer has to contribute to my school fees. He is far too preoccupied with his wife and his own children to care a jot about me."

Milandra saw the extreme sadness in her friend's face and had the urge to reach out and comfort her, but any physical contact at Hillsdale was forbidden. And, as Milandra looked at the other girls

446

walking through the gardens, she knew they were all starved of love and any human contact. Loneliness seeped through the place.

"Hello, girls! Why the glum faces?" said a sudden cheery voice and the girls turned to see it was Sullivan, the gardener at Hillsdale, who was busy cutting a hedge. Always in a good mood, Sullivan was the only person in Hillsdale who ever smiled and offered a friendly voice to the students.

"Mrs. Kellings wants me to be a nurse and I can't stand blood, Mr. Sullivan!" said Katie.

"Oh dear, that is a problem," said Sullivan before he broke out into a smile. "But, as my old dad used to say – you can get used to anything! And that works with the sight of blood as well, I reckon."

Milandra gave a little laugh and Katie giggled.

"That's more like it!" said Sullivan with a grin. "And I daresay if Mrs. Kellings says you should be a nurse, then a nurse you should be!"

Sullivan lived with his wife and four children in the gardener's cottage on the grounds at Hillsdale. Often he would sneak out his wife's home cooking and hand it to the girls during their walk.

At that moment, from around the hedge, Sullivan's son Ruairi appeared – he had been pruning the other side of the hedge. He got a start when he saw Milandra and he began to blush.

"Have you finished the other side of that hedge, Ruairi?" asked Sullivan.

Ruairi said nothing as he managed to go even redder.

"For goodness' sake!" laughed Sullivan. "Cat got your tongue? They are only girls, Ruairi – they won't bite!"

Ruairi shuffled on his feet and kicked a stone.

His father said, "Get along home, lad – your mother will have the tea ready soon."

Ruairi turned and began to walk away but, as he turned the corner, he took a quick look back at Milandra.

"Good day, Mr. Sullivan," said Katie as she and Milandra walked on.

Katie started giggling with delight.

"Did you see Ruairi?" she whispered. "He went red as a beetroot when he saw me! He always does! I think he's in love with me!"

"Katie! You shouldn't say such things!" admonished Milandra.

"Why? It's the truth!"

"Mrs. Kellings would go mad if she heard you even mention a boy, let alone talk about love. As for Bishop Staffordshire!"

"I know! I'm to be a spinster nurse! I can't help liking that he likes me though. He's so handsome, isn't he?"

"I haven't given him any thought," said Milandra.

The truth was she had given the raven-haired blue-eyed Ruairi some thought. She had noticed he did act in the strangest way whenever she and Katie bumped into him. And she had to admit he stirred a strange feeling in her, one she never had before and didn't understand. As the bell sounded, they headed back into Hillsdale for dinner.

Milandra sat in the huge assembly room with the other pupils, all eyes fixed on Bishop Staffordshire who stood at the top of the hall pontificating. He was making one of his frequent visits to Hillsdale. He would sweep in, do a quick inspection of the school and give a speech to the pupils before retiring to Mrs. Kellings' office for tea. This day he was accompanied by his young daughter Constance who sat at the top of the hall beside Mrs. Kellings.

"I hope each and every one of you understands and are grateful for the opportunity Hillsdale is providing you in life," said the Bishop loudly. "If it were not for Hillsdale, you girls would have nobody who truly cared about you, and what became of you. Your whole existence is reliant on the kindness of strangers who out of the goodness of their hearts provide Hillsdale with the funds to continue. Each night I think of you poor unfortunate girls and what dreadful fates might have befallen you if it was not for Mrs. Kellings and me. Without the proper guardianship we provide you, you might very well have fallen prey to the very lowest of society and ended up in houses of ill repute. Bear this in mind, girls – it is only the education that is provided here that saves you from being fallen women."

As the Bishop continued, his voice becoming louder and harsher, Milandra was concentrating on his daughter. Constance sat, beautifully dressed, and seemed distracted as she looked out the window at the gardens. Milandra knew if any of the pupils had dared look out the window as the Bishop spoke, Mrs. Kellings would inflict her cane on her. And yet Mrs. Kellings was looking fondly at Constance. Milandra felt herself becoming overwhelmed with an angry resentment towards the Bishop's daughter and the fact that she was cosseted and much loved, while Milandra and the other Hillsdale pupils were told they were inferior, unloved and unwanted.

After the speech, the Bishop, Constance and Mrs. Kellings retired to her office. Each of the pupils was on a roster to serve tea to Mrs. Kellings. That day it was Milandra's turn and she carefully held the tray, containing the teapot, china and an array of beautiful cakes, as another pupil knocked on the office door and opened it for her. Milandra walked carefully into the office where she found Mrs. Kellings seated behind her desk with the Bishop and Constance sitting on the other side of it.

They ignored Milandra as she set out the cups, saucers, plates and cutlery on the desk, together with the plates of cakes. Then she lifted the teapot and began to pour the tea.

"This is one of our brightest girls, Your Grace," said Mrs. Kellings, eager to impress. "We hope she will be a governess."

Feeling proud, Milandra smiled at the Bishop, but he simply ignored her as if she didn't exist and reached for his tea.

"How are religious studies progressing at the school, Mrs. Kellings?" he asked.

Crestfallen, Milandra finished pouring the tea and then quickly walked from the room. She felt a burning sense of shame. The Bishop had not deemed her worthy to even acknowledge. To him, she was a nobody and always would be a nobody.

Later that afternoon, Milandra sat in her bookkeeping class and, looking out the window, saw Mrs. Kellings seeing the Bishop and

Constance into their carriage. She watched, envious of the attention both the principal and the Bishop were paying to Constance. The pain of envy went deep. The pain of how she had been ignored as a nobody went even deeper.

That afternoon was needlework with Miss Simmons. Miss Simmons, who was half blind, would usually set the girls to work and then proceed to fall asleep for the rest of the class. Confident of this sequence of events, Milandra decided to do something she had never done before – to skip class. She knew Miss Simmons would sleep through the class and, if she woke up, wouldn't be able to see properly which girls were in the class, and so she wouldn't be missed. She was so humiliated by the Bishop's dismissal of her that she just needed to have some time on her own.

So, as the other girls made their way to class, Milandra slipped out of a side door and walked through the gardens towards the cliff. There she sat down on a rock and looked out at the wild Atlantic on that sunny afternoon. She felt she could stay there forever. She felt so lonely and wished with all her heart that her mother would come and visit her. But she knew her mother's next visit was months away.

Overcome with loneliness, she began to cry.

"Why are you crying?" asked a voice.

With a start, she looked up to see the gardener's son Ruairi standing there, looking down at her. She felt so shocked to see him and that he was talking to her that she quickly wiped away her tears.

She looked down at the ground, feeling ashamed.

"What's wrong, Milandra?"

She looked up at him, even more shocked. How did he know her name? She saw his face was full of concern – he looked nearly as upset as she was.

"Well?" he asked and moved closer to her.

"Nothing," she managed. "Nothing at all."

"You can tell me, I won't tell anybody," he said and he sat down beside her on the rock.

She was bewildered. Looking at him curiously, she said, "I didn't think you could speak. You never say a word when you're working with your father."

He turned beetroot-red as he always did. "I'm not supposed to speak to any of the pupils at Hillsdale. Strict orders from Mrs. Kellings."

"Why ever not?"

He shrugged. "I suppose I'm not good enough."

"Isn't the world a strange place?" pondered Milandra aloud. "We, the girls in the school, are told the same thing."

He smiled at her. "Not good enough to speak to the gardener's son?"

"Well, that was never said, but not good enough to speak to a Bishop and his daughter – amongst many others."

"'Tis a strange place all right," he said with a grin. "But tell me – why were you crying?"

"Oh, I just felt lonely – very lonely. You know, you're so lucky you're living with your lovely father and mother and family. I'd give anything to be with my mother all the time."

"Why aren't you then?"

"Because she works non-stop to help keep me here and lives a long way from here. She's fighting to give me the best chance in life."

"What use is all that when you're lonely?" he asked.

She looked at him, perplexed. "You're a most curious boy. But then I've never really spoken to another boy all my life so I can't judge."

He smiled and blushed even further.

"Why do you always blush? You're always blushing any time I see you," she said.

"I don't usually. It's because of you. You make me blush."

"I?" She was shocked. "But why?"

"Because – because I like you!" he suddenly blurted out and with that he jumped up and ran down the cliff path, back to the gardens of Hillsdale.

CHAPTER 81

After that, all Milandra could think about was her encounter with Ruairi. She was overcome with a sense of excitement when she thought about him. He liked her, he had told her so. She was overjoyed that it was actually her that Ruairi liked and not Katie, as her friend thought. Milandra had never given such things a thought before and now here she was exchanging secretive glances and looks with Ruairi.

The next week, when it came to Miss Simmons' needlework class, she chanced skipping it again and made her way down to the cliffs as before, hoping, and yet fearing that Ruairi would follow her again.

Sure enough he did and they met at the same rock.

"I brought you these," he said, handing her a beautiful bunch of flowers taken from the garden.

She was taken aback as she accepted them. "I can't take them back to the school, as they will wonder why I have them."

He shrugged. "Well, leave them here at our rock – our place."

She sat down on the rock, smelling the flowers, and he sat beside her.

They sat and talked for an hour, anxiously asking about each other's lives.

"I had better get back to school," she finally said. "I can't keep coming here to meet you. I will be missed and will be in grave trouble for missing classes."

He looked distraught at the thought of not seeing her alone again.

"You understand what is happening here – with us?" he asked cautiously.

"I think so – yes," she said as she looked into his eyes.

"It could be dangerous for both of us," he said.

"I don't know how I can meet you again," she said. "One of the teachers will miss me."

He nodded. "I don't want you to get into any trouble because of me." Then he smiled. "I'll figure something out."

She stood up and handed him back the flowers. "Goodbye, Ruairi."

And she headed back to school.

The upper floors of Hillsdale were divided up into tiny bedrooms and each one was allocated to a pupil. Milandra's room was on the second floor. One night she couldn't sleep and sat at her window even though it was after midnight, looking at the grounds lit up by the full moon. She suddenly got a fright when she saw a figure standing below her window and, as she peered out, she saw it was Ruairi. He was waving up to her and then, to her astonishment, he was beckoning her to come down. She shook her head vehemently but he persisted.

Then, as if in a trance, she changed from her nightclothes into a dress, put on a coat, and slipped out of her rom and down the dark corridors of Hillsdale to a side door. She took the key hanging beside it and, opening it, slipped the key into her pocket and hurried around the building to where Ruairi was. They stared at each other and then, as if they could read each other's minds, they turned and began to walk through the gardens to the cliffs.

"How did you know which was my room?" she asked when they finally reached their rock by the cliffs.

"You told me," he said, "when we met last. I've been standing under your window each night, hoping you would see me."

"I can't believe I've left the building at night. If I was discovered . . ." She didn't need to finish the sentence.

He reached out and took her hand.

After that, all Milandra could think about was Ruairi as she realised she had fallen in love. They had the same arrangement: she would creep out one night a week, sometimes two if they couldn't bear being apart. They would go to the cliffs or the stables. Milandra didn't think such joy could exist in the world. Why were the Bishop and Mrs. Kellings insisting a life of spinsterhood for all their pupils, depriving them of what love could offer?

She didn't think of the danger.

"I want to marry you," he insisted one night as they lay in the hayshed on the grounds.

"But – how?"

"We'll figure a way," he said, speaking with the assurance that innocence brought.

That night after leaving him, her heart soaring with joy, she rushed back to Hillsdale. As she crept into her room and closed the door behind her, she jumped when a voice spoke from the darkness.

"Where have you *been?*"

Katie was sitting on her bed.

"*Shhh!*" begged Milandra. She rushed to her best friend and sat down on the bed beside her.

"Well?" demanded Katie again.

"I've been with Ruairi," whispered Milandra.

"Ruairi?"

"Yes."

"The *gardener's* son?" cried Katie.

"*Shhh!* Yes. Katie, he loves me! And I love him!"

"How long has this been going on?" Katie was incredulous.

"A few weeks, months, I don't know, I feel I've known him all my life!" Milandra's voice was full of joy.

"But – but – but –" Katie didn't know what to say.

"Remember how he blushed when he saw us? He was in love with me all along."

"I see!" said Katie, feeling stupid as she had thought he had a crush on her. "But he's the *gardener's* son!"

"I think we're in no position to be snobs, Katie, not when we rely on charity at Hillsdale."

"It's all quite a shock," said Katie, thinking of the consequences should they ever be discovered.

"Love is a shock, Katie. You'll know yourself when it happens to you."

Not as a spinster nurse on a hospital ward, thought Katie.

The next week, Milandra rushed out of the school at the usual hour at night and into Ruairi's arms and they made their way to the hay barn.

As they began to undress and caress each other, Milandra wondered if she should tell him that Katie knew. She decided not to, as it might worry him. And she knew she could trust Katie with her life.

Suddenly the barn door swung open and in marched Mrs. Kellings, accompanied by half the school staff holding lanterns. Milandra screamed in shock as she went to cover herself.

"You – you harlot!" cried Mrs. Kellings as she grabbed Milandra by the arm, pulled her to her feet and threw her to two other members of staff. "And as for you!" She raised her hand and whacked Ruairi across the head.

She strode out of the barn.

"Bring her back to the school!" she ordered.

Milandra was marched out of the barn.

"*Ruairi*!" screamed Milandra as she was dragged away.

The rest of the night passed in a blur for Milandra. She was screamed at and shouted at and slapped across the face, not just by Mrs. Kellings but by other members of staff.

And all she could think about was Ruairi and what might be happening to him.

Milandra was sitting in Mrs Kellings' office.

There was a small parlour next door, with an interconnecting door between it and the office.

Bishop Staffordshire had been summoned and, when he finally arrived, Mrs. Kellings spoke to him in the little parlour.

A trembling Milandra could hear their conversation plainly

through the door which was very slightly ajar.

After Mrs. Kellings recounted the gory details to him, there was a prolonged silence.

Finally, he spoke, his anger clearly barely controlled. "I thought, nay expected, nay *demanded* that Hillsdale train respectable young girls for respectable lives, not train them to prostitute themselves for gardeners' sons! How long has this liaison been going on?"

"I cannot say for certain, Your Grace, but according to our pupil Katie who revealed the affair it could be a matter of months."

"Well, the girl must have a medical examination without delay to establish what her situation is – if the girl is pregnant it will be the end of Hillsdale! Summon the doctor!"

Milandra, listening, wished she could die.

An hour later the local doctor arrived.

"I shall fetch a female member of staff to be present," said Mrs. Kellings. "I'd prefer not to witness such a thing myself."

"Do not bother, Mrs. Kellings!" said the Bishop. "Any attempts to protect the girl's modesty at this stage are quite unnecessary! Proceed with the examination, Doctor!"

Mrs. Kellings showed the doctor into her office where Milandra sat quaking.

Trembling, ashamed and embarrassed beyond her worst imaginings, Milandra submitted to an intimate examination by the doctor.

The Bishop and Mrs Kellings waited anxiously on the other side of the door until the doctor emerged.

"Is she – intact?" asked the Bishop with a gulp.

"The girl is not pregnant, if that is what you ask, and quite – intact." The doctor looked at the two coldly before he hastily left.

"Thank goodness for that!" sighed Mrs. Kellings.

"Indeed! It will contain the scandal."

On the other side of the door, Milandra sat sobbing silently as she listened to them decide her destiny.

"So what are we to do now?" asked Mrs. Kellings. "Do you wish to see the girl?"

"I certainly do not, Mrs. Kellings! I have no desire to offend my eyes with the sight of a harlot!"

"Of course," agreed Mrs Kellings. "But what is to be done with the girl?"

"She must be thrown out of Hillsdale without further delay!"

"But – but what will become of her?"

"That is not our concern, Mrs Kellings. Where is her family? Has she got any?"

"Her mother is head cook in a Big House, her father is deceased," said Mrs. Kellings.

"If that is the truth! I've met many an illegitimate child who is passed off as the offspring of a deceased father," said the Bishop knowingly.

"But, if the girl is thrown out she will end up on the streets, or in a brothel!" cried Mrs. Kellings.

"If that is the girl's destiny, then we cannot save her. We've tried to do everything to give her a respectable life."

"But, Your Grace, the girl is young and naïve – should she have the rest of her life ruined because of a-a pervert?"

"Come, come, Mrs. Kellings!" The Bishop laughed cynically. "A strange kind of pervert it is that she rushed from her room to meet at night over and over again!"

"But, still, she has been an exemplary student up until now, never caused a moment's trouble and is one of our most intelligent students. I had high hopes for her. The girl has a fault in that she quite pretty – I always suspected it would land her in trouble."

"Her lack of morals and decency landed her in trouble, Mrs. Kellings."

Mrs Kellings never took on the Bishop or disagreed with him but she couldn't bear what he was recommending – that the girl be thrown to the wolves. She thought frantically.

"I think, Your Grace, that if we expelled her we would draw attention to the situation and people would want to know *why* she was expelled. By keeping her near we would contain the scandal. If we could just get her to graduation next year, then she would be off our hands and no longer our responsibility. I think that would be the wisest course of action, Your Grace."

The Bishop thought hard. "And what of the – pervert?"

"The Sullivan boy can be asked to leave the cottage we provide for his family and never return," suggested Mrs. Kellings.

"No, that is not good enough. Sack the gardener and have his family, including the boy, thrown out of the cottage and sent away from Hillsdale, with no reference."

"But –"

The Bishop slammed his hand on the table. "No, Mrs Kellings! Now, I have conceded in the matter of the girl for the reasons you outlined – to protect Hillsdale – but I cannot have the gardener or his family near the pupils again. The whole family must be removed from Hillsdale. They are not to be trusted. Why was the gardener not making sure his son was at home in bed instead of in the hayshed fornicating with our pupils? Give the gardener and his family notice to quit without any delay."

On the other side of the door, Milandra held her stomach tightly as she silently screamed.

The next few months passed with Milandra in a trance, trying to comprehend what had happened. True to the Bishop's word, Ruairi and his family were thrown out of their cottage at Hillsdale and she did not know what became of them. She thought about Ruairi all the time.

It was Christmas and any pupils who had nowhere to go for Christmas and a few of the staff remained for the holiday. Hillsdale was quite empty late on Christmas Eve and Milandra sat at her window, looking at the snow falling down. Suddenly she saw a figure standing below her window and her heart started to beat hard as she saw it was Ruairi.

She jumped up, opened the window and called softly down, "What are you *doing* here?"

"I had to see you! You are all I think about. Come down to me."

"I *can't*. I was nearly thrown out of the school last time! Where are you staying, where is your family?"

"In the workhouse. The Bishop wouldn't give us a reference and we couldn't get a position. There was nowhere to go. I can't bear it!"

"Oh!" Her heart sank on hearing the news.

"The thought of you is the only thing that keeps me going, Milandra. Please, I have to see you – please come down to me!"

"It's impossible, Ruairi! But you'll get yourself back on your feet, just you wait and see."

Ruairi started to cry. "I just came to say goodbye."

"Where are you going?"

"Away – I can't stay here without you."

"But – where are you going to?"

"Away," he said and he turned and walked into the falling snow that was turning into a blizzard.

"Ruairi!" she cried after him. "*Ruairi!*"

The next morning Ruairi's body was washed up on the rocks just below the cliffs where she used to meet him. Some said he lost his footing in the blizzard and fell to his death.

When Milandra heard the news she couldn't stop crying. She knew the truth as the echo of his last word kept ringing in her ears: "*Away.*"

PART 13

Sackville Street

1881

CHAPTER 82

Milandra continued to stroke Nicholas's hair at the bottom of the stairs of their house in Sackville Street as she finished telling him of her time at Hillsdale Abbey. She had a faraway look in her eyes as she spoke.

"Part of me died the day I heard Ruairi was dead. Any innocence or naiveté that I had just died away. If only I had gone down to him that night when he waited for me outside my window! I could have saved him – maybe. But I put my own self and fears first. It was all Bishop Staffordshire's fault, don't you see? He was so cruel, so unforgiving, so stubborn in his attitudes. He didn't need to be so vindictive to the Sullivan family, to Ruairi. We were only in love – is that such a crime? And when I came to Dublin and saw him – and his daughter so happy being engaged to you – well, I just had to . . . don't you see? Had to take their happiness, as he took mine. But I couldn't let anybody know, not even Flancy. Mrs. Kellings never told my mother about Ruairi and me, and neither did I. If Flancy had known the real reason I pursued you, she would have stopped me. She would have insisted no good would come out of it."

As Milandra continued to stroke his hair, she didn't notice Nicholas had closed his eyes.

"And tonight I couldn't just let you leave me and destroy everything that I have worked so hard to achieve in life . . . I couldn't just let you run back to Constance Staffordshire and take everything away from me again, even my daughter. You do understand, Nicholas, don't you?"

Milandra looked down at Nicholas and saw he was still. She reached down and felt for his pulse. There was none.

She bent down, kissed him and whispered, "I'm sorry, Nicholas."

She then pushed his head off the cushion and, getting up, put the cushion back on the chair. She went into the dining room and took a decanter of whiskey. Returning to the hallway, she poured half the contents over Nicholas before throwing the decanter to the ground, causing it to smash. She then quickly looked around for his packed suitcases and one by one she brought them up to the third floor and unpacked them.

Then she changed into formal evening wear and chose some jewellery. She tidied her hair as best she could without a maid's help and skilfully applied some cosmetics.

Then, wrapping herself in her richest hooded cape, she made her way downstairs.

Stepping around Nicholas, she quickly let herself out into the street.

CHAPTER 83

A hansom cab stopped outside the house on Sackville Street and Flancy and Petronella got out. It was nearly midnight.

"So you enjoyed that trip, pet?" asked Flancy.

"Oh, yes, Flancy. It was a wonderful show," said Petronella.

Flancy looked up and saw the light on in the drawing room upstairs.

"Is Mama back from France?" asked the girl.

"She should be, my darling."

"I hope *he's* not up," said Petronella.

"Ah, he's probably at that Club of his or gone to bed, love. Don't worry about that fool . . . but I'll tell you one thing –"

"What, Flancy?"

"Whichever he's at, he'll be drunk as a skunk!"

They both bust into giggles as she opened the front door and let them in.

As Flancy closed the door after them, Petronella stood stock still, taking in the scene in front of her.

"*Ahhhh!*" *she* screamed at the top of her voice.

"Whatever is the matter?" cried Flancy, turning quickly from the door.

Then she stared at Nicholas's lifeless body lying at the bottom of the stairs.

It was the early hours of the morning and Flancy stood at the door of the drawing room, watching Milandra with her arms around

Petronella, comforting her. There were several policemen in the house.

One policeman came out of the drawing room and came up to her.

"I think there is nothing more we can do now – thank you for your assistance," said the police officer.

"It's a dreadful shock, just dreadful!" said Flancy, looking over at Milandra and Petronella.

"The child finding him like that certainly was," nodded the policeman. "Lady Havington is very shaken. She said she left him drinking here before going to a function earlier in the evening."

"Ah, sure he was always drinking," sighed Flancy.

"Looks like he stumbled out to the landing with the whiskey and lost his footing."

"Sure didn't he come home from his Club here one night not that long ago and he collapsed at the top of the stairs. It's a wonder he didn't fall down that night. He probably would have only we were there to save him."

"We'll be back tomorrow in the morning to take full statements. It seems a tragic accident," concluded the policeman.

"Although, I wonder . . ." said Flancy, looking at Milandra.

"Yes?" asked the policeman.

"I wonder . . . did he mean to do it? It's very strange he told all the servants to leave for the night. Perhaps he had it planned. Suicide. He was an unhappy man – never felt he was good enough for his wife."

"It is certainly something to consider. However, it would be very unusual for him to throw himself down a flight of stairs carrying a decanter of whiskey with him," said the policeman.

"Well, he brought whiskey everywhere else with him, so why wouldn't he have brought it to his death with him too?" said Flancy.

"Certainly something to consider . . . We'll leave you in peace for now. Try and get some sleep. I'll position a policeman outside the house for the night, and I'll be back in the morning."

"Thank you," said Flancy and she watched as he and the other policemen left.

Then she stood, looking at Milandra and Petronella hugging each other quietly. Milandra looked up at Flancy, and it was if there were just the two of them in the world.

Constance sat looking out the drawing-room window in Mountjoy Square, anxiously awaiting Nicholas. She looked at the clock and saw it was nearly four in the morning. He should have been there hours ago. Milandra had been due back from France early the previous evening, Nicholas had said.

A litany of thoughts was passing through her head.

Milandra was obviously not going to take the news of his departure well. Perhaps they were still mired in the practicalities of the divorce. Anxiously trying to sort out a situation that would be beneficial to both of them. But as she remembered what Milandra was like, Constance imagined she would not take the news lying down. There would be accusations and recriminations. Perhaps she was threatening Nicholas. Or begging him not to leave. Perhaps she was persuading him to stay. Panic gripped Constance as she thought of this possibility. Nicholas had always been easily swayed. What now if he had been swayed to stay with Milandra? But he had seemed so certain that this was what he wanted to do. To spend the rest of his life with her and John. But perhaps the reality of walking out of Sackville Street and the life he had there had hit him when it came to telling Milandra. Perhaps he had not been brave enough to follow through with his plan. Perhaps he never even had the courage to tell Milandra he was leaving.

As the clock ticked on through the night, there was still no sign of Nicholas.

CHAPTER 84

Exhausted emotionally and having had no sleep, Constance got John ready the next morning as usual and dropped him off with Máire before setting off to work at Mrs. Cleary's. She could not concentrate on her work that day, as she fought her fears. The fact that Nicholas had not come the previous night made her realise that all was not well. For whatever reasons, Nicholas was not going to leave Milandra as he had promised. For the second time in her life, he was deserting her. Without even an explanation, a conversation. As she thought of the promises he had made to John and her, she became increasingly agitated and angry. Whatever about destroying her with his false promises, he had no right to do so with John, her son, their son.

"Whatever is the matter with you today, Constance?" asked Mrs. Cleary, standing over her work bench.

"Pardon?"

Mrs. Cleary took up Constance's work and inspected it. "This is not good, Constance! Not good at all!"

Mrs. Cleary was about to berate Constance for her bad work, but looked down at her and saw she looked exhausted, stressed and her eyes were red. She looked as if she was about to burst out in tears.

"Why don't you go home for the rest of the day and get a good sleep," suggested Mrs. Cleary. "Be back in the morning, in your usual form."

Constance nodded and quickly got up and left the premises.

As Constance hurried through the back streets, she wasn't heading home to Mountjoy Square but found herself instead making her way to Sackville Street. She knew what she was going to do. She was going to confront Nicholas. She would not just let him walk out of her life as she had all those years ago. She would confront him, challenge him and fight for him. This time, she would not be a walkover. This time she would end up fighting for what was hers.

With a nerve and determination she never knew she had, she stormed down Sackville Street towards Nicholas and Milandra's house. She wasn't sure what she was going to say or do once she got there, but didn't care. She needed to know what was going on. She deserved an explanation. The memory of Milandra came rushing back to her, but even the thought of confronting the indomitable woman did not put her off her mission. She would march up to the front door and demand to see Nicholas. She couldn't remember the last time she had been in Sackville Street. That day she didn't care what old acquaintances she might meet. Her heart started to palpitate as she neared the house. She was on the opposite side of the road and looked for a crossing to make her way across.

As she stood there looking across at the forbidding building, she suddenly spotted two police officers positioned at the front door. She watched, expecting them to move on, but they didn't. As she continued to observe, she saw the front door open and a constable come out and speak to the officers before returning indoors. Constance tried to figure out what on earth they might be doing there as she peered across.

"*Read all about it – death on Sackville Street – read all about it!*" called a newspaper boy as he walked down the street.

His words cut into her thoughts and she turned to stare at him.

"Read all about it, miss – today's paper straight off the press – death on Sackville Street!" said the boy, holding out a newspaper.

Constance reached forward and took the newspaper.

The words on the front page screamed at her:

'*Death on Sackville Street – Lord Nicholas Havington Found*

Dead at Bottom of Stairs by Daughter."

Constance's hands began to shake as she gripped the newspaper and then the street began to spin in front of her.

"Miss!" cried the newspaper boy as Constance collapsed on the pavement.

CHAPTER 85

The day of Nicholas's funeral was one of shock and disbelief for his circle of friends and colleagues. He was a man who had everything to live for. A beautiful wife, a wonderful daughter, a lifestyle many could only dream of. For him to be cut down in his prime was a tragedy. As Nicholas's coffin was laid into the ground, Milandra, dressed in widow's weeds and heavily veiled, held Petronella close to her. Everyone present thought it was a tragedy that Milandra had been widowed now twice at a young age.

Constance had kept a safe distance back from the rest of the funeral mourners at Nicholas's funeral. She was fearful that somebody might recognise her. She watched as Milandra conducted herself with dignity and grace throughout the service and the burial afterwards.

It did not seem real to Constance that Nicholas was dead. One minute they were planning the rest of their lives together, and now he was gone. To have lost Nicholas once had nearly destroyed her, to have lost him twice was unbearable. She had avidly read the newspapers since he had died to try and get some information as to what had happened. They reported that Nicholas had been alone in the house on Sackville Street when the accident had occurred. That he had been drinking heavily and fallen down the stairs. That his wife Milandra had returned from France earlier that evening and then left him alone in the house and his body at the bottom of the stairs had been discovered by the cook and his daughter. But it all didn't make sense to Constance. Only she knew what Nicholas was planning to tell his wife that night. And after he had told her he was leaving her, would she have casually left for the evening for a social occasion? And why would Nicholas have stayed in the house drinking heavily? Nicholas would not have stayed in the house a moment longer, but left straight away to come to her in Mountjoy Square as they had arranged. Deep down she knew he was determined to leave Milandra that night and that nothing would have stopped him. She knew that only his death would have prevented him from coming to her that night. So the course of events that was being reported made no sense to her. She pulled her hat further down her forehead and raised her shawl up over her face as she went and mingled amongst the mourners in the graveyard.

She overheard two men talking.

"Poor Nicholas, he had everything to live for," said one of the men.

"He did, he did," sighed the other man. "Of course he had been drinking heavily for a long long time."

"I know, he was an accident waiting to happen," said the other man.

As Constance heard them talk, she knew this was not true. Nicholas had not been drinking heavily. He spent most of his spare time with her, every evening, and never touched a drop. Where were these stories coming from? Who was spreading them?

She neared two women talking together.

"I don't believe the suicide rumour, do you?" said one of the women.

"Well, actually, it had crossed my mind," said the other.

"Mine too! He didn't strike me as the type, but one never knows, does one? Strange that he sent the servants away that night to be alone."

"Well, if he did kill himself, it was dreadful that he did it that way! Letting poor Petronella find him like that. She will never recover from it."

Constance's anger increased. Where was this suicide story

472

coming from? Of course Nicholas didn't kill himself. He had never been happier, about to start his new life with her and John. As Constance watched Milandra across the graveyard receive condolences from the line of sympathisers, her mind began racing. Nicholas's death did not make any sense to her. What everyone was saying made no sense. She needed to look Milandra in the eye. Only then would she know if Nicholas had told her he was leaving her and about his relationship with her.

Constance went and joined the long line of sympathisers. She studied Milandra intently as she drew closer to her. Milandra had just the right amount of sadness on her face. mixed with a determination to remain dignified and composed. But as Constance remembered, Milandra was a wonderful actress. As she neared Milandra she could hear her speak to the sympathisers.

"So kind of you . . . most kind . . . so kind of you," Milandra repeated over and over again to the people.

Constance was next in line and she prepared herself as the man in front of her offered his condolences and moved on.

Constance stepped in front of Milandra and Milandra smiled at her with the same vacuous expression she had worn for the others.

Constance pushed back her hat and brought down her shawl, exposing her full face to Milandra. Milandra's face dropped for a moment as a look of shock spread across her fine features.

As Constance glared into Milandra's eyes, she knew the truth.

Milandra quickly regained her composure and looked at Constance but looked at her as if she was a stranger.

"I sympathise with you for your loss, Milandra," said Constance evenly and clearly.

"So kind of you . . . most kind," said Milandra as her eyes were quickly directed to the next sympathiser.

Constance walked away and out of the graveyard. As she walked, she thought of Milandra's expression and her guilty eyes. Constance now knew that Nicholas had told her he was leaving her that night. He had been true to his promise and followed through. And Constance was now full sure that it was Milandra who had prevented him from leaving. He had not been drinking that night, or had an accident, or certainly not committed suicide. However, Nicholas ended up at the bottom of the stairs, Constance was sure it was not of his choice or by his design. And the only other person in the house that night had been Milandra. But what could Constance do, how could she air her suspicions? She had no evidence of foul play. The police had obviously investigated and had no suspicions. If Constance went to the police and told them everything, all she would be doing would be presenting herself as a whore. And a disgruntled whore whose married lover was now dead. All she would be doing would be bringing unwanted attention to herself, destroying Nicholas's name and jeopardising her own meagre existence. Milandra, she knew in her heart, had got away with murder – but nobody would take her belief seriously. Milandra was too powerful, too respected, too important. And Constance was a nobody.

As Constance reached Mountjoy Square, she was overcome with grief. Not just for Nicholas, but the wonderful future she was to share with him and John. As she climbed the steps up to the Staffordshire house, the door was now wide open. The property speculator had now taken over the house and as she passed through the doorway and into the hallway she saw children teeming around the house.

"Hello, missus," smiled the mother of the family who had moved into what had been their drawing room.

Constance nodded back and climbed the stairs. It was the same on the second floor, the bedrooms now one-room flats for large families. She walked up quickly to the next floor and down the corridor past the children there. She took out her key and let herself into her bedroom and firmly closed the door and locked it behind her. As she looked around her bedroom, she realised that this one room would now be her and John's life for the future. As she sat down on the chair crying, she faced the reality that she and Nicholas were never to be.

PART 14

1916

CHAPTER 86

Amelia abandoned her car outside Kilmainham Hospital and raced up the steps inside the building. She was not prepared for the scene that greeted her. Wounded soldiers lay everywhere, on makeshift beds on the floors being frantically attended to by medical staff who appeared to be overwhelmed with the extent of the causalities. There was nobody on reception and as she hurried down the hallway searching for somebody in authority to speak to, injured men desperately called out, some screaming for relief from their pain.

A nurse came rushing in her direction and Amelia grabbed her.

"I'm looking for my fiancé, Captain Rupert Perkins. Has he been admitted?"

"I don't know!" said the nurse as she quickly moved on.

Amelia continued down the hallway, grabbing any nurse or doctor she could find, asking if they knew was Rupert there. None of them knew, and were too frantic to even help her. Amelia realised that the hospital had never experienced an influx on this scale before, and all normal admittance procedures were being ignored as the hospital staff desperately fought to save lives. Amelia eyed every soldier, in the desperate hope it would be Rupert. But, as she saw the terrible injuries the soldiers had suffered, her heart began to race as her mind pictured the worst for Rupert.

She ran up the stairs to the next floor, where again soldiers were lying in the corridors. She ran into the wards, all filled with soldiers lying on the beds. Driven on now by the need to know what had become of her Rupert, she pictured how they should be now down the country enjoying their time together at his family home. Not her wandering the corridors of this grim hospital searching to see if he was alive or dead. At the end of the corridor she went into the last ward. She looked down the ward at the rows of beds occupied by the soldiers. Her eyes fixated on each face in the hope it would be Rupert's.

On the end bed she saw a brown-haired man lying, his face turned towards the nearby window.

She ran down to the bed and stood at the foot of it.

The man turned his gaze from the window.

"Rupert!" Amelia started to cry as she ran to him and flung her arms around him. "I thought you were dead!"

"Amelia," he whispered.

She pulled back and looked at him and saw his chest was bandaged.

"What happened to you?" she asked.

"It looks worse than it is," he said and started to cough, his face twisting in pain. "The bullet missed anything important, so the doctors say."

"My poor darling Rupert," she said and the tears were of relief as she gripped his hands.

"Stop that crying, will you, you'll upset everybody else," he said and managed to smile.

"I can't help it, you fool!" she said, quickly wiping away the tears. "You have my nerves shattered! Every day when you are at the front, I'm expecting a telegram telling me the worse. And then you come back on leave, and nearly get yourself killed here!"

"I'm not worth the trouble, am I?" he said with a smile.

"And if anything had happened to you, if you'd been killed – I wouldn't be ever able to forgive myself." She broke down again in tears.

He reached forward and took her hand. "Shush, darling," he said. "This is not the place to talk about that." He glanced around meaningfully at the neighbouring beds.

She lowered her head and whispered tearfully in his ear. "I had no right to speak to anybody about what you wrote in your letters to me. They were private letters between us. If you had been killed, I'd be responsible for your death."

He chuckled and then coughed loudly. "I think, Amelia," he murmured, "you might be giving yourself a little too much credit for your role in the rising."

She sat up, gripping his hand tightly, and said softly, "All I can promise you is that I will never betray you again. Regardless of any opinion I may have –"

"Of which there will be many," he interrupted her with a wry smile.

"I will always put you first. And whatever you want to do in life, even if it means going back to fight in France in this bloody war, then I support you. And always will."

He smiled at her. "That's all I can ever ask of you."

"So – so you forgive me?" she whispered.

He nodded. "When I was shot in Northumberland Road and fell to the ground, I thought I was going to die. And all I wanted was to see you again."

"Then marry me, Rupert!" she pleaded. "Let's not wait any longer – let's just get married!"

"But when I go back to the front – if anything happened to me, you would be left a young widow. I don't want to ruin your life."

"If anything happened to you, my life would be ruined anyway! Can't you see the state I'm in now?" She took out her handkerchief and furiously wiped away her tears.

"If you had any sense you'd walk away. I can't promise you a future. Seeing me like this, does it not prove it? That telegram will probably come one day, saying I've been killed."

"Well, I don't care! As soon as you are out of that bed, we are going to get married, do you hear me?"

"Yes, Amelia!"

"And I will never receive that telegram about my husband. I don't want you ever to talk like that again."

"Yes, Amelia!" He was taken aback by her determination.

"And another thing," she said.

"Yes, Amelia?"

"Just hold me!" She leaned forward and embraced him.

CHAPTER 87

"Staffordshire," Milandra repeated as she placed the wallet down on the table beside the bed Seán was lying on. "I knew who you were the first moment I saw you. Your mother is Constance Staffordshire, isn't she?"

"How do you know that?" he said.

"Because you are the image of your father, Nicholas Fontenoy, who was my husband," said Milandra. "When I saw you first standing on my landing with your revolver aimed at me, I thought you had come to find me, to kill me for the wrongs I have done, to your mother, to you – to Nicholas."

"What are you talking about?" he gasped.

She stood up, walked out of the room and returned carrying the bag that held the valuables she had grabbed from upstairs. She took out the album, and leafing through it took out a portrait of Nicholas and held it up to him.

"Do you recognise him?" she asked.

As Seán tried to focus on the portrait of Nicholas, he saw a man who looked very much like himself. But seeing Nicholas's portrait, he was jolted with a memory. Of when he was a young boy, living with his mother on Mountjoy Square, before their house was turned into a tenement. He remembered a time when this wonderful man came to visit each evening, always bringing wonderful toys and food for them. Yes, Nicholas had been this man's name. And then he had disappeared as quickly as he arrived and they had never seen him again, and his mother had never mentioned him again. Sometimes, Seán thought he had imagined the whole thing. That Nicholas had never existed. But here was Milandra showing him a portrait of him.

"Nicholas had come to me that evening and told me everything. He had been engaged to your mother Constance before he married me, and she had given birth to his illegitimate child. He told me the child was the image of him. He said his son's name was John. But you in your devotion to Irish republicanism changed it to the Irish form – Seán. Yes?"

Seán nodded.

"And you still are the image of him . . . he was going to leave me and live with you and your mother . . . well, I just couldn't let that happen. Don't you understand, I just couldn't!"

As Seán saw Milandra's face come closer to his, he blacked out for good.

Amelia was so tired and exhausted from the past few days that she lay down beside Rupert on the bed and fell asleep.

When she woke up, she realised she had slept through the night and it was early the next morning. Rupert lay fast asleep, and she quietly left his bedside and walked through the hospital. A stream of casualties was still flooding in.

"Excuse me, what is happening with the conflict?" she asked an officer who was just arriving.

The officer stopped. "The rebels have surrendered. It's over. We've taken back control of the city centre. There's a couple of outposts they still control, but it's only a matter of time."

"And what is the city centre like now?" she asked.

"Utterly destroyed," said the officer as he walked on.

As Amelia walked to her car, all her thoughts turned to her grandmother.

CHAPTER 88

Milandra walked through the ground floor of her house in dismay. Her beautiful house was now wrecked. She made her way to the front of the house and looked out what had been the dining-room window. She saw a heavy presence of British soldiers outside on the street.

One was speaking through a loud speaker. "*Citizens of Dublin, the city is back under government control. The rebellion has been quashed. The rebels have unconditionally surrendered.*"

She breathed easy with relief and returned to the hallway. She went down to the back where she descended the stairs into the servants' quarters. She went to the stove and set a light to the sticks and coal in it. Then she walked through the back corridor and into the footman's room and sat down beside Seán's still body.

She bent forward and nudged him. She nudged him hard again and suddenly his eyes flicked open.

He quickly looked around, trying to get his bearings. He had never felt so disorientated.

As he saw the old woman sitting beside him, the memories came flooding back. She had given him something to eat in the cake and he had passed out.

"What happened?" he asked groggily, struggling to sit up.

"It's all right now, it's all over. Your chaps have surrendered and the British are back in control, for now."

His head felt so heavy and he had a thundering headache.

"You drugged me," he accused her.

"Yes, I really had no other choice, you see. You were determined to go and get yourself killed. To fight a lost battle on the streets and be shot. I couldn't have that on my conscience, on top of everything else."

He remembered everything she had said before he passed out. Or had he dreamed it?

But as he glanced at the side table he saw Nicholas's portrait still lying there. He reached out for it and studied it.

"You are my husband's son. I had to save you from yourself, do you see?" she said.

"You had no right to drug me," he said.

"No, I haven't had a right to do anything I've ever done, but I've done it anyway. You're so like him, looks-wise. Nothing like him in manner, or personality. I imagine you've had the most dreadful upbringing and life, to lead you to want to get killed as was your clear intention these past few days. I think you grabbed on to this cause to give your life meaning."

"And our cause has failed," he said, sinking into depression.

"For now. But I suspect you have sown the seeds of something much bigger." She stood up. "Now we haven't much time. They will be looking for you and the other rebels who haven't surrendered. If they find you here, you will face execution."

He saw she had laid out causal clothes belonging to the footman on a chair.

"Change into these clothes as quickly as you can. I've lit a fire in the stove and we can burn your rebel uniform and anything else that links you with the rebellion. I'll wait for you in the kitchen. Do not be long."

He struggled off the bed, shaking his head, trying to focus. Whatever she had given him had knocked him for six. He didn't know how long he had been out cold.

He did as she bid and changed into the clothes she had left out for him and then made his way into the kitchen carrying his uniform.

Milandra grabbed his uniform and stuffed it into the fire in the stove along with the papers from his wallet.

"Where is your gun?" she demanded.

He reached into his inside pocket and took it out. She grabbed it from him and hid it in a crevice up the chimney.

She went to her bag and took out a bundle of money and handed it to him.

"Use this to get yourself to Cork and on the first passage to America. From your papers you are quite high up in this movement, so they will be looking for you. Travel under your birth-certificate name John Staffordshire. Do not refer to yourself as Seán again to anybody, do you understand me?"

He nodded.

"Well, what are you waiting for. Go!" she insisted. "Out the back door and through the garden gate which will lead you into the laneways. Don't stop until you are safely out of the city."

Seán reached into his inside pocket and took out the photo of Nicholas Milandra had shown him in the footman's room.

"Can I keep it?" he asked.

She nodded and he quickly put it back into his pocket.

"There's so much I want to ask you, about my father, Nicholas. About you," he said.

"Well, we don't have time for any of that. I will never see you again, so I wish for the rest of your life to be a happy one." She pushed him urgently towards the door.

As he was about to go he turned to take a final look at her.

"One thing," she asked. "What became of your mother? Is Constance still alive?"

"No. She died a few years ago, in the room she had lived in all her life on Mountjoy Square."

She nodded and waved him to quickly go. He opened the door and disappeared up the steps into the garden. Milandra let out a huge sigh and went to sit in the chair beside the stove.

CHAPTER 89

Private automobiles were not allowed into the city centre, so Amelia abandoned the car as close as she could get and set off on foot. As she got closer, the devastation became apparent. With the surrender of the rebels, the people were venturing out onto their streets for the first time and there was a general feeling of disbelief. The city had gone in a matter of the days from one of the finest in the world to a war zone. The military were everywhere, regularly stopping people to check their papers. Amelia's military pass enabled her to get past the checkpoints without too much delay. As she passed Trinity College and made her way to the river, she saw the *Helga* gunship still stationed there, its big guns now silent.

As she crossed the bridge and entered into Sackville Street, she looked around in bewilderment. It had suffered the worst of the shelling, and what had been fine buildings were now burned-out shells. Roofless, windowless, burned-out shells. She passed the General Post Office, the rebel headquarters, and saw that what had been once one of the city's finest buildings now was four walls. She began to pray as she hurried to the top half of Sackville Street. Her grandmother could be anywhere, if she had survived all this, but since Amelia had left her there on that previous Easter Monday, it was the first place to try and find her. As she got to the upper end of the street, she was relieved to see those buildings had not been destroyed to the same extent as on the lower half of the street.

She raced on and stood in front of Milandra's house. It was still standing at least, but just about, as part of the roof had fallen in and all the windows had been blown out. She ran up to the door and, taking her key, let herself in.

"*Grandmama! Grandmama!*" she called hysterically at the top of her voice as she picked through the falling debris. She saw the grand staircase in front had partially collapsed.

"*Grandmama!*" she cried out.

"Amelia!" came a faint voice in the distance.

"Where are you?" Amelia shouted, flooded with relief at the sound of Milandra's voice.

"The basement!"

Amelia ran down to the back of the hallway and nearly fell down the servants' stairs in her haste.

"Well – you took your time!" said Milandra who was standing at the bottom of the stairs.

"Oh, shut up and come here to me!" cried Amelia as she grabbed her, hugging her tightly.

"I've had the most hideous time. The house was invaded by rebels, can you believe it?" said Milandra in a nonchalant voice. "And then they started bombing us. I'm lucky to be alive, I tell you!"

Amelia was laughing through her tears. "I'm sure those rebels got more than they bargained for when they came into your house!"

Milandra nodded as she embraced her back. "That, I can safely assure you, my dear, is truest thing you have ever said."

Amelia carefully led Milandra up the stairs from the basement to the first floor. Milandra stood in the foyer on the ground floor, again surveying what used to be her beautiful house. Although it looked structurally still intact, everything was smashed and broken. The ceilings were destroyed, the chandeliers crashed to the floor.

"I'd like to fetch some things from my room upstairs," said Milandra.

"We don't know how stable the house is, Grandmama. It's best we just leave until we are told it's safe to come back," urged Amelia. "Let's just get home to Dalkey. We have everything you need for now there. Mama will be in such a state."

Taking Milandra's arm, she gently led her to the front door.

"Hard to believe that all this has happened in a short week," said Milandra.

"It looks worse than it is," said Amelia. "We'll have it fixed up in no time at all."

"Somehow I doubt that," said Milandra as she followed her through the front door.

Amelia turned and locked the door behind them. She wasn't sure why she was doing that, as all the windows were destroyed and the house could be easily entered. But, as Amelia saw all the British soldiers patrolling the street, she at least felt relieved there would be no further looting.

She took Milandra's bag and, taking her arm, began to lead her down Sackville Street towards the river.

Milandra's eyes took in the scene as they walked on. The street that had been her home for most of her life now lay devastated. The once fine buildings were now mostly demolished from the bombardment. The stores, General Post Office, hotels all were crumbled to the ground, with just occasional walls still standing.

"I'm sorry you have to see all this, Grandmamma," said Amelia.

"It's like Armageddon. If I wasn't seeing it for myself, I would never believe it."

"We will have you safely home in Dalkey soon," promised Amelia.

"Even your mother's cold hard beds will be a very welcome sight to me," said Milandra.

"And this will all be rebuilt. It will be rebuilt better than before. You'll be back here and it will be as good as new," said Amelia. She tightened her grip on Milandra's arm and they continued their journey.

"Perhaps . . . but I won't be here to see it," said Milandra. "I will never be back on Sackville Street again."

CHAPTER 90

The week of the Easter Rising drew to an end and Milandra recuperated at Petronella's house in Dalkey. She felt relieved to be there as the dreadful memories of that week flashed through her mind. Rupert had been released from hospital and was staying there as well. It was the Friday evening and, after having dinner, the family had retired to the drawing room. Milandra watched Amelia and Rupert sitting together on the couch. They had set their marriage date for the following Monday and now were excitedly discussing the details. Petronella and Amelia's husband Jordan seemed more affected by Milandra's brush with death than she was herself.

"Well, I always said you could put a bomb under Mother and she would come up smelling of roses," remarked Petronella as she refilled Milandra's wineglass and went to retake her seat beside Jordan.

"I wish we had Milandra over at the front – she'd scare off the Germans quick enough." Rupert grinned over at her.

"Please, Rupert, don't ruin the evening by discussing the war," pleaded Amelia.

"Well, at least Rupert doesn't have to return to the front for some time," said Petronella.

Due to Rupert's injury he had been given indefinite leave and did not have to return to the front in France for the foreseeable future.

"And maybe he won't have to return at all," said Amelia, squeezing Rupert's hand. "By the time he's recovered, the whole war may be over."

Everyone nodded, but silently realised the unlikelihood of what Amelia was suggesting.

As Milandra listened to her family's happy banter, her thoughts were firmly on Nicholas's son. She wondered had Seán, or John as she knew his true name to be, managed to escape arrest. With talk now turning to the execution of the rebel leaders, she hoped he had. She hoped he had followed her advice and set sail to America to start a new life. Or would his love for the suffragette keep him there? Had he followed his heart rather than his head? If he was like his father, Nicholas, she knew he would have followed his heart regardless of what danger it led him to. But she wanted to believe he had gone to America and was safe. After all the things she had done through her life she felt an unusual contentment about her actions the previous week. She may have destroyed Constance and Nicholas's life, but by saving their son decades later, in a small way she had atoned for her sins.

"Well," she said, rising from her chair. "I have had a very eventful few days so I am going to retire to my room."

"I'll escort you up," said Amelia, getting up.

"I'm quite all right, Amelia. You stay with Rupert and I can manage by myself."

"If you're sure," said Amelia and she kissed Milandra goodnight.

"Goodnight, everybody," said Milandra as Petronella rose and gave her a kiss as well.

"Goodnight, Milandra," said Rupert.

They watched as she left the room.

"The last few days were not what the old girl needed at this time of her life," commented Jordan.

"Mama is tougher than she looks," said Petronella with a smirk. "Far tougher!"

There was a knock on the door and the butler walked in.

"Pardon me, Captain Perkins, but there is an attaché at the door who wishes to speak to you."

"Oh, what now?" cried Amelia. "Tell him to go away and leave Rupert to recuperate in peace!"

"Now, Amelia, you know we can't do that," said Rupert, lifting her hand and kissing it before whispering, "I won't be long, I promise."

Amelia rose too. "I shall go too to make sure you won't be!"

Hand in hand, Rupert and Amelia walked out to the hallway where the attaché was waiting.

"Good evening, Captain Perkins, sorry to disturb you. How are you feeling now?" asked the attaché.

"Recovering, thank you," said Rupert.

"The city is now firmly back under our control."

"That is good to hear," said Rupert.

"I know you're on leave, Captain, but we need an account from you of what occurred at the battle at Northumberland Road. We are holding a number of rebels caught there and need your testimony. If you could report tomorrow?"

"Certainly."

The attaché turned to Amelia. "We also we have secured your grandmother's house on Sackville Street, Miss Robinson."

"What's left of it!" said Amelia.

"Indeed," said the attaché. His face became serious. "But I must also report that we have found a body in your grandmother's back garden."

"Was it one of the rebels? Or a looter?" asked Rupert anxiously.

"Well, neither. The body had been buried in the back garden for a considerable time by all accounts. But all the shelling dislodged the earth and the remains were uncovered. It's a police matter rather than a military, so we have handed the matter over to them. But I imagine the police will be calling to interview your grandmother."

Amelia was confounded. "But who on earth is it?"

"They found an inscribed pocket-watch on the body identifying him as a Lucas Hempton," said the attaché. "I am preparing a report for the police on casualties and am making enquiries as to who he might be and what was he doing buried in your grandmother's back garden."

Amelia's mind was racing. Lucas Hempton, the man she had been trying to write an article about, who she had spoken to

Milandra about, the man who had disappeared decades ago. The man whose fate Milandra had denied all knowledge of.

"But –" she began.

"I was hoping to speak to your grandmother to ask if she could shed any light on the matter?" said the attaché.

"Quite impossible!" Amelia said quickly. "She has retired for the night and is exhausted after her dreadful experiences this past week."

"I completely understand. Perhaps you could inform her and we'll . . . be in touch?"

"Yes, of course," said Amelia.

The attaché nodded at them and bade them goodnight as the butler showed him out.

"Whatever is that about?" mused Rupert, confused.

"I – I really don't know!" said Amelia.

Rupert took her by the hand to lead her back into the drawing room.

"Actually, Rupert, I just want to say goodnight to Grandmama, make sure she is all right. I'll be back to you shortly."

"Very well," said Rupert.

He kissed her and went into the drawing room.

Amelia stood for a while, trying to marshall her thoughts, before she headed towards the stairs.

She knocked on Milandra's bedroom door and entered to find her seated at an armchair at the window, looking out at the sea view.

"Hello, dear," smiled Milandra.

Amelia tentatively walked in and sat in the empty armchair opposite her.

Seeing her confused and concerned face, Milandra asked, "Is anything the matter, Amelia?"

"Yes, actually. An attaché from Rupert's regiment called to say they had secured the house on Sackville Street."

"But that's good news," said Milandra, puzzled.

"Yes – but also they found a body in the back garden – your back garden."

Milandra was horrified at the thought it was Seán, shot and killed before he had made his escape.

"A body? Who?" she asked anxiously.

"An inscribed pocket-watch on the body identified it as – Lucas Hempton."

"Oh!" said Milandra, shocked. "Lucas!" An inscription on his watch!

"They said the body had been there for a very long time. Which would be the truth as I know the man disappeared in 1869," said Amelia, studying Milandra intently.

"I see . . . well, I wouldn't know anything about that."

"But you told me you knew Lucas Hempton, that he was a friend of yours, when I asked about him. How on earth did he come to be in your back garden, and buried there all this time?" It was becoming blatantly clear Milandra was covering something up.

Milandra stared out the window.

"*Grandmama*!" cried Amelia loudly. "The police will back to ask questions. Tell me – so that I can help, if I can. Do you know anything about this? You must do!"

Milandra looked at Amelia. "I have many dark secrets. Vey dark secrets – that I have managed to keep hidden."

As Amelia looked at her she felt a chill run down her back.

"Do you really want to know everything about me?" asked Milandra.

Amelia nodded.

PART 15

Christmas

1869

CHAPTER 91

Lucas Hempton was seated having dinner alone at a secluded table in the Shelbourne Hotel. From where he sat, he had a clear view of Milandra Carter and Nicholas Fetherston having an intimate dinner but, as he was shielded by a large potted plant, they could not see him.

He watched them as they spoke intimately together, laughed quietly, occasionally reached out and held hands. It wasn't the first time he had seen Milandra and Nicholas together. They had happened to be at the same theatre as he was one night recently. From the vantage point of his theatre box, he had watched them, hardly seeing any of the play. For their part, Milandra and Nicholas seemed more preoccupied by each other than the drama unfolding on the stage.

Lucas was surprised to see that they were courting. They seemed an odd couple to him.

Milandra, the young wealthy worldly-wise widow, and Nicholas, who always appeared to him to be naïve and over-protected by his parents. What was more surprising to him was that Nicholas had rushed into this relationship so quickly after the ending of his engagement to Bishop Staffordshire's daughter. Lucas, like everyone else, had heard the ghastly and lurid stories about Constance Staffordshire. How she had affairs with Nicholas's best friend and work colleague behind his back. How she had brought such shame on herself and the Staffordshires that the Bishop and his wife had been forced to emigrate to Australia to escape the scandal.

Constance herself had disappeared from view. All such a tragic story, Lucas thought. He supposed he couldn't blame Nicholas for reaching out to find happiness with another party as soon as he could. But knowing Milandra, as Lucas now knew Milandra, he was certain that Nicholas was unaware of the kind of a woman she was. How stupid he himself had been with Milandra when she had arrived in Dublin, pretending to be a grief-stricken young widow, helpless and defenceless to the world! He had never met anybody less helpless and defenceless than her! It was clear to Lucas now that she had never had any feelings for his dear deceased friend, Ambrose Carter. She had merely used her marriage to Ambrose as an avenue to acquire his vast wealth. And then, once she had, she had used it mercilessly to carve herself a prominent niche in Dublin society. Milandra Carter was a bitch. That was what Lucas was now certain of.

He knew he sounded bitter. He knew he was bitter after his dealings with Milandra. He felt he had been used by her. Used to continue the smooth running of Carter Wines and the rest of Ambrose's business affairs after his death until she had acquired enough skills and knowledge of the affairs herself to dispose of him. Used him to introduce her to society in Dublin, until she had established herself. And once she had got what she needed from him, she had discarded him like a piece of rubbish. Rudely and ignorantly dismissing him, and telling him she had no more need of him. Lucas was not just bitter, he was furious. He had been a wise, shrewd and respected businessman all his life, and he had been outplayed by a woman who was not much more than a slip of a girl. Ambrose had relied on Lucas's business acumen all his life, and done very well from it. But his widow believed that Lucas was dispensable and surplus to requirements.

He watched as the happy couple finished their dinner and cheerfully left the restaurant. Milandra had now opened her lavish wine emporium on Grafton Street as she had promised, and seemingly it was doing a roaring trade. But Lucas wondered how well Carter Wines really was doing, behind the pomp and glamour. How well was the business doing with Milandra in charge? Now that she had got rid of all Ambrose's trusted management, now that he himself had no more involvement or say in the accounts or decisions? Just how good was Milandra as a businesswoman, or was it like everything else in her life, a show and an act?

Curiosity got the better of him. He called for the waiter and paid the bill, then he quickly left the restaurant.

He walked to Stephen's Green where hansom cabs were lined up, waiting for customers.

CHAPTER 92

The carriage brought Lucas to his home on Leeson Street. There he went to his key box and spent some minutes rummaging through the keys until he found what he was looking for. When Milandra had requested that he give back the keys to the wine premises and her house, she was unaware that he had always had a spare set. With a grunt of satisfaction, he pocketed the keys.

He waited until it was nearly midnight before he left his home and hailed a hansom cab outside in Leeson Street.

"To Sackville Street!" he instructed the driver, and as he sat back in the carriage he was alive with expectation.

Sackville Street was quiet. Snow had been falling all day, and now the street was covered in a thick blanket, only being disturbed by the occasional carriage bringing people back home from the theatre or restaurants.

Lucas stood outside the Carter Wine Emporium and admired it. He looked at the fabulous displays of wines and champagnes in the windows. The windows were shining and surrounded with opulent bronze edging. He looked at his reflection in the window, the falling snow all around him. He peered into the vast store stocked with every bottle of wine, spirit and champagne imaginable. Stepping back, he looked at words *Carter Wine Merchants* engraved above the stores. Yes, Carter Wines held its place proudly amongst the other stores and enterprises in Lower Sackville Street. Milandra had done very well from the marriage to Ambrose Carter.

He turned and walked down to the street until he came to a laneway that led down the side of the buildings. He followed the laneway down to the back of the buildings and made his way to the back of Carter Wines. Fishing out one of the keys he had taken from his key-box at home, he let himself in, closing the door behind him and locking it firmly.

He made his way through the stockrooms at the back and into the main store, quiet and dark. How many times had he and Ambrose worked late there at night, going through his business accounts, making sure that every penny was accounted for in the way Ambrose was noted for? If one penny was missing, Ambrose would fly into a rage until it was found. What would Ambrose say now to see his fortune, which he protected so fearsomely, being squandered on Milandra's frocks, parties and young fancy man? Lucas made his way through the store and to the central ornate staircase that led up to the first floor of the store. There on display were the most expensive of the vintage wines, reserved for the wealthiest customers.

Lucas continued on his journey past all these to the next stairs that led to the third floor. The third floor was occupied by the offices. There, during the day, the offices were filled with clerks – processing orders, organising deliveries, ordering imports from the major wine countries. At night, it seemed eerie in its silence. Lucas knew exactly where he was going: to the office at the end. This had been Ambrose's office, and Lucas knew it was the office Milandra worked from when she was at the store, and where the account ledgers were kept. He let himself in.

The office was at the back of the building, and he proceeded to light some candles so he could work. He went through the shelves and took down the ledgers from the last few months. Taking them to the desk, he laid them out before him.

He whispered to himself as he opened the first ledger and began to go through it. "Now, Milandra, we will see just how good a businesswoman you are. For I will not let you destroy my good friend Ambrose's business. As much as you don't want me involved, I will see what you are doing, and will try to save you from yourself, if it's not too late!"

As he continued to pore over the ledgers, his surprise changed to shock. Instead of finding the account books at Carter Wines to be in disarray, he found they had been kept meticulously since Milandra had taken over. Not a penny was not accounted for, not a pound missing. These ledgers had been kept in such a meticulous fashion they would put even old Ambrose to shame! What's more, business was booming since Milandra had taken over. They had got more orders and customers than ever before. It seemed Milandra's glamorous image and many friends in high places were actually attracting more trade to Carter Wines. Beyond that, Milandra had cut the prices she paid to the vineyards in France and had cut tighter deals with them which had dramatically cut the cost of the stock she imported. Profits were up, overheads were down, turnover dramatically increased. Instead of being a witless fashion plate, as Ambrose had thought, Milandra was a business genius! What's more all the entries into the ledgers were in Milandra's own handwriting. She personally oversaw every penny that came in and went out of the business.

Lucas conceded depressingly to himself that Milandra was correct. She really didn't need him – he did only get in the way. Sighing, he continued through the ledgers. But he could find nothing except excellent bookkeeping. Curious as to how Milandra had managed to bring the overheads down so much, he stood up and went to the filing cabinet where Ambrose used to keep the receipts of purchases. He found the cabinet locked. Thinking for a moment, he remembered Ambrose used to keep the key to the cabinet hidden on top of a shelf by the window. He went over and to his surprise found it was still kept there. He went to the cabinet and opened it and found that Milandra had continued to store the receipts there. He began to sift through the bundle of receipts which were mainly from French vineyards and was impressed by the deals she had negotiated with the vineyards and the very competitive sums she had negotiated according to the receipts.

Then. as he leafed through the bundle of October receipts, one grabbed his attention because it was such a large amount. He saw the payment was to a Tom Fitzgerald. From over the years he knew by heart all the wine suppliers to Carter Wines, all of them French or Italian or the occasional German name. He never remembered an Irish name among them before, and wasn't aware of any wine supplier of the name Tom Fitzgerald. Yet the name seemed familiar. In addition, the payment of one thousand pounds was way too large. With growing interest, he saw that the same amount of one thousand pounds was on the next receipt, paid to one George Fetherston. Lucas scratched his head as both receipts had been written out on the same day – October 14th – and signed by the recipients. George Fetherston – he knew the name well – he was the son of Sanders Fetherston at Fetherstons' Solicitors. Lucas knew that Milandra had employed Fetherstons' Solicitors. But the payment to them would come straight from her account, and not from the wine merchants' takings. And also it would be billed to Fetherstons' Solicitors, not to an employee of the company, even if he was the son. He tried to think of what merchandise could have been bought from him, but as far as he knew young George Fetherston had never been nor ever would be involved in the liquor trade. And why such an enormous amount? Lucas scrutinised the receipts, looking for some reason. On each receipt on file the reason for the payment was stated – six crates of champagne, ten boxes of wines and so on. But there was no reason for the payments entered into the ledger to either George Fetherston or to this Tom Fitzgerald.

As Lucas pondered on the name of Tom Fitzgerald, which seemed familiar, it came to him. He was Nicholas Fontenoy's friend. Lucas had met him at several parties at the Fontenoys'. A nice, pleasant sort of chap who didn't draw too much attention to himself. He was to be Nicholas's best man at his wedding to Constance Staffordshire, Lucas remembered.

Lucas suddenly looked up in horror as he remembered why else the name Tom Fitzgerald was so familiar to him. He was the man the scandal was about, who had claimed to have slept with Constance Staffordshire. As had George Fetherston. Lucas was stunned.

Recovering, he quickly took the two receipts and then placed the rest back as they were, before hurrying out of the building as fast as he could.

CHAPTER 93

The next evening was the night before Christmas Eve and Milandra was in the upstairs drawing room of her house. She had just finished decorating the huge Christmas tree she'd had delivered that day. Outside the Georgian windows, the snow was falling heavily, and in the fireplace the fire was roaring. She stood back and admired her work, the beautifully decorated tree. She sighed happily. She was due to attend a Christmas drinks soirée at the Fontenoys' that night, starting at nine, and she had already dressed for the occasion. In fact, the Fontenoys had invited her to spend Christmas Day with them. She had already become like one of the family, she mused. It had been a whirlwind romance with Nicholas, as she always knew it would be. She wondered if he would propose to her that Christmas. Flancy had warned it might be too soon to announce an engagement, with her not being widowed even a year, and Nicholas's engagement to Constance Staffordshire only months ended. But Milandra didn't care. And neither did Nicholas. She had transformed him in a short period from being a laughing-stock to being respected. People were beginning to expect him to announce an engagement to Milandra, and if he was to marry one of the richest women in Dublin, then of course they were going to respect him.

"*O Tannenbaum, O Tannenbaum, la la la la la la la!*" sang Milandra happily as she inspected the Christmas tree. Flancy had been down the country on a personal matter and was due back that night. And that day Milandra had given Kitty permission to go home to her family for the rest of Christmas. As Milandra was going to spend most of Christmas at the Fontenoys', she didn't need Kitty, and it was nice for the girl, who was quite a find actually, to have some time off with her family. Milandra's own happy life had filled her with the spirit of Christmas generosity.

"*O Tannenbaum, O Tannenbaum . . . AHHH!*" Milandra screamed at the top of her voice as she saw Lucas Hempton standing in the doorway of the drawing room.

"Good evening, Milandra," said Lucas.

"*Lucas!* What on earth are you doing here? You nearly gave me a heart attack!" she gasped, trying to regain her composure.

"My, that would be a pity, dear. I came to wish you a Happy Christmas."

"How did you get in?" she demanded. "You gave me back all the keys you had."

"I still have the key for the front door that Ambrose gave me to keep an eye on the house when he was living on the country estate."

"Well, you may leave it behind you this evening, thank you! Why didn't you knock on the door?"

"I did, but there was no answer," he said.

"The servants are away. Besides, I didn't hear you knock."

"Well, any time I do knock, what is the point? As Flancy always says you are not home?"

"Because I am not at home!" she snapped.

"I wonder."

"Anyway, you've wished me a Happy Christmas now, and I wish you one too. I really can't stay and chat as I have to be at the Fontenoys' for nine."

"Well, I also wanted to talk to you about Carter Wines."

"Lucas!" She lost her temper. "I have told you before, over and over, that it is none of your concern. It is being run very well, and I do not want to be rude but I wish you minded your own business."

"Oh, you are absolutely correct, my dear Milandra. Carter Wines is doing very well. Better than ever, I see, having studied the books."

503

Milandra was enraged. "What do you mean – studied the books? Do you mean you kept keys to my business premises as well? You have no business studying my books, and my staff have been told not to let you anywhere near them!"

"Yes, I let myself in with my spare key last night to take a look through the ledgers, just to make sure the business was not in jeopardy."

"You had no right to do such a thing!"

"I felt I owed it to Ambrose. Anyway, I'm glad to report that your business is booming and in excellent condition." He smiled as he advanced into the room.

"Good! Now you really do not have to concern yourself with it any more. And if you could leave your key to Carter Wines along with the key to my front door, I'd be very grateful!" Milandra's voice was vicious.

"As you wish."

"I wish!"

"But I must add that your business is doing so well that you can afford to give generous gifts of incredible amounts of money to perfect strangers."

"What are you talking about now?"

He reached into his pocket and took out the two receipts that he had taken from the office the previous night.

"A payment to Tom Fitzgerald and one to George Fetherston on October 14th last," he announced, holding up the receipts.

Milandra lunged forward but then stopped in her tracks.

"That is theft! Taking those from my office!" she accused him.

"No, it's proof."

"Proof of what?" she demanded, becoming scared.

"Proof of bribery . . . I know what you did, Milandra . . . I've pieced it all together. You bribed Tom Fitzgerald and George Fetherston to say they slept with Constance Staffordshire, your new beau's fiancée, in order to break up their engagement."

"Well – I've never heard of such a thing!" She laughed lightly. "I really do believe that you are going senile in your old age, Lucas. Have you spoken to a doctor about it?"

"I'm not senile, Milandra. I'm very aware, make no mistake."

"You have completely got hold of the wrong end of the stick as usual! Those payments are simply for legal work that both those lawyers did for me."

"Nonsense! I called into Ambrose's accountant today, who you haven't fired yet for some reason, and he said all your legal costs come directly to him and he pays them on your behalf from your account with him. He confirmed George Fetherston and Tom Fitzgerald never worked for you independently, and he has no idea what these costs relate to."

"He had no right to discuss my business with you!"

"He was under the impression I still had an active role in your business affairs. In fact, he said you never brought these payments to his attention. I think he wants to talk to you about them after Christmas."

"You interfering old busybody! Why can't you mind your own business?"

"Well, as any good citizen, it is my business when a great wrong had been done. And you have done a great wrong to Constance Staffordshire. I've checked the dates. You made the payments the same week Nicholas broke off his engagement to Constance, the same week her father the Bishop was forced to resign his position."

"Lucas, you have no proof of anything. Those payments could be for anything. In fact, now I remember – I bought some wine supplies off them!"

"You would have had to buy a whole vineyard in France from them for this kind of money, Milandra. It all makes sense to me. How you were constantly in meetings with Nicholas, how he was always at your house here for those meetings. I often came in and found you having a glass of wine instead of discussing legal matters. What happened, Milandra? Did you actually fall in love with him? Is there a heart in there somewhere? If so, true to form, you would do anything to get him, including ruining his fiancée's name and life."

"I refuse to talk about this any more with you! You are clearly insane! I wish you to leave at once. And please leave the keys to my store, my house and those receipts you took from my office as you go!" she commanded.

He folded the receipts over and placed them back into his inside pocket.

"What are you doing with them?" she demanded.

"I am now going to go to the Fontenoy house to speak to Daniel Fontenoy and his son Nicholas and show them this page, and tell them what I know. And what my suspicions are. I will then track down Bishop Staffordshire and his daughter Constance and tell them what I know."

"You can't!" she cried.

"I have to! I can't let that poor girl's life continue to be destroyed, all because of your desires! Somebody has to stop you, Milandra!"

"They won't believe you!" she said desperately.

"Of course they'll believe me. No matter what stories you make up! The payments speak for themselves!"

"But you won't be just destroying me, but Tom Fitzgerald and George Fetherston too!"

"Good! They need to be destroyed. They are as bad as you! You acted out of desire and they acted out of greed! I made my enquiries today and Tom Fitzgerald was virtually penniless at the time, a lowly clerk in Oakleys' and living in a tenement. He has since bought a smart house in Ranelagh with the money you gave him! As for George Fetherston, he is well known for having terrible gambling debts, all of which are now paid off thanks to you and your deplorable bribery!"

He turned and began to walk out.

She hurried to him and held on to his arm. "Lucas! Please, I'm begging you! I'll do anything you want!"

He shook her hand off. "Your charms are wasted on me, my dear. I simply do not care what becomes of you. If you take my advice, admit your sins and repent."

"Lucas! Please!" she begged as she hurried after him.

"Get away from me, Milandra!"

"*Lucas!*" she screeched.

"What?" he said, turning to face her.

To his horror he saw she was holding a letter opener that she had grabbed from the nearby table. She lunged at him and plunged it into the side of his neck.

Blood spurted out.

"Milandra!" he gasped as he sank to his knees.

He stayed a moment on his knees before falling over.

She stood staring at him, shaking, looking down at his lifeless body and her own blood-splattered gown.

"Well! I thought I'd never get here! The snow was so bad that the train had to keep stopping –"

It was Flancy.

She stood stock still as she surveyed the scene in front of her.

Milandra was standing over Lucas's still body, the letter opener still in her bloody hand.

"What – what – what is going on?" demanded Flancy.

Milandra stayed silent, shaking.

Flancy rushed forward, dropped to her knees and urgently began to examine Lucas.

"He's dead!" she declared.

She stood up and glared at Milandra.

"You murdered him!" she cried.

Milandra looked at the letter opener. "He gave me no choice!"

"What are you talking about?"

"He was going to tell them! Tell them all! Tell Nicholas!"

"You're making no sense! Tell Nicholas what?" demanded Flancy.

"That I bribed them."

"Bribed who?"

"Tom Fitzgerald and George Fetherston. To say they had sex with Constance Staffordshire. I only did it, because . . . Flancy, can't you see?"

Flancy slowly extracted the letter opener from her hand and placed it on the ground. Then she led Milandra over to the couch and sat her down before going to the drinks cabinet and pouring two large tumblers of whiskey. She came and sat down beside

Milandra and handed one of the glasses to her.

"Drink it! Drink it right back, you need it," she instructed.

Milandra raised the glass to her lips and took a large gulp while Flancy did the same with hers.

"Oh, Flancy, you've got to help me! What will I do? You've got to help me!" pleaded Milandra.

"Of course I'll help you. What else do you think I'd do, but help my precious Milandra?"

Milandra began to sob. "What will we do, Flancy?"

"We need to think fast. Are you expecting anybody tonight?"

"No," Milandra sobbed. "I'm due at the Fontenoys' at nine."

"You are in no fit state to go anywhere. I'll send a message up to them saying you're not going as you have a cold."

"What are we going to do about *him*?" Milandra pointed over at Lucas.

"Did anyone know he was here tonight? Did anyone see him come in?"

"I don't know. He used a key Ambrose had given him to let himself in."

"Good. It's unlikely he will have been noticed. If anyone asks, he did not come here tonight. You have not seen him."

"But – what will we do with him?"

"We'll wait until the dead of night, and then we'll go out into the garden and dig a hole and bury him there."

"In the garden! But it will be seen!"

"Nobody will see it. We'll get rid of the gardener. There's no reason for anybody to go out there. It will be spring soon and the earth will grass over."

"But, it's not right, burying him there!"

"If you had lived through the Famine like I did, then you'd have seen many things that aren't right, but you just forget about them, otherwise you'd go mad. And that's what we're going to do about this. We will forget about it after tonight and never talk about it again, do you understand?"

"Yes, Flancy. But, even if he hasn't been observed coming here, everyone will want to know where Lucas has gone – why he has disappeared," fretted Milandra.

"Let them – we will say we know nothing of it."

It was two in the morning and Flancy and Milandra were digging a hole at the back of the garden.

They had already cleaned any trace of blood in the drawing room and had destroyed Milandra's bloody gown.

"Now, that should do it – we'll go fetch him," said Flancy.

The two women went back into the house and up to the drawing room where they had wrapped Lucas up in a rug, having removed any papers from his pockets. They then dragged him down the stairs and out through the French windows and threw him into the hole they had dug.

"Is it deep enough?" asked Milandra.

"It will have to do," said Flancy. "We've hit hard ground and can't dig any deeper. We'd need men with pick-axes to get any farther down."

They started to fill in the hole and then covered the whole area up with snow.

"The snow is going to be here for a long time, maybe a few weeks – by then the ground will be hardened and nobody will know."

"Yes," said Milandra, staring down at their work.

"Now, come on inside," said Flancy, putting her arm around her and leading her into the house. "Forget about it now, Milandra. It's over. Promise yourself never to think of it again."

Milandra nodded as they went inside and locked the door behind them.

EPILOGUE

1916

Amelia sat staring at Milandra in disbelief as she finished telling of the events of Christmas 1869. She sat in silence for a long time, trying to digest what she had just heard.

"But you – you killed a man," Amelia said.

"Yes," nodded Milandra.

"And for no other reason than he was going to expose you for this – this – conspiracy you had engineered against this poor unfortunate girl – this Constance Staffordshire."

"It would have destroyed me if Lucas had exposed me at the time."

Amelia focused on this stranger who was sitting opposite her. The woman she had always loved and admired was now revealed as a murderer and many other things. She was a stranger.

"I'm not proud of what I did, of any of what I did. I acted out of survival instinct and vengeance. But I'm not proud of it," sighed Milandra.

"How could you possibly be otherwise?" Amelia was aghast.

"I did do something this past week to try to amend for my sins – not that it matters much, I suppose."

Amelia had never seen her grandmother cry or be upset but now saw her eyes fill up. But nothing could make her forget what she had just heard or allow her to offer any gesture of comfort to Milandra.

"What are you going to do?" asked Milandra.

"What am *I* going to do? The question is what are *you* going to do?"

"I shall do nothing," said Milandra. "Except live with my guilt."

"But the police?"

"When they ask about Lucas's body I will tell them I know nothing of it. My house on Sackville Street was a busy one with a houseful of servants, gardeners and guests who stayed. Any of them could be responsible for Lucas's murder. The garden was easily accessible from the laneways to the rear – anybody could have buried him there."

"And you think they will believe you?"

"Of course they will – who could ever suspect me, Lady Havington, of such a terrible crime?" challenged Milandra. "It's so long ago nobody is around who will even remember that I knew Lucas. Only when you were researching your article did I admit that I knew him, confident at the time his body would never be discovered."

"And that is the only reason you've admitted this to me now! Because you had already told me that you knew him well. And what if I tell the truth? If I expose you?"

"Then I shall cross that bridge when I come to it. But you won't say anything, Amelia."

"What makes you so confident of that?"

"As well as you being my sole heir, I know you wouldn't betray me." Milandra thought of herself and Flancy. "The women in our family have always covered for each other – no matter what. And you will do the same."

Amelia slowly rose from her chair. She felt she had to get away from Milandra. She could no longer sit in her company.

"Where are you going?"

"I-I'd better get back to Rupert. He'll be waiting for me."

"Of course," nodded Milandra.

Amelia quickly walked to the door.

"Amelia!" Milandra called as Amelia reached the door.

She hesitated before turning around.

"I love you, Amelia." There was a desperation in Milandra's voice, like she was crying out for her granddaughter not to reject her.

"I wonder do you really understand what love is, Milandra?" said Amelia and quickly left the room.

Outside, Amelia walked down the stairs in a daze. She slowly crossed the hallway and walked into the drawing room where she found Rupert alone, standing at the window looking out.

"There you are! I was beginning to get worried about you," said Rupert with a smile.

"Where are Mama and Papa?"

"They have gone to bed," answered Rupert.

"Is it that late? I hadn't realised," said Amelia as she glanced at the clock and saw it was after midnight.

She walked slowly across the room, her arms crossed, her hands holding each arm tightly.

"Is everything all right? You look a bit shattered," Rupert said, concerned.

Amelia's body gave a quick sharp shiver.

"Are you cold, my darling?" he said, coming and putting his arms around her.

"No," she said. "Somebody must have just walked over my grave."

He held her tightly and smiled down at her.

"There is nothing to worry about any more. I'm safe, your grandmother is safe – all here under the same roof with you."

"Yes."

"Do you realise when you came to me in the hospital and said what you said about putting me first before everything, it meant the world to me," he said. "That you were putting all this silly political stuff aside and realising that what matters most is us – you and me."

She allowed herself to be held. Yes, they were all safe under the same roof. Rupert and Milandra, the two people she loved most in the world. But their love was conditional. They expected her to obey them, and not betray them due to the love she had for them. Even if that meant not being true to herself and what she believed and knew was right and wrong. The past week had turned her world upside down.

She rested her head on his shoulder as she looked out the window.

"I think the world will never be the same again after this week," she said quietly.

"Of course it will be! We've quashed the rebellion. And we'll soon win the war in Europe – and everything will be the same as it ever was." Rupert spoke with enthusiasm. "That's what we're fighting for – to keep the status quo, to keep things as they were."

"But I don't think we're going to be able to stop anything," she said as a tear trickled down her cheek. "And I don't know if we should really try. The city is destroyed, Europe is destroyed. Everything is ruined."

"But we will rebuild everything. You'll see – put everything back to the way it was," promised Rupert.

"All the King's horses and all the King's men . . ." whispered Amelia as she held him tightly.

THE END

ALSO AVAILABLE

THE
FOOTMAN

From the country mansions of 1930s Ireland, to the decadence of 1940s wartime Paris to the courtrooms of London in modern times.

What the Footman saw . . .

In 1930s Ireland, Joe Grady becomes the footman at the stately home Cliffenden, owned by the glamorous Fullerton family. Joe is enthralled by the intrigue and scandal above stairs, and soon becomes a favourite of the daughter of the house, Cassie. There is mounting pressure on Cassie to marry American banker Wally Stanton. But Cassie is having a secret affair with the unsuitable Bowden Grey.

What the Footman did . . .

When Cassie and Bowden's affair is discovered in disgraceful circumstances, the lovers are banned from seeing each other. Joe risks his position at Cliffenden, becoming a messenger between them, until he finds himself making a choice that will change the lives of everyone at Cliffenden forever.

Decades later, Joe has achieved great success as a barrister. When suddenly Cassie is arrested for a sensational crime, he sets out to discover what happened to her in the intermittent years. He realises his actions at Cliffenden set off a chain of events that led to murder. But is Cassie guilty? Innocent or guilty, can Joe ever make amends for his part in her downfall?

A. O'CONNOR

ISBN 978-178199-904-2

The Secrets of Armstrong House

Present day – Kate and Nico Collins are filming a docudrama about life in their home Armstrong House in Ireland during its golden age at the turn of the century. When they discover a cover-up of a terrible crime involving Nico's great-grandfather Lord Charles Armstrong, they set out to solve a mystery over a century old.

1888 – Arabella Tattinger arrives to attend a glittering ball at Armstrong House as the family's younger son Harrison's fiancée. Her head is turned by the glamorous aristocratic family, and most of all by the eldest son and heir, the exciting but dangerous Charles. A chain of events unfolds from that night which casts the family into years of a bitter feud.

1899 – When American heiress Victoria Van Hoeven marries into the family, she is determined bring peace at last to the Armstrongs. But everywhere dangers are circling and secrets are ready to emerge from the shadows. Not just from outside the house but from within their golden circle. Victoria is stepping into the firestorm.

Kate and Nico press on in their efforts to uncover the truth – but are some secrets best kept hidden?

A. O'CONNOR

ISBN 978-184223-6260

ALSO AVAILABLE

The Left-Handed Marriage

Irish beauty Diana Cantwell meets Max Von Hoffsten, heir to a German count, and their romance blossoms in the carefree days before the First World War. But, when they become engaged, Max's father insists on a 'left-handed marriage', a custom among the German aristocracy in cases where the bride does not have the required pedigree. So, though Diana will be Max's lawful wife, neither she nor their children will have any claim to Max's eventual title or wealth.

Max and Diana agree to these terms and the newlyweds dazzle from Ascot to the Riviera. However, as the dark clouds of war gather across Europe, Diana becomes concerned by her husband's unpredictability and what she suspects are sinister secrets beneath his family's glamorous lifestyle.

When war is declared Diana finds herself caught between two sides, as her own Anglo-Irish family are fighting for the British and Max is an officer in the German army. When Max is reported missing presumed dead, Diana is rejected by his family. Widowed, penniless, she sets out to rebuild her life.

A.O'Connor once more spins an extraordinary tale that holds us spellbound, with the mixture of impeccable research and powerful storytelling that made *The House* and *The Secrets of Armstrong House* bestsellers.

A. O'CONNOR

ISBN 978-178199-9400